T0208423

Thank you for reading this Romance. I would like to dedicate it to my sister GK who helped me type and edit the story in its original format twenty years ago, long before computers were as efficient as they are today. She has always encouraged me to find my writing muse. When I did, the words came easily.

I feel blessed to have found my eternal muse who has given me the steadfastness to complete what I start, something I have not done consistently. I am moved to write from the heart by the music I listen to every day. This story, in particular was inspired by songs written by Jane Sibbery and ably performed by k.d. lang. 'The Valley' and 'Love is Everything' and of course, 'Please Help Me I'm Falling', made popular by Hank Loughlin.

The Will to be True

In The Shadow of the Blackbird

Judith D. Andrade

iUniverse, Inc.
New York Bloomington

The Will to be True
In The Shadow of the Blackbird

iUniverse books may be ordered through booksellers or by contacting:

iUniverse
1663 Liberty Drive
Bloomington, IN 47403
www.iuniverse.com
1-800-Authors (1-800-288-4677)

ISBN: 978-1-4502-1723-1 (sc)
ISBN: 978-1-4502-1724-8 (ebk)

Printed in the United States of America

iUniverse rev. date: 5/26/2010

Chapter 1

'Please don't do that.'

'I'm sorry Peter.'

'I've told you before…you will ruin your nails.'

'Yes…of course.'

As her husband resumed his study of the Toronto Stock Exchange report in the daily paper, Stephanie eyes were drawn to the sun streaming in through the kitchen window.

'We're up again! I knew the company's assets would rise after the merger but this is incredible.'

The words halted her fingers in mid-air. They had been poised to resume the impatient tattoo on the table top. Instead the tips turned inward pressing firmly into the soft palms.

'Did you hear me?' The clipped question held a touch of impatience.

Stephanie did not respond immediately. She waited until the paper was lowered and she could see her husband's pale blue-grey eyes.

'Yes, I did, Peter. You said your company's stock has been rising since the merger with PRA Associates. Why would you think I wasn't listening?'

'You're always so distracted lately. Whenever I talk, you don't respond the way you used to. Are you hiding something from me?'

'No…..I heard you. I don't have anything to hide either. I just don't know what the merger has to do with you personally.' Stephanie knew exactly what it meant – more work, more trips away from home, and more loneliness for her while Peter was climbing the corporate ladder to success.

She voiced none of her negative thoughts. It was a major effort to smile serenely waiting for Peter's inevitable assessment of her inability to understand corporate finance. Propping her chin on two fists, she leaned forward over the small, white arborite table, still littered with the empty plates that remained from their breakfast. Peter wanted her undivided attention. The morning paper was folded neatly before he continued speaking.

'It's everything to do with me. The opportunities for promotion are endless,' he paused, meeting her guileless look with one of smugness.

'I don't really expect you to understand anyway, Stephanie. You just can't seem to be able to grasp the finer points of the business world. However, as the wife of an accountant, you should try to take a little more interest in my work.'

He took a sip from his cup, savouring the fragrant percolated coffee. She felt his admiring glance sweep over the corn silk red-gold hair that seemed to fan about her face in a halo where the sun's rays caught its highlights.

'This coffee is delicious, as usual. You're so good here at home, fixing up things the way you do. As a woman you know the things a man likes instinctively.' He paused again. Stephanie knew he expected a smile. 'I know it's difficult for a woman to understand a man's world. I shouldn't expect that ….right?'

The clenched fists under the gently rounded chin tightened but her voice was steady as she offered a tentative reminder. 'I did start…my own business…'

'Oh, that. Sure, you did.' Peter did not hesitate she noted with a slight narrowing of her hazel eyes.

'Secretarial work is fine for a woman until she gets married, but now that you have me to look after you, your responsibilities have changed. Our needs here come first. You are happy, aren't you?' She knew the question hid a touch of insecurity in her husband but very little of it clouded his usual, firm, measured words.

'Yes, of course… I'm happy. It's just that I miss you when you have to go away.'

As the words left her mouth Stephanie knew they were lies. She peered at the face before her fighting an unexpected desire to cry. Stephanie knew that she was bored. She also knew that Peter would be very hurt and bewildered if she spoke her mind.

In the past, the demands of her job were a natural outlet for the active and vivacious red-head, but her natural vitality had slowly ground to a halt during the past year. The onset of spring in the late April morning seemed to bring a resurgence of energy, creating doubts and turmoil in a life that had previously seemed satisfactory, on the surface anyway.

She was thankful that Peter could not fathom her thoughts. Much as he would like to see her completely happy, she knew there was little more that he could do. He worked hard giving her everything money could buy. He wanted her to be proud of him.

'Each success I have reflects well on both of us. You should understand that' he often stated proudly. 'Travel is a necessary part of my job, Stephanie. Once I'm a junior vice-president I'll be home more.'

Frustrated by her inability to express herself freely, she turned her attention back to her husband hoping that he could read between the lines and discern some of her inner turmoil.

'I understand, Peter. It's just difficult finding things to do.'

'Work is too stressful for you, dear. We've been over that before. I can see that you've been much more relaxed these past few months. Didn't I tell you things would change for the better once you stayed home?' His smug look was back in place.

Stephanie frowned biting her lower lip, her eyes pleading.

'I don't want to discuss that business now Stephanie. We've been over it before and...'

'But Peter...n...nothing's happened yet. Don't you think I should see Michael?'

'No, Stephanie, I do not!' His voice had hardened.

'Michael's only going to send you for unnecessary tests. You don't realize how much you will be humiliated when he pries into details of our marriage that don't concern him. Just leave things alone. I don't see why you can't be satisfied with things the way they are. We are happy enough. It...will happen when it's time.'

Stephanie knew it was pointless to pursue that argument. 'I suppose your right.'

'I know I'm right. What you probably need is more exercise. Look, here's an ad for aerobics classes,' he said, handing her the morning paper. 'Why don't you sign up? It would give you something to do. There's even a 25% discount. You could go in during the day and still be home at night.'

'I'll look into it, Peter. Thanks.'

'I must go, Stephanie. It's getting late.' His quick glance at the silver Seiko watch brought a half-smile to her lips. It had been a gift from her on their first anniversary. It was the only jewelry Peter ever wore. His chaste kiss on the cheek was over almost before it began. He thinks I'll fall to pieces, Stephanie mused, shaking her head at Peter's retreating back. This skin of mine is as tough as nails. The alabaster skin, accentuated by the moss green robe she was wearing, seemed almost translucent. It gave her a fragile, delicate appearance which was very deceptive. She had been tempted to reach up and grab his head for a more lingering kiss but she knew that he would balk at any overtures from her. Peter hated aggressive women, in or out of the bedroom.

'Take care of yourself Dear' he called from the half open door. 'I don't want anything to happen to you. It might do you some good to join one of those women's groups though. Call them. I'll probably be late tonight so you'll have something to do today.'

A few seconds later, he was gone, tall and handsome in a dark grey suit, white shirt and matching grey and navy tie. His ash blond hair was close cropped and neatly combed. A black briefcase was held securely at his side. *A year ago I would have been on my way out the door with him,* Stephanie reflected staring out the window again. She pictured herself dressed equally well, in a neat grey suit, white blouse freshly pressed, a burgundy briefcase held securely at her side, looking just as business-like as her husband.

Time passed slowly as Stephanie Droga Atkinson sat gazing unseeingly out the window, images of the past chasing helter skelter through her head. In the end, the decision had been hers alone. Her job was always important she acknowledged with sadness but Peter was constantly telling her that she looked stressed and tired. Stress was making her irritable.

Was I really? she pondered. Looking back over the past year, she knew hard work only stimulated her to do more. Challenges were met head on. She finally conceded that Peter had seen something she had not been aware of within herself. She sighed wistfully, remembering his subtle hint that her failure to conceive was based on the fact that she was too overworked and too tired to respond to the natural demands of her body.

Bowing to the subtle but effective emotional manipulation of her husband, Stephanie soon conceded that she would be a better wife and mother, if she left the job. Within a few months, she gradually weaned herself away from the office. Without the demands of a full time working partnership in the busy translation service office, she hoped to be less stressed. Peter would display less resentment and eventually a baby would come. Repeating those words daily helped her to get through the final weeks.

In her mind's eye Stephanie could see the face of her friend and business partner Georgette. Stephanie knew that Georgette had been disappointed by her reason for leaving a growing lucrative business. Wisely she refused to completely dissolve the partnership. 'Take a year off if you want to. I'll manage in the meantime and then we can talk again. You may want to help out the odd day. Don't close all the doors at once.'

Stephanie had been grateful for her friends understanding but Georgette's final words seemed to be more prophetic than sympathetic. 'I hope you and Peter are able to reach a happy medium' she whispered close to tears on that final day. 'I can't see you having enough to do unless....?' there was a questioning pause, 'you are already pregnant?'

The question was merely rhetorical. Stephanie had bowed her head unable to meet the eyes of her partner. They had often discussed the possibility of a pregnancy and how it would affect their working relationship. Georgette would have been the second person to hear the news when and if it happened.

*My fourth wedding anniversary is almost here. Peter is happy enough but...*shaking her head, Stephanie saw herself in those first weeks at home. She cleaned, cooked and redecorated the condominium with the same zeal that she brought to her job. Looking around her now, from her seat at the kitchen table, she knew that it would take her less than one hour to tidy up and even less time to prepare Peter's evening meal.

The hazel eyes returned to contemplate the blue skies through the window pane. Pensively Stephanie realized the prophetic truth of Georgette's statement. It had been a year. The active young business woman was now a bored and restless housewife seeking in vain for ways to fill her days. There was no baby on the way and Peter surprisingly seemed to, not so subtly, avoid any discussion about family planning.

Getting up slowly from the table, Stephanie stretched her 5'10' frame. Her body tingled uncomfortably and she stood still for a moment, realizing that she must be badly out of shape if simple stretching could make her feel so light headed. She quickly cleared away the dishes and headed for the telephone, the ad from the health club in her hand.

Once her mind was made up, Stephanie wasted no time. Within two days she found herself standing alone, clad in a tangerine exercise suit, waiting for the class to start. She gazed around, noting the layout of the modern downtown Toronto Health Club Facility.

Initially, the idea of doing aerobics, in a group setting, had seemed a good one. Numerous young attractive women were now milling about the large exercise area. Stephanie had hoped that apart from the benefits of the exercise she would also have the opportunity to meet and make new friends. That idea was firmly quashed when she discovered that most of the participants came during their lunch break or day off. Almost all discussed business, seeming to scorn the domestic engineers who had too much time and too much money to waste.

Dismayed by their cavalier viewpoint, Stephanie held herself aloof unwilling to be exposed to any ridicule. She was just beginning to wonder if she made the right decision when out of the corner of her eye she saw a familiar face. Not sure if it was actually someone she knew or someone whose discomfort reflected her own, she took a deep breath before making her way over to a petite brunette whose arms were crossed over her midriff while a sneaker clad toe tapped impatiently on the hardwood floor.

'Have we met before?'

'If you were a man you wouldn't get to first base with that line for God's sake!'

'Excuse me?' Stephanie uttered, bewilderment written all over her face.

'Look, I'm sorry,' the brunette said, seeing that her smart remark did not go over well. 'I'm just a bit fed up today. I don't go out to work and most of the gals here think I'm from outer space or something. I just didn't want anyone else to ask me what company I work for.'

'I know what you mean. I don't work either and it's been difficult to find something in common with most of these women.'

'My name is Beth,' the brunette announced extending a soft red tipped hand. 'Well Elizabeth really….no that's not true either.

It's Elisabetta but everyone calls me Beth' she said laughing now. She looked up at Stephanie, her head cocked to one side. 'You said you know me from somewhere. Did you mean it?'

'I don't know you but I have seen your face somewhere before.'

'Well I don't think I've seen you before. You'd be pretty hard to miss…huh? Where do you live?' Beth speech pattern seem to run on quickly then stop suddenly hardly giving her listeners time to absorb the words.

The class had not yet started so the two women made their way to a nearby bench in the large mirror lined room. It gave them the opportunity to be at eye level with each other. As well, Stephanie needed a moment to think. Even though her smile eventually had been warmer, Beth was very tense, fidgeting with her hands all the time.

Once seated, they found themselves laughing as they discovered their shared home address.

'Isn't it ironic that we should live at the same place and yet end up meeting here? My name is Stephanie, by the way.'

'Nice to meet you Steph. This is going to be fun isn't it? I mean I've been coming here for weeks now, not really enjoying myself, you know, but just looking for something to do. Listen I'm busy after class today but how about us having lunch somewhere soon….if it's ok?'

'I'd like that.'

As the lively music signaled the beginning of class the two dissimilar women made their way to the centre of the room. Some of the more overweight women snickered about 'Mutt and Jeff' but the attractive pair bore no resemblance to the comic strip duo.

Stephanie carried her height well. Her full bust and hips were neatly balanced by a trim waist. The red-gold hair confined in a pony tail for the energetic movements usually hung loosely below her shoulders, softly curling tendrils framing her face. The golden highlights in her hair were repeated in the hazel long-lashed eyes which fanned upwards, giving the appearance of a absurdly blissful and seductive feline when she laughed.

Beth, on the other hand was a petit 5'1'. Her olive skin and full figure proclaimed her Latin ancestry. She had lovely full brown eyes that were very expressive in a classically Roman face. The thick dark shoulder length hair bobbed with a life of its own.

There was a similarity in the women however. Like Beth, Stephanie exuded an air of restlessness that seemed to preclude complete contentment. Their participation in the dance routine was almost frenetic as they pushed themselves to the limit, trying to exorcise curious unfulfilled needs.

*****

Despite the invitation for lunch, Beth didn't seem in a hurry to get together. She had several family commitments most days after class. They would talk casually at the club but each still maintained an air of cautiousness for about two weeks on the neutral ground. Stephanie did not push. It had been a long time since she made friends with anyone outside of the office. She followed Beth's lead until they met in the foyer of the building on their way to class.

'Are you busy after class today Steph?'

'Why no! I don't have any plans. What did you have in mind?'

'I just wondered if you'd like to go out for that lunch we talked about? I am kind of down in the dumps today. I want to try something different.'

Hiding her disappointment at the casual indifferent invitation, Stephanie nodded her head.

Deciding on a hot and spicy meal as an excellent way to sweat off any lingering calories, the duo made their way, on foot, to the nearby Bangkok Gardens Restaurant. Only cognoscenti of the unusual Thai cooking would seek out the unobtrusive little basement establishment.

As they descended into the cool cavernous area, Stephanie laughingly commented 'they should have located this place near a fire hall.' She knew that several glasses of cool water would be needed to wash down the piquant foods listed on the menu.

At the foot of the stairs, she was suddenly assailed by an eerie feeling. Looking at Beth in the gloomy interior she felt goose bumps rise on her skin and shivered. *A goose on your grave!* Stephanie muttered shakily, remembering her mother suddenly.

'Hey are you OK?'

'Yes, I just have a …difficult time adjusting to the change in light. I'll be fine. Just give me a minute.'

Forcing a smile Stephanie removed her coat and hung it up on the rack. Beth, thankfully, did not wait but hurried on to sit at a cozy corner table, pointed out by the waiter.

Stephanie did not move immediately. She stood, hand on the rail leading upstairs, staring at the only window longing to be back in the spring sunshine. She could not understand what was wrong with her. Having lunch with a friend should not cause her to feel so uncomfortable. *It's just lunch and yet I want to run up the stairs and never come back.* Her stomach was unsettled and nothing seemed to make sense. The dim interior only served to heighten this sudden sense of foreboding.

'Madam, are you ready to join your friend now?'

'What?...No… I…of course. I'm fine now.'

Seating herself at the table with a dazed smile, Stephanie decided against the temptingly seasoned foods and settled for something that would be kinder to her wobbly insides. Their lunch was served quickly and quietly leaving the unusual pair to become engrossed in a 'getting to know you' conversation that did little to dispel Stephanie's sense of gloom.

'Do you eat out a lot Steph?'

'No, why do you ask?'

'This is such a funny little place…kind of dark but the food's good. How did you find about it?'

'My office used to be near here. I did a lot of lunch time exploring and found it by accident.'

'Your office? You mean the office where you worked?'

'Yes, that's what I meant.'

'Greg doesn't care if I work or not. I like to stay home, but it does get boring sometimes. Anyway I wouldn't want to sit in an office all day typing. So what do you do for fun?'

'My husband works very hard so we don't go out much…but I do like…'

'Have you ever been to concerts at the forum Steph?'

'Ah… not really. My father, who was Hungarian by the way, had a real love of music, mostly classical. We used to attend the symphony performances at Massey Hall when I was younger but I haven't been lately.'

'I'm not into that classical stuff but I did hear that Johnny Mathis was coming to the Thompson Centre next month. I'd like to see him. Do you like his music Steph?'

'Yes I do. It would be wonderful to go.' Stephanie sighed glad that they could find something to agree on.

'I have quite a bit of his music on tape. If you are interested, we could get together sometime at my place.'

It was another tentative invitation. Stephanie did not answer immediately. Something in her refused to commit herself wholly to pursuing this friendship. Beth seemed too off-hand and unavailable unless it suited her needs.

'You know Beth. I have some earlier show tunes and some blues music from the 40's and 50's if you want me to…..'

'I just stick to the same old thing. Greg has all the other fancy stuff and monopolizes the stereo whenever he's home. He thinks he's the greatest songwriter since Mozzard or whatever his name was.' Her words were followed by a silly little laugh.

The comment seemed strange. Beth sounded as if she was demeaning her husband. Stephanie frowned wondering if she had misunderstood the delivery rather than the words. She was cautious, still feeling her way in this new friendship. She was fighting an unknown desire to never see Beth again. She had never met anyone like her before who was so outspoken and insecure at the same time.

They completed their lunch at a leisurely pace and parted company amicably. Beth headed for her sister's place in the Woodbridge area and Stephanie decided on a long walk to pass some time.

Out in the sunshine saying goodbye, Beth was very pleasant and most of the unreasonable fears evaporated. However a sense of loneliness could not be dispelled. The evening ahead looked very bleak. Peter was away and it was becoming too difficult to fill a day and a night with only her increasing sense of emptiness for company.

Chapter 2:

Stephanie and Peter lived on the second floor of the townhouse complex in the older established north east area of Toronto. Beth was situated directly overhead. The building was not new but had been completely renovated. There were three floors, in total, housing thirty units of two and three bedroom split level condominiums. The setting was unusual and had been popular with the young upwardly mobile groups who comprised the largest number of owners. As the 1980's were coming to an end, many young singles and couples opted for an urban lifestyle in elaborate condos rather than purchasing homes.

An invitation to her home for morning coffee and cake was soon issued by Beth. Bored and restless, Stephanie jumped at the opportunity to spend some time out of the apartment without being too far away.

The hostess had decorated in warm earth tones and safe beige brown upholstered traditional furniture. One living room wall was dotted with photographs. Stephanie would have loved to hear about the people behind the smiling faces. She did not want to pry but no offer to view the family gallery was forthcoming, so they sat in the breakfast nook, chatting

This cake is delicious I'd like to try it if you have the recipe?'

'Don't be stupid Steph. I bought it. Who has time for cooking all this fancy stuff? I never had to at home and Greg doesn't mind eating out when he wants something different.'

'I'm sorry. It's just so good. I...thought... you made it.'

'No way! We don't have to slave over a stove nowadays, you know. If Greg wants a home cooked meal every day he can get one at his house or go see my mother.'

Stephanie couldn't comment. She was offended at being called stupid then wondered if Beth really meant what she said. The unsettled guest smiled tightly, hoping her dismay would not be evident.

'I enjoy cooking. I used to help my mother a lot,' she offered at last, fighting the piece of cake which stuck in her throat.

'Didn't you hate all the work?'

'Hate the work?'

'Yeah, I mean having to cook for everyone….'

'I was an only child. Papa died when I was young and…'

The sentence remained incomplete. Beth had moved on to another topic quickly. *I seem to be out of touch with what people are doing and thinking these days. I just can't find the right thing to say. Is it me or them?*

The visit ended pleasantly enough but Stephanie continued to feel hollow and dissatisfied.

******

Two weeks later, Beth returned the visit. She rarely sat still, exploring the rooms and talking animatedly about the décor. It was the first time Stephanie saw her genuinely enjoy herself. She appeared to be absolutely delighted by Stephanie's home. 'You know, if I had to design something like this for you it would be just like this.'

Stephanie did not know if she liked to be predictable but looking around herself she mentally conceded that her personality was stamped everywhere. A large modern sofa invited guests to sink into its cushiony depths. Overhanging lamps created a cozy atmosphere and a reclining easy chair, set between the stereo and bookshelf, offered a comfortable alternative for soothing away tension while enjoying reading or music.

Peter had shown little interest in the decorating preferring his more austere den-study but he did appreciate his wife's unusual and innovative style.

'Your plants are absolutely thriving. How do you do it? My Dad would have loved this place. He had a green thumb you know.'

It would have been a perfect time to exchange confidences about families but as usual Beth rushed on. 'The colour is amazing. I'd never dare to match pink, black and grey like that but it works well for you.'

The tone of the words, Stephanie realized, made it seem less and less like a compliment. She tuned out the ramble of her guest and thought ahead to the snack she had prepared. She tried to be less formal than her usual style and served their brunch in the breakfast nook, located five steps up from the sunken living room. It had a light airy appearance with one mirror tiled wall reflecting the mid morning sun.

Despite the obvious differences in style, Beth seemed to prefer Stephanie's *lively pad* as she called it and was more often visiting there than vice versa. Stephanie too felt more relaxed at home. As the hostess she was able to follow Beth's lead. If the situation became uncomfortable, she could always get up and make more coffee or use the bathroom. As the visits continued Stephanie was able to accept Beth more easily and ignore the barbs that so often accompanied comments about 'Greg'.

It was inevitable that Beth, visiting one Tuesday afternoon in late April would meet Peter before the much maligned Greg became known. It seemed however that no introduction was needed. They had already met, not officially but as neighbours do, on a casual basis, saying hello and sharing opinions on the weather in the elevator long before the two women met. Beth seemed disappointed that Peter had not mentioned their meeting to his wife. Stephanie was not surprised however. His action was in keeping with the way he shared most events that occurred outside the home.

'Maybe he thought you'd be jealous, eh Steph?'

'Peter knows I'm not that type of person. It would have been great though to meet before now. I still find it ironic that we met so far from here and yet still share the same address.'

'Pete's so quiet Steph and you're such a lively person. I guess it true that opposites attract.' The whispered aside from Beth troubled Stephanie. She hoped that Peter didn't hear. Beth could be so outspoken. She had already ignored the subtle hint to change the subject.

'Imagine I have been talking to him for a year. I never would have pictured the two of you together.' Stephanie's heart sank as she offered a stiff smile in response.

'Pete even looked really shy, you know. It was a long time before he would even say hello much less a how're ya doin?'

Will she never stop talking? Stephanie wondered watching her husband's stiff back as he removed his suit jacket and put down the briefcase.

'Looking at him here, though he seems kinda …. different somehow.'

'He is different Beth. A man's home is where he can relax or be a tyrant if he chooses.'

Stephanie could tell that she had shocked Beth a little and was pleased about that. She was aware that most people wondered how she could have married so reserved a man. Many often mistook his calm and measured word for shyness. Peter was not shy however, diffident perhaps but he could make his presence felt when necessary. Extreme shifts of high and low were rare for Peter and he ruled his home firmly and consistently, with a chauvinist's attitude.

Stephanie felt she could get her own way if she wanted but trusted instead his good judgment. He was steadfast, faithful and trustworthy, all complements to her own restless and often turbulent personality. He wasn't a tyrant though. Stephanie needed something to halt Beth's flow of words. She wasn't sure why she chose that particular word and refused to analyze any Freudian connections.

As a courtesy, Peter joined them for a few minutes of polite conversation appearing a little uncomfortable as usual in the sunken living area. Their guest was still assessing his looks with a rather intense gaze directed at the man seated beside her.

'You're very tall Steph. I know next to me everyone seems big but Pete's not as tall as I thought.'

Peter's blue grey eyes sank out of sight as the lids closed slowly. Stephanie knew that he wasn't really conscious about his own height. He just felt that his wife should be much shorter than him.

'It's not that important really. I was more attracted to Peter's personality. He's kind and reliable.' It was an insipid compliment but the smile she directed at Peter was meant to add some warmth to the words. There was no answering response from him.

'I don't seem to be able to say the right thing today either,' Stephanie thought disgusted with herself.

'Oh yeah, not too many people bother with good manners today. I was really impressed when Pete talked back to me so nicely in the elevator. I wasn't working but I had to get up every morning for a month to help my...someone and I saw Pete every day. He was always...right on time. Isn't that right Pete?' she asked giving him the full benefit of her brown puppy dog eyes.

'Uh...uh...yes uh you were certainly punctual. It's a value not much appreciated today.' The reply was delivered in a tight monotone which puzzled Stephanie. She began to wonder if they had all entered the twilight zone. She gave her red-gold hair a shake. The conversation was steered into a discussion of the merit of predictability until, running a hand tiredly over his ash-blonde hair, Peter quickly excused himself.

'It was a pleasure to meet you properly Elizabeth. Please come by again.'

'Nice to meet you too Pete. Strange isn't it? Now we'll have more to talk about when we run into each other.'

'Yes…well… I've got some work here to check over before tomorrow. I'll leave you two, if you will excuse me.'

With a nod he left them. Stephanie was dismayed that Peter continued to have difficulty relaxing in mixed company. *Even though he had been engaging in polite conversation with Beth for nearly a year, he still behaved so formally. The dismay wasn't his entire fault. Beth was too outspoken for someone with Peter's sensitive nature. If she had made anymore remarks about his height or our unsuitability as a couple he would have been cold and withdrawn for days*, she thought defensively.

Sighing inwardly, she continued her mental debate oblivious to the chatter from her guest. *'He's tired I suppose, but then he's been like that with Georgette, for over four years. I guess he doesn't like Beth either.'* Shaking off the disquieting thoughts, Stephanie turned her full attention back to her guest who apparently noticed nothing unusual and continued to ramble on about the coincidence.

'The last link in the chain would be for you to meet Greg.'

'Yes, I'm looking forward to it.'

'How about you and Pete coming up after dinner next Sunday? We could have drinks and get to know each other better.'

Beth almost sounded like a child with a new toy. Stephanie responded to the unspoken plea and gave in but had some doubts about getting 'Pete' there. He never made friends easily and would not appear very enthusiastic this time if she correctly interpreted his manner so far.

As it turned out the evening was cancelled. Peter had an unscheduled trip booked to Vancouver on the Monday and felt it would be better to leave Sunday.

'The time change always throws me off schedule. Just explain to your friend. I'm sure she'll understand. Didn't you say her husband travels too?'

'Yes, but certainly not as much as you do.'

'I have to worked harder now Stephanie. I thought I explained why, the other day. It's very important for me to be on top of things while the company is expanding.'

'That's reasonable Peter, but I need an outlet too if you are going to be away so much' she countered quietly.

'Is that a threat?' His eyes narrowed a fraction.

'No, of course not! You know I love being here for you. I told you that a year ago when I gave up my job. It is just so difficult to fill my days Peter.'

'There must be things you can do here Stephanie. I just don't want you going back to that office. You had enough of that.'

'Does that mean you wouldn't mind if I did some translating work here at home?' she queried tentatively.

'Only if you promise that it won't interfere with our needs here.'

'I promise.'

They were not a demonstrative couple and Stephanie did not want to gloat over her little victory. It had taken a while to learn that compromise was the best way to get through to her husband. She had used the loss of the get-together to work out something to occupy her increasingly boring days. *'I'll square things with Beth,'* she mentally concluded. She kept her satisfied smile well hidden.

Chapter 3:

Quickly taking advantage of the chance to do a little work at home, Stephanie called Georgette who was more than willing to send over some straightforward but confidential business documents and letters that needed translating.

'It's a godsend, Stephanie. The office is busy and Jawahir is away for six weeks completing her diploma. I know the staff is good, but maintaining confidentiality is always a problem. Anyway that I can get your help is much appreciated."

'Thanks Georgette. Peter and I seem to have reached a happy medium and you were right, as usual, but I should be able to do more. He's indicated that he'll be very busy and the boredom is killing me.'

'Are you pregnant?'

'NO!'

They rang off with a laugh. Georgette was the only person who could be so blunt and get away with it. They had not spoken much lately and Stephanie missed their camaraderie.

Peter would be away several days. It meant that she could work undisturbed in the moribund apartment. It didn't take long to get a feel for the work that she had abandoned for months. Words flew around in her head as a clock ticked lazily nearby. It was the only sound she heard since the files had been delivered to her late Monday afternoon.

Meanwhile, the desktop computer stored and saved the steady stream of information pouring out of her fingers. *'It feels so good to be doing this,'* Stephanie realized. The smile on her face disappeared quickly when the telephone rang sharply, Her eyes widened and her hand went to tightened lips before she reluctantly reached for the receiver. A moment of guilt pierced her. She wondered if Peter could know how much she was enjoying herself. Placing the receiver cautiously at her mouth, she waited nervously for a response to her tentative greeting.

'Hello ...Hello?'

'Stebadee....zat oo?'

'Yes, it's Stephanie speaking, but who is calling?'

'Beds.'

'Bess?' Stephanie did not know any Bess. She was about to hang up, relieved that Peter was not the caller.

'Doe, Best!' the croaking words were followed by a spasm of coughing.

'Beth...Beth! Are you ill? What's happened?'

'Ah terribo code.'

'Good grief! You sound just awful! What can I do?'

A wheezy sigh at the other end told Stephanie that Beth would have found it difficult to ask for help.

'Grezz dot hobe,' a sneeze then a further attempt, '....Ah deed bedezid. Cad oo go?'

In all her years of language study, Stephanie had never had such difficulty translating simple English. The question was hard to decipher. In an effort to avoid further distress to the obviously sick woman, she replied, 'Yes, of course' deciding instead to allow her eyes to do what her ears could not. Beth needed help. That much was obvious.

She was greeted at the door of the condominium by an ill-looking and weepy woman. Beth appeared quite feverish and the unfilled prescription dangling from her hand told Stephanie all she needed to know.

'Go to bed, Beth,' she stated firmly. 'I'll be back as fast as I can.'

Scorning the use of the notoriously slow elevators, Stephanie headed for the stairs exit, barely noticing the tall man holding the door for her. She threw a breathless 'thank you' over her shoulder and quickly made her way down to the street where an all-night drug store was but a few minutes away.

Gregory Richmond paused at the exit door, allowing himself to savour the scent of the exotic perfume lingering in the air. He had barely caught a glimpse of the owner as she dashed past, red curls flying behind her. The fragrance was familiar to him and he realized that Beth must also be using that particular perfume. It was tantalizing and stirred his senses. He hurried down the corridor to his door. It had been a good while since he and his wife made love.

If she were wearing that perfume and one of her sensuous-looking negligees, he fully intended to make up for his preoccupation of the last few weeks. He strode purposefully down the corridor, anticipation making his body taut. Gregory Richmond felt good, having just closed a European shipping deal worth several million dollars that evening. Power and money were not always at the top of Gregory's list of priorities, but he did have a certain drive, for work-related success. The negotiations had been satisfactorily settled and other emotions were surfacing with a vengeance.

Beth really had no interest in his work. He even suspected that she was happy to have him preoccupied at times. It left her free to be involved in the many demands made on her from her family, without interference from a 'domineering or possessive' husband. As he inserted his key in the lock, he realized that he loved his wife with a gentle protectiveness that seemed to balance out the almost frenetic pace that her family expected of her. He hoped she had a quiet day at home however. Tonight he felt neither gentle nor protective.

Flush with his achievement, he opened his front door eagerly anticipating a cold drink, a hot dinner, and an even hotter wife smelling of jasmine and roses. Gregory's nose was assailed instead by the smell of camphor. As he entered their bedroom he could clearly see that the only heat in his wife was her raging fever and pitifully tortured red nose.

The implications were obvious. He bent over the sick and weeping woman, comforting her as best he could. It did not seem to be serious, only a common cold, but Beth liked a lot of attention when she was incapacitated. Thank God, he reasoned, that it happened now and not in the previous weeks when he was so preoccupied and unusually irritable about business matters.

'Honey, I'm sorry you're sick,' he crooned sympathetically.' I'd hoped we could celebrate a little tonight. Things went very.......'

'Grezz, feed so awfud. Cad tod aboud work dow'

'I know, Beth. It's okay, we'll celebrate when you're better.'

'Dever be bedder.'

'Of course you will. You just need to rest and drink lots of....'

'I deed bedezid. You…dot hobe. By fred's….gedding da bedezid for be.'

'Alright, honey. When Fred comes I'll give you the medicine and then you'll feel better. Do you want me to call your mother?'

'DOE!'and the coughing started ending any chance of further conversation.

At times she could be so stubborn he knew. A cold was not the end of the world, but to a sensitive Beth it seemed so and regardless of what was said tonight he knew that Mary Spinola, widow and matriarch, would arrive the following day dispensing her own brand of love and admonishments equally to her daughter. He also knew he would have to sleep elsewhere.

Hoping that 'Fred' would hurry up and deliver the medicine so that she could settle down, he swallowed hard on his own bitter pill of disappointment. A promising evening had been spoiled. For a long time he was so caught up in the might-have-beens that he failed to hear the knock on the door for quite a while. The insistent sound eventually penetrated his fantasy, chasing away the delightful outcome. His initial disappointment was replaced by anger and frustration. He ran to snatch open the door and grab the prescription from the delivery boy, probably relieving some of his mounting tension in the process. Frustration exploded as he was confronted by a flushed and panting Stephanie, exuding sex appeal, and assailing his nostrils with that heady perfume. She looked the essence of a high fashion model.

His insides dropped so suddenly, he almost felt compelled to bend over and pick them up.

'I've brought the medicine for Beth. I'm Stephanie, you're....'

'Who are you?' they both spoke simultaneously.

'I'm Stephanie.'

'Where's Fred?' again they spoke in unison, then paused.

'Fred who?' the goddess whispered eyes wide.

'The delivery boy.'

'Are you Gregory?'

'I'm Gregory.'

Try as they might they were unable to make any sense whether they spoke simultaneously or separately. By mutual unspoken consent conversation was suspended. It had not been particularly profound anyway. Gregory's eyes narrowed as he surveyed the beauty before him. He felt his already tightened muscles swell to a painful ache. He swallowed hard, seemingly mesmerized by the golden tipped hazel eyes that stared back at him in confusion. The arched brows were drawn together.

Gregory noted that he did not have to look down very far to see the image of himself captured in the depths of those eyes. In medium heels she was only 2 or 3 inches shorter. She took his breath away. Rational thought seemed suspended in time. Only the rapid beat of his heart forced him to acknowledge the necessity of taking a breath.

'Grezz?...Zat Stebadee?...I deed by bedezid.' The plaintive nasally whine from the bedroom broke the witch's spell long enough for Gregory to extract the small white bag from her hands, thank her with a nod, and close the door without further conscious thought.

Stephanie staggered down the hall feeling suddenly lightheaded. Putting a steadying hand on the wall, she realized she had been holding her breath. With a firm grip on herself and pushing her scattered thoughts to the back of her mind, she gasped tightly, stilling her trembling lips with an effort and continued down to her apartment.

Standing at the open door of her apartment, she could feel the emptiness echo around her. Stephanie knew a moment of panic. Alone and lonely were words that seemed to have been the sum and substance of her life for so long. She was unable to feel beyond the moment. She knew only an aching indefinable need. Foolishly reasoning that alcohol would be good company, she crossed to the liquor cabinet housed in one section of the book shelf unit. She poured herself a hefty scotch and drank all in three large gulps.

Stephanie was not a drinker, needing no stimulation to enjoy life. Liquor was merely a device which would dull her usually high spirits. As this was an anathema to her, she rarely drank. A demon was on her tonight, however stimulated by Beth's incomprehensible call for help; running to fetch the medicine, her active imagination working furiously overtime while she waited at Beth's door and lastly her meeting with Gregory Richmond. Stephanie had studiously avoided that particular avenue of thought until now, but her mind and heart rate had gradually slowed while the single malt scotch spread through her body.

Adopting an indifferent assessing attitude in her thoughts, Stephanie coolly examined him as she had seen him at the door. Never in her mind's eye did she look at him from her own natural reactions – a trick she employed when wanting to evade a personal issue. Objectively, he seemed to possess no startling qualities – above average height, well built, an obviously muscular athletic body, deep set light brown eyes, a healthy shine to his dark almost black hair worn fashionably long. It was a wholly masculine face, lean jaw lines, its starkness saved from austerity and coldness by a hint of dimple, or their adult remnants and a full sensuous mouth.

Stephanie hesitated at that point. Try as she might, her thoughts lingered on that mouth and she felt herself succumbing to unchartered feelings. Her traitorous body began to tremble and she acknowledged such a longing to feel that mouth on her own in a lingering tender kiss, working slowly on her own parted lips searching.......

She jumped up from the chair and ran almost screaming to her bedroom. Hastily throwing off her clothes, she had a quick shower and dove under the covers. In an effort to quell her thoughts, she grabbed a novel from her bedside table. The telephone rang just as she was half-heartedly settling into the story. Grabbing the jangling instrument like it was a life line to sanity, Stephanie was relieved to hear the clipped, calm tones of her husband's voice. She responded with uncharacteristic warmth, prolonging the conversation, much to Peter's surprise, as long as possible.

'Stephanie, you have the time to talk now but I don't!'

'I'm sorry Peter, I had forgotten about the time difference. Do you have plans for the evening?'

'Of course! You know that I usually go out to dinner with my colleagues after the meetings. They are waiting for me now. I have to go. Sleep well, Stephanie.'

'Night dear. Have a good....'

His surprise had eventually turned to impatience. As she held the dead instrument in her hand she realized that she could not stop the thoughts in her head from resurfacing.

For the umpteenth time her mind travelled back over the past year and objectively saw her recent existence as the exercise in futility, it truly was.

I've never been really unhappy, but I'm not happy either. This silliness tonight is just a prime example of what can happen to a bored housewife, she generalized unfairly. *I love Peter,* she also conceded thoughtfully, *but I'm not cut out to suppress my needs as an intelligent, contributing member of the working masses.*

The depth of thought startled her and for no reason that she could understand the tears fell, turning the lovely hazel eyes a translucent gold. Her resolve hardened with the release of her emotions and a determined woman pushed the *'silliness of tears'* to the back of her mind, deciding that some changes were definitely in order.

Over the next few days Stephanie saw little of the patient upstairs. The tall red-head was disgustingly healthy but she knew that her husband harboured some real fears about illness. She avoided any physical contact with Beth until the worst of the cold had passed. She did not want Peter to return and find her ill in bed. Although that was unlikely, she knew he would be upset to find she was even visiting someone sick.

Deep in the recesses of her mind she knew that she was just not up to seeing Gregory face to face again. Boredom or not, he had a profound effect on her system. It's intensity frightened her. She needed to get her priorities in order then she would be strong enough to laugh at herself.

In the cold light of day, following the unusual encounter with him she often wondered what had come over her. She couldn't blame him, nor her enforced absence from work for the feelings he generated. She must have been in a heightened state, missing her husband's comforting presence. Stephanie decided to wait until Peter returned before making any decision about the future. Dismissing the event, she felt that everything would be fine once her life included a little more of her own specialized work. In spite of the misplaced logic, she was also determined to avoid Greg.

So as not to appear unsympathetic, she maintained telephone contact with Beth. Each day she called. Beth was inclined to be tearful and easily upset by trivia.

'Do you know my sister hasn't even called to see how I am? I could've been dying and no one would care.'

Not having a sister, Stephanie tried to sympathize but was met with resistance.

'You wouldn't know how I feel anyway,' Beth continued. 'You're an only child. Everyone paid attention to you.'

Stephanie did not remind Beth that she had lost her father when she was very young. Nothing Stephanie said or didn't say mattered very much. No one was spared Beth's condemnation. Worst of all were the complaints about her mother.

'How could she talk to me about kids? I'm so sick. It would be impossible for me to think about having a baby now.'

Stephanie had just about decided not to inquire at all when surprisingly Beth called to announce, 'I'll be gone about two weeks Steph. I need a break and Mom will look after me.'

'Is there anything I can do Beth?'

'No. I'll call you when I get back.'

Just like that she was gone. Peter was also gone. He had come home and left almost immediately on a European trip for a further ten days.

Hating herself for the deceit, Stephanie took in quite a bit of work and went to the office a couple of times. Despite the guilt, she felt good. The see-saw of emotions, which constantly plagued her, disappeared when she was busy and productive. A testing time was necessary to help her decide what she would tell Peter. It would be the first major confrontation of their married life. She trusted Peter's innate kindness and common sense to be reasonable about her decision.

Chapter 4:

Three weeks later, Beth, fully recovered called to say that she had two tickets to the Johnny Mathis concert and asked Stephanie to attend with her.

'I'm sorry I was so bitchy when I was sick,' she apologized obviously aware of a certain coolness in Stephanie's response. 'You were really nice to put up with me. But, that's just how I am.'

Stephanie was at a loss for words by the uncharacteristic self candor. She wanted desperately to maintain this friendship, despite some undefined misgivings. None the less, she agreed. Besides, she could find no logical reason for refusing. She had already made a clear statement about her love of sentimental mood music and that singer in particular.

Hearing the hesitation, Beth continued, 'You know you'll love it. They're good seats. We should be able to see him up close at the Roy Thompson Hall. Someone also told me that the acoustics are great, whatever that means.'

'We should be able to hear him really well.'

'That 'we' means you are going to come right? Steph, I don't know if Pete wants to join us later but why don't we make a night out of it. We'll have dinner after and gossip for a bit. Would you like that?'

'Yes, yes I would but what about....Gregory?'

'Oh he's working late. He can pick us up later at the restaurant. He won't mind.'

But I might, thought Stephanie uncertain about facing him again. It had been a month, but the incredible feeling that their meeting had engendered still lingered. *Was it my imagination or did I really feel as if......*

'It ok Beth. I'll ask Peter to pick me up. His company landed a very big European contract recently and he's hardly home. He is sure to be working late and his office is very near to the Hall.'

'Do you want me to book a restaurant?'

'Yes, go ahead. Anywhere close is fine.'

The evening was a success from all points of view. Johnny Mathis gave a stirring performance, reappearing for several curtain calls. The seats were as good as promised and both women reacted like lovesick teenagers when those warm brown eyes settled in their direction.

In a mellow mood after the concert, they went to the Old Fish Market, a popular seafood restaurant with a cozy atmosphere and a lively clientele. Beth less, adventurous ate a salmon plate. Stephanie was ravenous and ordered a fisherman's platter. It offered a tantalizing assortment of seafood, set off with a tangy salad. It was enjoyed with a glass of white wine and followed by key lime pie.

'You know Beth, I've really enjoyed this evening. I never thought I'd get to hear that marvelous voice in person. Isn't it incredible that someone could actually fall in love with a voice?'

'Oh Stephanie, you're so different tonight. Anyone would think you never had a crush on anyone before.'

'I haven't!'

'Not even as a teenager?'

'No. There was never time. My mind was filled only with school work. Neither boys nor pop stars rated very high on my scale of 1 to 10.'

'As long as I can remember, all I've ever wanted was a husband and lots of babies.'

The comment revealed a serious side of Beth which Stephanie had not seen before. Her tone was sincere and retrospective. 'Greg and I have been trying to have a baby for quite a while. Once or twice I missed my monthlies but then it turns out to be nothing. I get so depressed.'

'Miss your monthlies?'

'Yes, you know. I'm as regular as clockwork so I always make my plans around the fertile days. Most of the time things don't work out because I'm tired or Greg has to work late then I have to wait another month.'

'Fertile days? I don't understand. What would you wait for?'

'Stephanie, you're kidding me right. Don't you check these things too?'

'Check what?' Stephanie was embarrassed by her lack of knowledge. Beth talked as if every woman in the world should know what was happening to her body each day of the month. Stephanie only knew that when her period came, she wasn't pregnant. That happened to her so regularly in the past four years that she eventually stopped counting the weeks some months ago. Beth's comments gave her serious food for thought.

'Beth! My God! It's been so long I can't remember. I've never been very regular or conscientious about….'

'You mean you might be……?'

'Oh no! How would I know? Just let me think for a minute.'

The seconds ticked by as Stephanie made an effort to think clearly. She really couldn't remember what happened in February and March. She very much needed to speak with Peter. On second thought she wondered what she would tell him anyway. They had been so patient at the beginning, then almost giving up. She just did not think it could be possible.

The thoughts jumbled around in her head. She began to feel nauseated even as excitement coursed through her veins. Weeks, days and numbers all tumbled over and over each other. She counted backwards and forwards, reaching a fairly conclusive end. Her mouth was one big 'O', but the excitement of the discovery was too much for her nervous system. Beth who was well practiced, soon had the white face of her dinner partner discreetly tucked between two very wobbly knees.

'Stephanie' she said softly, 'it seems like you haven't been paying attention to your own calendar. It would be really great if you were pregnant. I know it's going to happen for me too. Then we can be pregnant together.'

'Hold on Beth. I can't even process this information right now, if it's true. Pregnancy would explain a lot about my feelings lately.'

'You'll be fine in a minute. Breathe deeply. Imagine sharing all the ups and downs of a pregnancy together.'

'This is not one of the 'ups' I'm sure.'

Feeling better and not a little embarrassed by her need for the unorthodox table posture, Stephanie held up a hand to stop further talk. Clearly, Beth didn't understand how much of a shock it was to realize what had taken place. She had been bent over too long. Stephanie pushed back and sat up, looking around. She was sure every eye in the restaurant was looking at her.

'I'd like to leave Beth, if you don't mind.' She felt a moment of discomfort and offered a guilty smile in her friend's direction.

'No of course I don't mind silly. I mean this is great news. You've got to tell Pete right away. Wait here. I'm going to call Greg.'

'No don't! I mean, I'll just take a taxi.'

'Oh nonsense. We are going to the same place. Greg's downtown remember. All I have to do is call his office. Wait here.'

Beth disappeared before Stephanie could raise any further objections.

Too restless to sit still contemplating the possibility of her new status, Stephanie soon followed Beth to the front door where the petite brunette had the maître'd engaged in a lengthy discussion. Her mind was in a whirl of emotion. She continued to stare at the floor wondering what changes a baby would make in her life.

She gave no thought to the present. When the toes of a pair of well polished brown shoes appeared in front of her vision, she was forced to look up into the piercing eyes of Gregory Richmond.

Following their devastating previous meeting, Gregory had kept thoughts of Stephanie strictly out of his head on a voluntary basis. Often, however, the scent of her perfume would appear from out of nowhere and assail his nostrils. Visions of her would pierce his mind's eye. He felt foolish and tried to hide this heightened desire for a scent and a pretty face with extra physical work.

In some ways Beth was the happy recipient of most of this, and once her illness had run its course, Gregory made love to his wife as often as possible, both to exorcise a curious ache inside him and to try again to impregnate his wife. After four weeks when he seemed to be nearly inside out, the ache still felt more like a burning hole unquenchable and fully consuming. Beth had given no indication yet as to her status or lack of it. At times he wondered if he even cared anymore. Yet, standing here in front of this gorgeous redhead, he felt his veins catch fire and his senses stir like a frozen man finally being thawed out.

Her eyes were green diamonds. He saw the flush that spread over her face. *'She's not that indifferent to me. I really didn't imagine the look she gave me.'*

Realizing that his absorption with his wife's friend was becoming embarrassing, Gregory turned to face his wife. He could hear the rapid breathing, saw the tightening of the lips out of the corner of his eye. He frowned, trying to hold himself in check.

'What's wrong with you Greg? I told you I was going to call you after we finished eating. You said you would pick me up.'

'I'm here aren't I?'

'You don't have to look like that. Did you say anything to Stephanie?'

Reluctantly, Gregory turned his gaze back to the woman. He didn't particularly want to. His look was almost brutal as he tried to hide behind the façade of anger. He felt anything but angry.

His hand quickly found its way into the pocket of his pants. The fists were tightly clenched. The ache in his groin was almost unbearable. He felt a hand tug at his arm.

Startled, Gregory dragged his gaze from Stephanie's flushed face and bent head and tried without much success to let his wife's words penetrate the mists of desire choking his thought process. He held himself rigidly. Beth would misinterpret his actions. She always did. For once he would be grateful not to have to explain. His behaviour was out of character and churlish.

'Greg, Steph's not feeling well right now.' Adopting that mother hen attitude Beth placed herself between the two silent bodies, pushing her husband back a little.

'I haven't said anything Beth. I just want to get home. Are you ready or not?'

Beth pursed her lips and turned back to Stephanie.

'Are you alright Steph? Are you still feeling faint?'

'No I'm fine.' Aware of tension brewing between husband and wife she produced a wan smile. 'I'm just a little shocked.'

'Beth, are you ready or not?'

Beth gave her husband a silencing look while mouthing the word 'pregnant'.

He stared at his wife as if she were a stranger. His mouth opened to repeat the impatient request when her words penetrated his own fogginess. His gaze narrowed in disbelief as he returned to the beautiful green eyes before him. 'For God's sake let's get out of here then.' Gregory knew that Beth expected an apology. He could find none within. Instead he felt a knife turn in his stomach.

The green eyes staring back at him hardened. They washed over him with a look of loathing. The bottom lip trembled slightly but held firm. Gregory knew she was a better person than him at that moment. His anger was unreasonable. She was not responsible for his feelings. She had not asked him to pick her up. He was free to take his wife and go. He could almost see the words begging to be uttered and knew that he deserved every one of them.

'Peter's at his office too, working late. He…he's going to pick me up.' Staring defiantly into Gregory's eyes, she added pointedly 'it seems we have something to celebrate.'

Beth, who seemed forgotten, nodded and placed a soft hand on Stephanie's arm. She gave a gentle squeeze before turning to her husband. 'I'm ready Greg.'

Beth's tone was frosty. He knew she would have a few choice words for him. He could stop her tirade with a few phrases of contrition and an apology but instead he would listen patiently while she vented her fiery Latin temper. Beth usually hated arguments between them. She would often back down rather than endure his cold logic. It wasn't natural to her to have a disagreement without loud voices and recriminations on both sides.

As Beth's angry torrent of words washed over his head, he felt his need pass, only to be replaced by a bitterness that was almost physical enough to nauseate him. He felt bitterness towards the man who had access to that statuesque and enchanting body; enough access to impregnate her.

Gregory welcomed his wife's fury. Once they were in the car and away from that tantalizing redhead, his overheated emotions had cooled sufficiently to accept that his boorishness had been uncalled for. But, he had been so frightened by the depth of desire he felt for a woman he had seen only once before. Of course he couldn't admit any of that to his wife. A man's weaknesses were not for display. They made him vulnerable. That woman had made him weak and vulnerable. He wanted her with a passion he could not control and with each meeting, scarcely hide.

****

Stephanie shakily made her way to a comfortable chair in the waiting lounge. Peter was not too pleased when she called but his innate good manners would prevent him from any reply other than, 'I'll be there as soon as I can'.

Sometimes I wish he would blow up or lose his temper, even rage a little, instead of that calm, placid exterior. Even his lovemaking is confined to what he feels is within a limit of decency. At least he will be ecstatic about the baby. Stephanie's thoughts ran on as she waited. *Now he will have the best reason in the world for me to stay home.*

Her mind moved quickly, not allowing any other thoughts to intrude. It effectively kept the image of Gregory Richmond at bay. That incredible man! Despite her best efforts his image popped up anyway. She looked up expecting to see him in front of her but only the serene face of her husband was there, a frown marring his forehead.

'Stephanie, are you alright?' His voice held no concern, only a polite inquiry. The look she returned held a trace of tenderness for the father of a life barely defined within her and a devilish desire to kick the back of his knees to get him to unbend literally if not figuratively. The visual produced an inappropriate giggle. Peter quickly shielded her from other patrons in the foyer.

'I'm not drunk. I only had a glass of wine with dinner. It was hardly enough to make me silly.'

'Then why….?'

'In about seven months and a half months, you are going to be a father, if my calculations and suspicions are correct.'

'That's not funny Stephanie.'

She waited expecting that the news had not sunk in. She saw her husband frown then moisten his lips nervously.

'Being a father is a serious responsibility that I….that I….'

'……would be proud to accept' she finished hoping that he was truly astonished and not disappointed. She planted a light kiss on his cheek. It was an unexpected public gesture of her love.

Seemingly moved beyond words, Peter lifted her hand and squeezed it none too gently. He didn't seem to be as stiff as he usually appeared when confronted with highly charged emotional situations. Stephanie felt he was pleased even if he said little. She knew he would need some time to adjust. Deep down inside she hoped he would offer to stay and share a glass of champagne at a quiet corner table before they drove home but he pleaded fatigue.

'We'll celebrate another time. I've got some important business matters on my mind. Let's just go home.'

Peter made love to her that night with embarrassing haste. Stephanie felt shamed by his insipid efforts. Her rising desire, almost overwhelming at the outset, was very quickly brought to its knees. From somewhere in the depths of her being, she acknowledged often being disappointed before. For the first time she wondered if there was more to be experienced between husband and wife. Lying on her side, wide awake beside Peter, who had fallen asleep quickly, she longed for some undefined sign that this event would mark a change in their relationship. He had said very little more about the pregnancy. She hoped, in time, he would be able to express his happiness.

The next morning dawned clear and bright. Stephanie had not experienced morning sickness but she was overtired by the very emotional events of the previous night. Much to her disgust, she overslept and missed getting up to make breakfast for her husband. She was surprised that he didn't even call her. Peter liked to eat well and the hour they shared in the morning was usually the most pleasurable of the day.

It was hard to read his actions but she concluded that he was being considerate of her. There would be much to talk about in the coming weeks. Planning ahead to the dinner she would make, Stephanie headed towards the bathroom to take a shower. She halted at the door, reversed direction and went to the kitchen to make coffee instead. It wasn't long before she got caught up in visions of what her baby would look like. The shower was entirely forgotten.

The coffee pot was simmering nicely when a knock was heard at the door. Stephanie was sure it would be Beth, coming to discuss the evening. She opened it with a flourish, red hair flying, ready to greet her friend with a reassuring smile. The peach coloured negligee coat opened to reveal a silky concoction clinging to her curves. A deep V exposed already fuller breasts. Her gasp of astonishment and embarrassment could not be held back. She clamped her lips together to prevent any sound being misconstrued by the egotistical, ill-mannered man at her door.

Gregory stood stock still, his senses reeling. He had not really wanted to go to Stephanie's condo. All his common senses forced him to stay away. Now that he was there, he longed to wrap his fingers in that molten lava of red gold hair and press soft kisses into the long neck.

With difficulty he pulled himself together trying to retain some sanity. Gregory allowed himself one quick look down the shimmering length of Stephanie's body, pausing at the still flattened abdomen where life was growing. He felt himself shudder with distaste. His voice was husky but controlled when he inclined his head slightly and asked to come in.

Wordlessly, Stephanie stepped back closing the coat of her negligee as he passed her.

'What do you want?' Her demand forced him to turn around and face her.

'Uh...Beth seems to think I was rude and boorish last night. She read me the riot act all the way home and demanded that I apologize,' he recited dutifully, searching her face.

'There's no need, *really.*'

'But there is a need.' He paused allowing the cryptic remark to sink in. 'She feels your friendship is too new to withstand my arrogance.'

'Then she would be right.' There was no other response to his challenging statement. No apology had been tendered. He was merely paying lip service to his wife's demands. 'On second thought, I accept your apology in the spirit in which it was given.' She rolled her eyes pointedly at the door.

Gregory ignored the unspoken request and turned to survey the sunken living room of the condo. The basic colour was a light gray throughout, but cleverly set off by patches of colour which gave every area a special feeling. Several varieties of plants in the varying shades of green dominated one corner bringing it to life under the sun's morning rays. Colourful prints dotted the walls and large comfortable cushions were thrown in careless abandon like worn out gypsies along the couch.

A bookshelf filled with novels lined the wall, some lying at drunken angles, each begging to be read. A large burgundy arm chair provided comfort. The condo had a lived in look which appealed to Gregory's homely tastes. Stephanie was proud of her decorating and warmed up to the genuinely approving and utterly devastating smile which Gregory turned on her.

'Are you an interior decorator?'

'No, but my mother seemed to have a flair for matching colours and passed on her ideas. She tried to encourage me to develop a style I like and then build on it.'

'I like your style.' He laughed nodding his head to accentuate his approval.

It was impossible to be serious. Laughing along with him helped to ease some of the tension. Stephanie's naturally exuberance and optimism reasserted itself, allowing her to relax.

'Would you like some coffee?'

'I thought you would never ask. It smells delicious. My nose tells me it is perked, the old fashioned way.'

'It is. My mother insisted that everything be made from scratch. She told me I would never have to apologize for creating something inferior if I start with only the best ingredients.'

Leading the way into the kitchen, Stephanie paused asking politely if Gregory preferred to sit in the breakfast nook or living room. He looked very formal in a dark double-breasted pinstripe suit.

'I personally prefer the kitchen' Gregory replied taking his time studying her while she was busy pouring out the coffee. His desire seemed to have waned, confronted as he was by all the symbols of her domesticity with another man. He was determined to explore other avenues with her and see if they could be friends;

perhaps even find a fault or two that would make her less goddess like and more down to earth. Beth spoke very highly of her. His wife often found it difficult to make friends. He didn't want to spoil things.

'Tell me about your mother.'

Stephanie glanced at him quickly, expecting mockery but found only sincerity in the depths of the brown eyes. She needed no encouragement to discuss either one of her unconventional parents. She realized he was probably headed to work and cut down a three act play to one scene.

'My mother was British, upper middle class, not considered a great beauty but she was sassy and totally independent. She did costume design at a local theatre and went on to become semi professional in provincial repertory companies. Her own father never did approve of her choice of profession and refused to see her, although he did support her until he died.'

'Parents can sometimes be harsh and misguided even when they love their children. Did she have a successful career?'

'She was only mildly successful in London but with good contacts she was able to broaden her circle of friends and acquaintances. During the lean post war years she could fashion marvelous costumes over and over again with the same basic material so that what Cleopatra wore this week, Juliet wore next week. She really lacked ambition, perhaps because she never needed money, but enjoyed working only for the fun of creating.'

Gregory frowned. 'What war are you talking about?'

Stephanie laughed lightly. 'My mother wasn't young when I was born. She met my father very late in life. I believe they were both shocked when she produced me. I think she is still trying to recover.'

'Does she live here?'

'No she retired in England after I got married.'

'Is she still active in the Theatre?'

Stephanie laughed again in wry amusement. He wondered if he had blundered. He had no wish for her to stop talking. Her voice had a melodious lilting sound to it.

At his puzzled look she continued.

'The irony of it is that her retirement is being spent as a lady of the manor. She is hostess at her widowed brother's country home. Now she's all the things her father wanted her to be when he was alive.'

'Does she ever miss those days in the Theatre?'

'Good heaven's no! The thought makes her shudder. I never saw the backstage of a theatre when I was growing up. We only ever sat out front. I think marriage and motherhood killed the rebellion in her.'

Stephanie looked up, embarrassed at having told this man so much of her family history on such short acquaintance. Besides, she seemed to be monopolizing the conversation and his time. He did not however, look bored. He just continued to watch her.

Gregory stared fascinated at her unadorned right hand lying idly by the coffee cup. He studiously avoided the left hand with its simple gold band. Unable to help himself, he stretched across the small table and held her long fingers in his hand, admiring the shiny colourless tips which were perfectly manicured. His behaviour was unusual in the extreme, but her hands were so softly elegant and beautifully tapered. Gregory felt her resistance but did not look at her.

Stephanie for her part closed her eyes. She admired men with a lot of hair and Gregory's grew thick and rich. Some of it peeked out at the end of his shirt cuff on the back of his hand. She longed to explore the feel of it but held her eyes closed to block out the tantalizing action of his own fingers. She knew she should stop him but could not.

Her breathing tempo increased until she felt almost lightheaded. *What on earth is the matter with me?* As the thought ended, she felt a gentle tug on her hand forcing her eyes wide open. The desire she saw reflected in Gregory's eyes both repelled and excited her. Taking a deep breath she opened her mouth to utter some words of protest. They died easily on her lips as Gregory leaned over the kitchen table and planted a firm but gentle caress of a kiss on her cheek.

'Thanks for the coffee' he said simply and got up from the table leaving Stephanie staring at the door long after it had closed behind him.

Bewildered by the man and thoroughly out of sorts with herself for failing to put a stop to this guy who was obviously a practiced Romeo, she cleaned up the kitchen and went into the study to call Georgette with her good news.

Chapter 5:

Georgette O'Malley was a tried and true friend. She could have been Stephanie's sister to a less discerning eye. They were both tall, although Georgette still needed heels to match her friend's natural height and Stephanie had a slightly fuller figure but it was their incredible hair that was so striking. Strictly speaking, Georgette had straight thick auburn hair while Stephanie possessed the red-gold titian colour of her European ancestors but they turned heads wherever they went.

It was their similarity in appearance that had them laughing together at the first meeting, but gradually they had discovered a very significant common trait; a flair for languages. Pooling their limited resources they started an agency called International Temps which offered secretarial services in foreign languages on short notice.

Between them they spoke eleven languages, could read and write in eight of those and eventually found themselves so busy they had to hire additional staff. Five years later, the agency employed twenty women and one man and covered almost every known language if not once, then twice over. Those who were able to speak a language but had no secretarial skills were trained by the agency and expected to give at least one year's service, but few left.

Now the agency was well known and respected throughout Toronto's bustling business community with its international connections. The pair were the only shareholders in the business but since Stephanie's marriage and Peter's insistence that she stay home, day to day running of the company had been taken gradually over by Georgette.

Stephanie never liked the business side of things anyway. She always preferred to be working with clients and traveling to foreign countries with a business group if necessary. It was in this manner that she met Peter. He was a junior executive at the time, traveling with his boss to Spain. Stephanie had acted as both secretary and interpreter during the trip behaving as unobtrusively as possible working quietly and efficiently. It was always the rule never to get involved with clients on trips and her beauty was often a disadvantage. On the last night of her trip with Peter's firm, his boss became overly friendly after imbibing too freely at the hotel bar. Only Peter's tactful handling of the situation prevented any lasting unpleasantness.

It was some months before Peter and Stephanie met again, under different circumstances and allowed their friendship to ripen into love and marriage. Peter, however did not forget about the trip nor the outcome, and while he was never overtly adamant about Stephanie quitting altogether, he ruled out overseas trips of any kind during the first months of their marriage.

Since travelling was the most exciting part of the job, and Stephanie really had no financial need to work, she gradually cut back over the last two years, allowing the others to take the calls. Only when a major decision regarding the office required Stephanie's approval or when no one was available to take a request from a local client did she go to the office. This past year, however, she had stopped even that.

Sighing with some regret, she reached for the telephone. Stephanie jumped as the instrument shrilled unnaturally loud, or so it seemed to her. Clearly her nerves were on edge after a very eventful twenty four hours of emotional upheavals.

'Hello Stephanie. It's me Beth. I just called to see if you were still speaking to me this morning.'

'Of course I am. Why would you think differently?' Stephanie tried to infuse a more relaxed tone in her voice. She knew Beth was very sensitive to the slightest hint of unfriendliness.

'Did Greg come and see you today?'

'Uh…. Yes he did, but an apology wasn't really necessary you know Beth. I'm afraid I was a little foolish last night over the pregnancy and he was probably anxious to get home.'

'Are you sure Steph? I mean he was nice to you this morning wasn't he? I was very angry with him last night. I…'

Stephanie cut her short, anxious to put an end to the call. 'He was an absolute gentleman,' she put in hastily embarrassment making her face hot and red. '*Thank God people can't see through phones*' she thought.

'I'm glad everything was okay then. Would you like to have coffee with me later?'

At the mention of the word coffee Stephanie almost choked and hastily explained that she was busy getting ready to go to the office. An emergency had cropped up and she was needed at least for a couple of days.

'How come you have to work all of a sudden? I know you did some stuff at home but I'm sure they could get temporary help if they wanted to.'

'It's a specialized type of secretarial work that requires my language skills Beth. We haven't talked much about what I used to do. I'd much rather stay home and have coffee with you of course, but there is…..no one else.'

'Well they shouldn't take advantage of you.'

'You're right, but just this once, I have to give in. We can meet tomorrow night and plan something for the next day.' The positive note she infused into the rain-check seemed to satisfy both that all was well between them and they rang off on the best of terms.

Hoping that her partner would not make a liar out of her, Stephanie called the office prepared to beg if necessary for something to occupy two days, even if it caused some unpleasant repercussions with Peter. Right now Stephanie needed to get back into a world she knew and enjoyed, even for a few hours. She couldn't admit to any other motives but she knew that major changes were going to happen in her life and she needed to make one last stand for independence before matters were taken out of her hands.

Her silver grey escort was humming nicely despite lack of regular use. Within an hour, Stephanie pulled into the underground parking. The offices of International Temps were located on the fifth floor in a suite of rooms leased two years ago. As the company became bigger, offering services to clients from around the world as well as locally, it had become necessary to add more working space as up to ten staff could be typing, transcribing and even working with clients in the office.

Locking the car and walking briskly to the elevators Stephanie looked and felt good. Her favourite standard gray suit was offset by rust coloured accessories. The sleek lines of the outfit were softened by a high neck silk blouse. The overall effect of a feminine business woman was achieved with a minimum of fuss. A soft chuckle escaped her and she thought of how she had been about to pick up the phone for the second time, only to have it ring again. The second call was Georgette, trying to talk over the frog in her throat, begging for help. Georgette was rarely ill but Stephanie was happy, that she really would be needed for a few days.

There was no doubt Georgette was ill. Despite the watery almond shaped eyes and red button nose, she still looked lovely in a green blouson dress. Her lovely auburn hair was piled high on her head.

'Don't come too close' she cautioned, 'especially since my little niece or nephew is one the way. I wouldn't want you to get sick as well.'

'I am going to miss your hug today. I will hold you to it when you are better but I'll stay away.'

'And you don't need to look so happy that I am sick. I would have been happy for you to come in just to talk.'

'I know but you are sick and you need to leave right now. I am here to work today and you are going home, take aspirin, get into a warm bed and rest. I am calling Mrs. Orville to ensure that you stay there until you feel better. I'll pop in to see you this evening.'

Georgette held up a hand to protest, but she was forestalled by her relentless friend. 'I drove today. There's no problem. So unless you have something pressing to share with me, just go home.'

Georgette was not offended by the proprietary attitude. She really was feeling awful. When Stephanie got married Georgette knew their close friendship would end, although she hoped that the business ties would remain. She sensed possessiveness in Peter which would prevent Stephanie having too many absorbing activities outside. Obviously, things were not too bad yet or Stephanie would not be in to work. Georgette hoped that her time in the office would be a turning point.

Stepping out of her reverie, Georgette began to tell Stephanie about a client needing a Hungarian interpreter the following day. 'Yolanda is on a case right now, but should be finished tonight. If not, can you cope? The man we are dealing with is rather feisty and demands a firm commitment. Until I spoke with you I could not offer any guarantees. He will probably call sometime this afternoon to confirm but tread carefully. He sounds as tough as nails. His name is Gre....'

The warning cost Georgette the last of her voice. Taking a deep breath to try and get out the words only resulted in several sneezes.

'Never mind. I am sure he'll explain himself adequately. If you sneeze any more I'm going to run out of languages to say *God bless you* without repeating myself.'

With a watery smile and a weak salute, Georgette left. Stephanie sat down at the desk to see what needed to be done. Four hours later she had finally managed to catch up and sort herself out with the help of a very efficient part time typist. Their regular secretary was away but the young woman was quite good at her work. Only the problem of the Hungarian translator remained unresolved.

Realizing that she was very hungry and needing to keep herself well nourished, Stephanie decided to go to the small restaurant on the ground floor and have a decent lunch. Desk work was not her forte. The walk would give her a chance to loosen up stiff muscles. Half an hour later, on her return to the office, Karen, the temp, was looking frustrated. She was obviously trying to deal with a difficult client on the telephone. Motioning to pass the call to her, Stephanie quickly entered her own office and picked up the flashing line.

'Stephanie Droga speaking' she said calmly, automatically using her maiden name.

'Why is it that I have to deal with so many people regarding a simple matter?' the caller roared. 'Can you supply me with a Hungarian speaking secretary for four hours tomorrow or not?' Each word was enunciated carefully, as if he were speaking with the hearing impaired.

Stephanie was stunned. The angry voice at the other end of the telephone was the same voice that had thanked her for coffee in the morning. It was the voice which caused so much turmoil inside of her each time they met. Hoping he wouldn't know it was her, she hastily lowered her tone to respond 'yes'.

Suspicious of such an easy victory after so much uncertainty, Gregory Richmond said in a deceptively calm voice of his own, 'do you mean that after two days of indecision, two days of giving my secretary half hearted assurances, you are now ready to give me a firm commitment?'

'Yes of course! We do like to guarantee services whenever possible, but we cannot break a contract with one client to satisfy another.' Stephanie found a voice which she hoped was businesslike and firm, but as totally different from her own as she could make it. The attack on her company, whether justified or not, set lights flashing behind her eyes. At that moment, there was more red than gold in her hair. 'These days we rarely get calls for the Uralic languages. Usually our staff compliment is quite adequate.'

'My dear lady...'

Stephanie winced at the patronizing tones. There was an insult implied in the words. 'Droga, the name is Droga Sir!'

'My dear Droga,' Gregory started to say, obviously missing the first name. He laughed realizing the absurdity of continuing with a futile argument. 'Can you have someone at my office at 1:30 tomorrow? I'll need some letters translated and a product monograph to be made up. Tell the person to ask for John Burke. He will handle all the details and arrange for an office to work in. Will that suit you Droga?'

Stephanie lost herself after hearing his deep laughter. She was imagining a pair of pale brown eyes, the perfect row of white teeth, and the lean expressive face. A second 'Droga' brought her back to earth. Forgetting the voice she had used before, she quickly answered in her normal tones. There was a puzzled silence at the other end following her brief 'that will be fine.'

'Have we spoken before Droga?'

'No sir. I think not' she replied adding a slight accent. Since she would probably never see him in the office, Stephanie felt a little deception wouldn't hurt. She did not want this man invading her life 24 hours a day. Their sexual attraction was overwhelming. It frightened her to feel so much physical awareness for a man she barely knew. They were better off keeping as much space as possible between them.

Stephanie quickly ended the call, giving her firm assurance that someone would be there the following day. Confirming the address and name of her contact she rang off with a sigh. Her relief was only short lived. At 5:55 Yolanda called in only to confirm that she would be tied up at least another day with her present client. With a sinking feeling in her stomach, Stephanie closed the office. She headed over to Georgette's condo to report on the day's happenings and check on her friend's progress. It was a wasted trip. Georgette was exhausted and sleeping soundly.

Disappointed that she could not spend time with her friend, Stephanie, reluctantly, made her way home.

At precisely 1:23 p.m. the following afternoon, Stephanie entered the office building which housed the large maritime firm. Wayfarer Shipping Co Limited was founded by James Wilson over 35 years ago. He continued to be CEO and of course Chairman of the board. He had four daughters. Three of them worked within the company but James felt that shipping was a man's world and was very pleased that his sister Dora provided him with the male child to carry on after his retirement. Gregory Richmond was the heir apparent, but he worked hard learning his trade. He spent at least a year in each department, sometimes in very junior positions absorbing every facet of the business. At present he was Vice President in charge of operations.

Armed with this information following a few discreet telephone calls, Stephanie approached the receptionist in the lake front headquarters. The structure was old but the interior had been modernized with a nautical flair in keeping with the services offered. The receptionist sat at a large desk. She seemed overwhelmed with papers and a computer. She raised her eyebrows at Stephanie's approach. At least it seemed that way. In fact she had plucked her eyebrows too high, giving her a perpetual surprised look. Stifling a laugh, Stephanie announced herself and asked for John Burke. A hasty glance around the busy open area assured her that the clerical staff was housed on the ground and the executives were upstairs. She was getting nervous and wanted to be safely ensconced in an office before Gregory Richmond showed up.

John Burke was stubby and balding. He appeared to be on the aggressive side. Stephanie wondered if the nature of the business encouraged the men to approach everything so assertively. He barely glanced her way before motioning to follow him. He did not wait for her assent or pause to see if she was behind him. The boorishness of the two men she met so far astounded her. She longed to make some protest but restrained herself. She was glad she said nothing. John Burke halted and turned to look at her, absorbing her looks for the first time. His double take was comical. Stephanie's striking looks penetrated his self absorption. He began to act as if she were the answer to his prayers despite the fact that she towered over him. His change from boor to groveling servant only served to incense her further. He obviously had no interest in her or her capabilities.

Ignoring his attempts to be nice to her, she instructed him to take her directly to the office where she would be working. She wanted to get on with the job. His company was paying the bill. It took some time for her to settle into the work. John Burke was making a nuisance of himself. Each time she needed his help with technical words he was inclined to linger. Then, the office, although attractively furnished with a stunning mahogany desk and Royal blue carpet and curtains, was a little cool, making her under worked fingers stiff and slow. The two hours stretched into three before the letters were finally translated, replies drafted, and the product monograph completed.

To Stephanie's relief, John Burke regretfully said that he had been called away to attend to some other business in another section. She could leave all the necessary papers with the receptionist. Dismissing him with a smile, the first since their first encounter, she settled thankfully to a final review of her work.

****

John Burke had just used the exit door to go upstairs when Gregory stepped off the elevator, incensed over the wasted afternoon. He had no desire to meet with any clients. His desk was littered with paperwork pertaining to the loss of a Greek ship during a fire. His company information and signature were needed for the insurance company to investigate the mishap and settle the claim with the owners. He wanted John to dig up some vital details for him and hoped he would be free to do the necessary research. Hearing that Burke was tied up in a meeting for some time, he returned to his office.

When he asked about the Hungarian translations and heard they were not yet completed, the news sent Gregory's secretary scurrying out of the office to avoid hearing the expletives that Gregory rarely used but needed at that moment to let off steam. To his credit he did apologize later but the few words barely released the tension within him. Getting up from his desk he paced back and forth wanting to find some meaningful work to release his pent up energy. It was hopeless. He was unable to settle down and concentrate on any detailed documents.

Stephanie, finally satisfied with her work, stood up, stretched lazily and took a few deep breaths before sitting down again. Massaging tired fingers, she bent over to pick up a sheet of paper which had fallen to the floor. She had no need to look up as she grabbed the errant page. The hairs on the back of her neck began to prickle. She knew it was Gregory Richmond who had opened the door. He was staring at her back. *He couldn't know that I am here today. Should I get up or not?* Much as she wanted to avoid a confrontation with him she could not stay head down forever.

'What are you doing there? Do you need help or what?' The voice was curious, impatient then suspicious. Stephanie reluctantly raised her head from under the desk and stood up hoping to face him with as much aplomb as she could muster. She felt that he would be too much of a professional business man to bait her, or assault her senses in a public place. The hope died instantly as she finally looked up, encountering the shock, the smile and that incredible sexual pull. *It's too late,* she thought. A wave of dizziness washed over her as her body adjusted to the hasty change in posture. She swayed slightly on her feet and he, realizing she was ill based on the sudden pallor in her face, was at her side in a few quick strides, gathering her in his arms.

No need now for any quick measure to prevent her fainting. At the touch of his hands on her body, warmth began to flow through her. Stephanie never knew when the help and comfort became sensuous in nature, but the vigorous movements became slower, patterned following invisible pathways to the core of her womanhood. She wondered that the caresses on her back could give so much pleasure. Stephanie was melting into this man, feeling in the touch, his increasing ardency, an inexplicable anger and tension and his physical need of her. She clung to him burying her face in his neck, afraid to see what was in his eyes.

Gregory needed more. He needed to see if an answering response was in her face. Gently pushing her away from him and speechless since those first terse words, he looked into her eyes, searching her face with shaking fingers. 'Do you realize what I am feeling right now?' His whispered voice was filled with awe.

Stephanie's only reply was an affirmative nod of her head. She was bemused by his eyes, unable to speak. Afraid to utter any sound, she kept her hands flat on his chest, just below his shoulders, neither aggressive nor defensive in posture. She sensed that one word or gesture would activate passions within both of them that would have far-reaching effects.

'He must be the one. I desire him. I feel a need in me to give all and more to this man. I don't understand it and I can't control it.'

Gregory saw the up and down emotions. He was afraid too. With the upper halves of their bodies apart but the lower halves touching he knew that Stephanie must be aware of how much he desired her. That desire could also be interpreted in a purely physical way. He wanted her to see that his ardour went beyond the physical. He bent forward, avoiding as much physical contact as possible. He bestowed a light kiss on her lips, then another and another. He teased her, checking himself, hoping her need would be as great as his.

The light kisses became unbearable torture. A driving hunger possessed both of them. Their lips met and opened allowing free exploration. Bodies met and strained towards each other. Hands roamed freely, hers in his thick hair, at times caressing, then pulling and tugging. His hands removed the pins securing the knot at the top of her head savouring the long strands in his fingers. With her head thrown back, Gregory had access to the creamy neck, the curves and hollows from ear to shoulder and he explored all of them, his lips and tongue creating sensations Stephanie had never experienced in her life. His hand found its way to caress a sensitive breast, reveling in the fullness and hardened peak.

Stephanie's hands did not remain idle. She undid the middle buttons of his shirt, exploring the hairs on his sculptured chest, drawing the garment from the waistband of his trousers and putting her arms around his torso. Her hands felt as if they were being caressed by the movement of the muscles in his back. Feverishly they clung together and kissed, neither mindful of anything except their mounting passion. Gregory felt himself losing control. He had not felt like this since his teenage years. Clinging to Stephanie, his body shuddered and convulsed while he held her tightly, his face buried in her soft scented neck.

Frightened by his sudden stillness, Stephanie tried to look into his face, but he continued to hold her, whispering apologies into her ear.

'I'm sorry I lost control like that. Having you in my arms just seemed to be the continuation of a dream. Your perfume haunted me for weeks before I met you. I imagined over and over what it would be like to capture your scent from the warmth of your body.'

Stephanie heard the tenderness in his voice. The intimacy implied in his words woke her senses to the reality of the situation. As awareness surfaced, and she understood what passed between them, she struggled to control her breathing. Trying desperately to push him away and put some space between them, her hands released his shirt and crossed over her breasts in a protective posture.

Feeling embarrassed and not a little uncomfortable Gregory sought to hold her for a little while longer but common sense dictated that his intimate proximity could only ignite them further. Holding her shoulders for an agonizing second, and seeing the clear signal of her distress, he moved away to straighten his clothes. He leaned tensely against the wall near the door. With the width

of the room between them Stephanie stammered, 'I....I'm...so...
sorry. I don't know what came over me. I've never done anything
like this before. I must have been out of my mind.'

She tidied her hair and clothes, hastily grabbing her bag and
hoping to leave with as much dignity as she could muster. There
was no doubt that she was frightened by her response to him and
the feelings he aroused in her. 'I need some time to think. I must
get away from here....now!' She almost shouted the last word.
Years of being left unfulfilled by Peter and now this satisfying yet
incomplete encounter was rubbing raw nerves together.

Gregory sensed her agony. 'Stephanie, please listen to me. We
have to talk. I know this is not a good time but will you meet me
somewhere in about half an hour....just to talk? He did not want
to beg but was aware of the refusal on the tip of her tongue. She
shook her head before he could utter another word.

'Please, what happened here is too important for us to pretend
it never occurred.'

'No! Can't you see this is all wrong?' There is nothing to
discuss. It should never have happened. I intend to forget it and I
suggest you do the same.'

Stephanie made to leave but he blocked the door. He didn't
touch her but a look of real terror began to show in her face. 'Look
I won't touch you again. I've made you that promise. I don't make
a habit of seducing every pretty woman I see but I feel something
for you that I just can't explain. It won't go away because you
wish it would.' His eyes pleaded for an understanding of the
incomprehensible. 'I know that feelings got out of hand here but
you wanted me as much as I wanted you.'

Stephanie chose not to confirm or deny the blatant truth of
his words. She had wanted him with a passion she never knew
existed within herself and she was deeply ashamed of her actions
and more so of her reactions. She hated being backed into a
corner. Right now she needed air.

'Yes, I admit it, but it changes nothing. It was just a moment
of weakness and lust. I have never, ever behaved like that in

my life. I was just overwhelmed.' Her voice softened a little in acknowledgement of her surprising next words. 'You are, after all, a very attractive man.' Stephanie held up a hand to stop him saying a word. Her tone hardened again as anger and self disgust overcame the previous mindless desire. 'Have you forgotten you are married, I'm married and expecting a baby?'

Gregory looked as if she had slapped him. He had indeed forgotten her pregnancy, even her husband when she was in his arms. Beth was always at the back of his mind but he struggled to keep her there, while the unexplained emotions for the beautiful woman in front of him demanded his immediate attention. Her words made him aware of the rest of the world, even the office in which they were talking. For a few moments he had been on another plane, oblivious to anything but the feel and smell of her in his arms, her lips on his. Gregory felt desire mounting in him again. He searched her face once more hoping for some sign that she would change her mind and stay to talk. The green-gold eyes were like ice chips. Wordlessly he stepped aside for her to pass out the door.

Chapter 6:

A quick trip to a nearby powder room at the deserted reception area affected some temporary repairs before Stephanie returned to her office. During the drive back, her skin had enough time to react to the passionate assault on her face and she was horrified by her refection as she stumbled into the private bathroom in her own personal office.

Her eyes were red rimmed and puffy, the lips swollen and bruised in some areas. Her face was totally devoid of makeup and her hair, normally unruly looked like she had an encounter with a light socket. There was no joke though in the electrifying feelings that Gregory Richmond ignited in her. That thought was firmly quashed. Stephanie fervently sent up a prayer to offer some thanks for the empty offices. She did not want anyone to see her in this state.

It was getting late. Like an automaton, she made a cup of tea to quell her heaving insides, continuing to evade any but the most necessary thoughts as she checked and signed the day's work sheets for the accountant. But it was impossible. Tears of shame and humiliation fell with vengeance born in her guilt.

I must see Georgette tonight she moaned aloud. I must find some measure of control before going home to face Peter. After splashing her face with cold water and completely redoing her makeup, Stephanie closed the office and hurried down to the underground parking to get her car.

****

Georgette O'Malley was one of nature's unusual combinations. She had a mixture of modern chutzpah and ancient culture. The former developed from years as a navy brat and the latter, she inherited from her Chinese mother.

Ryan O'Malley, her impressive, gruff father was a British navy man through and through. He spent his early years travelling from port to port enjoying his experiences fully. Women had no part in his life except the odd 'girl in every port'. He was essentially a man's man and only sought female company when his physical needs got the better of him.

He was eventually stationed at Hong Kong for an extended period of time. While enjoying life there he became fascinated by the most exquisite fragile looking Chinese beauty named Jin Sung.

After months of alternately wooing her ardently or trying to maintain some distance from her, Ryan finally succumbed to the irresistible web of love and presented himself to Jin Sung's father. Hat in hand, Ryan begged the old man for permission to seek her hand in marriage. Many obstacles were put in the way of the couple but Commander O'Malley's credentials as a navy officer were impeccable and Jin Sung, being well over 30 and unlikely to find anyone else, despite her father's money, were married. There were weeks of deliberations within the family. The old people shook their heads but everyone agreed that they seemed a well suited couple. Their complete love for one another was obvious. Separations were inevitable in a navy marriage but Ryan continued to worship his wife throughout their life together. On his retirement, they settled in England.

Jin Sung devoted herself to making her husband's time at home as relaxing and worry free as possible. He never knew until long after they were married, that beneath the docile exterior was an adventurous woman who longed to travel, see the world, and escape the tyranny of a male oriented society that had no use for an intellectual woman. With her horizons broadened and complete security in her husband's love they became the most popular and respected couple within the elite navy officer circles.

With their life style, they felt a child would be an encumbrance. Both were basically joined in an intellectual and passion free relationship. Their couplings were infrequent and really only for Ryan's pleasure. Neither enjoyed the act particularly but merely performed well together just as they did everything else. It was a complete shock when Jin Sung found herself pregnant after five years of marriage. Their dismay was later replaced by complete resignation, calmly accepting the changes that would be made in their life. Providing the baby was healthy, they both hoped for a daughter who they felt would adapt more fully to the life they shared.

Georgette, so named for a popular British author, became a focus for her parents. She was loved, cared for, educated and adored by the single unit they became. Looking back, Georgette confided to Stephanie that she longed more than anything to be let into their magic circle, but they were as one. She was secure, well travelled, well bred and physically a perfect balance of her mother and father, inheriting his auburn hair and commanding stature and her mother's almond shaped eyes, full lips and a porcelain perfect complexion.

At age eighteen, Georgette left home, tired of trying to see her parents as individuals. Their closeness seemed to exclude her as a person. They had raised her beautifully, giving her insights into life and living but nothing specific about her role as a woman, nor a man's role in her life. Her intellectual, asexual and passionless parents created a void in her life. She knew of the pain and pleasure of physical love by reading and hearing stories but there was very little physical contact within the family. Rather than be hurt by the unknown Georgette choose to remain aloof, an observer of life's mysteries but never a participant.

****

It was almost seven o'clock in the evening when Stephanie rang the chimes to Georgette's condo. She wondered how she could have let so much time elapse without a social evening in the company of her friend. Looking back over the past few months Stephanie could clearly see that she had avoided any personal contact with Georgette, confining their communication to business.

There wasn't much point in using Peter as an excuse. The enmity between her husband and best friend existed from the day they met and yet until a year ago, Stephanie had always successfully run the gauntlet between them. If any changes had taken place, they were within Stephanie herself. Deep in the recesses of her mind she knew that in four years of marriage her personal growth had been at level zero, but she refused to acknowledge that the stifling effect of her husband's mono-faceted personality was largely responsible for this.

There was still no answer at the apartment and Stephanie was having some difficulty keeping her negative thoughts at bay. Georgette had been so ill the previous day. Surely a message would have been left at the office if anything serious happened. The day had been fraught with too many sensations already. Searching frantically in her bag for the spare key she kept, she failed to hear the door open or see the look of concern on Georgette's face.

'Stephanie, whatever are you searching for? Come inside for heaven's sake. You look absolutely weary. I am sorry I was so long but I was trying to get rid of a very persistent suitor on the phone.' The words were said with neither great surprise nor reprimand. She always maintained a cool, calm stoic air.

'How are you feeling?' Stephanie inquired delaying the inevitable questions that would surface once Georgette saw her face in the light.

'Much better thanks.' It was followed by a shrug. 'No matter how sick I was yesterday, today I feel well. But you…?'

Stephanie held up a hand to ward off verbal swords with her friend. Georgette would be absolutely blunt and demand to know the truth. Stephanie would tell her and seek advice, but she wasn't ready yet. There was complete understanding between the two women. Georgette would wait. Stephanie was in need of a hot meal first.

Over an hour later, replete from a dinner of poached egg on veal cutlet, spinach salad, tiny new boiled potatoes and a small glass of wine, the two women were seated at either end of a large plush white sofa. Café au lait sat steaming in cups on the coffee table. They were staring into an artificial fireplace which gave every appearance of being real. Over dinner, personal topics were avoided and only business was discussed. Stephanie had been appalled to discover that she could not even talk about current events. It had been so long since she did more than give a cursory glance at the newspaper or listen to the nightly news. Peter never discussed world events with her.

The red and yellow lights of the logs began to have a hypnotic effect on Stephanie. She carefully recited in a monotone the events of the day, leaving out only the most intimate details. Neither shame nor regret was evident in her voice.

Georgette knew and understood how she was feeling. She held out her hand and Stephanie moved across the length of the sofa to sit on the floor. Silent tears streamed down her cheeks. Georgette stroked the red gold hair, whispering word of comfort. It had always been thus. The older more travelled Georgette, the mentor, the listener, offering stability to the turbulent often volatile personality. Complete devotion and trust was shared between both.

The sobs subsided quickly, most having been spent earlier. 'I just don't know what came over me today.' She paused then added a disclaimer. 'That's not really true Georgy. I have been attracted to this man from the first day I saw him. I could no more resist what he offered today than breathe. It frightens me.'

'Sometimes,' her friend offered, 'the chemistry between two people just exists without cause, without reason, but with disastrous result if the two people belong to others.'

'I understand all the repercussions,' she replied massaging her aching temples. 'I don't intend to let this feeling get the better of me. Wrapping her arms around bent knees, she rested her head back trying not to relive the feel of being in Gregory's arms.

'The only way to avoid that is to avoid the man.'

'I know but how can I when his wife and I are friends? If I make any attempt to break off our relationship now it will be taken as a personal affront to her and only make me feel guilty.'

'Which situation makes you feel more guilty?'

Stephanie felt her restlessness return and she stood up then, pacing the room in her agitation before she spoke again. 'There will be no other situation, Georgette!' Stephanie's eyes flashed, not so much in anger as determination. 'I have a husband and he loves me. I'm pregnant for God's sake!' The determination was turning into anger directed at herself and Georgette was concerned. Stephanie rarely blew up in the past, but lately she always seemed to waver between apathy and barely controlled hysteria. Getting up and putting her arms around her trembling friend, she led Stephanie back to the couch forcing her to sit and try to calm down.

'Georgy, you never liked Peter. We've been married for four years now and still, you barely speak to each other. You never visit me if he's at home, and we don't go out together in a foursome. Why Georgette?'

The older woman was puzzled by the change in topic. She could not understand why she was being questioned at this time. Her dislike of Peter was solely based on his unsuitability as a husband for her friend and partner. She knew someone of Stephanie's temperament needed strength and forcefulness in a man. Essentially Peter was weak and he stifled all the natural vitality of his wife, hoping to increase his own stature.

Georgette knew from observing Stephanie this evening that her personality was being submerged in the same boring mould of her husband's so as not to provide him with competition in any way. It was having a disastrous effect on her emotional stability.

She knew that Gregory Richmond was probably exactly what Stephanie needed, but not under this type of circumstance. None the less she offered a lame comment. 'I've told you before that I just didn't think you were right for each other; but I guess after four years, I may have to revise my opinion.' A tinkling little laugh followed the lie.

Stephanie was not amused. 'You don't fool me you know. You've never said that before but you know as well as I do that if Peter were all I needed in a man I wouldn't be running into the arms of someone else.'

'A lot of what you said is true but I don't honestly think you can pinpoint any specific reason for your feelings towards this man. Examine your relationship with Peter and see what you can do to fulfill your attraction for Gregory in other ways.....with your husband.'

'That sounds like good advice.' Stephanie said getting to her feet. 'I must get home and get a good night's sleep. I'm sure that Peter won't be pleased to find me out this late again. I'm sorry that you've been sick but he had to back down when I insisted that one of us needed to be at the office. I'll be in tomorrow. I intend to continue working, even half days for awhile. I never thought I would if I was pregnant but somehow I just need to get out of the apartment.'

Georgette remained smiling for some time after Stephanie left. Wanting to work was a good sign. Whatever was the catalyst, she was pleased that her partner was beginning to show some signs of taking control of her life again.

Chapter 7:

Stephanie wearily let herself into the darkened condo. It was obvious that Peter was not home yet. The telephone was ringing insistently. Stephanie hated the situation. The caller invariably would hang up on her just as she picked up the handset. Nevertheless she made a bee line for the phone in the kitchen area.

As she shut the front door with her foot, the strap of her purse slipped from her shoulders. Ignoring the dangling bag, she rushed to the kitchen mounting the first two steps with one bound of her long legs. The bag unfortunately got tangled in her left foot and she was thrown off balance. Stephanie still negotiated the last step but was almost completely off balance as she stood in the kitchen hopping on one foot, the telephone still jangling in her ear. She was wavering dangerously between the kitchen table and the wall, her legs seemingly controlled by some master puppeteer.

By now the strap of her bag was hopelessly tangled in her leg almost to her thigh. Stephanie knew she was going to fall. She veered to her left in hopes of hitting the wall and protecting her unborn child from the sharp edges of the kitchen table. Mere seconds had passed.

Miraculously she hit the wall, taking the brunt of the blow on her back and left shoulder but the hand that came up in a self protective action hit the edge of the wall by the stairs. Incredibly, there was only a moment of pain and then it was gone.

Gathering up her scattered and frightened senses, she realized that the telephone was still ringing. Swearing in frustration she reached for it muttering that *'this had better be good or else'* and almost but not quite shouted *'hello'*.

Beth, on the other end of the line, was peevish and upset. Her mother had called and ruined a perfectly good day with endless complaints; Stephanie seemed to have forgotten they were getting together tonight. To top off a miserable day, her husband had come home irritable, refusing to sympathize with her. It seemed like the last straw to talk to someone else in a bad mood.

At first she thought she had dialed the wrong number but ventured on tentatively, 'Steph is that you? I just called to find out what happened. We were supposed to get together remember?'

There was a long pause. 'Beth I'm very sorry. Really, I did forget, but something came up at work. I should have....I should have....I...'

Stephanie felt a moment of contrition when she heard Beth's voice. It was followed by an incredible feeling of guilt, which washed over her in waves. She raised a numbed arm to wipe her brow and through hazy eyes saw her hand. Its appearance shocked her. It looked like a blood vessel had burst but where was the pain she wondered, staring at her hand fascinated. It hit with an impact so sudden, the throbbing so violent, it took her breath away. Further waves of nausea washed over her. A terrifying scream could be heard echoing around the condo, long after she was lying senseless on the floor.

Beth heard the agonized scream. She thought, at first, that Stephanie was angry with her, but the subsequent crash and banging of the phone told her that something was seriously wrong. She called into the receiver a few times, scared, then shouting.

Gregory meanwhile was slumped over the desk in his den, head in hand. His agony over the day's conduct was raging through his mind meeting head on with a desire still smoldering at his core. The sound of her name echoed hollowly in his ears. It took some time before he realized that his wife was in fact calling

Stephanie's name. The tone was one of desperation. He wondered, in sudden overwhelming guilt, if Beth knew. Did Stephanie call and tell all? He laughed mirthlessly to himself. The one time he strayed, although, he amended silently there was no excuse at any time, he was going to get caught. Lifting the glass in front of him to take another deep draught of the neat whisky, he thought, *'I can't help what I feel. Surely it was just a physical reaction I'll conquer in time'.*

The voice from the other room however was beginning to sound very strange now, even to his own guilty ears. Deciding to face Beth with whatever accusations she had and put Stephanie out of his mind and life for good…or at least to the back of his mind, he went out into the living room, totally unprepared to find his wife screaming at him in a frightened voice.

'Greg, you've got to do something. I've just been talking to Stephanie on the phone and something has happened to her. I know….I just know…. Please do something! Now Gregory!'

'What happened Beth?' He spoke calmly seeing that his wife was getting hysterical.

'I was talking to her and suddenly she screamed… real loud… and…. and then I…. h…heard a big crash….oh My God Gregory! Do you think she was attacked?'

'Stay here Beth until I call you. If you don't hear from me in ten minutes, call the police. Do you hear me Beth?'

'Yes, yes OK…but be careful please.'

Gregory wasted little time examining any more of his feelings. He knew his stomach was somewhere in his throat and bile was threatening to choke him very soon. He also knew a profound relief that Beth had not found out about today. Beyond that his mind refused to even function until he saw what lay ahead.

The apartment door was closed but not locked. He opened it cautiously. A dim light was glowing in the kitchen area and all he could see was a pair of long legs in his line of vision. Throwing all caution to the wind he went inside and dropped to his knees beside the inert form. The phone was still hanging from its socket and he spoke to Beth briefly, giving her a list of things to bring before hanging up.

Once he ascertained that she was breathing, Gregory quickly checked her for any sign of injury around the head. Eventually his gaze fell on the injured hand. It was too much. The bile was checked, but tears spilled onto the bloodless face beneath him. This was not a time for weepy sentiment. Gregory knew the tears were a result of several factors surrounding the events of the day but he did not want to examine his feelings or motives any further. His first priority was to get the ring off the rapidly swelling finger and try to make her comfortable until she revived.

He gently took her hand and placed the ring finger in his mouth. He tried to avoid pulling hard. It was clear the hand was badly injured. He removed the ring, shoved it in his pocket then picked her up. He staggered slightly before making his way slowly to where he had seen the couch on his early morning visit the previous day. As he moved, Stephanie began to stir, moaning softly at first then with increasing clarity. Gregory realized that she was regaining consciousness and the pain in her hand was beginning to make itself felt. The moans became louder and her body began to shake. Wave after wave of undefined feeling passed through him. Her pain made him ache to absorb it. He couldn't do much more than just whisper words of scant comfort as he lay her gently on the living room couch. He was kneeling over her trying to find a comfort spot for her hand when the light came on flooding the area and startling Gregory who had not heard the door open.

'What are you doing with my wife!?'

Peter, angry and defiant stood in the vestibule far enough away, but the scene which confronted him must have been shocking. He obviously had no idea what was going on. To Gregory's sensitive eyes, he didn't seem as if he wanted to know either.

'I've had a hard day with all kinds of pressure to deal with. I...I asked you a question. What are you doing with my wife?'

Gregory had not reached his position in life so quickly without being able to read people well. Confronted with a similar situation he would not be hovering in the doorway asking questions nor explaining himself. Although the words were aggressive, Peter's questions had been uttered like a spoiled child talking to a bully. Rocking on his heels, Gregory spoke with quiet authority.

'Your wife was talking to mine on the phone. Beth heard a scream and thought someone was attacking Stephanie. She asked me to come down and investigate. I found your wife on the floor in the kitchen. Somehow she seemed to have injured her hand, then passed out.'

He moved slowly away from the whimpering figure on the couch as he spoke, gesturing at the same time for Peter to advance. To Gregory's surprise, Peter merely took a few steps forward then leaned over and peered at his wife.

'She looks awful!' he stated unnecessarily. 'Is she going to alright? My god! Her hand is swollen all out of proportion. It is broken?'

'I am not a Doctor but it would seem so. I think that if you are unable to assist me here, perhaps you would be kind enough to call a doctor.'

Resuming his position at the couch, Gregory continued unable to keep the sarcasm from entering his voice. 'My wife should be here any minute with some ice and blankets. I had no idea where to find them here. Would you please call a Doctor?' he added with increased emphasis as the man continued to stare without moving.

'When Beth gets here they can lean on each other', he thought disgustedly. *'They're two of a kind in this respect anyhow'*.

Stephanie opened her eyes cautiously. Her body seemed to be one big ache that centered solely on her left hand. She was disoriented and confused but one fact was clear, Gregory was here, holding her good hand, putting something cold on her head, whispering words of comfort.

She relaxed under his ministrations knowing from previous experience that Peter, with his almost phobic fear of illness, would not be able to do anything. Her mind was apart from her body, avoiding the pain, finding only the solace.

****

Hours later, between bouts of consciousness, Stephanie awoke in the hospital, safe and comfortable at last. The throbbing hand was a dull ache. Full memory returned, but she was pleasantly drowsy. The weathered face of Dr. Czerny was above her, stern but concerned.

'You seemed to have given us all a scare Stefania. Do you remember what happened?'

She gave a brief account of the accident up until she lifted the telephone receiver. A look of fear entered her eyes and her hand automatically felt the slight almost imperceptible swelling of her abdomen.

The Doctor, who had known her since childhood and whose busy practice included many such moments, accurately interpreted the questioning gesture.

'You've been lucky Stefania. Why haven't you come to see me before now?'

'I realized that I could be pregnant just two days ago. Is it going to be alright?'

'The baby's fine' he stated confidently. 'They are very well protected from external stress. The water surrounding them buffers most shock waves. From what you tell me, your lower back did not actually receive the worst of the first blow and the second was slight. I am still very surprised not to have seen you for such a long time. Even if you didn't need me as a doctor, I am still your friend…but we will discuss that tomorrow.'

'What about my hand Michael?' she asked plaintively, subdued by his professional manner and gentle rebuke for the neglect of their relationship.

'The blow to your hand cracked the bone below your third finger and ruptured a blood vessel. The pressure on a nerve caused the initial numbness. This will last until some of the swelling subsides. You have wrenched your shoulder. No doubt you will have quite a few bruises tomorrow. I'll have a specialist look you over tomorrow for the hand and the baby but you'll do fine for tonight.'

With those final words, he gave her uninjured hand an affectionate squeeze and quietly left the room but Stephanie had fallen asleep almost before the door closed behind him.

****

The next day passed quickly. Stephanie remained in bed giving her body time to recover. Despite the doctor's reassurance, he wanted to avoid any possible risk to her unborn child. The hand continued to be intermittently painful and numb, but the periods of pain were longer and longer. 'A good sign' decreed the specialist who breezed in for an early morning consultation.

Georgette visited in the morning with lots of magazines to occupy Stephanie who was getting increasingly restless. Peter also came early, but was very ill at ease and merely stayed long enough to assure proprieties. His wife understood his fear and dislike of hospitals. She knew that he had spent his life with a demanding invalid mother alternatively resenting then loving her. He was feeling very dispassionate towards her when she died. Guilt warred with relief for a long time after her death, but the sight and sound of anything medical reduced him to a quivering insecure boy.

Beth also arrived early but walked around the hospital room as if she were afraid to touch anything. Stephanie was happy to be in a private room. She didn't know how either Beth or Peter would have reacted to another sick person. Beth seemed to want to talk and relished her part in the drama, repeating each second of it. Every member of her family had heard the story and Gregory's daring rescue at the bidding of his wife.

Stephanie was certainly grateful to Gregory and Beth but she had not seen him since the accident and could not really remember much of the subsequent events. Only the scene earlier in the day, when she had been held captive in his arms, replayed in her mind. She wondered with deep guilt if any of her feeling had been exposed during her semi-conscious moments. Stephanie hoped that if Gregory did come to visit, it would be with Beth or with someone else present. She dreaded facing him again. In spite of her feelings, it would be expected that she offer her own thanks personally.

****

Georgette had returned for an evening visit when Gregory finally arrived. She was, however, on the point of leaving for a date. She refused to be detained, even by the beseeching look which Stephanie sent in her direction. Georgette was actually consumed with curiosity to meet and speak with this man who could turn Stephanie into a weeping passionate woman. No amount of curiosity however could displace good manners. She had committed herself to a date. Gregory and Stephanie would need some time to talk and sort through the events of the past twenty four hours.

Gregory thought so too. He came without his wife.

Georgette acknowledged the stilted introduction made by Stephanie with a gracious nod and a few polite words. She departed in a swirl of silk and perfume to meet her date at an exclusive art showing. An awkward silence fell between the two who remained in the room. They both looked around uncomfortably, observing with unwarranted attention, the bland beige walls, the fluorescent lighting, and the safety windows darkening in the twilight sky. Gregory had only concern written over his face, but Stephanie remembered little of their last encounter. Only the time spent in his arms came into her thoughts. Her eyes remained lowered, nervous fingers pleating the crisp white cotton material of the bed sheet.

'Perhaps, I shouldn't have come?'

'Oh no!' Stephanie exclaimed looking up. 'I'm not sure what happened at home but Beth and Peter have both told me how helpful you were when I fell. I wanted to.. uh…thank you personally and I do…thank you…I mean.'

'Your thanks are accepted. It was an unfortunate accident, but you seem to be on the road to recovery.'

'Yes, yes I am.'

Another silence fell across the room. Gregory moved nearer. Stephanie raised a hand as if to stop him.

'We have to talk, Stephanie. I know this isn't the time or the place.' He hurried on before she could stop him. 'I don't want you to be afraid of me. Please just hear me out. I don't know what is happening to me or between us but we have to talk about it.'

Stephanie raised her eyes to the ceiling to gaze unseeingly at the metal runners for the bedside curtains. She knew she was not afraid of him. She was afraid of herself and the strong feelings she felt towards him. She was married and pregnant. *Why would this be happening to her now? Could she tell him her thoughts?*

Gregory's eyes never left her face. Glancing at him quickly, she searched his features for any signs of deceit but the look he returned was open and honest. Satisfied that he was sincere, she sighed and said 'I am afraid, Gregory. Not so much of you, although the intensity of passion between us has scared me. But more than that I'm afraid of where this is leading. I am not the kind of person…or at least I didn't think I was the kind of person…who would have…an…an affair.'

Gregory knew she was feeling as guilty as he did. He searched for some reassurance to offer her. 'Stephanie, none of us, I think, actively go searching for lovers. I've never…since Beth and I have been together, but there is something about you that….'

He trailed off the rest of the sentence leaving his protestation unsaid. It still was not the right time. The restless fingers were threatening to shred the tortured material on the bed. During the silence which ensued, he casually surveyed her profile. Even without makeup she was magnificent. Pale but composed, the cupid's bow mouth look sensuous and inviting. A barely perceptible movement alerted him that she was saying something and he had to refocus his attention on the whispered words, before he realized that she had been speaking for some time.

'…hates anything to do with hospitals you see. His mother was an invalid for most of his life.'

Stephanie paused for some time. She was wondering if Gregory would understand the point she wanted to make. 'Usually he's pretty good' she continued tentatively, 'but this type of situation would have been impossible for him to handle'.

Gregory frowned.

She could not be certain if he was puzzled, angry, or indifferent. She gave him a beseeching look, searching for some understanding. His first impression of her husband could not have been good. She knew that Peter would have been hopeless if he had found her on the floor. That wasn't a measure of her husband's character and she didn't want Gregory to blame Peter for her uncharacteristic *lapse of moral behaviour.*

Misinterpreting the pathetic defense of her husband's inexcusable conduct, Gregory enunciated carefully to suppress his anger and stated, 'the important thing was to get you to the hospital Stephanie. You were drifting in and out of consciousness. It was really your doctor who made the decision to bring you right in'.

She was disappointed. Gregory seemed to have lost the drift of the conversation. He had dismissed Peter simply by not mentioning his name. She should have been angry, but she was not somehow and changed the subject to avoid any further chance of controversy or misunderstanding between herself and the patently sexy man leaning against the door jamb.

'Dr. Czerny has been a friend since my childhood. He was very angry with me. I hadn't been to see him yet about…well… you know.'

Gregory nodded, not wanting to speak and break the slight ease of tension between them. He felt he had disappointed her somehow but he could not condone her husband's behaviour under any circumstances.

She sighed tremulously. He was about to leave but she motioned for him to sit in a vacant chair closer to the bed. He cautiously lowered his lengthy frame into a comfortable position on her good side, near enough to touch her. He knew he could not, and let out a deep sigh matching her own.

A slight chuckle from the bed was reassuring. Her fears were under control for now at least. She didn't seem to want him to leave. Trying to find a safe topic, he searched his brain. His eyes noted her hospital bracelet. The difference in her last name confused him. She had said her name as *Droga* but the bracelet clearly read *Atkinson*. Curious, he sought a way to introduce the name without reference to their encounter at his office.

'Tell me about your father,' he demanded quietly. 'I had only half the story before.'

Stephanie felt a sudden pain as she jerked her head around to look at him. She waited for the pain to subside, breathing evenly for a few seconds. Gregory stayed the hand that automatically reached out to comfort her and waited patiently for her to begin.

'You seem to know that I love to talk about my parents.'

'I'm also curious about why you have two last names?'

'This one belongs to Peter. I started the business in my maiden name and never felt a need to change.'

'I'd still like to hear about your father.'

'It's a sad story with a happy ending. My Papa was very tall, very slim, and kind of bookish in appearance. He was married before completing university but continued his studies to become a professor of languages in his native Budapest. He taught English and French. Papa was a well respected teacher and colleague. During the tumultuous years of the Hungarian revolution his upper middle class background seemed to make him an enemy of the people. Those, who he thought were his friends, suddenly turned against him, but he would never have left Hungary.'

'Is it painful to talk about?'

'No, but I ache for the pain my father must have felt when his wife and young son were accidentally killed during a particularly violent street protest. Feeling broken and alone, he escaped relatively easily to England and settled there. With little effort he obtained a teaching post near Nottingham at a private boy's school. He never thought to find love again and was content with his life as a widower. One joy however was his love of repertory theatre. At first he used to go there solely to improve his skill in colloquial and conversational English. Then it became a genuine pleasure. Finally it was to find love. He always said that a performance, rich with Hungarian scenes and costumes, so stirred the dying embers in his heart that he had to meet the creator of such beauty from his homeland.

My mother was exactly one foot shorter than my father but it was love at first sight. They were both over forty and neither expected love or a family.' There was a wistful quality to Stephanie's voice as she concluded her story.

Unwilling to break the mood but curious to hear the end of the story, he prompted, 'how did they eventually arrive in Canada?'

Allowing her parent's love story to wash over her gently, Stephanie went on, more thoughtful now, her eyes misting over in memory. 'Their marriage was not opposed in any way. Mama always said Papa was such a kind and gentle man. Everyone who met him could not fail to be attracted to his soothing personality and cultured manners. There were no other real social barriers. Papa's family history was as acceptable as Mama's but both felt that her domineering father might interfere. They decided on Canada for a honeymoon and just stayed on in Montréal. Helen, my mother, conceived on the boat trip over and I was born eight months later. My father lived until my 16th year.' There was no rancour in her tone. Gregory knew those sixteen years had been happy and secure.

Intuitively, he probed, 'did your father na..?' but he never finished the question because she turned her head, looking at him fully for the first time since he entered the room and simply said 'yes, I was named for my half brother Stefan.' It was actually my mother's wish to honour the family my father lost. She named me Stefania Maria for both of them.'

Gregory was stunned by the almost ethereal beauty in those eyes. He knew sadly, in that instant that she had tugged his heart strings, opening a passage for her to enter and nestle safely in a corner of the softly beating organ, blissfully unaware of the loving damage to its owner.

'O what a tangled web', he quoted softly to himself.

Taking her good hand in his, he held it palm up, longing to kiss it softness. Instead he placed her wedding ring at its centre.

'I had to remove it to save your finger.' Gregory leaned forward and kissed her forehead before silently exiting the room.

Long after he had gone, Stephanie lay awake pondering, for the umpteenth time, the vagary of life which can bring two such unsuitable people together, too late for lasting happiness. As the heat from his body, captured in her wedding ring warmed her hand, she wondered if she was referring to herself or to her parents.

Chapter 8:

Two weeks later, Stephanie returned to work. The feeling in her hand was fully restored. Healing was taking place and apart from a slight dull ache and the need for a light supportive bandage, there seemed to be no lasting effects. The bone was knitting nicely according to the latest x-ray and an ultrasound had confirmed 'a healthy viable fetus at 13 weeks'.

Her unexpected arrival at the office was greeted by protests all around but Stephanie soon set their fears at rest. Georgette was not as easily mollified.

'You really shouldn't be back here you know.'

'Oh leave off, Georgette' she muttered. They both laughed at the British Cockney accent.

'Stephanie, you always manage to make me laugh. It is almost impossible to be angry with you.'

The titian hair fell forward over a face suddenly clouded. Georgette knew that look. Instead of her usual sarcastic or biting comment she said gently, 'is Peter having a hard time adjusting to the changes?'

'Well yes…. I haven't been able to do a lot of things myself and each time I ask him for something I sense an emotional and physical withdrawal from me.'

Georgette realized that there was a lot more unsaid but replied with what she hoped was a reassuring tone. 'I am sure he is bound to feel some tension but it will ease in time. Anyway,' she continued in a brisk tone,' we are pretty busy and I could use an extra hand.'

'A hand is all you're gonna get.' She responded to the blatant lie easily but decided against any further confidences and entered into the mutual deception. 'Is my office empty today?'

'It is for the morning but there will be some clients in later to arrange our services for a designer convention, so perhaps you could deal with them. There's also some translating work that needs to be double checked. Andrea is new here and while she's quite competent at best, she does get confused with some of the technical terminology. It's about medical matters and that's your best subject.'

'French to English?'

'Yes, it is our famous Dr. Beaumont.'

'But oo else could give us zee work so dificil?' Stephanie mimicked showing an amazing talent for reproducing accents at will. Chuckling at a vision of the almost stereotypical Francophone Doctor with the pencil thin moustache, she headed towards her office, pausing only to throw a quiet thank you over her shoulder.

Jawahir, their highly competent Ethiopian secretary was back after a study leave and greeted Stephanie with a dazzling smile. She herself spoke four languages and was able to work in several capacities. Officially, she was executive secretary but handled cases where Arabic was required.

'We have missed you Stephanie. I hope that you are feeling better.'

'As alamoo ahlaykum' Stephanie ground out phonetically trying to respond with a traditional Arabic greeting. 'I am pleased to be back. Congratulations on passing your courses and may I say that your dress is positively stunning. You are very talented Jawahir.'

The coffee coloured East African woman accepted the flattering comments kindly before promising to bring in the files that Stephanie would need. *'I really must learn to sew,* thought Stephanie entering her office. *I know she makes all her clothes but they look as if they come straight from Paris.'*

The room seemed a quiet haven to gather her thoughts together. The gold and green colours were muted in the early morning shadows. The window faced west and she had initially chosen this office for that very reason. Essentially an evening person, the afternoon sun seemed to warm and caress her, bringing out the very best she was capable of. Early mornings, like today Stephanie would perform well with mundane and repetitive boring tasks.

The deep beige leather executive chair beckoned and she sank into it with a careless abandon that her mother would deplore. There was no time for much reflection as Jawahir brought in the requested files. Thanking the tall slim woman politely, Stephanie removed her navy jacket, then sorted through the priorities facing her for the day. It suddenly seemed to be an overwhelming task and she paused wondering if she had come back to work too soon.

That pause was her undoing. Getting up from behind the walnut desk, she locked the door, sank down into the patterned love seat in her office and sobbed bitterly, releasing two weeks of mounting frustration and anger.

****

Georgette brought her home from the hospital the day after Gregory's visit. Stephanie never expected Peter to go out of his way to be helpful but he almost totally ignored her refusing even to assist with meals. In addition, he had moved out of their bedroom saying that he did not want to do anything to hurt the baby. It was hardly a legitimate excuse at this stage of her pregnancy.

The final straw occurred three days ago when she woke up feeling unusually nauseated and fumbled to the bathroom with her queasy stomach. Peter had heard the sounds coming through the open door and shouted at her from the hall. 'For God's sake close the damn door. You are making me sick with all that noise.'

Sides heaving, fighting wave after wave of nausea, Stephanie looked at Peter standing near the open bedroom door and realized that he was looking worse than she felt. White faced, hands clenched at his sides, he looked the picture of a frightened child trying to make the horror before his eyes go away. There would be no reassurance from Stephanie. With one last heave her stomach was finally granted its wish. She heard from somewhere in the vague mists of her mind, the front door slam with as much power as he could muster.

Later, warring between disgust and sympathy, disgust won out. She called a homemaker's agency and hired a housekeeper to care for her and Peter for a month or more if needed. Stephanie realized she probably should have done it initially but basically as a wife, she failed to recognize or acknowledge the depth of Peter's problem with illness. There was very little easing of tension between them. Peter neither apologized nor attempted to explain himself. The incident lay like a dead weight between them.

A discussion with her family doctor was only slightly reassuring. Unless Peter was willing to discuss or explore his problem it may worsen. With a fatherly pat, Dr. Czerny also said that Peter may be able to deal with things better given time but it was best that she not push him.

'Treat your pregnancy as a normal function then in time he may feel the same. It is possible that he may not have told you the full story. It could be what you don't know that will cause the most problems for you'

Stephanie gave it a lot of thought before deciding to return to work and recreate the early less tense atmosphere of their married life. It would still be some time before she would start to show. Staying home and trying to pass her days without even some companionship from her husband would be unbearable. Peter did not offer any strong objections, perhaps realizing himself that a crisis was approaching in their relationship.

She maintained a calm and placid air at home trying successfully to suppress any outward anxiety but it cost her dearly emotionally and the early morning weepiness was not entirely caused by hormones. If Peter did not accept this pregnancy, termination was out of the question and every other alternative was unthinkable.

Feeling better after her mini flood of tears, she washed her face and reapplied her makeup with extra care. '*Work was the panacea*,' she thought and immediately focused on the tasks ahead.

A lively and informative discussion with the Italian designers restored all of Stephanie's good humor by mid afternoon. Typical Latin compliments on her beauty and personal tastes, even when taken with a pinch of salt, proved a boon to her ego. Ushering the impeccably dressed gentlemen out the door after the tenth *arrivederci,* she hurried back to her desk to answer a summons from the telephone.

Her breathless '*hello*' was followed by a lengthy pause. Just as she was about to check with Jawahir, a tantalizing male voice was washing over her in endless waves, almost like a lover's caress. There was no hesitancy in the tones. It was a final balm to a day that was getting better by the moment.

'You must be feeling well again if you have returned to work. Am I calling at a bad time?'

'Not at all Gregory. I've just had an entertaining hour with two Italian business men. They have agreed to use our agency for a convention next month. I'm sure it will lead to other lucrative contracts.'

'They must have been very impressed. There's an air of excitement about you.'

'I don't know about how impressed they were, but they were particularly generous with their compliments. It does a gal's ego a world of good.'

'I can't believe that someone as versatile as you would need that kind of reassurance. You astound me with the number of languages you speak fluently.'

'Ah Gregory, language is like music. It only requires a good ear and a sense of timing.'

'I can relate to that statement. I can also understand why those men would be so impressed. You say things in a way that gives your listener a familiar analogy.'

'Thank you Gregory, that's a lovely compliment too.'

'How are you feeling Sunny?' he asked seriously, changing the subject.

She laughed at the name he had adopted to call her, and went on to vaguely explain her reason for returning to work.

True to his word, Gregory decided to suppress whatever sexual attraction lay between them. Under no circumstances could they develop or explore anything except the most platonic of relationships. Even a daily call was dangerous because it could set a precedent for other things but Gregory felt he had himself well under control.

After a courtesy call to her when she left the hospital, he had tentatively asked if he might contact her again. She had agreed mostly out of a sense of gratitude for his help. Their hospital visit had paved the way. She accepted his final assurance that they would only discuss matters of everyday life, nothing personal unless she decided otherwise. Stephanie seemed to enjoy their daily talks while confined to the apartment. With her working now, it would add another dimension to their developing friendship.

She laughed delightedly at his own mimicry of her ancient housekeeper but offered no real explanation for the lady's presence at home. None was needed. Gregory understood her problems better perhaps than she did herself. With a final witty comment, Gregory ended the call, pleased that she had shown no sign of wanting to discontinue this tenuous link between them.

'You must have had your milk direct from the prize cow' Georgette commented dryly. The carpeted floor had given no indication of her presence.

'Don't be silly Georgy.'

'And don't call me Georgy.'

The two eyed each other for a moment in silence. The attractive woman, narrowed her lovely green, almond shaped eyes, while raising a questioning eyebrow. She observed Stephanie's flushed face intently.

'We are not having an affair! I promise.' she said raising her right hand.

Gliding gracefully into a fabric covered chair facing the desk, Georgette softened her look with an enigmatic smile but could not avoid a return to her sharp caustic wit. 'God knows it would probably do you good to have a real man for a change.'

'That's not true or fair and you know it.'

'I am not going to apologize or argue with you Stephanie, but any relationship you have with this man is not going to make things better with Peter.'

'I am not looking for a relationship as you call it.' The red in her hair seemed to stand out suddenly.

'Well maybe you don't need to look. You obviously have one going. Can't you see how vulnerable you are right now? You are facing some major changes that could lead to a crisis in your marriage. Any dependence on another man will only compound the problems in your current situation.'

'You don't have to tell me that.' Stephanie softened her stance. 'You are a good friend Georgy, the best anyone could ask for. I am sure you knew when I came in here this morning that I was lying. Things have not been going well with Peter.'

Georgette nodded, holding her tongue with great difficulty.

'Talking to Gregory is like talking to you, I don't feel any pressure to explain or apologize for who or what I am. It's just a friendship. Really! I promise not to allow myself to get too involved. We've agreed to be telephone friends only. For a few minutes a day, it seems harmless enough.'

The smile Georgette gave was forced but she had to be content with those reassurances. They went on to discuss the day's work in detail. They parted amicably after a shared warm hug.

A month later, Stephanie was leading a double life. Her days at work were full and rewarding. With her increased input, physically, the company was able to take on more work. Georgette was ashamed to admit how much she had missed her friend and partner around the office. Stephanie filled every room like a wild and balmy tropical breeze. She was in her stride, meeting with clients, charming them, and then prying as much business as possible from tight pockets. Stephanie did it all, remaining pleasant and cheerful to everyone who came in contact with her.

Her daily call remained prompt, short and to Georgette's keen eye, still a pleasure. But during those quiet times, when others could not see Stephanie's inner torment her dearest of friends could read the sadness and bewilderment behind the translucent green gold eyes and was afraid.

****

Evenings were a continuing drama in the Atkinson household. Peter had become a different person. He pushed himself at work coming home tired and irritable. He found fault with everything his harassed wife did and didn't do. Damned either way, Stephanie racked herself trying to find some way to reach the cold, impersonal stranger her husband had become. In desperation and longing for some physical communication she greeted Peter with a spontaneous hug and kiss one night when he came home early. Too late she realized it was the worst possible gesture.

Flinging away her hands and pushing her violently to the floor, Peter shouted, 'don't touch me! Don't ever touch me!' Turning on his heel, he stalked out of the still half open door without another word.

Much later, huddled in bed, trembling from head to foot and trying desperately to get warm in the dreary September evening, Stephanie realized that she needed some answers. Peter cold and withdrawn was one situation, but Peter violent and out of control put her and their unborn child at risk. She was not seriously hurt during the fall, but she had been badly frightened by his loss of control then bewildered when he failed to show any concern or remorse. He did not even return to the apartment.

Her desperate longing for some physical comfort remained unfulfilled. The coldness of Peter seemed to penetrate every pore of her body leaving her more vulnerable and lonely than she had ever been in her life. Seeking comfort in her thoughts only conjured up visions of Gregory. With an ache that was almost painful and not recognizing it as desire, the terrified woman spent several moments trying to realign her senses to the very serious crisis facing her. Another woman's husband was not the answer to her short term or long term needs.

Fortunately, she had a regular Doctors appointment the following day and was not expected at the office. A long weekend, and she had laughed at the time, but it was turning out to be very long indeed.

Dr. Michael Czerny was appalled by his patient's story. He had known her parents for years and harboured a deep love and admiration for the *'professor'* as he had called Piotr Droga. They were both Hungarian men who shared unhappy pasts yet maintained a firm commitment to the eventual freedom of their homeland. The two expatriates often spent long hours discussing many things while a much younger Stephanie sat at her father's knee.

Michael and the professor met during his second year at university. He gravitated naturally to the older Hungarian who understood the problems of the young refugee, orphaned prematurely, but still struggling to try and complete his education. Those days had been tremendously difficult. Michael often reflected on the sadness he felt, even as hope lived within him. He never failed to remind Stephanie of the thanks he owed to the professor. His sanity had been saved by the warmth and love he received in the Droga home.

Now lapsing into Hungarian in his anger and distress, Michael felt his native tongue would bring back some of the most reassuring memories of that beloved man. In part Dr. Czerny was successful, not because Stephanie became sentimental, but simply because whenever she spoke a language other than English, she automatically adopted a businesslike manner. Her mother's tongue was her natural outlet for expressing deep feelings but Stephanie did maintain a calmer posture while they discussed her dilemma.

Once again the growing child seemed to have suffered no ill effects from this further assault on its mother's body. An ultrasound showed a normal growing fetus now 20 weeks whose heartbeat was strong and steady. Stephanie was awed by the miracle of lines and shadows which allowed her to see the life growing within.

Back in the Doctor's office with the result, Dr. Czerny asked 'how much do you know about Peter's background Stefania?'

'Not much Miklos Basci' she answered each reverting to the appellations of her childhood. 'His mother was an invalid as you know, confined to bed since his 7th year. She died six months before I married Peter. He never really committed himself seriously to our relationship until after she was gone.'

'Has he ever talked about her manner or behaviour?'

'Only that she asked an awful from him, was rarely affectionate. She seemed to make him feel guilty over something, so I don't know if he may have been innocently responsible for the accident that killed his father and crippled her.'

'My dear, if you hope to save your marriage, I think you must get to the bottom of the mystery. I believe that therein lies the core of your husband's problems.'

Later, on the way home Stephanie pondered the words of her friend and physician. In her absentmindedness she narrowly missed hitting a pedestrian. She entered her apartment on shaky feet, realizing that she was not in any condition to investigate her husband's past. She knew she was incapable of handling herself rationally with this tense high strung situation playing on her mind.

On the table top was a terse note from Peter.

Trip to Texas today. Will be back on Monday. Sorry about last night.

She was only vaguely reassured by the apology. It seemed more of an afterthought, but it was better than nothing.

Chapter 9:

By noon, with a good meal inside her, and feeling much better, Stephanie thought perhaps a long drive might be just the thing for her. Peter's family home had been near the shipping town of Collingwood. She knew small towns rarely change. There had to be someone in the vicinity who would remember the Atkinsons. Small town tragedies were repeated like litanies for years.

Impulsively, but feeling justified, Stephanie changed into a warm beige track suit noting her thickening waistline with a tremulous sigh. The door was closing behind her when she heard the telephone ring. There was only an instant's hesitation. *Once bitten-twice shy! They'll call back* she noted ruefully looking at the still slightly reddened mark on her left hand.

Getting off the elevator in the basement she ran full tilt into a rock solid body. Somewhere she registered that she was certainly headed for a disaster if she kept up the unaccustomed clumsiness. Somewhere else, she registered the warm and comforting arms of Gregory, which closed around her for what seemed like an eternity but was, in reality, only a few seconds.

'Sunny, slow down please. Where are you going?'

'Why do almost all out conversations start with you asking me a question.' she said asking one of her own. Stephanie was suddenly irritable and could not find a reason.

Gregory sensed the tension in her body. Searching her face he did not like what he saw. 'Sunny, please, I am your friend you know.'

Relaxing a little and adopting a nonchalant pose she was far from feeling she ground out, 'I have to get some important information.'

'Is it for work?'

'No!' She dropped her eyes.

'The truth please' he demanded, hands on her upper arms.

Realizing the futility of trying to lie to Gregory, she explained hesitantly, 'I must get…I need some information up north about… Peter's having some problems and….I….'

Giving up trying to explain she soon found herself in his arms. 'Where ever you are going, I'll take you. No questions asked. You're not in any condition to drive.' The tone of voice brooked no argument.

A quick glance at his feet revealed a briefcase and she stirred, looking up at him to question its presence. He forestalled her with, 'I was taking an early weekend off, partly to study some new contracts. Don't worry about it. I'm going up to change. Promise me you'll wait here. I won't be long.'

Promises extracted from Stephanie were a dime a dozen these days, but she gave him her word and fully intended to wait, knowing that at best, her impulsive trip could end in disaster, if she could not concentrate. Too late she remembered Beth!

Their friendship had fallen off since Stephanie's return to work and she had not pursued it. There remained at the back of her mind enough guilt to prevent complete honesty between them. Stephanie was able to admit only to herself how much she needed those daily telephone calls. She wondered now if he would bring Beth. She didn't want to examine how she felt about that.

The object of her thoughts reappeared quickly and alone. Dressed in navy slacks and a white polo shirt, he advanced oozing latent sex appeal. Straightening quickly from a casual pose against a car she felt so drawn to this tall, warm and self assured male that her arms, almost of their own volition, were raising to welcome him. It was a silent and poignant gesture not missed by Gregory. Stalled only by the flutter of a tiny growing life within her, the hand instead went to her abdomen in an age old gesture of communication between mother and child and the spell with Gregory was broken.

There were no words between them at first, each aware of a near emotional disaster. Once out of the sprawling metropolitan area, the wide open spaces along the northbound Airport Rd. seemed to work magic and both passengers relaxed. They moved along steadily unimpeded by an early afternoon lull in traffic. Music played softly from the stereo. Gregory was confident and comfortable behind the wheel of the luxury car.

'If you would like something else, there's more music under the dash.

'I'm not much for modern music Gregory. I had older parents remember?'

'How far back do you go?'

'Not that far. The 50's if I have a choice. Papa weaned me on the music of his era and of course the classics.'

'I'll pass on the classics thanks. I really enjoy big band music, especially for dancing, but usually I make my own combinations picking songs I like rather than singers who are popular.'

'And is there someone in particular?'

'You know, from your era, I like Brook Benton and Dinah Washington.'

'I haven't heard of them. What did you like about their music?'

'Harmony! It was beautiful between them. Dinah sang with a crystal huskiness in her voice which embraced but controlled a song and Brook's voice was as smooth as cream. Words flowed from him. They sang together and individually but both had remarkable voices.'

Stephanie was startled by Gregory's descriptive musical analysis.

'They weren't mainstream early in their careers but I do have a few of their songs on one of the tapes unless you'd like someone else?'

'I'm partial to Johnny Mathis but I don't mind trying something new.'

'An exceptional singer but Beth has his tapes in her car.'

The mention of her name startled Stephanie into a return of her guilty feeling. She looked at Gregory, a question in her eyes.

'Didn't you know she was away? One of her sisters is having another baby. True to form, she's run off to play nurse and nanny.' The tone was derisive and Stephanie gained a little insight into the marriage of this couple. She remembered that Beth had not shared his musical interests among other things.

'Beth never talked much about her family and I didn't want to pry.'

'She's the middle child in a family of five girls. I used to date her older sister in high school. Beth is a few years younger than me. Our house faced theirs across the street in the east end of Toronto. After I completed my MBA, I noticed that Beth seemed to have grown up suddenly. We began seeing a lot of each other during the summer and one thing led to another. We were married before Christmas.'

Gregory's tone was very matter of fact, almost resigned. Nothing like a man in love relating the story of his courtship, but Stephanie kept quiet, listening intently to his story.

'Beth's family are second generation Italians, very close and with five sisters, very competitive. As she's the only one without any family, they expect her to help out. This is the eighth time she's been pressed into service. I'm expected there for the weekend since Antonia now lives in Burlington but I'm not leaving until tomorrow morning.' His tone had a quality of finality.

Nothing verbal passed between the couple enclosed in the car for quite a while. Gregory said enough, without being disloyal, to give Stephanie ample food for thought. Between the lines lay the unspoken need for Beth to have a child. It could be anyone's fault but with four sisters competing and producing, Beth must feel that the fault was not hers. She wondered silently if Gregory blamed himself and hot on the heels of that thought came, unbidden her own condition and his attraction for her.

To cover her embarrassment due to those thoughts, Stephanie turned her attention once more to the tapes. A trembling hand was quickly captured and held.

'It's not me Stephanie. I had myself checked out. I've never been able to tell her because I know it would break her heart if she thought it was her fault and I do care about her feelings in this.'

The admission cost Gregory a lot. He was in many ways very protective of Beth. His wife was obviously vulnerable where her family was concerned, but he felt some measure of honesty was required with Stephanie. His unconventional relationship with her still rested on very shaky ground and any deception would certainly be ill-advised.

The answering squeeze from her hand reassured him. Wisely, Stephanie kept her own counsel about the wisdom of his action.

****

They reached the verdant, undulating hills of Hockley Valley. After selecting a cassette which Gregory had made with several of his favourite tunes, they suspended conversation by mutual consent and allowed the songs to wash over and envelop them. Lulled into complete relaxation by the movement of the car climbing and descending the roads with ease, Stephanie was able to absorb the beautiful words of an early 50's hit written by the Gershwin Brothers and sung by Dinah Washington.

Love walked right in and drove the shadows away.
Love, walked right in and brought my sunniest days
One magic moment and my heart seemed to know
That love said hello
Tho' not a word was spoken.

Tears pricked behind the eye lids. The movement of the titian head was barely perceptible. Gregory and Stephanie knew and understood the words, but his eyes remained resolutely on the road ahead and she feigned sleep. Only the clenched knuckles on the wheel and her irregular breathing gave any deeper credence to the words.

****

'Where are we?' Stephanie was awakened by the stillness of the car.

'Feeling better?' Gregory asked admiring her face, relaxed and unmarred by the lines of worry he had seen earlier.

'Yes I am. But are we there?' she repeated looking around at the nearly deserted crossroads.

'No, we have a way to go but I think you need to be more specific about the destination.'

He had pulled over to the side of the road, reluctant to waken her but not wanting to head in the wrong direction.

'Do you know anything about Collingwood Gregory?' she asked seeking his guidance.

'As it happens, I do' he bragged grinning from ear to ear. 'It used to be a ship building port years ago but like a lot of older industries became moribund when competition from foreign markets produced less expensive goods than those made locally. With the loss of contracts, the industry virtually died. The craftsmen unable to find work left or settled into other jobs.'

'What happened to the area if such a major employer was unable to provide enough work?'

He was impressed by her thoughtful question and answered directly. 'The area is located on the shores of Georgian Bay and provides summer fun for most people but it's the Blue Mountains that are famous for winter skiing.'

'So now it's a resort area?' He nodded but she added before he could expand, 'there's something else associated with the area isn't there? The name Blue Mountain rings a bell here,' she said tapping her head with a coral painted finger tip.

'Have you seen the aquamarine and black figurines in the stores?'

'Of course I have. Papa had some exquisite pieces in his office at the university from a grateful student.'

'I don't think exquisite is quite the word. Sturdy perhaps and certainly unique...but...'

He stopped and looked at her. They both began laughing. It had been an interesting conversation, slightly different from their usual telephone dialogue which more often than not centered on the day's events. Gregory was knowledgeable without patronizing her, and Stephanie had shown more than just perfunctory interest in his mini travelogue. The laughter had dissolved any lingering strain. For the first time there was no tension marring the relationship between the occupants of the car.

'What do you need in Collingwood Sunny?' He ached to hold her even as he asked the question.

'I have to find the registry office for the area surrounding Collingwood. It should give me some clue to the whereabouts of Peter's family home.' She looked at Gregory with a silent plea in her eyes, hoping that he would understand her needs without too many questions. She felt that loyalty to her husband was a priority, yet she was aware that it was asking an awful lot of the handsome, thoughtful man facing her to drive aimlessly around the southern Ontario countryside without good reason.

He was silent for a few minutes. 'Sunny I don't know if we are headed in the right direction.' He glanced at the clock on the dash noting carefully, 'it's about 3:10 now. I don't think we can afford to waste time. Most government offices close by 4:30. You'll have to trust me on this. I believe the information you want would more likely be available in Barrie than Collingwood. Despite its size, it is still part of a County and will not have the registry office. Barrie has the County seat. We are more likely to find the information for Simcoe County there.'

'Do you really think so?'

'I'm pretty sure. We are about equal distance from both places Sunny, but we will only be able to reach one today.'

He said no more, giving her the opportunity to make the final decision.

Stephanie did what he had been longing to do since he had stopped the car. Taking both his hand in hers she looked him fully in the face, pausing for a few seconds to admire the planes and grooves crafted in such stark, but well defined simplicity. Her look was neither inviting nor sexual but conveyed a wealth of faith and confidence which spoke volumes.

'I know what I need Gregory but as usual I've rushed headlong into it without planning ahead. I think under these circumstances I must accept that you are in a better position to make the choice. I trust your judgment to go where you think we'll most likely succeed. In our short relationship I've never had cause to doubt you or your word.'

The words were significant. She was talking about more than just the immediate issue.

He squeezed gently before releasing her hands. The serious atmosphere in the intimacy of the car was affecting him deeply. He did not want to make light of her words, but Stephanie had spoken with an innocent air, seemingly unaware of the havoc she was creating within him.

Gregory gazed over her shoulder at the colourful early autumn scenery through the car window. He drew a ragged breath before replying. 'Thank you Sunny but I think we'll be better off finding a phone. Then we'll be sure.'

'Oh Gregory, I wouldn't have liked you any less if you were wrong.'

Thank god she didn't realize what was happening to me, he thought shifting uncomfortably in his seat. 'I couldn't afford to take that chance' he said laughing. 'Come on lady. Let's check the gas station across the road for a phone.'

He quickly opened the door glad to put some distance between him and the enticing young woman staring at him with an alluringly naïve smile on her face.

The gas attendant directed the couple towards a telephone perched precariously at the outside of the building. Gregory directed a sharp stare at him. He noted the undue interest of the young man as he watched her walk towards the phone. The look sent the attendant scurrying back inside. He kept a discreet distance from her allowing for privacy while she made her call.

Stephanie phoned Collingwood first with the help of a nasal voiced operator, who wasted time verifying the details of the call, which had to be billed to her home number. Then there was the inevitable transfer from desk to desk and a repeated request for the same information. It was some minutes later that a soft spoken man came on the line, sounding pleasantly official and speaking with a quiet air of authority.

'How may I help you ma'am?'

'I'd like to see the birth and death records of a particular family. Would that information be available there?'

'I'm afraid not.'

'You mean I have to go to Barrie?'

'You misunderstood me ma'am. All births and deaths for the Collingwood area are recorded here but the information is not available to the public without legal authorization.'

'You mean that I couldn't check the records to trace my family.'

'Not here or in Barrie for that matter.'

'But I need the information. It's very important.'

The kindly man could hardly resist the plea in her voice, but laws were laws. He relented a little to ask, 'what type of information do you need? Perhaps I could suggest an alternative.'

'Could you Mr....Uh?' Stephanie breathed out. Relief gave her voice a husky purr.

'Mr. White, Stanley White,' he stated, almost choking as he pictured a Marilyn Monroe likeness on the other end of the line.

'My husband's family had a farm near here. I'd like to find out exactly where it was. His father was killed at home so I had hoped the death records might give an address.'

'There's always the newspaper notices which keep records of the obituary sections, but you would need a date. What is the name if I may ask?'

The hesitation was brief. Stanley White had already shown respect for proper procedure.

'Atkinson.'

'Atkinson. You mean Minnie Atkinson?'

'Why yes. Did you know her?'

'Not personally. I grew up in the area. Everyone knows the story of the tragic accident.'

'I don't want to put you on the spot...uh... Stanley but can you give me the name of the town where the farm was located.'

'I can do better than that Mrs. ...?'

'Sunny will do nicely,' she interjected smiling at Gregory who was leaning casually against the wall.

'How appropriate! Well, let's see now. The farm was pretty near Singhamptom but I believe Minnie settled in Creemore. There may be a sister still living there on uh....Hall St. Would that help you?'

'Stanley, you've been very kind and helpful. This information could help save a life. Thank you so much.'

'The pleasure was mine,' he responded gallantly, fervently wishing that the owner of the angelic voice could by some miracle appear in his office.

Gregory wished too in that moment. If only he could keep that smile on her face forever.

'Thanks for being so patient, Gregory,' she acknowledged gratefully as they made their way back to the car. True to his word he asked no questions. He was merely content to chauffeur her wherever need be but she was bursting with excitement and once back in the car elaborated a little feeling that Gregory deserved some explanation.

'Peter's well being depends on me being able to unravel a childhood trauma that he cannot or will not discuss,' she admitted cautiously, still loyal to her troubled husband.

'Is it important to you too Sunny?'

'Yes, yes it is. I may have overestimated Peter's ability to cope with ….certain situations. I need to understand what motivates him before I can help.

Gregory was surprised at her depth. Like a lot of people he assumed that she was just a warm, passionate woman, instilling sunshine and joy wherever she went, but still shallow enough to bypass life's more serious matters in favor of the easy way out. *Was I wrong?,* he thought. A little jealousy was creeping into his feelings. He suppressed that immediately as she continued to speak.

'His family home was near Singhampton but he eventually settled in Creemore with his mother and, I gather, a sister of someone, but the man on the phone wasn't clear about that.

'Let's see he mused searching a road map for the names she had mentioned. 'We can continue north here and turn on the County road for both Singhampton and Creemore. Do you want to go to both places?'

'If you don't mind, Gregory.'

'No, I don't mind.'

Stephanie gleaned a little more information in Singhampton at the general store. The elderly couple who remembered the tragedy shook their heads sadly. 'Was terrible Miss. Minnie and the boy never recovered. Bill was a real nice man too. Worked hard you know.'

'Is the sister still living in Creemore?'

'Oh yes!' the bird like pair chirped up readily. 'Poor Katherine devoted her life to the care of those two. A real jewel, she was.'

'Would you have the address?'

'Uh let's see now. No need for numbers. Sixth house down on the left. That right Marian?' The wife agreed nodding thoughtfully.

Stephanie thanked them politely for their trouble and hurried back to the car before they could ask her any questions.

Creemore was a small village in the foothills of the Blue Mountains. Hall St. was the town's main road and Gregory quickly located the neglected looking house where Minnie Atkinson had lived. By mutual agreement Gregory decided to wait in the car. He had already selected a Benny Goodman tape and waved Stephanie on. She hesitated for a fraction of a second.

'Are you sure you don't want me to go with you?' he queried noting the slight delay.

A moment of indecision and deep sigh was her immediate response before she said, 'no Gregory but if I need you I'll call. And please don't make me promise okay?'

'Okay, good luck' he whispered but she had already gone.

Chapter 10:

An hour later Gregory, who had finally given into sleep, was brusquely awakened by an urgent rap at the window.

'Your sister's feeling a bit poorly. Can you come in and give her a hand?'

Peering at the thin almost emaciated face before him, it took a few seconds for Gregory to orient himself. As awareness hit him, the words penetrated his murky brain and he flew out of the car almost knocking over the old lady.

He found Stephanie seated on a musty old couch of an indeterminate chintz pattern. She was looking decidedly queasy. He wasn't sure how long he had been asleep or what happened but absurd thoughts of *'Arsenic and Old Lace'* flew through his head. He knew he was being melodramatic but this dark, dank house had death written all over it, in the faded curtains, the lifeless wall hangings, the dried up plants and the threadbare carpet.

'Do you want to go now?' he asked gently bending over her.

'Gregory, please give Katherine some money for me after I get to the car. She is living so poorly.'

He had no heart to argue. Her whitened lips frightened him in turn. There was no standing on her feet. Gregory picked her up as if she were made of china and carried her to the car. He turned on the engine, air conditioning blowing to dispel any lingering mould from the house and left her head down breathing deeply.

He dipped into his wallet and took out a reasonable sum of money for the old lady and wished her a good day. He couldn't get out of town quick enough.

'She didn't do anything wrong Gregory, The story she told me was a long and horrible tragedy. I was heartbroken listening to it but the place was so musty and I haven't eaten in quite awhile. I just felt faint.'

'I didn't mean to overreact Sunny but I was dozing and she startled me. You have to admit she looked kind of creepy.'

Stephanie chuckled half-heartedly at his sheepish tone and apologized in turn. She debated silently whether to relate the sad story to this wonderful man who was fast becoming a very important factor in her life. In the end, she decided against burdening him for she knew intuitively that he would only increase his vigilance over her and further complicate her already ragged emotions.

'Gregory I need some time to…..'

'Don't explain Sunny. I think I made it clear this afternoon that I would help in any way I can. When and if you want to share this with me, I'll be glad to listen but don't apologize if you are not ready now. I'm more interested in getting you something to eat then heading home. You need to rest.'

'You are so incredibly kind.'

'Not usually. You bring out the best in me.'

They stopped for a delicious but simple meal in a nondescript eatery near Mansfield called 'Harry's Home Cooking'. The quaint roadside restaurant lived up to its name. The buxom and matronly looking cook served up portions big enough to satisfy its only two patrons. Afterwards Stephanie excused herself to put through a long distance call to Georgette. On her return to the table she spoke quietly to Gregory. 'One last favour, if you don't mind. I'm going to stay with my friend Georgette tonight. It's a bit out of your way but I don't want to go home just yet.'

Gregory was consumed with curiosity but he did not press her for details. Nevertheless he reiterated his promise to be available to help in any way he could. Stephanie was warmed and grateful for his continued support and promised to explain as much as possible when she sorted through the potential repercussions this dramatic tale would have on her life.

With that, he would have to be content.

****

Georgette was relaxing in an over-sized chaise lounge when she received the long distance call from her best friend. Stephanie did not sound anxious on the telephone but the older woman knew that something important had occurred. Quickly calling her date to cancel what had promised to be a mediocre evening at best, she settled down to wait for the arrival of her friend.

'I'm fine.' Stephanie stated. 'I'm up north near Collingwood and I need to talk with you. Will you be home this evening?'

Hearing the plaintive appeal in the voice, Georgette had silently dismissed her escort as unimportant and quickly lied reassuringly. Stephanie was the one person who Georgette had really allowed into her very private world for as long as she could remember. Always introspective, the Captain's daughter had needed to be very self contained in the face of her parent's total self absorption as a couple.

In addition, the Eurasian beauty was probably more qualified to sort through the psychological jumble of Peter's life. Unlike Stephanie's fine arts degree, Georgette was a psychology major at university. Her flair for languages was developed during her years of travel with her parents. Through her mother, she spoke three Chinese dialects; German from a two year stay in the booming post war years, Japanese from another posting and Greek due to her close proximity to the world of shipping. Self study had improved on her rudimentary skills and later she added French, Portuguese, and Italian to her repertoire. Georgette was as accomplished as she was beautiful.

The doorbell interrupted her reverie and she quickly hurried to answer it.

Still not fully recovered from her earlier fainting spell, Stephanie was quickly drawn into the stark simplicity of a small and seldom used den. Mothered with some jasmine tea and comfortably ensconced in a lazy boy chair, she sat silently gathering her thoughts into a cohesive story. She knew Georgette had an orderly precise mind that would deal better with the facts as opposed to a highly emotional fantasy.

Stephanie felt herself being observed silently and intently as she haltingly began to relate the pathetic story of Peter's childhood.

****

The Atkinsons had not been a typical farming couple. Bill, Peter's tall scarecrow looking father had inherited the family land. He was the eldest child and only son of a family of four. He was also semi-illiterate but hardworking and honest.

His marriage to Minnie Everette had been a surprise for she was the delicate and fairly well educated daughter of the strict local Baptist minister. A farmer's wife needed to be strong people had said. The Atkinson's were short on healthy males and long on delicate women. They did not need another one!

Minnie, however, loved Bill with all her heart and desperately wanted to escape her father's imagined tyranny. Bill had been so totally captivated by her delicate peaches and cream complexion that he uncharacteristically held his own against all opposition.

To everyone's surprise, Minnie produced a healthy oversized son, ten months after the wedding. Her status in the small community was elevated enormously but few knew the cost to her. She was confined to bed for a month after the birth because Peter who was named after his paternal grandfather had been a difficult delivery. It was complicated by a retained after birth and an extensive post partum hemorrhage.

'No more babies for awhile!' decreed the doctor in a stern warning. No one in farming communities knew or cared much about birth control in those days. Within a year Minnie had miscarried twice. A specialist, consulted, at last, warned them that any more attempts to

increase their family before Minnie had a chance to recover would result in her death.

Frightened and desperately afraid of losing his bright and pretty wife, Bill, disdaining contraceptives, withdrew from any intimacy with her. Frustrated and angry at the loss of physical comfort both turned their attention elsewhere; Bill to his beloved land and Minnie to her young son who became smothered by his mother's excessive love.

Resuming their erstwhile sex life some four years later, Bill, who by now was drinking heavily managed to impregnate Minnie quickly. Nature however intervened with a vengeance. They were not able to resume a normal relationship and the events that followed moved them to an emotional dimension beyond their control. Young Peter, by now six years old was caught in the maelstrom of confusion.

****

Here Stephanie paused, knowing the end of the story but giving her enigmatic friend time to digest what she had heard so far. The fragrant tea was topped up and with a sigh and a nod from Georgette, Stephanie knew without words that the psychologist in her friend had carefully sifted through the information given and was ready to hear more. No questions were asked. The narrative continued.

Minnie was not to have a normal pregnancy. At 10 weeks she started spotting and that effectively put a stop to her now loutish husband's unwelcome attentions. The unborn child became the beneficiary of Minnie's complete attention and fierce protection from Bill's clumsy sexual advances on her body.

As she daydreamed endlessly about the beautiful child she would produce to restore her lost self confidence and self worth, she virtually ignored Bill and Peter's needs except for the basics of food and clothing.

Confused by this about face, a desperately lonely Peter turned his attention from his preoccupied mother and spent those warm summer days instead watching his father plough and harvest.

During the day his father was not so bad and did not call him 'mama's boy'. But at night, Peter hid in his room trying to cover his ears against the harsh words his father would yell out when under the influence.

In Minnie's eighth month of pregnancy, she woke up one morning feeling achy and weary beyond belief. A violent quarrel the night before had left her drained and confused. She wished that she had asked Bill's sister Katherine to come in from town earlier to stay with them. Katherine, an unmarried school teacher, was often good company for the lonely woman, but Minnie avoided and discouraged frequent visiting because of Bill's behaviour. She was not expected for at least another two weeks.

It was too late however for the might have beens because as Minnie staggeringly made her way to the kitchen, her water broke, flooding the floor.

Young Peter, hearing his mother's cry, ran into to see why she was afraid. He was quickly dispatched by a shaky Minnie to the fields to call his Papa. Bill, in the throes of the harshest hangover in his life and nipping steadily to keep the worst of it away saw his son come running. He was by that time too drunk to really operate his machinery safely. He was still sober enough however to realize the frantically waving arms of his son meant trouble.

'Bill had turned off the machine. Katherine had been certain about that when she was relating the story in that sad little house in Creemore. Peter had said so. She repeated that emphatically, but somehow, when he was getting up, the machine tipped over crushing Bill beneath its deadly weight.'

'Is there more?' Georgette intervened quietly.

'Oh yes. There's more.'

Concern showed in the green eyes for the mental and physical well being of the agitated woman before her and standing up abruptly Georgette decided to call a very firm halt to this poignant and sad story. With firmness she was famous for, Georgette said 'no more tonight Stephanie. It's late. You are completely worn out. Nothing is going to happen to change things overnight.

It's a good thing that Peter is away. Even if you didn't want to, I would have to insist that you sleep here tonight. We'll resume in the morning.'

Realizing the wisdom and common sense of her friend's words, Stephanie who was exhausted relented. She got to her feet and followed Georgette the few steps down the hall that led to a small second bedroom.

It had been a long day with several highs and lows for a woman in mid pregnancy. *'Georgette is right'* she thought. *'Nothing would change overnight'*.

****

It was late in the bright September morning when Stephanie awoke to the smell of percolated coffee permeating the air. After a quick shower, she followed her nose to the kitchen where Georgette, resplendent in an ivory coloured caftan, waited patiently for her sleepy friend to surface. Georgette had hoped that a goodnight's rest would restore some of the younger woman's natural vitality and she was not disappointed.

Her *'good morning – feeling better?'* was perfunctory as was the expected affirmative reply.

Most of the shadows and lines of fatigue were gone from her face. Only the inner torment caused by this incomplete relationship with her husband was evident and then only to those few people who knew and loved her.

Helping themselves to coffee, toast and a poached egg, the partners faced each other across the glass topped table in the small kitchen

'Any comments on last night?'

'Not yet Stephanie. I want the whole story first. You know my background, of course, but I have never practiced professionally. While I am prepared to offer what I hope will be sound common sense advice, I hope you will seek professional help if needed.'

'Bless you. You have my word that I will. Your common sense approach however, has helped me through many a crisis; nothing of this magnitude of course, but my approach to life has always been the impulsive one step at a time method.'

Nodding at the reality of this accurate self analysis, it actually seemed at variance with the troubled woman's usual personality. Georgette added, 'you are in your own way, most adept at getting things done quickly and orderly. You have been such a wonderful business partner these last six years and I have missed you terribly.'

Warmed by the rare compliment, the two striking redheads hugged without words, quickly finished their breakfast and returned to the den. There Stephanie resumed her narrative, the words dropping like stones in the sunlit room.

****

Peter seeing his father fall and remain trapped beneath the huge piece of machinery, screamed endlessly, terror overriding everything else.

How long he stood there no one knew except the now frantic Minnie feeling the labor pains coming quicker and stronger and knowing time was running out. A quick call to the doctor and ambulance service only increased her panic. Both were immediately unavailable. The nearest ambulance was in Barrie 50 kilometers away.

Almost an hour and half later, Peter finally reappeared covered in blood, his little mouth working endlessly. Out of the mists of her pain and fear, Minnie could only make out the words 'tractor fall.' The blood on his hands and clothes told the final tale. Minnie knew no more.

For years after, when madness overtook her, Minnie would relive the horrific scene over and over in her mind.

The ever faithful Katherine, after giving up her teaching job, devoted her life to the care of her half-crazed sister-in-law and her, figuratively if not literally, orphaned nephew. His incapable and highly strung aunt could never cope but struggled on valiantly for over 20 years, trying to compensate the little boy for all he had suffered.

Tragically she was never able to shut out Minnie's accusatory screams from the ears and eyes of the growing boy.

'What happened to the baby?' Georgette asked, slivers of sympathy piercing her usual stoic countenance.

'The ambulance attendants, it seems were ill equipped for the scene which confronted them. Minnie lay on the floor unconscious, her newborn baby dead at her feet. Cowering in a corner of the large kitchen was a small boy covered in dried blood. Running up through the fields, were passers-by who had seen the overturned vehicle and realized that the occupants in the farm house were too far away to have heard a sound.'

'Please Stephanie, no more! I can feel my whole body trembling. I don't know how you could listen to or relate that episode in your condition.'

'I don't know how either but that little boy is now my husband. With this knowledge comes understanding and rather than hurt me more, it opens up a previously closed avenue.'

'Ever practical and optimistic fool,' thought Georgette crossly. *'A trauma this extensive was unlikely to be buried too deeply. Whatever barriers Peter had erected, they served him well in the daily routine of an uncomplicated and controlled life. There must have been some earlier counseling. Apart from a definite withdrawn air and tightly coiled emotional mainspring, Peter held himself well in check.'*

Georgette continued to ponder all she had heard. A frown marred her forehead.

'Are you going to share your thoughts with me or not?'

'Sorry Honey, but you've given me quite a lot to think about. Three lives may be at stake here.'

It wasn't the best comment to make and Georgette knew that the moment she saw her friend's face.'

'Not physically Stephanie, emotionally and mentally.'

The look on Stephanie's face mirrored her fear because she knew and was remembering the last encounter with Peter.

'He hasn't hurt you already has he? Has he Stephanie?' The hazel eyes shifted.

'My God…he has hasn't he? Why didn't you tell me?'

Stephanie knew their long standing relationship demanded complete honesty. She was nervous and placed her hands around her belly, rocking herself back and forth. She nodded affirmatively.

Warm arms embraced the trembling body. Unlike Stephanie, who spoke words of love in English, Georgette, for all her western look and behaviour, lapsed into the sing song mandarin tongue of her mother. Stephanie didn't understand the words but the softness was a balm to her fragile condition.

They both agreed to suspend any further discussion until after a break and took themselves off to a lunch at a nearby Italian restaurant. A long walk along Queens Quay did much to restore their equilibrium.

Later that evening, Georgette discussed the situation, voicing her earlier concerns and encouraging Stephanie to discuss those areas of Peter's likes and dislikes which he could explain comfortably. If she experienced any further signs of stress or violence Stephanie was to leave the apartment immediately and come to her friend – no questions asked. 'You have a spare key, use it!.'

During the taxi ride home, Stephanie's thoughts were not on Peter but on his bird like and fidgety aunt. She had related the story easily enough, but seemed distracted and disoriented otherwise. It was curious that Peter had never mentioned her, but he must feel some sense of responsibility because Katherine Atkinson had raised him and cared for his mother.

Things were getting more and more complicated. Where would it all end?

Chapter 11:

Except for a note from Gregory that was left under the door of the condo, the next 24 hours were spent in total isolation. Mrs. Jaruscek, Stephanie's aging housekeeper would be in Monday for her final day so no dusting or cleaning was required. Stephanie passed the day lazily, reading books, and practicing Portuguese for a Monday morning community meeting. Most importantly she was resting.

There was also time to explore her rapidly expanding abdomen. In front of the bathroom full length mirror, Stephanie observed the slight protuberance from all angles, picturing herself in the months to come. A small throw cushion strategically placed brought inexplicable tears to her eyes. The moment passed quickly but she realized that she had sadly neglected her prenatal education and must book herself for classes soon. Georgette, she was sure would be her coach or whatever was appropriate.

Also completed during that quiet time was a long overdue letter to her mother. Stephanie had already sent a note announcing the pregnancy. The reply had been somewhat stilted for Helen Droga, like Georgette saw beneath Peter's superficially urbane manner.

Despite the obvious formality of that earlier reply Stephanie knew she had to apprise her mother of the facts. Lying was an unforgivable sin. Those words had been drummed into her from childhood. If anything happened to Stephanie or the baby, Helen would be most displeased.

Stephanie knew that returning to England had been a heart wrenching decision for her mother. There was no overt hostility between Helen and Peter but her mother had hinted at signs of possessiveness in Peter that Stephanie failed to understand. Rather than destroy any relationship between husband and wife, Helen left, warning Peter in her outspoken way that her daughter's happiness was her primary concern. Stephanie had been embarrassed at the time but now realized what it had cost her mother to separate herself from her only child to ensure a peaceful marriage.

Peter had not returned by Wednesday but during a Monday evening call he explained the deal. Peter sounded cheerful and his response to her tentative 'are the negotiations going well?' was an uncharacteristic chuckle.

'So far we've got them on the ropes. The CEO here is really anxious to get a foothold in the northern paper industry and we are offering the best prices of any of the other reps present. This will be a big contract for us if we land it.'

There were no personal references in their conversation. Relieved that they ended on a positive note she rang off thoughtfully. Her spirits had been raised a bit and she hoped it would carry over until his return home.

Tuesday and Wednesday were beautiful days, holding the promise of an Indian summer. At the office there were quite a few calls for Georgette's expertise and Stephanie held the fort in her absence. Gregory called only once. Their conversation had been a lengthy one. The new baby was born with some heart defect and not expected to live. The whole family was already in mourning. Beth was staying on to help her sister.

Reassured by her confident yet sympathetic comments, Gregory ended by letting her know that he would be back in Toronto the following Friday. He promised to call then. Long after he hung up the phone, Stephanie sat quietly in her office wondering about the heartache of carrying a child for nine months only to lose it and suffer the heartbreak. A small prayer escaped her lips for the unknown mother and father. She patted her own belly sending a message of reassurance to the tiny life growing within her.

****

Wednesday evening found Stephanie curled up in the lounge chair reading a highly recommended mother and child book. She was amazed at what she did not know about having babies. Even though her own childhood had been warm and secure, she was not sheltered. She was however an only child and matters of sex and conception did not really interest her in those early teenage years.

The loss of her father when she was sixteen effectively shut down her immature emotional system for a while and all Stephanie's energy was directed at getting an education. A year after completing her degree in languages, she met Georgette. For the next two years they both worked very hard to start the agency. Because they had little business experience between them, most days they spent juggling clients and nights taking management courses at the local community college. It was a heady period and left very little time for socializing. There had been occasional snatched dates and parties and the inevitable corporate Romeo's but very little time for serious commitments. Looking back, Stephanie realized that she had denied herself the normal growth process of crushes and flirtations. When Peter arrived on the scene she was overdue for love.

Unfortunately, her alabaster skin and clear hazel eyes gave people the impression of ethereal beauty and emotional fragility. To Peter who was emotionally sterile, she seemed to represent his ideal mate, cool and untouchable. Stephanie mistakenly followed his lead in their relationship and effectively suppressed any tendency to give or seek warmer more passionate responses.

Eventually the passionate sexual side of her withered and virtually died and their marriage maintained the status quo. While reading a chapter on sexuality in pregnancy, Stephanie was shocked to discover that some women actually felt more stimulated during the second trimester of pregnancy. Her eyes remained glued to a sentence which read; *have sex as often as you are comfortable but stop and consult your doctor if any pain or bleeding occurs.*

'As often as I am comfortable? How often is that?' Stephanie queried the sense and nonsense of the statement. Peter no longer slept with her and even before he left the marital bed they rarely had sex more than three or four times per month.

Quickly seeking the chapter on conception again, she reread the details and wondered: *'how on earth did I ever get pregnant in the first place. It's not a shock but a downright bloody miracle! I've been practicing abstinence birth control for years!'*

Still amazed by her ignorance she dropped the book and stared at the ceiling as if seeking divine advice. The gesture was a mistake. Gregory came to mind unbidden. Gregory who made her head swim, her senses reel, and her stomach turn over and churn endlessly. Stephanie knew what was happening now and jumping up, she let out a few uncharacteristic expletives. She began to prowl and pace the living room floor. Her breasts ached, her back hurt, her hands clenched and the auburn hair flew in all directions as she tried desperately to shake off the sexual languor that was overtaking her.

Reality however did what self control could not. Startled by the sound of a key in the door, Stephanie, with a groan of frustration realized that Peter was home. It could have been almost funny were it not for the pathos of her new knowledge. Peter sometimes made love to her after a long trip. *'I need to unwind'* was his usual apologetic comment. Now Stephanie needed to 'unwind' but she doubted that Peter would even touch her. All these thoughts raced through Stephanie's mind at supersonic speed so that in reality she and Peter had faced each other across the space of the living room for less time than two heartbeats.

Apologies were not easy for Peter. Time and distance had given him as clear a perspective on his actions as he was capable of and he was ashamed. On a conscious level he did not want to hurt his wife, but sometimes memories just exploded in his brain and would not go away.

With her recent knowledge of his childhood, Stephanie could clearly read the look on his face. The glance held a touch of possessiveness as if she were an object to be admired and showcased but never touched. '*Why have I never realized it before?*', she wondered.

Peter stretched out his hand saying nothing. His cold blue eyes softened a fraction and Stephanie went to him slowly. Ever mindful of Georgette's warning to follow his lead, she merely clasped his hand in her own.

'It's good to have you home. Are you tired or would you like something to eat?' Just like a dutiful wife, reciting all the proper phrases, she thought bitterly and suddenly wondered if she could live with a walking time bomb.

'Thanks Stephanie, just some tea.'

They both sat in the breakfast nook silently sipping the freshly brewed liquid, neither speaking. There was no tension, surrounding them, only an air of expectancy. Peter was the first to speak.

'Stephanie, I never meant to hurt you. I hope you'll believe that. The last five days have been difficult for me knowing I should apologize. I wanted to do it over the phone but it wasn't the right thing to do. My reaction was well...was...' His hands spread in a helpless gesture unable to articulate his feelings. 'You have been pretty understanding about the sickness thing...you know, hating the sight of blood.... but the other night well...I...', he finally trailed off having given his longest personal speech in quite a while.

Praying for the wisdom to say the right thing, she took a deep breath and said with a calmness she was far from feeling. 'I try to understand how difficult it is. You were as honest with me as possible when we met about your difficulty with blood and hospitals and so far we have managed quite well.' This was accompanied by a slight smile to reinforce her words. She allowed them to sink in then continued. 'I was very frightened both for me and our baby when you pushed me. I want you to promise me Peter that you will tell me when something bothers you because I can't cope with your rejection of my affection, especially now.'

Peter was thoughtful for a long time. Tears had come unbidden to Stephanie's eyes and her body tensed waiting for his reaction.

'You may be asking too much.'

'I don't think so.' The reply was firm.

'I'm not sure I am ready for this Stephanie.'

'Ready for what Peter? We've been married for four years. We are financially secure. Surely you expected that things would change sooner or later? We talked about having a family.'

'But I wasn't ready.'

Stephanie knew her tone was rising and Peter was becoming petulant. Her gamble had been lost and she made as if to rise from the table.

'Aren't you going to ask if we got the contract?'

The words, *'I don't give a damn!'* ached to roll off her tongue. She contemplated the look on his face if she were actually to say them. Instead she asked with weary resignation, 'how did it go?'

'We got it!' Peter looked so pleased she smiled in spite of herself.

'We'll go out Friday night to celebrate, but I have to go back to Texas, then Seattle to iron out some technical details. Okay?

She knew that the *'okay'* was meant to encompass their entire conversation but Stephanie felt defeated and only replied, 'dinner will be fine.'

Later in bed alone, the tears could not be held off any longer. They fell and soaked her pillow. Stephanie wondered what her future would hold.

****

The Friday night dinner did not seem to hold much promise. Peter had been more kind than usual since their talk but remained physically and emotionally distant. There was an air of excitement about him however while they were getting ready. It was very unusual in that Peter was more talkative, but the topics were strictly work related.

As Stephanie stood in front of the mirror applying light touches of makeup to her face, Peter came into the bedroom unannounced to see if she was ready. 'Come on Stephanie, it's almost seven now. If you don't hurry we….'

Stephanie turned around clad only in a slip, the bulge of her pregnancy evident. 'I only have to put on my dress Peter' but she was talking to the empty doorway. Sighing she finished her task. The dress she had chosen was a straight sheath with pleated shoulders that gave fullness at bust and hips then settled softly at her knees. It hid most of the pregnancy bulges. The black shaded pattern gave her skin a delicate fragile appearance. *'Why do I have to cover myself up? It is so frustrating.'* she thought taking one last glance at herself in the mirror. The matching hip length jacket which she had not planned to wear was taken out of the closet and worn despite the early autumn evening.

There was no doubt that the pair made a handsome couple. As they entered the Tower restaurant a short time later many heads turned as the maître'd escorted them to a table for two near the window so that they could observe the city by night. Peter had spared no expense. Stephanie was surprised by his choice. The CN tower's revolving restaurant was expensive and exclusive. At least if conversation lagged, the view of the city was a spectacular ever changing panorama of lights. There would be dancing later but getting into Peter's arms even in this innocent situation seemed unlikely.

Peter ordered picking, as usual, the least adventurous entrée on the menu; steak and baked potato with a salad. He was as predictable about his palate as night and day. He did not even bother to look at the long list of delicacies. Slight frowns early in their relationship had warned her that exotic foods were a no-no when dining out as well as at home.

Conversation was desultory as they ate, but Stephanie knew the prospect of a promotion for Peter was in the offing and showed appropriate praise when his comments warranted it.

'It seems that someone up there noticed how hard I've been working at last. I don't know why my skills weren't appreciated before.'

'You have worked very hard Peter. You deserve every consideration for promotion.'

'I certainly hope it's more than consideration, I'm not doing it just for the love of the job. It is such a large corporation. There are numerous vacancies available since the merger. I want to be in top management though. Research and development is only one small but significant division. You know I...' Peter stopped talking abruptly and began staring over her shoulder, a puzzled look on his face.

'What is it Peter?' she inquired, good manners prohibiting her from turning around.

'I see a man sitting a few tables behind us who came over from England earlier this week to negotiate some new contracts with our company but he's sitting with...Elizabeth's husband I believe.'

Stephanie did want to turn then but could not move for the life of her. '*Gregory here!*.' She felt heat rising in her even as Peter raised a hand to respond to some movement behind her.

'He's seen me Stephanie. Do you think I should go over?'

Peter's problems meeting people comfortably in social situations continued to be a problem.

'If you feel it's appropriate. I'm not sure what your connection is with the man.' Stephanie refused to turn around.

'I told you he's been in our office all week. I saw him yesterday. But what is he doing with uh….Gregory…is it?'

'Yes that's his name. Peter if you want to go, just go.'

'There's no need to adopt that tone with me. Anyway, Gregory's coming over. I'll see what he says.'

Clenching her hands under the table and breathing evenly to still her pounding heart, Stephanie waited nervously for the sound of Gregory's voice.

'Good evening Peter, Stephanie. Nice to see you both here.' he smiled affably as he shook Peter's hand.

'Uh good evening Gregory….G..g..good to see you again.' Peter was nervous but trying to cover it up. Stephanie said nothing, merely nodding and smiling.

'I hope you are fully recovered Stephanie?'

'Yes, yes, I am thank you Gregory.'

'Peter, Andrew tells me that your company has been doing some negotiation with him?'

'That's correct. Is he negotiating with you too?'

'No we are old friends. His father was the head of our European shipping agency. Andrew and I have known each other for years.'

'I see.' Peter visibly relaxed. The competition was removed.

'Andrew asked me to see if you both would care to join us. I can ask the maitre'd to find us a table for four.'

Peter hesitated. It would be the first time he mixed business with pleasure. His wife had never met any of his colleagues and all his working lunches and dinners were confined to the negotiating teams.

'We're just about finished here. Maybe I'll just go over and say hello. Stephanie is tired and doesn't want to prolong our evening.'

Peter missed his wife's frown. Gregory did not.

'Yes, well why not have a few words with him? I'll keep Stephanie company while you're gone.' His tone was clipped and did not invite further comment or rebuttal.

'I'll be right back.' he warned, his comment directed at Stephanie. She sat like a stone, embarrassment written all over her face.

'Can I sit down Sunny?' She looked up locking eyes with Gregory. His voice had lost its tautness as he observed the hurt bewildered look on her face. Once again, Peter had shown himself in a bad light.

'How's Beth's sister?' Stephanie rushed on, not wanting to discuss Peter's behaviour.

'They are still very upset. It's a troubling time but as a family they really support each other well.'

There was a pause before he continued. 'You look lovely tonight Sunny. The name seems to fit more than ever.'

'Thank you Gregory. The compliment means a lot to me.' Involuntarily her glance strayed over to her husband who appeared to be deeply engrossed in a conversation with Andrew.

'I hope I'm a good substitute while he's away.' Gregory's voice had a teasing tone hoping to encourage a smile. He hated to see even a moment's pain or unhappiness mar the face that was so dear to him.

She smiled in response. 'Of course you are. Better than good in fact. Why don't you tell me about Andrew while we wait?'

Gregory obliged knowing it was just a stop gap tactic enabling them to avoid personal issues, but he made the story humorous, adding some details about his youthful days that held Stephanie's complete attention.

'Was that your first trip to England?'

'Yes and very nearly my last. My mother felt I was getting too much attention from Uncle James and that it was spoiling me. The following year Andrew came over here but we didn't behave much better.'

'I find it hard to picture you pulling pranks like that.'

'We were so bad that Andrew's father wouldn't let him anywhere near the company's shipping accounts ever again. The scolding he got directed Andrew towards a career in corporate law instead of accounting. He avoids the operation side of the business altogether.'

Stephanie laughed, genuinely enjoying herself. She failed to see Peter and Andrew returning to the table. Peter appeared angry and Andrew had a puzzled look.

'Stephanie, Andrew has asked to be introduced to you. Stephanie, Andrew Hume-Mills.

'Pleased to meet you, Mrs. Atkinson.' Admiration warmed his voice as he extended his hand to shake hers. The laughter induced by Gregory had added a sparkle to the green gold eyes. Stephanie saw a puzzled look in his eyes and wondered what Peter had said about her supposed 'tiredness'. She knew that she felt as well as she ever did and it showed in her face.

'Sorry to hear you're not feeling well. I would have enjoyed expanding our evening to include you and your husband,'

Peter was fidgety, obviously hating this conversation, while Gregory sat impassive watching the interplay.

'Yes, I am sorry too but I'm expecting a baby and it's been a difficult pregnancy.' She lied to protect her husband. He was neither grateful nor remorseful until Andrew grabbed his hand pumping fiercely. 'Oh say, congrats old man. Have to look after the little heir.'

Peter gave a surprised smile. Gregory was now thunderous. Stephanie rose gracefully from her chair, forcing Peter to assist her.

'Nice to have met you, Andrew. I hope we see each other again. G'night Gregory. Thanks for your company.' She made her way out, head held high. She was angry and hated her husband at that moment.

Behind her retreating back Andrew turned to Gregory, a frown marring his forehead. 'Please explain to me Gregory, how a man can be so uptight and nervous while his pregnant wife looks absolutely glorious?'

A puzzled Andrew received only a curious tense shrug from his friend whose narrowed eyes longingly followed the departing couple as they made their way out of the restaurant.

****

Stephanie remained silent in the car on the way home, ignoring Peter's comments until he mentioned Gregory. 'I don't see how that man could be married to a woman as flighty as your friend Beth or whatever she calls herself. I don't actually see how you could be friends with her either. She's not your type Stephanie' he said glancing at her stony shadowed profile in the confines of the silvery Buick Regal.

'Who is my type Peter?'

'Oh I don't know. At least Georgette has her head screwed on right but you can never tell with those Orientals.'

'What do you mean by that?' The effort to keep her voice down and even was nearly impossible.

'You know. She's very secretive.'

'We all have secrets Peter.' Her voice dripped ice.

Even Peter could tell that he had gone too far. 'I won't say any more. You would only defend her anyway. But I don't want you to see Beth anymore. She's not a good influence.'

'I haven't seen her for weeks.'

'Well that's alright then.'

Stephanie knew that Peter did not want her to see Gregory either. Gregory could make her laugh. Even that competition was too much for her husband.

A tense silence settled in the car for the duration of the short trip home. Once inside the apartment, Peter made some overtures which Stephanie knew would usually precipitate their infrequent couplings. She also knew she had no heart for any intimacy. She felt totally rebellious. His change in manner from one minute to the next confused her. His controlling ways put her off. He had already indicated that intimate contact during her pregnancy was something he found intolerable. Stephanie went immediately to her room as soon as they entered the condo. Her dress and slip came off quickly. One look at her bulging belly was enough to send him scurrying to his room. It was the only time that she could truly say her husband was consistent.

Chapter 12:

A month later on the surface anyway, everything seemed the same, but subtle changes were taking place. No longer able to hide her pregnancy and tired of feeling that she had to, Stephanie gave up and wore instead figure flattering maternity clothes. She ate well, rested for an hour during the day and slept soundly at night. Her last check-up with the doctor was reassuring. The baby kicked hard and frequently, a constant reminder of its health and well being and source of wonderment to its mother.

Stephanie completed her mother/baby book and shared all the ups and downs of pregnancy with Georgette. The prenatal classes were booked and as expected, Georgette was both pleased and flattered to be asked to coach. Peter became increasingly withdrawn. There were no signs of violence but he avoided almost all physical contact with his wife. The Texas deal had lead to more and more lucrative contracts and much to Stephanie's relief, they were out of town. He called often while he was away but his conversations were work related and he rarely asked about the baby, although he did ask how she was feeling.

One Wednesday afternoon in early October, Stephanie, Georgette, and Jawahir, were discussing the upgrading of the secretary's position. Stephanie's due date was in early January and with an increasing workload both her managerial and translating skills would be missed. The trio worked out details of a salary increase commensurate with added job responsibilities, then decided on the title of Office Manager.

Jawahir was pleased and said so, thanking them politely for their confidence in her. She had travelled a long way from Addis Ababa to this point. Her story had similarities to many early Ethiopian refuges. She had been a member of Ethiopia's nobility. After the death of the Emperor, Haile Selassie, the country went into turmoil. Like other Monarchies, those who had been privileged were chased from their lands in ongoing civil wars. Jawahir and part of her family escaped. Those who didn't get away were killed or imprisoned. She herself had been well-educated and highly skilled, but adapting to life in Canada had been a struggle.

She eventually obtained her university equivalency in economics and worked with International Temps when jobs in her field were few and far between. The partners were aware they were getting more skills and hoped that the offered salary increase and job title reflected their acknowledgment of this. Satisfied by the mutually agreeable conclusion, they were cheerfully celebrating with a glass of bubbly white grape juice when the telephone rang. Closest to the receiver on Georgette's desk, Stephanie quickly answered it.

'International Temps, Stephanie Droga speaking.' Her knees turned to water and she quickly hid her face as the deep husky voice she had not heard for over a week began to vibrate through the instrument, touching her whole body.

'No I can't,' was all she said.

Hanging up abruptly, she excused herself from her puzzled companions and left explaining that she had to take the call in her office. When her private line rang, she hesitated for a fraction of a second then cradling the instrument close to her, waited for the familiar feelings which accompanied these calls to wash over her.

'I've missed you Sunny.'
'And I, you.'

'Is Peter out of town?' She nodded her response forgetting that he couldn't see her, then whispered 'yes'.

'I need to see you Stephanie. I need a friend to talk to. I've been trying to avoid adding any of my problems to our conversations but there seems to be so little time to talk even then.'

'We have been so very busy Gregory. The company's reputation is growing. It seems like I have been in and out of here a lot lately.'

'I hear you loud and clear. With winter coming we're also trying to get all our ships through before the St. Lawrence closes. It never fails to bring numerous headaches.'

'How are things with Beth's family these days?'

There was a long pause. He was choosing his words carefully. 'It's part of the problem. I'll explain later but I'd feel better if we could get together to talk. Will you have dinner with me this evening?'

He could not keep the earnestness out of his voice and she could no more resist it than she could stop breathing. He had remained true to his word and never put any pressure on her. This was the first time he had asked to see her and she agreed.

'I'll meet you downtown,' he said naming a spot close to their respective offices. 'Then we can decide where we would like to go.'

On an impulse, she stopped herself acquiescing to his wishes. 'Gregory, if you don't mind, I'd like to go over to the Island Restaurant.'

'Hiding?'

'No it's just a favourite spot and the ferry ride and short walk will do me good after being in the office all day.'

He agreed with her assessment and arranged a time to meet before ringing off.

Not long after, Georgette came in. She was wearing an earthy green sheath type dress and very high heels. The extended shoulder pads gave her upper body the appearance of strength. She looked like a tigress ready to defend her cub.

'No lectures Georgette, please.'

'No lecture intended. I don't pry into that relationship as you know. I am aware that he hasn't called much lately.'

'No he hasn't. He's been busy and so have I.' Her tone was decidedly defensive.

'Honey my head tells me this is all wrong but my heart smiles when I see the look he brings to your face. Are you going to see him?'

'Yes, he has never asked me before. Something is worrying him and he needs to talk about it. He was there for me when I needed someone so, I can't do less can I?'

'No you can't but please be careful. I couldn't bear to see you hurt anymore.'

****

Stephanie's wardrobe for the office centered around navy, beige-browns and greens in either dress and jacket or two piece suit. She had added a couple of pants suits with the maternity wardrobe as panty hose were becoming increasingly difficult to wear. Sitting comfortably was also a problem and the pants gave her some added leeway. Her tan suit and beige silk over-blouse were ideal for the often chilly ferry ride from the city to the three small islands just ten minutes away. She had a wool shawl in her car which would keep her warm if it got too windy.

The Toronto islands were a summer playground with numerous activities for the kids. A few year round residents were fighting an on-going battle for the right to live there permanently but Stephanie had no interest in any of those things. Looking out from the upper deck of the ferry with Gregory at her side, she was enthralled as usual by the skyline of the city from the lake. She was warmed by the final rays of the evening sun. She never failed to be moved by the Canadian sunset in October and this evening she knew it would be significantly poignant because the man beside her was equally moved.

'It's beautiful isn't it?' he said responding to the look of serenity on Stephanie's face.

The lake was crystal clear and despite the chilly breeze from the open upper deck of the ferry boat, Stephanie felt a sense of peace and calm settle over her. She leaned her body against an upright post and contemplated the fast receding city. Unconsciously, perhaps, she had tested Gregory and not found him wanting. This had been a favourite ride for her and her father as long as she could remember. They both had an affinity for this particular view.

Peter had not been impressed, hating even the quick trip over, liking only things tangible and solid. In their courting days, it hadn't mattered, she thought. Peter had been special because.... because... and here she stopped short. In a flash of insight she now knew what had attracted her to her husband. It was his incredible, but superficial, physical resemblance to her father. She had never looked deeply into his character. She just remained fixed on the uncanny feeling that her Peter had been sent to replace her beloved Papa, Piotr.

What a fool I am! She thought contemptuously, frowning at herself assessment. '*There was not one ounce of Papa's kindness, intelligence, humour, or joie de vivre in Peter. Only the deep hidden traumas that so marred both their early lives was evident. Papa dealt well with his; Peter had not.* **Stephanie you have grown up at last.**' She could almost hear her mother's voice and knew that Helen Droga had correctly read four years ago, what Stephanie only realized this instant.

She gazed at the dark vibrant hair of the man leaning over the protective rail happily watching some ducks negotiate the wash from the flat-bottomed ferry. '*He is not like Papa either but it doesn't matter because he has many other wonderful qualities. He can make me laugh, comfort me, protect me, stimulate and arouse me to heights I have never known. Oh my God! I've been a fool,*' she reiterated fiercely.

The power of her thoughts and the intensity of her gaze must have disturbed him because Gregory turned suddenly and stared at her very hard, eyes unwavering. Enfolding her hand in his, he whispered 'hello Sunny.'

****

Dinner in the little restaurant on the island was cozy. The October evening chill held off until the eastern sky began to darken so they were able to eat among the Weeping Willows surrounding the jetty where the restaurant was located.

In spite of her astounding self revelation, Stephanie was able to set aside the repercussions and enjoy both the company and the fresh fish meal. Towards the end, they were completely relaxed with each other, sharing jokes and getting to know each other's likes and dislikes. They created a small space of intimacy into which they were both drawn, forgetting everything.

'My uncle thinks I've become obsessed with work lately.'

'And are you?'

'Well he has the right feeling but the wrong object.'

'Is that why you haven't called?'

'Mmmm'

'Because you have been obsessed with work?' she prompted.

'No.'

'Don't be deliberately obtuse Gregory.'

Raising his hands in mock horror, he looked at her with a silly smile. 'Please don't use those big words with me. I'm just a humble seaman' he lied cheerfully.

'You know I have to,' she pleaded. 'I'm an English major and I must or else I'll forget them.'

Standing up Gregory offered a mocking salute. 'I am at your command Major Droga.'

Stephanie was happy to join in their little game and made to stand up but sank back in her chair. She raised a hand to forestall his concern. 'I think I have overeaten and my baby is protesting the onslaught of calories. I believe a walk would be in order.'

He understood completely. They took a leisurely path that would ultimately circumnavigate the Centre Island and end up at the ferry dock. It was getting chilly but they held hands and kept up a brisk pace until their bodies were acclimatized.

'What's happened to Beth, Gregory? You promised to tell me. I haven't seen her for over two months.'

'Remember the sister who lost her baby. Antonia's her name. She took it really hard. She and Mike have two boys and desperately wanted this little girl.'

'Was Antonia the sister you dated before?' she interrupted.'

'Yes, but she's happier with Mike, believe me. He's completely Italian.' Stephanie chuckled. It was well known by anyone growing up in Toronto, that Italian girls were expected to marry Italian boys. Gregory would have been out of the running early especially if she was the oldest daughter. Stephanie sidetracked to the issue not thinking that it would also apply to Beth but she quickly apologized for getting distracted by her thoughts.

'I interrupted. I'm sorry.'

'That's ok. Anyway, Antonia wants to go to Italy for three months or so to recuperate. She won't leave the boys behind and wants Beth to go with her to help.'

'How does Beth feel?'

He sighed deeply. Stephanie knew that Beth would go anyway regardless of his wishes. 'The family always comes first with her. Probably if I were Italian, I could understand better how she could leave me for weeks on end. It wouldn't be the first time. She never seems happy unless she is in the middle of everything. Her own periods of hypochondria are just a way of getting back some attention. Of course if she were having babies it would be different.'

Stephanie was silent for some minutes after he finished speaking, trying to absorb what he had said. He does love her, she thought. It shows in his concern for her welfare. She could understand his feelings but could not understand why Beth didn't realize that he was also unhappy and lonely.

'Are you angry with me Sunny?'

'No! No, only concerned about you even though I have no right to be.'

Stopping suddenly and turning her to face him he ground out, 'there are no rights and wrongs for us. We care about each other and we are friends, but because our relationship is unique, we've got to be completely honest and open with each other. Aren't you like that with your ravishing friend Georgette?' he teased reducing some of his intensity.

'Yes, I suppose I am. I'm sorry.' She looked at him steadily before tilting her head to one side. 'Do you really think she's ravishing?'

'Jealous?'

'Yes,' she pouted, a teasing look in her eyes.

'There's no need. She is but a pale imitation of you.' He recited gallantly, his hand over his heart.

'Oh Gregory, even when you lie you make me feel good.' She gave him a light push to emphasize her words.

They walked on slowly each immersed in their own thoughts, still holding hands. This stolen time was too precious. The western twilight fell slowly enclosing them in a purple and orange glow. It added a sense of fantasy to their evening stroll through the Island's park. It wasn't long before Stephanie halted and doubled over, clutching her abdomen. She didn't seem to be in pain but Gregory expressed concerned and quickly led her over to a nearby bench facing the lake.

'What's wrong?'

'I feel so foolish. Sometimes when she kicks I feel like she's going to fall out somehow. I know it's impossible but it's a funny feeling I just can't explain.'

'Is the baby kicking now?'

At her nod, he looked at her expectantly. She nodded again and gently placed his hand on her rolling abdomen, glancing at him curiously waiting for the fear or rejection to show. The baby continued to move. Surprisingly he appeared to feel no disgust and the warmth from his hand seeped into her body seeming to calm both mother and baby.

'Is this your first time Gregory? I mean.... to feel a baby move.'

'No, but this is your first baby and that's all that counts. This is such a special time in your life, when you need to be lavished with care and attention. If I can do anything...'. He was halted by the look on her face.

The ready tears had come again as she stared deeply into his eyes. Raising her hand she used her fingertips to trace the wonderful square jaw with its slight stubble. She explored the grooves at the sides of his face, smoothed the straight silky eyebrows, slid gently down the long proud nose and rested tenderly on the full but firm lips.

Gregory's hand stayed still though he desperately wanted to reciprocate, but this moment was initiated by her and she would set its pace and limits. He closed his eyes to shut out her intoxicating beauty. Too many senses were being attacked. He had to keep control. He was fighting so hard to maintain a calmness he was far from feeling that he never knew when her lips replaced her fingers. Goaded beyond endurance and past caring about the consequences, he gave an agonizing moan and wrapping his arms around her deepened the kiss.

Stephanie sensed the change, knew what was coming and welcomed it. She had no idea how far it would go. The public setting precluded the ultimate outcome but right now she no longer cared. His hands roamed freely, exploring the curves of her very sensitive breasts. There was aching tenderness but she gave it no mind. The whimpering sighs and sounds she made were clearly begging for more.

His lips left her mouth to blaze a trail of fire from her shell like ears to the hollows of her shoulders. He buried his face in her fragrant hair, crying softly, 'Sunny, Sunny I want to love you so badly.'

He found her mouth again, but this time her lips were open and waiting. Their tongues clashed hungry for contact with each other, seeking, seeking. Stephanie knew she was lost, realized that she could love this man and would do anything for him.

Clutching his shoulders tightly and digging into the flesh through the material of his suit she buried her head in his neck.

'Gregory, I'm so scared. I've never been so scared in my life. I know what I'm doing, but I don't know how. You're making me... You're...I want..she trailed off, gulping and near hysteria.

It took some time to calm her down. Her frightened face effectively dampened his fervour and sudden awareness of their location forced his reeling senses to a complete halt. He continued to stroke her hair and whisper softly to try and still her trembling until only a few hiccoughs marred her even breathing.

'Let's walk Sunny, if you feel up to it. We're still quite a distance from the dock. It will be better if we keep moving.' Nodding her assent he helped her to unsteady feet and placed a supportive arm around her back and waist. He held on to her firmly as they made their way through the gardens now shrouded in moonlight.

They were silent for some time before Stephanie found her voice. 'Gregory, I just want to explain my reaction. The first time we were together my reaction was pure instinct. You took me completely by surprise and I didn't have time to think. Tonight was different. I had an awareness of what I was doing. I really thought I had myself under control. I'm sorry if I hurt you.'

Gregory was incredulous. He murmured some words of comfort but his mind was in turmoil. He couldn't believe she was a married woman. Her pregnancy was a public testament to some sexual activity but she talked almost like a virgin on her first date. Decency would not allow him to question her about what she expected from him in response, nor the activities she pursued with her husband but something was not right.

He loved her. He knew that long ago and he certainly desired her but apart from friendship, did she need more from him, want more? He was confused by her invitation to engage in intimacy which allowed him to lose control. Was it to her seduction or her innocence? Both were heady temptations. Knowing that he could not continue to live in limbo, he decided to try and talk with her friend Georgette. He hoped she might give him a better understanding of how to proceed.

Chapter 13:

Stephanie returned home that night, thoughtful and worried. She was no longer sure what she wanted. The evening had been a source of discovery for her emotionally and mentally. Gregory's lovemaking had fired her blood to incredible heights but she was still frightened by the intensity of her response and her desire to initiate a change in their relationship. Stephanie wasn't sure if she was just starved for love and physical affection or did she really love him. If she did, where would it all end? Neither of them was free but their relationship had now gone beyond the point of acceptable friendship.

When he dropped her off at the office to pick up her car, they had shared one lingering kiss. There was a wealth of sweetness given and taken yet it contained without words the apologies and explanations for their emotional maelstrom earlier.

They had both agreed to arrive at the condo complex separately. It was the only consciously furtive moment in an evening which had started out so innocently. She wanted to berate herself for precipitating the change in their relationship but she could only speculate about the consequences of her actions. The extraordinary sensation of being in his arms left an afterglow which lingered and begged for more.

While Stephanie sat in the comfortable lounge chair in the living room pondering the events of the evening, she glanced idly at the untouched mail she had collected from the letter box on her way in. She shuffled them around and noted that there was a UK postmark on a pale blue airmail envelope. She eagerly tore open the letter, knowing it was from her mother.

Dearest Daughter
Sorry to be so long in writing to you but your uncle and I traveled to the continent for a short holiday with some friends. We left before your letter arrived.
I was most distressed to read of your discoveries about Peter's past. I'm sure you realized that I had some misgivings about the marriage at the time but never wanted to voice any concerns as you seemed to be happy enough until now.
I'm very worried about the effect that this will have on your pregnancy dear. I had an easy time with you but one never knows. Your father treated me like Dresden China but I doubt you will enjoy the same. You deserve more than Peter is capable of giving.
I know I have commitments here, my love but I am prepared to come over and stay if you need me.
Please write or call immediately if anything changes,
Your loving mother,
Helen.

This was an unusually short missive from that dear old lady and Stephanie knew her mother was deeply concerned. The letter contained not one proverb or truism which was Helen's trademark when corresponding with her daughter. Placing the delicate onion skin paper next to her face, the lonely and worried daughter curled up in the large chaise and inhaled the warm, ever present scent of Helen's favourite Blue Grass perfume. She had echoed Gregory's words without even knowing the full situation. There was scant comfort however as the tears fell.

****

Georgette was only half surprised to receive Gregory's call the following week. She knew that some profound change had taken place in Stephanie after her evening with Gregory. The preoccupied woman had admitted as much but little else. Georgette was too much of a friend to probe deeper, uninvited and too much of a professional to force any confidences.

She rightly hesitated about meeting Gregory who was an unknown quantity. Their brief encounter previously, in Stephanie's hospital room, left only a superficial impression but both would be equally disadvantaged. After weighing the matter carefully she called him back and agreed on a time and place the coming Friday. She arrived promptly and was shown in without a wait.

'Thanks for coming Georgette' said Gregory standing and extending his hand as she entered and greeted him across the gray patterned carpet. They had arranged to meet at his office. Georgette did not want to be distracted by the rules of etiquette in a public place. If Gregory turned out to be nothing more than a shallow two-timing husband she fully intended to let him know it in no uncertain terms.

He was, she could see, a man used to command, but Georgette was tough and not easily intimidated. Her deductions about his character were not based on the rich walnut and black leather furnishing, nor the essentially masculine nautical air in the silver decorations, but solely on that indefinable air that marks men who lead by nature.

'Can I offer you something hot or cold to drink?'

'Juice would be fine thank you'. Georgette sank gracefully into a chrome and leather armchair facing the desk.

Later, when the beverages had been served by a confused looking young lady with raised eyebrows, the two took their measure of each other.

'Do you mind if I ask you a personal question?'

'I don't mind if you ask.' There was a coolness to her tone. Gregory was not deterred. He never expected this interview to be easy.

'You and Stephanie are so much alike but I gather you are not related?'

'That's correct. We are just good friends.' The taunt hit home. It was a standing response to public couples who consistently deny private relationships.

'Touché.' Gregory acknowledged her jibe but remained calm.

Georgette was suddenly ashamed of her attitude towards this man. It was not all his fault. She knew that, and had no right to bait him.

'I'm sorry. I think my hostility is misdirected. As a navy brat I'm very cynical about platonic relationships between married people.'

Relenting a little, they faced each other across the expanse of his desk both resolute in their desire to help the woman each loved. Gregory spoke again, more clinically, than emotionally.

'There are at least five or more people who stand to be hurt by any relationship Sunny and I continue to pursue.' The admission was difficult.

'Sunny?'

'Stephanie,' he corrected with a devastating grin. 'She seems to glow with all the colours of the setting sun.'

Georgette waited for him to continue but he seemed lost in memories.

'What do you do here?'

Gregory was surprised by the question and the abrupt change in topic. He recovered quickly and gave a detailed account of his history. 'My Uncle, who is chairman of the Board, started this firm 30 years ago. It's not a shipping company as such, but a local agency for various European and Middle Eastern shipping firms. We handle affairs locally when vessels come into Canadian waters. The problems could range anywhere from damage to the ship itself to illness or trauma to a crew member. We have to be ready for anything.

My uncle has no direct male heir so I was trained to take over when he retires. I received an MBA at U of T and worked my way up from the bottom; no favours given. At present I am COO.'

Gregory had not questioned her reason for wanting to know but she elected to tell him anyway.

'You seem to be a man of contradictions.'

'In what way?'

'Your reference to Stephanie's colours doesn't fit the image of a high powered business executive.'

'Would you believe that I also took music at university?'

'Singing, writing or playing an instrument?' she queried seeing in his smile some of the aura that would make him attractive to Stephanie.

'All of the above!'

'So how did you come to be ensconced in the world of shipping or is this your real passion?'

'You are curious aren't you? There was really no option. I love music. I would never have been able to make a living as a singer or songwriter however, so this job satisfies my intellectual side and music still satisfies my artistic and emotional side. It's as simple as that.'

'I've enjoyed our preamble and I've also learned a little about you but that wasn't why you wanted to see me, I'm sure. Please tell me what I can do for you.' She invited him to open up to her. She was gracious and gratified by his honesty and direct answers, so far.

'I love Stephanie,' he stated evenly and clearly. 'I don't know where our relationship is headed and I don't want to hurt her but….I also do not want to lose her.'

'It still doesn't explain why you wanted to see me. I think I surmised some of your feelings already.'

Getting up from the plush black leather chair, the tall, good looking man began to pace distractedly, his right hand running strong fingers through the thick dark hair. The expanse of windows framing him from behind the desk, provided a spectacular view of the lake and the diminishing Friday evening traffic below. Coming around the desk to face Georgette, he stopped in front of her.

'The situation is untenable. We're both married, she's pregnant, and my wife can't have a baby. Her husband seems to be a cold fish with some serious mental problems yet none of these things can justify our relationship. I care so much for her, but she's delicate, fragile emotionally and very inexperienced.'

Georgette's head was reeling from the depth of emotion Gregory displayed. He really did love her. That much was obvious but what did he mean she was inexperienced. She stared hard at him trying to seize on a fleeting and disquieting thought. 'Do you think Stephanie is using you?'

'Not consciously no. I'm afraid that if I question her motive for continuing to see me, she may find too many reasons for us to stop being friends. A discussion of her sex life is also completely out of the question. There's a naïve and innocent air about her, almost as if...as if...'. Gregory found he just could not say the words.

'I understand what you are trying to say. Like you, there are certain things I don't pry into. I've never questioned her intimate life and I don't intend to change that now. If Stephanie cares to tell me anything I'll listen but there I draw the line.'

It was a gauntlet of sorts. She still was not wholly reassured that his declaration of love entitled him to expect a detailed discussion of Stephanie or her marriage.

'I'm not asking you to betray anything, Georgette', he cautioned, admiring her loyalty. 'Whether you agree or disagree with what is happening between us, I'm sure that you would put her happiness first.'

Georgette mentally conceded that he was absolutely correct. She relented a little knowing that in spite of their unorthodox relationship, clearly he was deeply committed to Stephanie. Georgette thought carefully for a few seconds before deciding on what she could say without betraying the confidences of her friend. She decided her own observations were best.

'Stephanie never dated much as far as I know. I met her about seven years ago, just after she completed university. Her father's death had hit her very hard and she was still upset that he never lived to see her graduation.'

Gregory, captivated by this glimpse of a younger Stephanie, sat in the other chair in front of his desk, giving Georgette his undivided attention.

'We struck up an immediate friendship based almost exclusively on our resemblance at first.' She smiled now, acknowledging this more expansive response to his first question.

'It didn't take long to discover all the other interests we share despite the fact that we are complete opposites in personality. The idea to start the business was mutual and we worked very hard for the first three years to get it under way.'

'I'm impressed. I had no idea that you both built the business yourselves. Sunny is always so modest about her contribution.'

'Too many people can't see beyond her pretty face. She's always stereotyped as the ultimate, decorative secretary no matter what she says. I can assure you that since her return to the office, our business is up twenty percent.'

Gregory nodded but said nothing more, waiting.

'Stephanie didn't date much, if at all. There really wasn't any time. Peter was the first and only man that I actually saw her with at any time. They were never really demonstrative and I admit that I had some misgivings but they seemed content with each other.'

She shrugged her shoulders lightly and a certain body language told Gregory that she would not welcome any more questions. He got the message and read between the lines of her little speech.

Rising slowly, he murmured a polite thank you and saw her to the door of his office. He halted with his hand on the door knob and observed her for a moment.

'I have some thinking to do. If anything should happen, call me if she needs me. Please.'

Georgette moved off towards the elevators. Gregory returned to his desk and gazed unseeingly at a framed picture of him and Beth in happier days. He could not figure out what had come over him. His current situation with his wife was unsatisfactory but by no means hopeless. He wondered what it was about Stephanie that triggered such a response in him. He never thought of himself as a philandering type of husband, but from any angle that he viewed the situation it was wrong.

In many ways Stephanie could still be very naïve if what Georgette had implied was the truth. He doubted that Stephanie was using him to fulfill some fantasy, but it meant that his involvement in her life was a complication she would be unable to deal with if she did not know or could not accept the repercussions. She had innocently triggered a change in their relationship. The effort of trying to understand her uncontrolled response would be too much stress for her already tense situation. Stephanie had not confided in him about the trip up north but he could see that her husband was possessive and jealous. Any hint that his wife was involved with another man could incite all kinds of reactions in a man with that kind of personality. Her safety would be at stake.

They both needed time apart, he acknowledged sadly. Whatever the reason for her sexual awakening he could not take advantage of her artless but stimulating touch. That joy belonged to someone else, not him. The thought turned his insides into a tortured knot that twisted painfully as he contemplated even a day without the sight or sound of her.

****

Some days later, an aggravated and tense Stephanie was staring idly out the window in her bedroom. Her mind was not on the view below but centered on the man whose framed photograph was gripped tightly in her hands.

'What can I do to help you.' She begged silently. But his picture remained as unyielding as the man himself.

His interest in the growing baby was nil and his long suffering wife fared little better. Each trip he took became longer and each stay at home shorter and more frustrating for her. His temper seemed to be out of control one minute followed by long cold silences the next. He never moved to strike her since the fall, but Stephanie wondered what happened to the man she married. Pride would not allow her to share the sham of her marriage even with Georgette. She smiled at work but doubted that anyone was really fooled.

It was another lonely evening or Stephanie. A sudden knock at the door startled her out of her preoccupation. She was in no mood to see anyone, although she conceded that a break might be just what she needed to stem the negative thoughts which seemed to pervade her every waking hour. On her way through the living room, she realized that it had to be another tenant otherwise the buzzer from the ground floor would have sounded.

Gregory, she thought silently. He hadn't called since their dinner.

She peered carefully through the peephole, surprised to see Beth standing there. Hesitating with her hand on the knob during another insistent rap, Stephanie finally opened the door.

'Oh Steph, you got so big.' Beth stood on the threshold, twisting her hands and looking so agitated.

The exclamation was neither a true nor accurate statement, because the tall well proportioned Stephanie carried her pregnancy quite well. The oversized peach coloured top all but obscured the growing abdomen. Embarrassed and feeling somewhat guilty by her involvement with the smaller woman's husband, Stephanie nevertheless invited Beth in. She was curious about what would bring her to the apartment this evening after weeks of no communication.

'You haven't seen me in quite a while, you know.'

'I've been really busy with my sister. Greg told me that he ran into you and told you about the baby. It is such a terrible tragedy.'

Yes, that's right, he did.' Stephanie was grateful that Beth introduced Gregory's name first. It made it easier not to lie.

'I haven't been around much. Tonia's very upset and needed me to help with the boys.'

'I am very sorry Beth. Please accept my condolences.'

The condolences were waved away by a nervous gesture of the hand. Stephanie wondered how she could have like this woman who now seemed so shallow.

The petite brunette launched into her speech almost as soon as she had taken her next breath. 'Greg's been giving me a really hard time you know. I mean we've been married for so long now. It's not like he needs me all the time and we don't have any kids. If my sister wants me to help her I don't see why I can't and he's acting up as usual.'

With her own knowledge, Stephanie understood the rather muddled dialogue but chose not to comprehend.

'I'm sorry I don't know what you mean.'

'It's all so simple, you know. Tonia wants me to go to Italy with her while she recuperates because Mike her husband, you know, can't go now. She really needs a break and so do I. I don't see why Greg can't understand that.' Her voice was ringing with frustration.

'You've been away quite awhile. Maybe he misses you.'

'Don't be silly Steph. He never misses me. A family is important too. What's a few weeks more? If I had a baby it would be different but I don't', she ended on a defiant sob.

The continued repetition of not having a baby was beginning to wear on Stephanie's nerves. And, her own growing baby seemed to be angrily protesting its own mother's increased stress. Uncomfortable and irritated by this unwanted and embarrassing intrusion, Stephanie blurted out, 'If you've been married so long and nothing's happened why don't you see a doctor?'

Beth, who had begun to pace haphazardly about the living room, halted in front of Stephanie, eyes blazing and said hotly, 'I don't need a doctor. I've got four sisters who get pregnant whenever they want to. Besides I was pregnant when I married Greg but I miscarried so there's nothing wrong with me. Greg's the one and he won't do anything about it.'

Stephanie was shocked, not so much by the revelation which she knew to be untrue, as the delivery of it. She chose not to utter one word in response.

'I should have known better than to come here anyway. You are so smug with your own pregnancy that you don't care about anyone else. My sister said I should divorce Greg if he's no good and I will if he doesn't let me go to Italy.'

With that parting shot, she stormed out of the apartment, leaving Stephanie surprised and pondering the implication of Beth's outburst. Even with her newly acquired knowledge of conception she felt the selfish woman failed to come to realistic terms with her own problems. 'How blind can she be?', Stephanie wondered staring at the closed door. Beth had the opportunity to seek help and a willing partner to support her. She didn't sound as if her husband was a priority at all.

Stephanie had no time however to dwell on either the encounter with Gregory's unhappy and distracted wife, nor on his continued lack of communication. She had reasoned that he only wanted to find someone to fill in the gap left by his wife's preoccupation elsewhere and their disastrous outing had proven that she was an unsatisfactory replacement. Her pregnancy, her marriage, and her inexperience all combined to make her undesirable.

'*It's just as well*', she reflected bitterly '*but I did think that he cared for me even a little*'. Anyhow, a meaningful friendship was out of the question and she couldn't be his mistress, not now maybe not ever. Her thoughts, she knew were unfair to Gregory in some respects, but other more immediate concerns occupied her troubled mind.

Resigned to making the best of her current situation, she concentrated on immersing herself in preparations for the birth of the baby. Stephanie started prenatal classes in her 30th week with Georgette, who was surprisingly nervous.

Yet all the while, subconsciously the image of Gregory remained a persistent and nagging hunger that nothing would assuage.

Chapter 14:

With six weeks to go until her expected date of birth, Stephanie was determined to clear out as much paper work as possible. Michael Czerny had advised her to take a couple of weeks off before the birth. With so much emotional stress in this pregnancy he wanted her to take things as easily as possible.

She decided to work late on a Tuesday evening at the beginning of a wet unseasonably warm December. Some overdue translations for a linguistics colleague needed to be completed. The work was not difficult, just tedious. By eight o'clock her head was beginning to ache and mistakes were being made in an uncharacteristically sloppy handwriting.

The sharp jangle of the telephone startled her. Stephanie was sure Georgette was checking to see if she was still there. Cross and ready to snap, she grabbed the receiver.

'Hello, who is this?' she muttered annoyed at the interruption then stunned by the caller.

'It's Peter.'

'I didn't know you were coming in today. When did you get home?' Despite the pounding headache, she tried to infuse a lighter and more welcoming tone. He had said his name in such a terse fashion she immediately felt wary.

'Never mind that now. You're always busy with something whenever I need you.'

She frowned into the telephone wondering if it was really Peter, her ever absent husband, or some practical joker.

'You haven't needed me for quite a while now Peter,' she stated as evenly as possible, her red lights beginning to flash.

'If you didn't go to work you'd be here when I come home.'

She chose to ignore that comment. 'Was there any particular reason you called?' she asked softly hoping some degree of concern might have prompted him to find her.

'I'm going up north. A distant relative died and I'm in charge of the will so I have to go.'

'I'm sorry Peter. Do you want me to go with you? Is it someone close?'

'No!' He shouted frightening his puzzled wife. 'I told you she's no one important.'

'Why do you have to go tonight? You must be tired and it's already so late. Get some sleep and leave early in the morning.' The request was not unreasonable. He sounded very tense and more irritable than usual.

She correctly surmised that it was his Aunt Katherine who had died. The old lady had seemed so frail when Stephanie was there in the late summer. She wondered why he said she was *no one important*. It made no sense, but she could not betray her knowledge without upsetting him further.

She held the receiver some distance from her ear as he continued to berate her and her concern. 'Is it so difficult for you to understand? I am going to go and get it over with because I have a lot to do tomorrow at the office before I leave town again.' He had calmed down a little with that statement, but his voice was belligerent. Rather than prolong a useless argument, she resolved to try and encourage him to open up a little when he returned home.

Peter's relationship with his aunt surely held the key to his character development after the tragedy. Perhaps her death would unlock some of his tightly held secrets.

With a final admonishment to drive carefully in the early, totally unpredictable December weather, she also asked him to call, if he was held up, before she rang off. She knew he wouldn't. Her hand remained on the receiver as she sat lost in thought, feeling that somehow nothing would ever be the same after this night.

****

Peter was furious. Numerous unnecessary delays had kept him in Collingwood long past the time he had expected to return to Toronto. He was angry, very, very, angry and so cold. It was already after seven in the evening. Heading out to his car from the motel room in Collingwood, where he had spent the long lonely night, he shivered. The lawyer had refused to see him the previous evening. Sure it was late he acknowledged angrily but the lawyer should have realized that he wasn't a little boy anymore. He had an important job. He made it clear he could not wait around. As he got into the car he shivered again, glad to be getting away and hopeful of being somewhere warm the following day.

He turned on his engine and headed for the Airport Road and home. He kept his eye on the white line, forcing the painful memories to the back of his mind. Snow was falling but the powerful car clung to the slick asphalt, handling the rise and fall of the road with ease.

The windshield wipers swished back and forth, clearing the glass and revealing the darkened sky. Ahead lay the crossroads, defined by a solitary flashing red light commanding all drivers to halt. Peter did not.

The sign post clearly said Creemore. He had no desire to make even a perfunctory stop anywhere near the town of his nightmares. He continued on, fighting desperately to keep the demons of his past at bay, but every action seemed to bring forth those mocking ghosts.

Like a song which plays over and over, the swishing of the wipers became a hypnotic refrain....cold...cold ...aunt Kath....cold.... mommy cold....papa cold.... On and on it went. Peter was afraid.

He had been afraid all his life. 'No one loved him except Stephanie but when the baby came she wouldn't love him any more either.'

The refrain continued and Peter felt chilled to the bone. The snow fell faster now. He had to turn up the speed on the wiper but then the refrain played faster.

'No!' he shouted in an effort to stop the noise in his head. It was too late. They were there. The ghosts he fought to subdue. They surrounded the car enveloping him.

Peter laughed in defiance. 'I don't want to go,' he thought rebelliously. 'Stephanie needs me. I need her. I can outrun them. All my life they've chased me, hunted me. Now Aunt Kath's gone. She wants me too but I'm not going!'

The car sped forward, seeming to glide with ease through the white mist. Peter leaned back in the seat a smile on his face. The white mist parted easily as the car sailed into the inky night. Deep in the recesses of his mind, Peter heard a baby screaming. 'Mary Margaret, my sister, this time I'll save you. Don't' cry......'

****

Peter Atkinson died instantly when his car swerved off the road during a blinding white-out of swirling snow so common north of the city. It was barely twenty four hours after the call to his wife. Sudden reduced visibility was a common enough phenomenon even this early in December, but the OPP were puzzled by the failure of the driver to slow down in the prevailing conditions.

The tall somber looking constable who was escorted directly to the condominium door by an obliging building manager was glad that he had been able to see the victim's widow instead of announcing his presence through the intercom. He never knew what situation he might find especially since it was close to midnight. The stunning auburn haired beauty who greeted him warily was his first mother-to-be. Ever mindful of the effects of severe shock in an advanced state of pregnancy he nonetheless recited the information according to protocol and promptly caught her as she fell into his arms.

When she recovered a little, Stephanie gave the kindly policeman Georgette's home telephone number. He had already called the doctor whose number was listed by the phone, but the officer knew that the young woman would need a friend and stayed with her until they arrived full of concern and fear for her and the unborn child. Both appeared very competent and quickly reassured the police officer that they could handle things from here.

'Officer, I hope that there will be no need to disturb her with any details. I can identify the body if necessary.'

'Thank you doctor. The coroner will let you know. Here's my card if you need to reach me. Good night ma'am, miss.'

Georgette escorted the policeman to the door while Michael led Stephanie to her bedroom. 'I want to give you a mild sedative Stefania. It won't harm the baby but you need to rest.'

'Whatever you think is best Michael. I just want to stop hurting so much.'

Later when Stephanie finally settled, Michael and Georgette sat in the living room discussing the situation.

'Is the baby going to be alright Michael?'

'I do not know Georgette. The sedative is safe enough but this stress could precipitate premature labour. The baby is healthy otherwise but there are some risks, even at this time for a premature baby.' His tone was unlike anything Georgette had heard before. He held his head in his hands, fighting his own feelings.

'We'll just have to keep a close eye on her. Is there anything I should be aware of?' Georgette spoke with a calm she was far from feeling.

'Just check with her from time to time that the bay is moving and kicking. I am going home now but I will be back by mid morning. If there is any change in the heart rate or activity at that time I will admit her to the hospital.'

Michael left, but Georgette was unable to settle down to sleep right away. He mind was in a whirl. She had calls to make. Each one was weighed carefully in her mind first.

She put through a long distance call to Helen Droga to give her the news. Fortunately the time difference meant that Helen was up having breakfast.

'I am worried Helen. You can speak with Stephanie first before you make your travel plans but if you can't stay with her now, perhaps it's best to wait until she gives birth but I will leave that up to you.'

'Is the baby in any danger?'

'So far, Michael is quite satisfied.'

'I'm so glad he's there Georgette. I know you will both look after my daughter. I plan to book a ticket now but certainly I will call back later today.'

After completing the call, the ever efficient Georgette made a quick list of other things to be done. Michael would be back soon and she wanted a couple of hours sleep before he returned. There would be many difficult hours ahead.

Working quickly later in the morning, the pair organized funeral arrangements and consulted Stephanie only when it was necessary to get her approval. She knew she could trust these two dearest of friends and raised no objections to the simple service planned for two days time. She shared a few words with the kindly funeral director but it was clear she was satisfied to leave the details to her friends.

It was essential for Stephanie to rest as much as possible. Georgette left the running of the office in Jawahir's capable hands and devoted herself entirely, in her no nonsense way, to seeing that things ran smoothly,

She made two other significant calls later that morning. One was to Gregory Richmond informing him of the death. He was stunned by the news. Georgette was unsure if she had done the right thing but she remembered his request when they parted at his office. She offered no stipulations about him visiting. She asked only that he call before. The second call was to the lawyer whose name was found listed on the scattered papers in Peter's car.

****

Gregory could not breathe deeply after the call from Georgette. Thankfully he had been alone at the time. He could not begin to guess at the implications this would have.

Beth was still away in Italy. Their final parting had been in anger. He had not forbidden her to go but made it clear that she had spent enough time away from him and that he needed a wife at home. It made little difference to her. After six years of marriage she could not just sit around doing nothing, she had declared.

In the end, he had given up. During that time he had steadfastly refused to call Stephanie, putting her at the back of his mind, trying desperately to give his marriage the undivided attention it would need if they hoped to salvage anything of the relationship. Beth had not cooperated at all and he had felt an impotent rage at the injustices of life. And now this!

It was mid-afternoon before he could take a couple of hours away from the busy office and, as promised, he called beforehand. Georgette quickly put Stephanie on the phone. Her cracked and pain filled voice tore at his insides, but she wanted to see him and that was all that mattered.

He arrived at the condo half an hour later. Tactfully, Georgette left them alone on the excuse of urgent business. Stephanie was in her bedroom sitting in a mauve pattern loveseat staring out the window at the overcast sky. Her eyes were red rimmed and swollen, the irises resembling fathomless pools.

'Gregory, please come in.'

'I'm sorry Sunny. Sorry for the pain you feel.'

'I don't know what…I feel. My hearts aches for the lonely and frightened boy my husband was. My arms ache to hold and comfort a man I never really knew. I feel the pain of lost dreams and hopes. It all seems so meaningless now…to plan…..to want things…'

'It had meaning Sunny. The dreams and hopes are part of what makes life worthwhile. As short as your marriage lasted he was very much a part of you and your dreams.

'No ….no, Gregory. He was never …a part of me. He wanted to be but the past held him too tightly…for me….. to share his life.'

Gregory hesitated but a few seconds before enfolding her in his arms. He didn't really understand all she said. He did know, however, that she seemed to come to terms with the kind of man her husband had been. He stroked the cascading titian hair and murmured words of love and comfort.

Before long her ragged breathing quieted and became even. He knew she was sleeping. Moving slowly, so as not to disturb her, he gently carried Stephanie to the double bed and laid her tenderly on her side. She protested feebly but he stayed beside her until she settled into a deep sleep again then covered her with a gaudy multicolored afghan which seemed to mock the solemnity in the room.

Georgette had not yet returned so he sat and observed the delicate young woman for some time, wondering how he could love her so much. Her alabaster skin stood out starkly even on the snow white pillows and he was actually alarmed by her pallor. Only the even rise and fall of her chest above the bulge of her pregnancy reassured him. As his gaze wandered around the room, he noted with some curiosity the lack of masculine appointments in the room.

'*So they didn't seem to share the room*' he thought. It meant nothing. That growing baby was not an immaculate conception. Suddenly he was angry.

Leaving the sleeping figure on the bed, he returned to the living room just as Georgette was opening the door.

'She's asleep now. I put her on the bed. I hope she'll get some rest for awhile. Is the doctor satisfied with her condition,' he asked anxiously.

'The baby's heart rate is fine so far. It has been steady. There's some decline in the baby's activity and that has Michael worried, but not unduly since she has been sedated. We just have to keep a very close eye on her.'

'Does anyone know what happened?' he asked sitting down on the brightly patterned cushiony sofa. As he looked around he remembered his first visit there and his own feelings.

'Not really,' Georgette responded heading to the kitchen to make tea. 'The OPP felt that he must have been speeding. He knew those roads and was aware of the hazards of sudden snow squalls at this time of year. I do know that his Aunt died and he went north to arrange things. Stephanie shared that with me. I've called the lawyer who saw him yesterday to inform him about the accident. He seemed very upset at the news. In fact, he is driving down this evening after court to see Stephanie.'

'It's very strange isn't it, that Peter should have kept that part of his life almost completely hidden from his wife.' Gregory joined Georgette in the kitchen.

'It may have saved her life Gregory. She would have been in the car with him otherwise.'

It gave them both pause for serious thought.

****

Stephanie woke feeling much refreshed by her sleep. The effects of the fogginess caused by the sedative had worn off and her head was clear. She was done with tears for now. Peter was dead. Her biggest regret lay with the unborn child who would never know her father. Stephanie was almost sure it was a girl. She dreamed of giving him a daughter. As she felt the reassuring movement of the baby she wondered what kind of father Peter would have been. She liked to believe that he would have loved his child wholeheartedly with a passion that he lacked in his relationships with adults. For the benefit of his now fatherless child she would maintain that principle, allowing Peter to have some dignity in death that he would never have in life again.

The two women ate a light early supper while they discussed the final arrangements for the funeral. Georgette was heartened by Stephanie's apparent acceptance and encouraged her to discuss both her positive and negative feelings.

'You know Georgette, Peter and I have not had a proper relationship for some time. He was my husband and I cared about him but not for him. He rejected everything I had to offer.'

'It's a very difficult time Stephanie. You are angry and hurt. The things that seemed so important before will probably have less importance as time goes by.'

'I can't hide the fact that we had gone beyond even being civil to each other most of the time. His last call was the most he had spoken to me in weeks. Even then he was harsh and uncompromising.'

'I am not making excuses for Peter or his behaviour towards you. We don't understand what was going on in his mind. There's no point blaming yourself though. You did all you could. Perhaps given time he might have changed.'

'I don't want or need false reassurances. If I was not pregnant it might have been over eventually but the fact that I am hastened the deterioration of our relationship, Georgette so let's not pretend otherwise.'

'Stephanie!'

'Don't look at me like that. I'm not bitter towards Peter. He was what he was. I'm more angry with myself for not opening my eyes to the reality of....life before. My optimism was a fool's way of facing problems.'

The older woman's relief while observing Stephanie's calm manner earlier soon turned to concern as she perceived a colder hardened personality emerging from beneath the hurt. The echo of words, which Georgette often thought to herself, were so out of character for Stephanie. Looking deeply into the hazel eyes, the loving friend was dismayed by the loss of that indefinable quality of innocence that made Stephanie unique.

They went on to discuss the arrival of the lawyer.

'Do you feel up to talking with him honey?'

'It has to be done. I just want to get everything over with as quickly as possible.'

Knowing the consequences of trying to reason with Stephanie who was clearly getting tense and looking for some outlet to redirect her anger, Georgette wisely avoided any antagonizing comments while she searched for some topic that would not fan the flames of frustration seething within her friend.

Georgette felt inadequate. She was too close to Stephanie to be objective. The changes she noted in her friend required a tact that she was unable to adjust to. *'I've known Stephanie in many moods,'* she reflected shaking her head, *'but this is almost frightening!'*

Thoughts of Michael, then Gregory flashed through her mind. She was about to call the Doctor when the intercom buzzer sounded. Gregory's voice floated up through the speaker calm and confident.

'I'd like to come up Georgette unless this is a bad time?'

Georgette knew he might come back after his earlier visit. He said he had some urgent work to finish at the office but hoped to return by early evening. She took one look at Stephanie's face, and saw the relief mirrored there. She quickly gave her consent.

His arrival brought an immediate change in the tense atmosphere. Stephanie gradually calmed down relaxing in the easy chair while they waited for the arrival of the lawyer.

Stephanie was ashamed, under the circumstances, to allow even her best friend to see the naked and desperate need she had for Gregory to be near her. She had remembered his earlier visit and the physical comfort he brought to her, just by being present. She was floundering in a sea of sensations that were foreign to her usual nature. Stephanie needed an anchor. Gregory was there.

No intimate remarks or gestures passed between them but somehow Gregory and Stephanie seemed to communicate instinctively. In the end, as the final details of Peter's ragged childhood unfolded from the lawyer's lips, Georgette was ever thankful for Gregory's presence.

Chapter 15:

Mr. Campbell was an elderly and scholarly man who probably should have retired long ago from his legal practice. His involvement with clients always went beyond what was required or expected. He was universally loved, so kind and generous was he; but that type of giving nature often worked against him too.

As he wearily made his way out of the taxi, he mentally rehearsed the possible scene about to take place. He never knew Peter had been married and wondered what kind of woman could live with a past as complicated and incomplete as the one Peter brought. *'Perhaps time had helped the boy to achieve some equilibrium in life'* he thought wistfully. A normal healthy relationship that was stable, seemed as farfetched to the lawyer as anything Peter could accomplish with respect to his personal life.

The portly, balding man severely dressed in the black suit and white shirt required in court, was greeted at the door of the condo by a rather exotic looking beauty with lush auburn hair. Despite his small town background, Leonard Campbell had travelled extensively in his youthful days. An army posting in Korea had given him an appreciation of the Orient. He discerned this in the face bidding him to come in, but was puzzled by the incongruous colouring. Never believing that Peter could have married anyone not wholly Anglo Saxon, he held his initial greeting in check waiting instead for her self-introduction

'Good evening Mr. Campbell. I'm Georgette O'Malley. We spoke on the phone this morning. Please come in.'

Years of training and keen observation stood him in good stead. Her melodic voice was as pleasing as her face but she was not Peter's wife.

'Thank you my Dear.' Any further speech was halted as he observed a rather wan looking titian-haired Amazon stretched out on a chaise lounge. Unable to avoid a double take between the two striking women, he was escorted to her side where she gracefully rose and extended her hand, almost dwarfing his own adequate height.

'Mrs. Atkinson, my deepest sympathies to you at this time.' Her nod and polite 'thank you' touched the elderly man deeply. He was awed by her stature and almost, but not totally, dumbfounded by her advanced state of pregnancy.

The third occupant of the room also rose to greet and be introduced to the lawyer. He was very tall, handsome, and gave every indication of being an athlete. Leonard Campbell sensed a feeling of anger emanating from the brief handshake. Its cause was inexplicable to the kindly man, but dismissed as unimportant in that moment.

'Pleased to meet you Mr. Richmond.'

In fact, Gregory found himself annoyed buy the use of 'Mrs. Atkinson'. He always seemed to delude himself into the thought of 'Sunny Droga' single mother. He inwardly cursed his childishness and replaced the frown with a slight smile as he sat down. He quickly realized that he had no place in what was essentially a private family matter, but if Stephanie needed him he was prepared to stay and be as unobtrusive as possible.

Some casual conversation was exchanged about the accident and funeral arrangements while refreshments were being served. Mr. Campbell had elected to travel to the city by commuter GO bus. He hailed a taxi from the local terminal, leaving him no time to have even a hurried meal. He was grateful to the Georgette for sensing his need for nourishment. He needed to settle much in his mind before he could proceed.

Each member of the trio kept a watchful eye on Stephanie prepared to end any conversation which brought on the slightest distress. During a lull in the conversation, the lawyer who was quickly tiring decided it was time to state his business and go, if the widow was up to it. She was, but he proceeded cautiously.

'Mrs. Atkinson, how much did you know about Peter and his family?'

'I know the whole story Mr. Campbell. You see, earlier this year I had an accident at about the same time that I found myself pregnant. Peter's behaviour towards me changed and I felt there was more to his story of a chronic invalid mother than he had originally led me to believe.'

'How did he change, if I may interrupt?'

'He withdrew physically and emotionally at first then showed signs of unprovoked violence towards me. My doctor suggested that Peter might have deeper emotional problems that I should probably investigate.'

'I see. Please continue.'

'Mr. Campbell, I am not on the witness stand. Please don't treat me as if Peter and I are on trial.'

Appalled by his courtroom demeanor, he apologized quickly not wanting to further offend this beautiful woman who nonetheless seemed very tense. She smiled her acceptance and continued as he requested but uninterrupted this time.

'Some months ago, I travelled north to find, I had hoped at the time, a neighbour or friend who could give me a general picture of the tragedy. I was surprised to find not only his home but also Katherine Atkinson, who was largely responsible for his upbringing. I hadn't even known that she existed. After hearing her story I was torn between pity and fear. I tried my best to avoid confrontations with Peter and encouraged him to discuss his feelings with me. It never worked. He continued to live in a private hell, the only comfort was his job.'

Stephanie paused and took a deep breath, shifting her body slightly and placing a hand on her abdomen before she resumed. 'My one last hope was that this child would make a difference. If not, I was prepared to leave.' Her words dropped like stones into the silent void.

Georgette, who knew the whole story already, remained calm and watchful of her unhappy friend. Gregory's anger, long since under control, returned full force and was now directed at the deceased husband who had dared to hurt his pregnant wife. The greatest shock, however was sustained by Leonard Campbell, whose mouth stayed open, and whose pallor changed. He muttered 'Oh My God!'. His words were heard by all but Stephanie alerting the others to some further tragedy which was known only to the lawyer.

A cramping backache had suddenly intensified and she was in the process of trying to shift into a more comfortable position yet again. The older man debated within himself whether he wanted to pursue things further or just discuss Peter's estate. He opted for the latter but was forestalled by a demanding request from his widow to give her information about her late husband's teenage years.

He hedged somewhat but was unable to avoid some conciliatory words. There was about Stephanie a look that seemed to bore into his head insistently trying to pick out answers that she needed for her peace of mind. He realized, however, that nothing he knew of Peter's youth would be reassuring or comforting to her.

Gregory and Georgette became alert but secondary players in this sudden drama and clash of wills between an increasingly hostile and fidgety Stephanie and a dismayed, defensive Leonard Campbell.

He began tentatively. 'Peter had to leave home at about age fourteen. I was lawyer to his maternal grandfather whose increasing concern over his troubled grandson knew no bounds. Minnie was legally incompetent you know, brain damaged from the hemorrhage. Katherine refused to give up care of both of them and smothered Peter with love to make up for the times when his mother called him...er... names.'

'What names?'

'You know,' he prevaricated, with a short list of harmless appellations that did not fool Stephanie for a moment, but she let him continue.

'There was some peer pressure on the boy and one or two serious incidents finally led the social services to remove him to a boy's home in Barrie to receive some long overdue counseling.'

'I don't suppose you care to tell me about those incidents?'

'No, Mrs. Atkinson, I don't. He's dead and the worst details of his life with him.' Leonard carried on relaxing a little now that he had gained the upper hand again.

'He spent two years there, in the home, but never relived in detail or resolved the traumas of his early life. The best they could do was to suppress the horror of the incident and encourage him to get on with his life. In part they were successful because he became cold, withdrawn, and entirely self-serving. That, I believe, is consistent with what you noted?' He waited for her acknowledgment.

'While that was not ideal either, it was a far cry from the severely disturbed boy who had first arrived there. He was eventually placed in the care of his grandfather, a fair but autocratic man who preached endlessly about putting the past behind you and having faith in God. That, too, may have been misdirected counseling, but again it worked. Peter was able to finish school, go on to college and hold his demons in check.'

'Were you surprised to find that he was married?'

'Yes I was very surprised, but from what you say it seems to have been reasonably successful.'

'Up...until...I.. got... pregnant,' she enunciated carefully. Her eyes were boring into the face of the lawyer, challenging him, engaging him in a battle of wills.

Leonard Campbell was well past his prime. It had been a long day and he was tired, burned out really from a long life of similar stressful situations in which he had to tread carefully. He couldn't engage Peter's widow any longer. Her strength was his undoing.

'I am surprised that he did allow you to become pregnant knowing that the sound of a crying child triggered his worst nightmares and his worst behaviours.'

Those final words, unthinkingly uttered by a much-fatigued man, broke the tenuous hold Stephanie had on her pregnancy. The increasing backache became a sharp abdominal pain and the ensuing gush of water a sure sign that Peter's unborn child would no longer be denied entry into the world. The baby seemed to be the only one of the dismayed group with a clearly defined purpose.

Leonard Campbell, horrified by his error in judgment, apologized profusely. He was barely able to gather himself together. In the ongoing melee, he left hurriedly to get a taxi to a downtown hotel, knowing that he could not make the return trip home.

Georgette, quickly reacting to a situation she had mentally rehearsed numerous times, gathered together a few things after alerting the hospital. She had prayed for happier circumstances but tried not to be deterred by her increasing concern for Stephanie's mental anguish and physical discomfort.

Gregory gently laid Stephanie on the couch after she collapsed into his arms. He waited until the initial pain subsided, then tried to make her relax and take some deep breaths. He too, was deeply concerned. Stephanie was close to hysteria. The contractions he knew were not the problem. Whatever final pitiful hopes she harboured about Peter had been lost.

All the words of love and reassurance that he could find within him poured from his lips as he desperately tried to help keep her from falling over the edge. It was to no avail. The agitated and pain racked body tossed and turned while she moaned and cried.

'I knew it! Deep down inside I knew it! He could never have loved this baby and now he's dead ……..and my child will be…..

fatherless just like me. It hurts so much. Please help me. Mama…..
Mama, where are you?'

Gregory could see the grief over the death of her father released
in this new moment of acknowledged loss. He felt helpless and
hopeless. He quickly called out for Georgette, and then dialed
911 instructing them to send an ambulance. He knew he could
not possibly have driven her safely in his current state. It was a
wise choice.

****

Two hours and fourteen minutes later, Stephanie exhausted but
happy, held her premature son in her arms, stroking the down
covered body while cooing and crying at the same time. She
was disappointed that he had to be taken away so quickly but an
overzealous pediatrician, on hand in case of a problem wanted to
give the squalling, but premature baby a thorough examination.

Georgette, wide-eyed and awed by the miracle of the delivery
said little. She and the tired mother hugged, weeping copiously
while Michael and the obstetrical team completed their work.

Later in the very early morning hours, clean, warm and
comfortable in a private room of the large downtown hospital,
Stephanie welcomed Gregory with an outstretched hand. He
appeared strained and worn out. Much of the time was spent
pacing restlessly in the father's lounge while awaiting the baby's
birth. He was cheered immensely to see the glow surrounding the
new mother, but the ravages of the past twenty four hours could
not be hidden. There were deep dark circles beneath the now
luminescent hazel eyes.

'You've been an anchor to me this night Gregory Richmond,'
she said softly receiving his chaste kiss and hug. 'In a world gone
completely upside down….you kept me steady and I love you
dearly.'

Her endearing little speech disarmed Gregory, but he gave
minimum credence to the words. From his experience with Beth's
sisters he knew that in the first few hours after giving birth women

generally loved everyone in sight who had helped with the delivery but he was pleased and touched by her lyrical wording just the same.

'You need to get some sleep Sunny,' he whispered close to tears. 'I'm going to take Georgette home and then get some sleep myself. I'll come back later.'

'Don't be long but sleep well my love.' The last two words were barely perceptible as sleep finally overtook her. He covered her shoulders smoothed the hair from her face and with one last kiss on the sore but softly parted lips, he left the room.

Never in a life of ups and downs, problems and decisions, hurts and happiness, did Gregory Richmond feel as he did this night. He knew that neither mother nor baby belonged to him. He knew that Stephanie had yet to bury her husband. He also knew that she must still complete her grieving and give all her attention to her newborn son. He also knew that sometime in the near future, he would have to make a decision about his own life, because his happiness lay in her hands and he could not under any circumstances continue in a marriage such as his. For the first time in many a year Gregory cried in mourning for himself, for all that was lost and all that was yet to be found.

****

Peter Atkinson was buried four days after the birth of his son. Despite protests from all parties, Stephanie insisted on attending. No one would have questioned her absence in the circumstances, but she merely delayed the funeral until she was strong enough. She laid her husband to rest, at last, with as much dignity as death would allow. As she watched his coffin lowered into the ground, she thought *'Peter's sins lay not in his actions during his life but in pretending that a normal life was possible. Sooner or later the traumatized child would surely seek revenge for its hurts.'*

Stephanie accepted the condolences of his colleagues with quiet grace. Few of them were known to her but she had a sense from them that Peter had been well respected for his abilities if not well liked.

The overflow of milk from her aching breasts gave her the opportunity to escape early and Georgette quickly sped her off to the hospital where Peter's wailing son was beginning to rake up the sheets in his incubator. Stephanie had been upset when the pediatrician told her that the baby would be in the hospital for four to six weeks.

'He's premature you know,' the bulky young doctor said in that patronizing tone reserved for anxiety prone mothers.

'I am aware of his birth date Doctor,' she cut in sarcastically.

The young man straightened immediately and continued in a more reasonable manner. 'We are very pleased with his weight, just over 2200 grams but there can be some developmental delays especially in the lungs so we need to observe him in the controlled atmosphere of the incubator for at least 72 hours. Then we will reassess his status. He will lose some weight at first and he's a very long baby so we would certainly prefer to see him gain four to five hundred grams before going home.'

'What should I feed him doctor? I want him to come home as soon as possible.'

Quickly assessing this recent widow and knowing her professional status, he had suggested a popular bottle feed that would supply all the baby's nutritional needs. But Michael Czerny, who because of the circumstances had to relinquish control of the infant's care, would have none of that and told the young doctor and the puzzled mother that breast milk was best and superior to any cow's milk formulated commercially. Support was forthcoming from all sides and as the young mother sat quietly nursing her infant after his father's funeral; she knew a peace and contentment that she never expected from so simple a function.

One week later, the baby came home amid cheers and bouquets from all those who rallied around to support Stephanie. Helen Droga had arrived from England two days earlier. She had been reassured by Georgette that her presence was needed when the baby came home. Gregory drove the car and ran errands as requested, but left soon after to spend the holidays with his family.

It was Christmas Eve and while the family was subdued, the presence of the baby in the condo brought untold joy to each of them. He would be christened on New Year's Day but for the family gathered around a small tree, seemingly hypnotized by the colorful winking lights, the all important naming of the baby was to take place.

'Have you decided yet Dear?'

'Yes Helen, I have. It was a very difficult decision, but one I can live with. Few people know me as Atkinson so the baby will have Papa's name. He is Peter's child but that family name seems to have brought little happiness to any of them and lastly this time of year is a time of love, hope peace and forgiveness. My son will be called Christian Peterson Droga.

Chapter 16:

Christian Droga thrived happily in the warmth and love of the three women who lavished him with care and attention. If the masculine faces of Michael Czerny or Gregory Richmond intruded now and again, he did not seem to mind much because they were always smiling.

Helen Droga appeared to be the most enchanted of all, delighted as she was by her satisfactory role as grandmother to the tiny bundle her daughter allowed her to spoil shamelessly.

His feeding demands taxed his mother but she refused to relinquish her breastfeeding more than once or twice a week so that Helen or Georgette could feed him. 'There are lots of other things you can do,' she chided them. Stephanie produced abundant milk and had a freezer full of stored bottles if needed. His weight gain was as rapid as the passing weeks and before long the grey days of winter had given way to the colourful promise of spring.

Stephanie soon realized the necessity for making some serious decisions. Her relationship with Gregory was in limbo. He came and went as a friend only, while time helped to heal the emotional and physical wounds of her ill-fated marriage and the untimely death of her husband. The horror of Peter's life had been laid to rest but the after effects were not. A visit to Michael's office soon settled a major concern for Stephanie.

Seated across from her physician and friend she gave voice to her fears. 'The possibility of inheriting certain genes has been bothering me Miklos Basci.'

'In what way Stefania?'

'I just wondered if...there is any possibility that Christian could inherit any of the troubling mental problems that plagued Peter's life.'

'Not likely Dear. I understand your concern but your late husband's problems were rooted in psychological trauma. Other mental problems such as schizophrenia are physiological, meaning that it comes from changes within the body and therefore can be inherited.'

He forestalled her next question with a raised hand and continued, 'I can't promise that Christian will be 100% normal. No one could do that. His development will depend almost entirely on his environment and the factors affecting it.'

Adopting a less official pose the kindly doctor patted her hand, kissed her cheek and reassured her that many women expressed less specific but similar concerns and the best they could do was to go out and give their child equal measures of love and discipline. The rest would take care of itself.

****

Heartened by the long talk, Stephanie then turned her attention to the problems of Peter's estate. She had received a congratulatory card from Leonard Campbell along with a sincere note apologizing profusely for his clumsiness that evening. Much less tense now and realizing that she had unknowingly been in early labour and very irritable, she accepted the apology and tendered one of her own with a further note to say that she would drive up to his office when the weather improved.

By mid April, the warmth and sunshine presaged a beautiful summer. Helen, Christian, and Stephanie made the trip to Collingwood by car, stopping at the place where Peter's car had gone off the road to throw some flowers at the spot where he had died.

She was composed and smiling when shown into the rectangular shaped office by a gray haired, rotund woman who appeared to have been with the lawyer for years. Helen elected to remain in the cozy reception area keeping an eye on Christian who was sound asleep in his car seat.

Seated before an antique mahogany desk and surrounded by pictures, certificates and the inevitable law books, Stephanie exchanged pleasantries before allowing him to get to the specific details.

'Mrs. Atkinson…'

'Stephanie, please?'

'Stephanie then…your late husband cared little for his properties up here and rarely drew money on his account. There is a sizeable profit from the sale of the farm which has been gathering interest over the last twenty years. As well, the house in Creemore has multiplied its initial value many times.'

He allowed her to digest this information before continuing. 'Peter's maternal grandfather will leave a fair sized estate in Collingwood and your young son is the only heir that I know of.'

Stephanie's jaw dropped considerably.

'You can always find someone to handle your financial matters, Mrs….er…Stephanie.' Mr. Campbell became flustered wondering if he had blundered again and tried to reassure her.

'Financial matters? No that is not what interests me Mr. Campbell. Did I hear you correctly? *Will leave*, you said?'

'Why yes' he responded.

'Mr. Campbell, I am a student of the English language as I hope you are. Does this mean that Peter's grandfather is still alive?'

'Why yes' he repeated still puzzled. As realization hit, he shook his head and murmured, 'you didn't know even that did you? How could Peter have kept these things from you?'

Neither had an answer.

'Can the …uh …Reverend…I believe you said, receive visitors?'

'Why yes' he repeated for the third time never believing in his wildest dreams that his old friend, John Everette could be so blessed. That his troubled grandson could pick such a generous and forgiving wife seemed the answer to a prayer.

The happy duo quickly concluded the business of Peter's estate. All money was to be held in trust for young Christian, except for the funds required to completely refurbish the house in Creemore. Stephanie realized that real estate never loses value, but money could. In time, when the worst memories faded, the house could be used as a summer or winter retreat for the family.

****

The nursing home where John Everette had chosen to spend his final days was set in the sprawling park near the edge of town. At a glance, one could see how ideal it was for the elderly residents. It had the appearance of a resort rather than an institution.

Leonard Campbell had wisely called ahead asking the administrator to gently prepare the Reverend for his unexpected visitors. Heart disease, and a subsequent stroke had weakened the old man considerably but his mind was alert. He had been further debilitated by the series of shocks sustained in the last few months.

Stephanie asked to be allowed to go in alone first. There were private things she wanted to say to the elderly man. They had stopped to feed Christian and he sat happily playing with his few toys. She smiled and kissed her mother before heading down the hall.

The room was standard sized with a single bed, dresser and washbasin. Numerous religious artifacts were carefully set out on the chest of drawers next to the bed.

'Come in child. My bark is long gone and I never did bite.'

Smiling nervously Stephanie entered the room and seated herself on the bed, unable to stop the tears which filled her eyes. If Peter lived to old age he would have been exactly like the thin, proud man seated before her. Only a slight droop to one side of his face marred an otherwise handsome countenance.

'Don't cry for me child or for my grandson. Peter probably had more happiness with you than he felt he had a right to. The hurt was just too deep for him to put it behind him completely and live a normal life. Tell me about yourself instead.'

And she did quickly for she knew that Christian would not behave forever and the old man despite an impressive visage was in reality very ill indeed.

He asked a few question about Peter but reassured her with these surprising words. 'I made mistakes with that boy. I tried too hard to please his mother ....when her mind was clear. Firm when I should have been soft and soft when I should have been firm.'

'I'm sure the decisions you had to make were very difficult. It couldn't have been an easy time for any of you.'

'No Stephanie…it wasn't…but I was very hard on Peter after he left the boys home. In my heart I did believe that without my discipline and faith he would not have survived even as long as he did.'

'I had my weaknesses too Reverend…'

'It would give me great pleasure to hear you call me Grandfather, Stephanie.'

There was no hesitation. She felt his request to be a privilege. 'I had my weaknesses too Grandfather. But without the knowledge of his history I was powerless to understand or help him.'

'Strange that you should say that. When he came up here to see me after his Aunt died, he was so angry with the world that the news of his death wasn't unexpected. He told me about you for the first time. He still knew, despite everything, that he could not share his secret with you.'

'I wonder…..'

'Don't my dear. Peter could not endure a life with the baby. You see, the death of his little sister at birth was the hardest thing that he faced that terrible day. Her screams echoed in his mind all the time.'

'I thought that she had been a stillbirth?'

'No child. She was very much alive but Minnie was unconscious and unable to direct him to help her. He had already been so frightened by his father's accident. It was too much.'

Stephanie sat still for a few minutes, digesting the information. 'I always believed that I was going to have a daughter, you know. I think I was trying to make up for his loss but I realize now that it wouldn't have made any difference. I can only hope that he has found some peace.'

They both paused for a moment of shared silence.

'Now then, bring my great grandson here and let me give him my blessing. I'm an old man and time is short.'

The return of some of his former assertiveness cleared the air of further melodrama so that Christian, full and contented smiled toothlessly bringing tears to the old man's eyes.

'Don't come this way again child unless that's your wish. But if you can drop me a line now and again, I'll be glad to hear how my great grandson is progressing.'

Stephanie promised to maintain the link. She would keep the house in Creemore and the correspondence for the sake of her son. She left Collingwood feeling as if the most terrible weight had finally been lifted from her shoulders. She took with her only a small picture of Peter aged 5, to set aside for Christian to see. It was the last photo of Peter Atkinson taken in joy and innocence before the loss of his father and sister scarred him forever.

****

The next few days after her return from Collingwood, Stephanie belatedly realized that she had not seen Gregory for some time. She tried to recall his last visit and found that she could not. Nor could Helen, when questioned. Mother and daughter never discussed the role that the charmingly handsome man played in the latter's life but the older woman had been around for quite a while and could see that he cared deeply for her grieving daughter.

Helen had never been an interfering parent and did not intend to start. She did know that the grief would gradually lessen and her daughter's natural desire for love and companionship would soon reassert itself. Helen was beginning to see signs of that already for there was a restless haunted look about her child that could not be hidden.

'Are you thinking about returning to work dear?' she inquired one evening as they sat around talking.

'Uh....yes ...Mama. Summer's are usually quite busy.'

'I didn't plan to stay quite this long but I could hold on another few weeks until you find a nanny and she settles in with Christian.'

Giving heed at last, Stephanie looked at her mother. She wasn't really seeing or hearing. Her mind was not contemplating the decisions that needed to be made.

'*Where was Gregory? Maybe I should call. I wonder if Beth is back.*' Her mind wandered again without responding to her mother.

'Stephanie, are you paying any attention to what I've said?'

Jumping up from the sofa where the two women had been relaxing after dinner, she stared hard at her mother trying to focus on the matter at hand. To make things worse, her milk started leaking and she was embarrassed. It had been some time since it last happened. The usual trigger was Christian's movements or crying. No sound emanated from his room.

'I have to feed the baby Helen,' and she walked away abruptly leaving the puzzled mother to ponder her daughter's strange behaviour.

The little room that had been the den was now converted into a green and yellow nursery filled with childish toys and equipment from his doting godparents. The young baby was scarcely ready for most of them but they gave the room a cheerful atmosphere.

Georgette and Michael had purchased his crib and dresser set but a belated shower added many colourful, wind-up, glowing, walking, and talking toys.

Christian was not crying but he was awake staring at his bedside music box. Time had improved her mothering skills and she felt very confident as she looked into his delighted eyes.

'He's a good baby' thought the proud mother. She searched his face for some feature that would identify him as her baby or Peter's but he steadfastly refused to look like either of them, maintaining instead his own identity, including a nondescript thatch of brown hair.

He nursed steadily and was soon asleep after a final burp from his satisfied stomach. Usually Stephanie claimed this hour as her own and no one intruded on her time. It was always special. From three months on, her young son had slept peacefully until the early morning. With a final kiss she left him to sleep. There was no comfort for Stephanie. Reluctantly leaving the darkened room she returned to the living room to face her mother.

'I'm sorry Helen. I was very abrupt before, but I still feel very wound up. Now that things have been resolved as far as Peter's concerned, I should be more relaxed.'

Stephanie's use of her mother's given name and maternal appellation did not concern Helen. It had been like that since her daughter's early years. They jokingly agreed to be best friends as the girl became a woman. Helen often stated truthfully, 'I am far too old to be your mother!'

More often than not these days however the *'Mama'* slipped out and Helen was worried. There seemed to be so many more events which happened in the past year but as yet Stephanie had not confided anything.

Patting the couch beside her, she held her daughter by the hand trying to infuse some peace. Stephanie was far too big for the much shorter woman to envelope in her arms, but Helen could sense a need for comfort.

'As I said before dear, I think you may be ready to return to work, at least part time. Your interest in the business is not just as an employee. Being a mother does not preclude other interests....'

'I know that Mama.'

'Then what troubles you my pet?'

Still hesitating but determined to talk to the one person whom she knew would judge her kindly, Stephanie said, 'when I was young we never talked much about sex. It just didn't seem to interest me and well..... you were.....'

'So old?' Helen interjected softly as her daughter faltered.

'I'm sorry Mama. I know you and papa loved each other deeply but....'

'Did you feel that your sex life with Peter was unsatisfactory?' It was not really a question. Helen sensed a need to be frank.

'I really had no comparison to make Mama. He was my first man but I read some books and....'

'You met someone else who turned your world upside down.'

'Yes but I never...' She felt so inadequate, unable to put her feelings into words.

Patting the fidgeting hands tenderly, Helen took a deep breath. 'I'm not so old that I can't remember those wonderful feelings. I lived too long around the passionate, emotional environment of the theater world to expect less, but when I married you father he was everything I could have wanted and more.'

'But I didn't know what I wanted!'

'Peter lacked your father's passion dear and it would have been impossible for you to respond naturally to something you did not receive.'

'Then it's not abnormal for me to want to have sex? The desire I experienced sometimes made me feel....cheap.'

'But you said you met someone that you care for. Usually those feelings will be expressed in a satisfying sexual relationship.'

'Oh Mama, that was the problem. I cared for Peter but sex was almost incidental in our marriage and to me that was normal. When I met Gregory I thought I just wanted to have sex with him. I was confused by my deeper feelings….feelings I couldn't control or understand.'

'He loves you dear.' Helen was still puzzled by a wary look on her daughter's face.

'Does he Mama? But he's married too. Being in love doesn't justify anything. I can never be happy while he is with someone else.' She shrugged. Having put her feelings into words, she felt more despondent than ever.

****

By the beginning of May a nanny had been found for young Christian. She was a French Canadian girl, the eldest of a very large family, who had recently completed a course in baby and child care. She felt more comfortable in her natural French and an obliging Stephanie encouraged her to use it as often as she like. Helen agreed to stay for one more month to supervise, but England beckoned. She felt her presence would prevent Stephanie from getting on with her life.

There was still no word from Gregory and a desperate call to his office only confirmed that he was away. *"I knew that already'* she thought crossly, slamming down the phone.

During the rest of that day Stephanie worked herself into a fine temper angry with everything and everyone. Young Christian, unused to this tense and angry stranger reacted accordingly crying, sobbing and refusing all comfort. Wisely Marguerite, on the job just two short weeks suggested that Madame might like to take a walk.

Realizing the wisdom of that but still in a temper, the fiery redhead took herself off. Too impatient to wait for the elevator, she headed for the stairs. Her feet stood rooted to the tiles on the small landing, almost refusing to descend the two flights to the ground. She knew Gregory was not home. Her eyes strayed up the one flight. Without conscious thought, she found herself standing outside his door. Anger and fear ebbed within her body.

'If Beth answers, I'll make some excuse', she thought desperately. *'I have to be near him right or wrong. I want to know if he's playing games with my feelings.'*

She raised a trembling hand to knock at the door when it was suddenly opened. The unexpected action nearly toppled her over. Standing before her was Gregory. The fear and frustration she was feeling washed away to be replaced by a need so strong it took her breath away.

Drawing a ragged breath she could not still her shaking body nor bring back the rage that had been burning in her before. Questions needed no answers. She wanted something else. The look in his smoldering brown eyes told her that he felt the same and understood.

Gregory held himself in check. His angel had returned to him, standing as before, breast heaving, hair askew, eyes wide, their hazel colour a tiny ring around fully dilated pupils. But this time it was different. He was free to follow his instincts and his insides soared communicating without words a powerful message of need, of love of desire. *Would she want what was offered?*

She took a step backward, her body visibly trembling. A sense of déjà vu held them, as time stood still with memories of their first encounter. Her retreat shook him, scared him and his left arm snaked out to capture the red-gold tresses and wind its way sensuously around the delicate alabaster neck. There was some resistance but ever so slowly the hand encountered the tense muscles in her back and drew her forward, not into his arms but within the circle of his love.

A trembling hand lightly stayed his finger on the wall switch. 'No…no lights, please,' she whispered, hardly daring to glance his way. He complied but continued to draw her forward into the depths of the sunken living room.

A warm tropical glow emitted from a large aquarium set up against the far wall. It was surrounded by a stereo set with all kinds of music paraphernalia lined up on shelves. It looks different here she thought inconsequentially. Her eyes seemed to be mesmerized by the yellow and black fish swimming aimlessly in the spacious tank.

'Music Sunny?'

'He speaks so few words sometimes but he knows what I need.' She smiled softly as she watched his shadowy figure move effortlessly to the stereo tuner and press the buttons.

Immediately the room was enveloped in the shimmering sounds of a violin symphony playing versions of popular songs. As the notes caressed her aching body, the tension oozed away slowly leaving her aware of a throbbing ache to immerse herself totally in the body of the man who now stood, legs apart, arms outstretched, beckoning to her.

She swallowed her irrational fears as her eyes adjusted to the dimness of the room. She sensed rather than heard his beseeching *'come dance with me?'.*

She glided into the space he offered, closing her arms about his neck.

No need to ask. He wanted her as much as she wanted him, but he seemed content to wait until she was ready.

'Gregory, I…'

'Don't talk Sunny. I just need to hold you in my arms like this for a minute. I can't think straight just yet.'

They danced, not as lovers do but as partners and she fitted herself to him, moving step for step around the centre of the living area, he leading, she following as if they were one.

As the introduction to the beautiful haunting melodious 'Mona Lisa' played, he tightened his arms sending fireworks shooting through her body. Their pace changed and four feet became rooted only their bodies swaying, sometimes as one but increasingly in opposite directions as his soulful tenor voice seduced her senses one by one.

She was touched by the depth of emotion he vocalized. 'Have I hurt you Gregory?' she asked as the final note lingered on his lips.

'No my darling, but we've both been hurt by circumstances beyond our control.' His whispered reply brought tears to her eyes. He was deeply aroused, could not hide the fact, yet he refused to release her or increase his responses to the continued stimulation of her body swaying teasingly against his.

'Beth?'

'She's not here. She's....' A finger tip at his lips stopped him.

'I don't need to know now. I want you too much to care.'

Gregory might have been glad to hear that she desired him above all else right now but the finger stayed and was soon captured by hungry lips and a seeking tongue, licking gently, words forgotten.

'Gregory you are tormenting me. Can I...?'

But her sexuality finally overtook her consciousness. *'I can't think when he does that'* was the final blur before she gave into the sensation.

The tongue travelled to the palm of her hand where his lips planted gently kisses before capturing the mound of Venus below her thumb with perfect teeth. The skin was held until waves of desire forced her to drag her hand away and rejoin the other around his neck to keep her from falling.

The husky tenor now almost hoarse with erotic tension found her ear and breathed out between driving kisses, 'I've waited... never a...woman like you. Oh my God!...you are everything, everything.....I have ever dreamed about...for so....so long ... Sunny.'

Overflowing now with pure lust, denied the joy of sexual fulfillment for years, Stephanie let out an agonizing cry, begging for release from a thunder building within her.

Whatever controls Gregory harbored left him. Clothes were unbearable torture. He removed his own, tearing what failed to give way easily. Her own went the same until she stood clad in her sturdy bra and lacy high-cut panties. Dimly, he was aware that she was still nursing Christian. He knew it was no barrier to their coupling but would leave it to her. The bra was off before he could blink but he stopped the hands removing the lacy triangle. He would not be denied that pleasure.

Her eyes widened at the sight of him. Taking her hand, Gregory drew it forward silently encouraging her to explore his body at will. He moaned with surprise and delight as her slim delicate fingers wrapped around him after a very brief hesitation. He was too far gone to see the fascination on her face, but his body jerked spasmodically with her manipulation and he almost climaxed. He captured her hand and brought it to his lips for a quick kiss.

It was a moment in time but their breathing tempo quickly became erratic as his eyes and lips blazed a trail of fire from the top of her neck down the centre of her body. 'The milk, she gasped reminding him of her abundant flow. He paid no mind. Nature's evidence of her motherhood only captivated him as he watched her face grow softer and glow with sweat.

She began to sway on her feet, eroticism seeking an outlet for the pounding pressure at her core. He knew he must hurry before frustration stifled her.

The white lacy concoction was soon headed downward past her trembling thighs and on his knees in front of her he finally removed it burying his face in the warmth and softness of her abdomen. He planted a few kisses there, holding her firmly. A quivering hand slid up her inner thigh ever so lightly and made it way to the moist satiny edges of her womanhood before slipping within to massage tenderly, reveling in the wetness a as liquid proof of her need. He was not prepared for the second scream that tore out of her body as his fingers found the bed of her sexual being, awakening and arousing her to such an incredible heights that she fell to her knees, hips bucking, sobbing wildly as a thousand sensations washed over her.

Stephanie thought she was dying and cried aloud for the death was sweet. The large sofa beckoned but there was no time. She gripped his shoulder in mindless passion kissing him over and over as her response continued. Gregory was ignited by the sensuous twisting of her body.

Straightening his legs and propping his back against the sofa, he sat her on top of him, allowing his throbbing manhood to enter her quickly. If she was shocked by the unorthodox position it was only for a fraction of a second. He filled her completely.

She needed no lessons. Unable to think, she allowed nature to take its course. She moved rapidly up and down, knees bent beside his hips, head thrown back savoring the feel of him inside her. She was caught up in the dominant position, while they now danced as all lovers ultimately do, this time she leading, him following.

He watched her face in the glow light, shadowed but expressive, as he kissed her lips and neck and any other parts of the inviting skin. As another shock wave washed over her, she fell back but was caught firmly by a pair of powerful arms and held, until sanity returned. Gregory knew he could not control his own release much longer. He was a man starved but wanting desperately to have the ultimate fulfillment of a mutual climax.

He laid her flat on her back, giving them a breather, but not for long. Her eyes beseeched him to come back to her. He paused, however, opening her knees to tenderly place a kiss on the surprisingly golden triangle of hair before entering her again. Her legs wrapped themselves around his torso and she drew his lips to her, opening her mouth and welcoming his thrusting tongue as she welcomed his thrusting body.

He barely heard the whispered, 'I love you Gregory, as he plunged into her warmth and wetness, rocking them both with powerful strokes. Her body arched and fell as she clung to him arms and legs entwined about his glistening back. Their mouths met, hungry for increased contact, tongues slashing at each other fighting with a life of their own as words failed them.

Sweat sparkled on their bodies in the sensuous dimness and their only awareness was the feel of him inside her, ravaging her welcoming warmth deliciously, faces twisted in the tortuous climb to the heights of mutual gratification.

'Stephanie, oh my love,' he cried as they entered the vortex of heaven and hell. Gregory knew that if he died in that moment, he would have already been to both places in her arms.

****

Stephanie woke with a start. She could never remember feeling such a powerful sense of satiation. The unfamiliar sounds of violin music assailed her ears. The hand resting heavily across her breast scarcely moved as she lifted it easily and placed it next to the man sleeping beside her.

She turned slightly to ease the cramp in her back from lying on the floor. She knew she should leave but was held in check by the opportunity to observe Gregory undisturbed.

Studying his face as it lay in repose, she felt an overwhelming tenderness for the handsome man who had given her those wonderful intense feelings. Much as she loved him, however, what they had done was wrong. It had been wrong from the beginning and now that she was a widow it was still not even half right.

She quickly gathered herself together, dressed and left the condo surprised, but not overly concerned, when Gregory slept on.

'It's better this way' she reasoned. *'Everything just came together at that moment and our desire got the better of us but it won't happen again.'*

It was after midnight and all was quiet in her own place. She peeped in on her sleeping son, thankful that Helen and Marguerite had not waited up to witness her disheveled reappearance. Those stolen hours with Gregory would be something for her to relive in her private moments, but not to be shared.

A warm shower quickly relieved the achiness of the unaccustomed activity and she soon fell into a deep satisfying dreamless sleep.

****

The sounds of Christian, agitated and hungry soon had her scrambling out of bed in the early morning. She had a lot to make up for. Their usual evening hour had been missed the previous night and the little guy had suffered from his mother's distraction the previous day. As she nursed him quietly in the early morning sunlight, the promises to herself the night before faded and she could feel the pull of Gregory's attraction even as she denied it existence.

She burped the drowsy infant and returned him to his cot, where she knew he would most likely sleep another two hours. She headed for the shower again but the stinging water failed to wash away the lethargy that always seemed to accompany thoughts of Gregory. She decided that action would be her best bet.

Refreshed, she followed her nose to the aromatic smell of coffee perking and found Marguerite already busy in the kitchen.

'Bon Jour Madame. Ca va bien?' The polite greeting was the only reference to Stephanie's uncharacteristic behavior. As an employer, she was grateful and pleased by the young girl's discreet demeanour and knew that they would get along well.

The pair discussed a few matters pertaining to Christian's care and the introduction of solid food. They shared fragrant cups of coffee and warm buttery croissants. Stephanie decided to take a real walk when they were finished. It would help clear away her cobwebs about the future and give her time to evaluate what had happened with Gregory the previous night. A call to Georgette when she returned would set the wheels in motion for her return to work. Beyond that she refused to speculate about her future.

A warm fuchsia track suit which was a gift and clashed horribly with her hair, suited her mood of the day and she headed out the door, just as the telephone rang. She knew that Marguerite or

Helen would answer it. *'I am not in the mood to talk with anyone,'* she thought peevishly. And, closing the door firmly, *'if it's Gregory, I'm not ready to face him yet.'*

****

The condominium block, although located downtown in Toronto was not far from one of the numerous parks dotted throughout the city. On this crisp May morning she headed for the winding path where few people would be at this time. The brisk pace she set for herself seemed more like running away than relaxation but jumbled impressions from the time spent in Gregory's arms continued to plague her until she could have screamed in frustration. Stopping to bend over and take some deep breaths brought no relief. She turned to retrace her steps home and found herself confronted by the reality of the man, more potent and more powerful than any vision her mind could concoct.

It an unknowing soul had chanced to observe the pair in the park, he or she could have drawn only one conclusion. The tall, dark haired man with an incredible, lithe and intense attitude must be a musical conductor. His hands and arms moved through the air with ease and authority seeming to coax the very sweetest notes from the early morning sun.

As the melody of the sun played around the golden highlights in the hair of the slim, graceful, titian beauty, she swayed gently to and fro as a dancer might when performing a tune created for her alone.

One mistake the observer would never make would be to believe that the man was merely the conductor of the song. When the hands fell to his side and the dark head bowed forward, he waited tense and taut. He seemed to care little about his performance. Only the approval of the dancer mattered. She alone could dance so perfectly to the song he created for her.

The observer's eyes closed in silent prayer.

Chapter 17:

The pair returned quickly to Gregory's condo eager to be alone with no ghosts past or present to haunt them. A quick call to Helen assured her that Christian was well taken care of.

'You needn't hurry back Dear. It is more important to devote some time to yourself and your own happiness. Christian is playing on the floor. He's quite happy.'

'Thanks Mama, I love you.'

'And I love you too', sighed a deep masculine voice at her ear. 'Is everything alright at home?'

'Yes, Helen seems to have things under control.'

'Good for her!' He dismissed the doting grandmother easily but not unkindly. 'There's far too much control here though' he concluded pulling off her colourful top.

She hadn't been ready to fall into his arms when they returned from the park. It was important for her to know where she stood in his life. He explained his actions of the past few weeks with the best news of all. Beth was no longer a part of his life. He had been away in Italy trying to tie up the loose ends of his futile marriage.

'You must have sensed that I was back Sunny. I had only just dumped my suitcases in the bedroom and was on my way down to you when I heard the knock.'

Stephanie was overwhelmed that Gregory was free at last to be with her but she needed to check on her son before she could allow herself to savor the implications of all that Gregory was telling her. The reassurances of her mother and the warm approving tones of her voice satisfied Stephanie that she was free to follow the dictates of her heart.

As these thoughts raced through her head, Gregory's hands had not been idle and she was mildly shocked to realize that they were both nearly naked, in broad daylight.

'Gregory, we are in the living room,' she protested laughingly.

'How quickly we forget?'

She blushed remembering snatches of their lovemaking and soon found herself caught up in the erotic sensations of the night before. She directed a look at Gregory that would have melted the Swiss Alps. He scooped up her 5'10 inch frame and made his way to a bedroom, simply furnished and lined with shelves. In the centre and occupying most of the space was an enormous water bed inviting them to lie down. The curtains and the carpet were designed in a bold African print. She landed with a bobbing thump on the waterbed, awed by this new glimpse of him.

'Your tastes are not what I expected.'

'I hope this balances my ultraconservatism in the office.'

'Are you a Libra Gregory?'

'Yes, I am and I don't need to know your sign. What I know is that Venus was rising on the day of your birth and bestowed all her beauty and charm on you.'

It was an extravagant compliment. 'You have a way with words,' she sighed, with a long look at her lover.

Gregory drew her off the bed to join him, standing enjoying the length of her body against his, reveling in the points of contact. He lightly rubbed her back as they kissed tenderly, exploring and learning each other's needs. Her hands roamed his body, loving the feel of the well defined muscles. Neither made comparisons to others, they were merely getting to know each other intimately.

It could not last long. Memories of their first lovemaking intruded and the movements of the pair soon became insistent, sensuous, consuming. Growling at his inability to savor her slowly he soon placed her back on the undulating bed joining her quickly.

'I don't want to enter you for a moment Stephanie. Can you wait?'

'Why Gregory?' she asked curiously not offended, because she knew how much he wanted, just what he was denying himself.

'I've dreamed about your body for so long, been haunted by its hidden loveliness. Last night it was dark and I saw so little of you. I need to look at you, caress your skin, taste all the tantalizing curves that have driven me wild for months,' he explained stroking and rubbing the golden triangle while he murmured softly at her ear.

'I want to massage your back, legs and feet and watch you twisting and turning under my hands. Can you wait Sunny?'

'No Gregory. I can't.'

Shocked but obliging, for he knew that he would have plenty of time for exploration, he raised her long legs over his shoulders entering her suddenly and fully, anticipating and enjoying the lust, the love, the agony, and the joy on her face with each forceful thrust.

She cried out and then wept wildly with the strength of her climax. And Gregory, satisfied for now after his own powerful release cried with her, unable to hide the joy after months of frustrating delays.

****

Much later, enveloped in the warmth of Gregory's arms and cocooned in the soothing water bed, a contented Stephanie talked comfortably with him to clear away the misunderstandings. Their unconventional relationship had given them no chance to share feelings as lovers do and they must be freed of the past if they were to have a future.

'I think Beth wanted to be married more than she wanted me, and kind of forced the issue. We got along pretty well, but her failure to get pregnant seemed to cloud her whole life and consequently our marriage.'

'Did you know what she had in mind when she went to Italy?'

'No not really, but I knew that if she went, our marriage would be over.'

'Do you think the annulment will take long?'

'No we have valid grounds with the problem of infertility and she seems as anxious to get on with her life as I am with mine. The man she met is a widower with two small children and I think he'll accept her on those terms but not with a divorce.'

'I was so angry that you went away and didn't tell me.'

'Ah my love, you were preoccupied. I thought it best not to place any more burdens on you. If things didn't work out with Beth, I wouldn't be able to offer you any future with me.'

'Will you mind Gregory…about Christian, I mean?'

'I may mind that he's not my son but never that he is Peter's son.'

Grateful for his honesty she showered him with several passionate kisses.

'Hold on', he cried when he could breathe. 'He's also your son, you know and I'll have the privilege of raising him if his mother will have me.'

She happily agreed and punctuated her words with more hugs and kisses until things got out of hand, but Stephanie held back a little wanting to settle one final matter.

'Gregory, I….I…'

'What is it Sunny?'

'It's so difficult to explain. I'm not very experienced sexually I mean.'

'I would never have known that last night', he teased, but she refused to let the matter drop.

'At first, I thought our attraction was just...well sex...you know, because I'd never experienced those feelings before and I thought I should have. I guess I've just never truly been in love before. I did care for Peter, but you will have the best of my love Gregory and all that I am is yours.'

He tenderly traced a line around her mouth before replying. 'I first fell in love with your scent. Since the first moment I saw you, I have never been so overwhelmed by feelings of love yet so powerless to act on them. Last night felt like the first day of my life.'

As the final words to the Dinah Washington anthem played softly from the stereo in the living room, they surrendered the best of themselves to each other.

One look and I forgot the gloom of the past.
One look and I have found my future at last.
One look and I have found a world completely new,
When love, walked in with you.

Epilogue.

Almost a year later, with all their troubles apparently behind them, Stephanie and Gregory made the final preparations for their wedding. It would be two years to the day they first met. Gregory's wedding to Beth had been a lavish affair that he did not want to repeat. Stephanie on the other hand had settled for a civil ceremony in the JP's office at Peter's insistence. She wanted a more elaborate setting this time.

They agreed on a twilight chapel ceremony with about 60 family and friends present, followed by a late supper at the romantic Old Mill Restaurant. A week's honeymoon in Jamaica would give them a much needed rest before they returned to their new home purchased just days ago in an Oakville suburb.

Helen had gone back to England but found it hard to be parted from her adored grandson. Gregory was a different man from Peter and welcomed his fiancé's mother with undisguised pleasure, soaking up stories of her theatre days and Stephanie's childhood.

He introduced his own mother Dora, a widow like Helen, into the warm circle of love that was the three women and a little boy who would be so much a part of his life. Dora Richmond was happy to find companionship in her lonely days and grew to love Stephanie as much as her son did.

The happy couple wasted little time regretting the past. They had spent the year in a traditional courtship avoiding the pitfalls of living together until they felt entirely comfortable with each other.

Gregory had to obtain a civil divorce to go along with his annulment. He was not a strict orthodox Catholic but he had married Beth in good faith believing it to be forever. Spiritually his conscience was clear.

****

As the day dawned crisp and clear in early May, Stephanie stood just beyond the chapel entrance dressed in a simple antique drop waist wedding dress. The frothy edges of the ivory coloured material fanned about her calves as she turned to smile at Michael Czerny who would give her away.

'You are a beautiful woman Stefania, everything your father would have wanted in a daughter. Today as I perform this small but highly significant task for him, I know he smiles because I finally see in your face, the complete happiness he would have wanted for you.'

'Thank you Michael,' she beamed accepting his kiss and blessing.

Turning to face her maid of honour and best friend she was moved by the suspicious moistness around Georgette's eyes.

'Be happy Stephanie. You were both made to be together.' The rare show of high emotion touched her deeply.

'Thanks Georgy, shall we go now?'

Entering the small chapel behind the measured steps of Georgette, who was resplendent in a peacock blue silk dress, the bride stared ahead meeting the welcoming warmth of her groom.

She knew that she had laid the ghosts of the past to rest and in Gregory she had found her future at last.

Part Two

In the Shadow of the Blackbird

Chapter 1:

The small ache was no longer a minor irritation that could be ignored. Dropping the gold Cross pen absently, Georgette placed two slim fingers at her throbbing temples applying counter pressure to the balloon that was threatening to explode inside her head. It was a useless struggle. The agonized face staring back at her from the depths of the highly polished Rosewood Chinese design desk reflected pain, sorrow, and disgust. Refusing to face herself any longer, she turned away from the desk and loosened the pins which secured her hair, letting its auburn glory sail heavily down her back.

Tense and nervous fingers threaded their way through the thick mane and along the scalp, instinctively massaging the tender spots before fanning out to smooth the nearly waist length hair. It was easier then to lean back against the soft, black leather chair. Unwelcome and unwanted, tears fell. Georgette knew that she was very weepy of late. She hated the weakness even as it relieved some of the stress and tension.

She opened her lovely almond shaped eyes and stared at the oriental style furnishing in her office. She knew that it was not totally appropriate for business but after her mother died she felt a need to be closer to her roots. That was then. Within months she hardly knew what she wanted. Her thoughts were so out of character. Georgette O'Malley prided herself on her ability to remain independent of thought, stoic in demeanour, and realistically objective in her daily life. All those resolutions, developed up to the age of eighteen, held her firm for the next 15 years of her life. By age thirty five, everything was falling apart.

Stephanie her friend and business partner was married, happy, and a mother. Their translating service was now a successful business which allowed her to pick and choose work as she pleased. The passing of her parents within months of each other challenged her resolve. They were together in death as they had been in life, excluding her. Georgette perceived herself to be redundant in that relationship, a feeling which lasted until to the end of their lives.

The relatively young woman knew she was depressed and understood the implications of allowing the debilitating mental lethargy to engulf her. Yet, she failed to act on it, treating the tears, the retreat from social activities, the constant headaches as mere self pity because her safe and orderly world had turned upside down.

'If I were Stephanie, I could have faced myself with a fool's optimism and discovered a way out.'

At that moment there was a light tap at the door. Georgette knew it was the object of her thoughts. No one else would have been brave enough to ignore her warning. *'No calls! No clients!'* she had said. Stephanie Richmond, ever fearless, entered with a flourish, not waiting for even a perfunctory 'come in'.

'Georgette, I thought you were going to meet with me and Dr. Zahavi this afternoon?' Stephanie knew her friend and business partner was depressed. The loose hair, tumbling over one eye and rippling down her back, spoke volumes. The professional woman was always correct, always the picture of elegance and sophistication. Waist length hair hanging loosely about her body was not within Georgette's acceptable dress code for the office.

'Don't look at me like that Stephanie. I asked not to be disturbed. My head feels like that American liberty bell, crack and all.'

'You could have let me know you weren't coming Georgette.' Stephanie wasn't angry. There was only deep concern in her voice despite the gentle rebuke.

'Would you have postponed the meeting if I did call?'

'No.'

'Didn't you get on with the proposal without me?'

'Yes.'

'Then what difference did it make whether I was there or not?'

Stephanie narrowed her lovely hazel eyes. She knew she would get sarcasm, even anger but this indifferent self pity was unusual. 'None except that we are partners here. New contracts are negotiated together as a matter of principle.'

'When you weren't here, I did them alone. Now you can do the same!'

The shaking fingers threaded the auburn hair nervously. The full lips tightened. Georgette had yet to look up.

'Georgy?' Stephanie moved nearer to the desk. There was no response. She sat down staring at the averted profile, its oriental loveliness now almost obscured by the curtain of burnished red hair.

'It seems incredible to me Georgy that you would harbour a grudge.'

The deep hazel eyes looked up then startled by the coldness in a voice whose every nuance was as familiar to her as her own slightly British accent. The eyes of the partners locked across the desk. They had fought before but weathered each storm with a minimum of fuss.

'I don't bear any grudges. It was simply a statement of fact.'

'You're shooting me a line of crap Georgette.'

'And your language has deteriorated since you married that sailor.'

'You are looking for a fight but you won't get one with me. I know you too well. If you don't take a break from this office soon Georgette...'

'You'll what?' The challenging words were met head on. Stephanie did not flinch. Georgette relented and gave in realizing honesty was the best policy.

'I'm so tired Stephanie. Some days I don't know one language from the next. All the words jumble up in my head. Nothing makes sense any more. You know the saying, *stop the world I want to get off*? Well someone stopped my world and I got off. Now I don't know how to get back on again.'

'Georgy, please take a vacation. I was away so long and you managed. Surely I can do the same. Nick can handle the accounts. Jawahir is doing a superb job as office manager and I will be in every day.'

'Won't Gregory mind?'

'My sailor is no ordinary mortal you know. He actually appreciates my skills. We don't plan on another child for at least a year so there's no reason or excuse for not taking some much needed time. No less than four weeks. I insist!'

'Where would I go Stephanie? I can't even think straight much less plan a holiday.'

'Planning and organizing is what I do best. Let me take care of all the arrangements.'

Getting up from behind the desk she came around to stand in front of her friend. In low heels, Stephanie was 5'11'. She was a very impressive woman and difficult to ignore. Georgette who stood 5'9' was unable to avoid looking up.

'I heard you Stephanie,' she mumbled gazing into the beautiful face which none the less had a determined look.

'I mean what I say Georgy. For years you have been the closest person to me. My marriage hasn't changed my feelings towards you nor made you any less dear to me.. .'

'I know Stephanie. It's not you that's changed. It's me. Suddenly my life just doesn't seem to have any purpose.' Stephanie pulled up her friend from behind the desk and sat her down on the love-seat installed for comfort in each partner's office.

Holding both her hands, Stephanie spoke softly but earnestly. 'Too many things have happened in the past year. I know you feel that you weren't close to your parents but still, their loss must have affected you deeply.'

'I suppose.'

Georgette had refused to acknowledge the pain or even allow the normal grief process to invade her life. Two trips to England within months to bury first her mother then her father had taken a heavy toll, finally wearing down the protective armour she carefully erected years ago.

A navy brat! That's all I have ever been,' she thought idly trying to find some words that could expand her careless, 'I suppose.'

Finally, as her friend waited patiently, a virtue which escaped Stephanie most days, she spoke out from her heart. 'Stephanie, all my life I've always felt like an outsider, standing watching as other people like you move through life, accepting the hurts, the happiness and the uncertainty which confronts them each day. Yet still they rise above all that.' Getting up from the mini couch she kicked off the red kid shoes and padded softly over to the window to gaze at the ant's nest of humanity moving aimlessly about the busy downtown Toronto streets ten floors below.

Stephanie watched her friend noting with some relief the thoughtfulness and introspection which was a sign of release. She remained seated, waiting and saying nothing.

'Mama Jin and Daddy always seemed to be a self contained unit, one with the universe so to speak.'

Raising her arms to demonstrate the words, she threw back her head as if in supplication to some unseen power. 'What did I know about ups and downs? Life was neatly ordered according to Mama Jin's correct way of doing things and Daddy's strict military scheduling.'

Turning to face her friend, there was a hurt little girl about her. 'The predictability of my day to day routine continued even when I had the opportunity to break free. Despite their life style, they were an anchor to me.' She laughed amid new tears. 'Commander O'Malley would have loved the anchor metaphor.'

'Commander O'Malley would not have been pleased to see his daughter falling to pieces because her once ordered life has undergone some changes.'

'Well his daughter has lost it!'

'I don't think so. You are just too stubborn to admit that their loss has left you feeling lonely. They loved you Georgette and did the best they could to raise you to be independent. Mourn their passing honestly and openly then get on with you life. Develop some new interests, look for new challenges, allow people into your life.'

Georgette sighed, resuming her seat in the old leather chair behind the desk. 'I think that for years I've deceived myself into believing that I didn't really need them Stephanie. You know as long as they were there, everything was fine. Now they're gone and I do miss them.'

'Accepting the loss is one thing Georgy but still you need some time to get a new perspective on things.' Stephanie paused trying to find an opening to offer balm to the bruised and aching heart. 'Come over this weekend. The weather looks good so we'll barbecue and I will tell you where you are going,' she announced firmly.

'How's Christian Stephanie?'

'Spoiled rotten I shouldn't wonder. Helen and Dora won't let him be alone for five minutes,' she grumbled. 'Marguerite tries her best to intervene and gets caught between the two grandmothers. Just as everything gets settled, in comes Gregory and swoops him up. With everyone doing things for him all the time, he'll never walk, talk or have an independent thought until he's ready for university.'

Georgette laughed, the first genuine smile exchanged during the past hour the two women spent in the office.

'I don't believe a word of that Stephanie. It hasn't been that long since I last saw him and even at 21/2 years he's quite advanced.'

'Believe it or not,' Stephanie said with a deceptively indifferent shrug. 'You better come and put a stop to all this nonsense before he gets out of hand.'

The little banter about Christian did what no amount of cajoling or pleading could do. Christian Droga-Richmond was loved by Georgette as passionately as his mother or stepfather. She had been present at his birth barely twenty-four hours after the untimely death of his biological father.

Stephanie had a traumatic and unsatisfying marriage that was further complicated by her unexpected pregnancy. The death of her husband followed by revelations about his unstable childhood sent her into premature labour. Georgette and Gregory had been with her at the time but Gregory, still legally married to his first wife, remained in the background. Witnessing the miracle of birth had been an astounding experience for Georgette and her role as Godmother to the little baby opened avenues of feeling she had never explored before. Looking back now Georgette realized that for the first time she had given love unconditionally to another human being, expecting nothing in return. It was an unusual departure in a life that had previously steered clear of any emotional commitments.

Georgette dated often. She was attractive, well-read, cultured and very intelligent. She was able to hold her own and be successful in the business world or in the arts. She made an ideal evening companion despite a tendency to hide her insecurities behind sarcasm. But no man ever pierced her inner core nor saw beneath the smooth, sophisticated veneer. As soon as escorts or dates started making demands or expecting more she gently but firmly sent them on their way. Granted, Christian was a child but in her unguarded moments, playing on the floor with him, laughing as he bounced on her knee, or cuddling the sleepy body, her true, warm and giving nature would lay naked for the world to see.

'I haven't seen him for awhile.' The confession shamed her. 'I'll be there on Sunday Stephanie but I want him to myself for awhile.'

A responsive smile could barely be concealed.

'I hate it when you outsmart me you know.'

'As long as you don't hate yourself,' Stephanie warned getting up. She could no longer hide the satisfied smile on her face. 'Come early. Helen goes to church until noon and I'll give Marguerite the weekend off.'

'Thanks Stephanie.'

The week-end was still three days away. Habits die hard though. No sooner had the door closed behind her friend than Georgette drew a piece of paper forward. She began making a list of the things she would need to do. At the very top she wrote 'present – Christian'. *Stephanie will kill me* she thought gleefully. She ended her notes with a light-hearted chuckle.

Chapter 2:

The day of the barbeque started out very chilly. Everyone hoped the Sunday morning sun would soon make its presence felt in a month that had been damp and unseasonably cool.

Georgette awoke at 7:30 am, listless and headachy. She'd tried to maintain her optimism for the weekend invitation but couldn't quite overcome the mental lethargy which seemed to permeate every aspect of her day to day life.

She knew that canceling would cause untold repercussions with Stephanie but she still contemplated legitimate ways of excusing herself . Her mind, once sharp and orderly, tumbled endlessly over vague excuses. None satisfied even her own pitiful desire to stay safely cocooned in the large polished four poster bed. The hand-made furniture had been fashioned in rich teak, set off with a gold carpet, matching drapes and a softly feathered Duvet in burnt orange and gold colours. Her glorious bedroom projected the best image of her own sense of self.

Georgette's parents hadn't been wealthy but in the bustling world of Hong Kong, her mother's family had been fairly well to do business people. Jin Sung's life style continued in the upper hierarchy of the British Navy where her husband had commanded his own ship. They were both accustomed to the best things in life and had raised their daughter with a connoisseur's eye. Georgette worked hard to afford and maintain a lifestyle which she accepted as the norm. She saved and accumulated every collector's piece to decorate her home, gradually creating a luxurious setting in a two bedroom, split level condo she purchased eight years ago in the new waterfront development area of Toronto.

The death of her parents left her financially secure but it was too late to mend the fences frequent early separations from her parents created. As a family they never hugged or kissed often. Georgette would have found it difficult to cross that barrier and yet it seemed such a natural function for Stephanie who gave so much of herself even in a simple handshake. If it hadn't been for her vivacious partner, Georgette would never have learned the joy of human physical warmth given freely. She knew those thoughts were self destructive but could not avoid them. She buried her head beneath the covers hiding her face from an unseeing world, shedding her tears in private.

The phone at her bedside rang softly. Reluctantly her hand snaked out to grab the offending instrument.

'Hello'

'Hello Georgette. It's Michael Czerny.'

'Michael?…Michael…why are you calling? Nothing is wrong I hope?'

'No nothing's wrong. I understand from Stefania that you are spending the day there.'

'Yes, I was planning to.'

'Was Georgette?'

'Did Stephanie tell you to call me?' There was a suspicious note to her voice.

'Yes, she said that if I was coming you may prefer to drive with me instead of taking your car. Do I presume too much to call you?'

'Of course not Michael!' Her hasty reply sounded false. She expanded on her initial denial. 'Stephanie knows I have been feeling depressed lately, I just wondered if she solicited your medical opinion on my behalf.'

'I am not a psychiatrist Georgette.'

'I am sorry Michael and yes, I would like a lift. You know how much I hate to get behind the wheel of a car.'

'Good, I will come there in one hour.'

****

Georgette rang off thoughtfully. Michael was Stephanie's friend and physician. He was also Christian's Godfather and over the 21/2 years since the birth of the squalling premature infant, she and Michael had bonded closely. First, they saw Stephanie through the loss of her husband then the birth of her child. Watching Christian grow had been an unbelievable pleasure for the childless pair.

When Stephanie married Gregory a year after Christian's birth, they guided her down aisle, Georgette in front, Michael giving her away. It was a moment of happiness for both of them. Stephanie had been severely traumatized by her first marriage. In return she was so beloved by her son's godparents that they would have done anything to ensure her happiness.

However, like every other aspect of her own life, Georgette had allowed both her responsibilities and pleasures to lapse. She hadn't seen Michael since March when she returned from England after her father's death nor Christian since his parents wedding anniversary party in May, which Michael had not been able to attend.

'Well, I am definitely committed to going now.' The decision was made. She had an hour to get ready. Her hair alone would take half that time.

Slipping out of the silken pajamas, she made her way to the ensuite bathroom. The long auburn braid was loosened. Georgette hated to see her face reflected in the mirror these days. She seemed to look every one of her nearly 36 years. The dark hazel irises had lost almost all their glow. The beautiful almond-shaped eyes, swollen and puffy from crying, appeared more Chinese than ever. The porcelain fine skin was a stark white. High cheek bones only accentuated the shadowy circles beneath the eyes. She had inherited her father's height but not his bone structure. Her long slim fingers and size 6 triple A feet were more in keeping with Jin Sung's race than Ryan O'Malley's huge Irish/Scottish ancestors.

Looking down at her naked torso, Georgette felt that few men would be attracted to the small breasts, narrow waist but over full hips. Never in her life would she admit to anyone that she was still a virgin. It seemed wholly incompatible with the life style that she projected. Rarely did she go out with young men in the first flush of youth where sex was the inevitable conclusion to the second date. Her escorts were usually much older established men who were far too cultured to force themselves on a woman.

Georgette was not intimidated if they didn't call back. She wanted no complication in her life and got none. Sex however was not a secret rite which she avoided due to fear or ignorance. She was a psychology major in university and understood very clearly the actions and interactions involved in the act. She simply wanted no part of it for herself. *Ice maiden and frigid* were terms that failed to impact upon her in any way....until now.

Stepping under the running water, she donned the plastic shower cap to protect her hair. She simply didn't feel like expending the energy to be ready on time if her hair didn't dry quickly. Georgette checked her closet for something casual to wear. Rows of dresses and suits hung, neatly and visually catalogued by colour. Matching shoes were laid out evenly beneath the rows of dresses on a double shelf shoe rack. Finding something was not a problem, but finding something casual seemed an insurmountable chore. Georgette never wore a pair of jeans, had never felt anything except the finest silk, wool, or cotton next to her skin.

Eventually she found a pair of older style grey pants with a matching raglan top. The outfit was a little big but seemed the most appropriate attire. She was surprised at the amount of weight loss since the last time she had tried on the outfit over a year ago. It crossed her mind that something physical could, in fact, be the cause of her feelings and overall depression. She would consider that thought later. For the present she looked and felt somewhat better.

The buzzer for the intercom sounded just as she completed the final twist in the long braid that was the least troublesome style these days.

Normally Georgette kept her hair at the level of her shoulder blades. She always felt slightly longer hair gave much more versatility in styling. But since her mother's death over a year ago she had refused to do more than trim the ends. Lately the queue or braid of the ancient Chinese culture became a symbol and whether consciously or unconsciously she wore the style away from the office, seeming to want to accentuate her Chinese roots.

'*Identity crisis*' her mind screamed but she ignored it and made her way to the intercom to let Michael in.

'Hello Michael, punctual as usual. Come on up. I'm almost ready.'

She waited by the door and opened it when she heard the firm knock. She stood stock still. Michael had changed. His brown hair, lightly peppered with grey flecks a few months ago was now silvery grey. The eyes which might have been considered nondescript were a starling blue-green in a face which shone, bronzed by the summer sun. Its weathered cragginess disappeared, replaced by lines and grooves which added immense character to the quiet, caring dignity that he brought to his busy family practice.

Time had made him seem taller until Georgette realized that in the frequent foursome with Gregory and Stephanie, Georgette and Michael although above average height were often dwarfed by their friends imposing statures.

'You look so different,' she commented, surprised at the awareness she felt.

'I've been away. I went home to Hungary for six weeks this summer. Returned only just last week,' he added entering the stark white living room but not before slipping off his loafers in the uninviting foyer.

The couple exchanged a European style greeting of air kisses on both cheeks. She was more stiff than usual. Her introspective thoughts of the last few weeks added an unwarranted awareness to physical intimacy and she was suddenly shy. Michael sensed this immediately but made no comment other than to note her tiredness.

'I haven't been sleeping well Michael.' She dismissed his concerns with an obvious statement then moved on quickly before he could interject any further comments.

'Would you like a coffee before we go?'

Michael hesitated. He wasn't sure if he wanted to create any intimacy with Georgette or force any confidences. She actually looked ill and he was as shocked by her thin figure and subdued manner as she had been by his new and improved appearance.

'I think not Georgette. I was instructed not to delay you.'

'Stephanie is not my keeper you know.'

'She is your friend and our godson is waiting impatiently I believe.'

'Your accent has deepened, Michael'

'Yes that is natural I think. I found it difficult to remember much of my Hungarian words at first. As their beauty returned to my conscious mind I cared little about speaking English again.'

'I understand that. My mother's Mandarin tongue pleases me so much. I often use it in my thoughts instead of English.'

An awkward silence filled the room. Georgette made no move to leave. Michael could see that she was deeply depressed but could find no words of comfort. The Georgette he knew would never allow a moment to pass without filling the breech. She quickly turned her back to him to stare out the window which extended the length of the living room. Her shoulders were hunched and trembling.

'I'm sorry Michael. It doesn't take much to make me cry these days.'

'Are you worried about anything specific Georgette? Something, I could perhaps help?' Unseen to her, he extended his hands palm up.

'Can you help me face a premature mid life crisis.... the loss of my parents? I was ashamed to admit how much their deaths hurt me. Did you know that...how inhumane I am?'

'I did not know you were ashamed but I can see how much you are hurt by their loss.'

'I didn't realize it was that obvious but for the first time I am confronted by feelings I can't control. It frightens me Michael.'

'Have you talked...with anyone?'

'Not really. Stephanie and I had a long conversation earlier this week. She told me I was human after all and needed a vacation.'

'Do you think she is correct in her assessment...of the need for a vacation?'

'Yes, I need a vacation, but she also told me that I must grieve for my parents.'

'What are your own thoughts?' he asked gently.'

'I am still thinking about it, trying to resolve the ambivalence of my feelings towards them over the past 18 years, with this sudden desire to have them back and tell them how much I really did...' Georgette frowned and then halted.

'You really did love them?' Michael concluded the sentence in a soft voice.

'No! I respected them. They only cared about each other. I was a by-product of their complete love, not an extension.' She was angry now, hating the weakness and see-saw emotions that loosened her tongue.

'Let's go Michael. I have some things to take with me. Will you give me a hand?'

She looked at him then seeing a vague disquieting look on his face. She ignored it and hurried to the kitchen to collect the packages for young Christian.

****

The thirty kilometer drive to the small but rapidly growing town of Oakville took less than twenty minutes on the highway, free of traffic, in the early Sunday morning.

Georgette and Michael avoided personal topics commenting only on world events. Michael was pleased to see a return of some of Georgette's former assertiveness as they discussed the plight of children in war torn countries. They were still debating the use of United Nations intervention for the orphaned children, a subject close to Michael's heart when they approached the driveway which led to the large modern home of Gregory and Stephanie.

Alighting from the car, they were met at the door. Their hostess was glowing. She was carrying Christian, plump and healthy looking on her hip

Hugs and kisses were exchanged while Michael and Georgette exclaimed delightedly at the growth of the young boy.

'He's quite a size Stephanie. It is normal for them to grow so fast?'

'If the way he eats is any indication of growth I would say yes,' she laughed handing over the boy to his beloved Tante.

'Hello Darling', she crooned pleased that he showed no signs of the shyness that often sent him scurrying behind his mother's long legs.

'Have you been a good boy?' The little head bobbed then shook side to side as he contemplated an incomprehensible question.

'Tante a un cadeau pour toi mon chéri,' Georgette teased kissing the soft cheek.

'Qu-est que ca?' he responded clearly.

'Un oiseau!'

'A bird, Georgette?'

'Don't worry. Not the real thing, but I think he'll enjoy it.'

Stephanie left Georgette and went over to Michael who had observed the exchange with warm eyes before retrieving the gifts. He gave an imperceptible nod of the head to the daughter of his dearest friend and mentor before receiving a firm hug and kiss.

'How is she Miklos Bacsi?' she whispered in Hungarian.

'We'll talk later Stefania but I can see why you were worried.'

'Come on then,' she replied aloud. 'Gregory's trying to set up the barbeque out back.'

The trio entered the large front foyer where their images were reflected in the mirrors lining the hall closet. Straight ahead was an ornate staircase leading to the second storey bedrooms. It was a beautiful home where bright and shiny ceramic tiles reflected shafts of light everywhere, bouncing rays of the morning sun on the walls and into every corner of the house.

'I think I'll go upstairs with Christian and set up the bird cage Stephanie. Tell Gregory I'll see him in a few minutes.'

'Ok Georgy, come down when you are ready.'

Taking the little hand, Georgette guided Christian upstairs to his room while the others headed out through the kitchen to the back yard patio where Gregory struggled valiantly to start a fire in the brick oven that he built at the beginning of the summer.

Georgette slipped off her shoes at the top of the stairs and made her way along the carpeted second story to the blue and yellow room which she and Michael had furnished for their Godson. She sat on the floor, legs apart, a big smile on her face as Christian moved about clapping his hands, bending over, eager to see what was in the big box.

'Vite, vite Tante' he implored when her slow fingers couldn't remove the paper fast enough.

'Un moment, you little rascal' she laughed adopting his French-English speech.

She marveled at his skill in comprehending everything, although it shouldn't have been surprising. Mother and Godmother were both multilingual and had pooled their common resources several years ago to start their own International Temporary translating services. Stephanie was younger and more vivacious. She was born to do public relations work and spent most of her time getting new clients for the firm. Georgette was all business and handled the day to day operations of the Agency. They worked well together except during the last year of Stephanie's troubled marriage when Georgette ran the business almost single-handedly. They had weathered that storm successfully when the birth of little Christian brought them closer together than they had ever been.

In order for Stephanie to return to work she had employed a French Canadian nanny who spoke to her young charge almost exclusively in French. It did not present a problem for Stephanie and Georgette, but Gregory, and the two grandmothers, Helen and Dora struggled at times to understand him. They were reassured that there would be no confusion for the young boy if they spoke in English. After all, both Georgette and Stephanie had learned to interact in the language of a non English speaking parent early on. Georgette in particular had lived in so many places that she learned languages by osmosis. She was fluent in eight languages and the three major dialects from her Chinese mother. She was also a psychology major and was able to support Stephanie in her decision to encourage her son to be multilingual.

Listening now to Christian babble excitedly she knew that by age three she had been able to speak to her mother in Mandarin or her father in English. Looking back she realized that it was only during those moments in the early years when she could clearly define two separate people from the couple who in later years traveled on one indivisible wavelength.

The box opened at last and inside was a wooden bird cage with an indigo feathered black bird inside. When the light caught its iridescent plume, it glistened with many colours. She showed Christian how to pull a string at the bottom and watched happily as his eyes lit up went the bird sang, twirled and bobbed its head.

'Oh…more Tante…' he laughed. Too excited by the treat, he ran to the stairs, 'Maman vite,! Un oiseau. Elle chant.'

Stephanie, hearing Christian call out, ran to the stairs. His happy face and pointing finger invited her upstairs to discover the source of his unrestrained delight. An entreaty to pull the string again was done by his obliging Aunt.

'Where did you get that Georgy? It is delightful.'

'I found it in a little store in China Town. I thought it would amuse him.'

'Quite an unusual gift!'

Christian was allowed to pull the string the next time and his delight at the predictable outcome had his mother and godmother in stitches. Georgette lay back on the carpet genuine happiness in her face.

'I am going back down. Gregory's having trouble with the BBQ. I may have to cook.'

'I won't be long. Michael will think I am monopolizing Christian.'

Georgette remained on the floor watching her godson spread his toys all over. He spent some time showing her those special ones he cherished. They spent nearly half an hour sharing the merits of each treasure. For a child so small he was remarkably poised and patient.

Reluctantly she knew that she couldn't hide away forever. She hadn't even said hello to her host. Gregory would understand but bad manners were never acceptable to Georgette.

She helped Christian return his toys to the wooden box in the far corner of the spacious room. The bird cage was left on his dresser. She knew Gregory would find some way to hang it up later. As she placed it on the flat surface she saw herself as the bird, caged, longing to sing but waiting for the right person to pull her string. '*What fanciful nonsense,*' she chided herself.

'Let's go see what Mommy and Daddy are doing,' Georgette urged patiently. Christian pleaded silently to be lifted. She picked him up cuddling his little body close, for a moment, before she headed downstairs.

Chapter 3:

Gregory, Stephanie and Michael were seated comfortably in patio arm chairs under a large umbrella, supported by a glass top table.

'Here's our favourite aunt,' Gregory announced getting up to greet his absent guest. 'How are you Georgette?' he asked hiding his shock at her appearance with a light peck on her cheek. Her only reply was a slight smile. She had no ready answer and the perfunctory 'I'm fine' wouldn't work with a man as sensitive and perceptive as her best friend's husband.

Gregory was a man in a million. He was kind, firm with a gentle understanding of people and human nature. He and Georgette had combined to support Stephanie through her worst problems. Their shared love for the troubled woman brought them closer together and they remained solid friends.

'Call me if I can do anything,' he whispered hating to see the limp, apathetic attitude behind the forced smile.

Georgette knew the simple words were sincere. He had said them to her before and meant it. When she called him, he was there. Gregory spoke very little when he was emotionally sensitive to a situation.

'I will but I am trying to work through this on my own,' she stated, nodding to emphasize her determination.

'Sometimes we need a friend' he cautioned easily then added, 'you won't find any better than those here.'

'I know Gregory. I am just not ready, but I won't forget.'

Nodding his agreement, he guided her over to the vacant chair. His offer to take the sleepy little boy was refused. Georgette sat down pulling Christian comfortably onto her lap, his tousled honey gold curls, resting against her breast. He had captured her long braid and stroked it softly as his eyelids drooped.

'Would you like me to take him Georgy?'

'No I'm fine. Let him settle. I will take a cold drink though.'

Stephanie got up to pour out the drinks from a nearby table leaving Georgette and Michael together.

'I am sorry Michael. I seem to be monopolizing him.'

'I saw him earlier this week. They met me at the airport the night I returned from Hungary. "Christian and I will have time to talk and play later Georgette.'

'Here's your drink,' Stephanie said handing her a pink concoction.

'I think I'll see if Gregory needs a hand.' Michael got up from his seat. It was clear he was leaving the two women to talk. Once he was out of ear shot, Georgette made an unusual inquiry, her eyes following his back.

'How old is Michael? He seemed so old before.'

'Before what?' Stephanie asked puzzled by the question.

'Before his vacation. He has more gray hair now than he did six months ago but he actually looks younger today.'

Stephanie was pleased by the interest Georgette was showing but kept her face neutral. 'He works too hard. This vacation was the first real one that he's ever taken.'

'You always call him uncle.'

'You know that's just a term of endearment. When I was young Papa insisted and now it's just a good habit but I only use it when we speak Hungarian.'

'How old is he Stephanie?' Georgette persisted. She knew Stephanie had a knack of adroitly avoiding something if it suited her purposes.

'He's about 43 or 44 I think. Michael was a brilliant student you know. Papa always felt he would go far, became a scientist or a researcher but he went into private practice as soon as he graduated, then devoted himself to his patients.'

'You told me he was orphaned very young?'

'Yes, his parents were killed during the Hungarian revolution and an uncle sent him over here to continue his studies. I was just a young girl when Papa first brought him home. Even in his youth he moved about with a kind of intense, quiet dignity.'

'That would sum up his general attitude today.'

Stephanie was curious about the sudden interest. The pair had known each other quite a few years. Like Georgette, Stephanie had considered Michael to be a staid middle aged man who always seemed to have a worried air about him but the recent vacation had worked wonders giving his thin weathered face a fuller look and straightening a back that looked permanently stooped from carrying the concerns of his patients.

****

The day passed pleasantly enough. Christian slept for some time so that his parents and godparents could eat an early lunch undisturbed. Later in the afternoon he went for a short walk with Gregory and Michael allowing the two women to discuss the holiday plans.

'I had a difficult time trying to find something for you Georgy.'

'I thought you said planning was your best skill.'

'It wasn't the planning but the place.'

'So what did you decide?'

'Gregory and I had such a wonderful time in Jamaica that I thought you would probably enjoy a month there but in a slightly different setting than a honeymoon hotel.'

'I should hope so.'

'I do indeed so......' she halted drawing out the suspense.

'Stephanie, will you never grow up?' Georgette asked quite exasperated and amused by this effervescent friend who finally blossomed into the blissfully contented, outgoing, woman with a big smile on her face. Love certainly does work miracles she thought, feeling relaxed by the quiet undemanding day.

'Oh what for Georgette? I've already been old. Now I need to be young for awhile. Don't deny me that.'

'No of course not.' Georgette held the hand that seldom remained still. 'I would never want to see your high spirits dulled but I would like to know where I'm going before I get too old to travel.'

'St. Ann's Bay. It is a small town on the north coast of Jamaica. It isn't really a tourist spot yet but there are several points of interest close by. I have booked a two bedroom condo unit with full domestic service. Included is a full time limousine service to pick you up at the airport and ensure that you are able to sightsee as much as you would like. I have sent a fax to Gregory's agent in Jamaica in case you need anything not easily available or accessible. You can call him at anytime and I have booked a first class airline ticket leaving Wednesday morning.'

Stephanie paused to take a deep breath and held it. Her face mirrored some anxiety but she was hoping for a positive response.

'Do I need any shots?'

'No!'

'I'll go. As usual you make it to difficult to refuse the offer. That's a big reason why our business is so successful Stephanie.'

'TCB means being thorough Georgette. We both do it in our own way. Now if I am not mistaken Gregory is singing inside. Let's join them,' she urged rising and linking arms with her friend. They made their way, arm in arm, to the downstairs den where all manner of musical accoutrements lay about. Gregory received a musical minor at university, boasting a better than average tenor voice. Stephanie urged her husband to sing and entertain as often as possible, loving his ability to wring every nuance and emotion from a song.

'I see that Christian has his request in early.'

The sounds from the room bore no resemblance to the usual childish tunes one would expect a toddler to enjoy. As the two women entered the large fully furnished basement, they were greeted by the sight of Gregory and Christian marching purposefully around the open centre of the room, one fist at their mouths and the other hand moving up and down, playing an imaginary trombone. The sound of Robert Preston singing '76 Trombones' from the Broadway show, The Music Man, blared from the stereo.

The women joined Michael on the couch placed against a wall clapping vigorously, encouraging the impromptu performance. This type of activity was not unusual in the Richmond home. Stephanie and Gregory often found themselves in the music room together singing dancing or a combination of both. All family members participated at one time or another and no guests were excluded from the fun.

Christian was inundated with praise for his participation then settled shyly beside his mother as Gregory was asked to sing some other popular show tunes. He sat at the piano accompanying himself with a medley of hits finishing with 'The Impossible Dream', his personal favourite.

Noting the somber looks from his audience he declared 'no more sad songs'.

'That's hardly sad Gregory. It was meant to be uplifting.'

'Well everyone looks sad so it didn't serve the purpose did it my darling?' He walked over to kiss his wife, removing any sting from the words. Little Christian, always sensitive to his parents, looked up at his mother.

'Danse Maman!' he begged.

'Come on Michael. I think it's our turn,' she said handing Christian to his godmother. Gregory moved over to the stereo selecting a tape with Hungarian folk songs. Stephanie had been taught the dance routines by her father and often performed with Michael when they were younger. The pair was energetic and exciting, giving themselves to the music.

Helen Droga, Stephanie's mother had slipped in unnoticed. She had enjoyed the day with friends giving her daughter an opportunity to entertain without her presence. Pride filled her as she watched, enjoying the sight of her daughter and her husband's protégé dance passionately to the very music which had brought her together with Piotr Droga. Their love had been a middle-aged miracle.

Leaving the intense faces of Michael and Stephanie, her gaze fell on her son- in- law. He appeared proud and very much in love with his wife. Helen smiled. Her snow white head tilted to one side as she silently thanked God again for delivering her precious child into Gregory Richmond's capable hands. Her gaze moved on to Georgette and she could not still the involuntary gasp. Ignoring her grandson, she was dismayed by the loss of animation from the face of her daughter's best friend. Even though Georgette appeared much more relaxed than usual, it was a measure of the depth of her problems that Helen could easily see the drastic change over the last few months.

Looking back, Helen remembered clearly when Stephanie first brought Georgette home. The Eurasian girl was striking even then, well dressed, well mannered. She had been a picture of perfection. At first glance the two women appeared so much alike, slight varying shades of auburn hair, tall and slim. Stephanie's own almond eyes inherited from her father's Slavic ancestors gave them a remarkable resemblance. As the years passed, Georgette's long straight hair had darkened slightly and her oriental features became more pronounced, turning her into a striking and unusual woman.

It had not taken Helen long to see beneath the sophisticated veneer which Georgette presented to the world. Stephanie always seemed to be drawn to strong quiet types but Helen knew that unlike her daughter's first husband who was cold and unemotional, Georgette possessed a warm and giving nature. In Helen's mind, her devotion to Stephanie and the obvious love she felt for young Christian were traits, only people who care deeply, can sustain.

The music ended with a flourish. Helen seen now by Georgette exchanged a quick hug before joining the exhausted dancers in the centre of the room.

'Miklos, your holiday has done you a world of good it seems.'

'How so Helen?'

'I've never seen you so light on your feet.'

'My partner makes me appear to be the better but it's not so, that I am good.'

Huffing slightly, his English faltered but everyone understood the compliment to Stephanie. There was more light hearted banter but Christian feeling tired after a long and busy day began to fuss, trying to decide who should come upstairs with him. Helen settled the matter firmly.

'Come on young man. Nana hasn't seen you all day. You can tell me everything that happened to you and I will tell you all about my day. OK?'

Christian went willingly. Nana's firm tone brooked no argument. Even at 75 years of age, with snow white hair, she commanded complete respect by her bearing alone. She was dwarfed by everyone except her grandson, yet cared little. She was never mean spirited. She knew her place in her daughter's home. She could clearly see that the younger adults wanted to be alone.

'Come and see me before you go away Georgette.'

'I will Helen.' There was no hesitation in her reply. The older woman left, with the young man in tow, to a chorus of goodnights. Georgette returned to the couch.

'None of that is allowed Georgette. You've been sitting down all day. What's your choice here?'

Gregory waved his arm in the direction of the rows and rows of tapes and albums which lined almost one full wall.

'Is there anything you don't have Gregory?'

'Nope!'

Georgette didn't really feel like dancing. She was happy enough to watch and observe. Her physical apathy was as debilitating as her mental torment. Gregory, aware of the soothing effects of music, wanted to encourage her to participate.

'Since I'm going to Jamaica, I wouldn't mind a little of the Caribbean sound.'

'There are two types of music that I know of,' he said heading for a low shelf and fingering a couple of albums. 'This,' he announced showing a colourful album, 'is calypso, a fairly common type of beat throughout the Caribbean but Jamaica has evolved its own style thanks chiefly to Bob Marley who introduced reggae to the world but...'

'Gregory!'

'Sorry Sunny,' he said sheepishly. 'I do get carried away don't I?.'

'Yes you do. Let's have the music before the coach turns into a pumpkin again.' Stephanie laughed knowing her husband could talk for hours about his consuming hobby. Gregory subsided quickly and placed the album in the stereo. The rhythmic sounds of Calypso filled the room.

'My dance, I think Madame,' he said nodding at Georgette. She was too well mannered to play coy and rose gracefully.

Gregory was a superb athlete, moving about with ease. Michael and Stephanie joined them on the floor and the foursome soon got into the pulsating rhythm, hips swaying.

The music ended leaving them breathless and laughing. They switched partners and Georgette went into Michael's arms with a shock. She had never danced with him before, never felt the warmth of his embrace. He always seemed so thoughtful and preoccupied. Even at Stephanie's wedding he hardly relaxed, but spent his time watching the newlyweds carefully to make certain that Stephanie was indeed happy. The holiday had been good therapy for him and he held her with purpose moving easily to a slightly slower tune. Georgette looked up surprised to note that he was watching her intently. She frowned.

'You have had a good day,' he observed, ignoring the tightness in her face.

'Yes thanks. I do feel a little better.'

Georgette hated the formality in her voice. She had known the man for almost a decade but suddenly his hand at her back felt different, suggestive. Her breath was getting short. She knew her cheeks, so colourless before were hot and red. Just as she did earlier in the day, her body stiffened but Michael executed a deft turn forcing her to cling to him or lose her balance.

'Relax Dear,' he commanded softly.

'I…I am. I just haven't done this for awhile.'

Looking into his face, Georgette tried to understand what she was feeling. Michael's startling blue-green eyes stood out starkly against the golden honey tone of his skin, slightly flushed with the exertion. She desperately wanted him to pull her closer, hold her tightly and before she could draw a deep breath, it was happening as she wished. The tempo of the music changed again, slowed even more but her breathing pattern accelerated. As she rested her head against his shoulder, she could feel her heart pounding wildly.

The heat from his body sent waves of his clean male scent to assail her nostrils and her senses, attacking her equilibrium making her dizzy.

Fighting for control, Georgette, clung to him, hiding her face in the hollow of his shoulder, pretending she was Christian, a child, safe and secure. Beneath her make- believe she was also fighting to deny other unfamiliar feelings.

There was nothing childish in her reactions and she was dismayed to find herself succumbing to a desire to be kissed and stroked gently at first then with increasing passion. The song ended abruptly it seemed.

Georgette released Michael quickly fearing that her thoughts may have been communicated in her body language. The blue-green eyes searched her face for a fraction of a second. His arms continued to hold her shoulders firmly. Unable to meet his questioning look, her eyes dropped and he released her without a word.

****

Stephanie had not been giving her full attention to Gregory. He was about to voice his complaint when she stopped him with a poke.

'Hush Gregory. Turn off the music. I want to offer some refreshments.' She rolled her eyes in the direction of the couple standing stiffly nearby. It took a few seconds but he saw what had been distracting his wife.

'Sunny you don't think that they...?'

'Gregory I wish with all my heart. I love them both dearly but Georgette will not let her armour down and Michael seems so set against another relationship that it might not work.'

'You can't make it happen because you want it to, my love.'

'I know, but she's so vulnerable right now. It may be...'

'Stephanie you may need to leave this alone. You know how she guards her inner self. She reveals little except what she is comfortable exposing. Hard for a man to get past that.'

'Right now she's exposing a need that only the least sensitive man would fail to notice. Turn off the music and then help me in the kitchen.'

Gregory gave up. He blamed himself for making his wife so happy that she wanted the same for everyone. The smug smile was quickly suppressed as his wife divined his thoughts. She gave him a quick kiss before speaking aloud.

'This dancing has given me an appetite again. Gregory and I are just going up to tuck in Christian then we'll fix a light snack and come back.'

Her smile was guileless.

Chapter 4:

Georgette and Michael sat down on the couch. There was a touch of awkwardness between them. Nervous and not a little afraid of the sudden upsurge of desire, she studied the pattern of the ceramic tiles searching for some way to avoid anything personal.

She surprised herself by asking 'do you prefer Michael or Miklos?'.

'I'm comfortable with both, Georgette.'

'Oh,' the floor continued to absorb her more than ever. 'Who looked after your practice while you were away?'

'I accepted the need for a junior partner, a younger man, more in touch with the youth of today.'

'I never considered you that old, you know.'

'But I am, much too old to be able to understand the many complex problems facing teenagers today.'

She looked at him out of the corner of her eye wondering if he were fishing for compliments. Seeing the open honesty portrayed there she gave a little half smile.

'What are you thinking about?' he questioned, leaning forward in response to her smile.

'It is not within you to prevaricate or aspire to things that go against your nature.'

'I am happy in my own limited way Georgette. Once ambition seemed to be the first step on my ladder to success but I found very early that the rungs are often oiled. It makes the ascent very difficult.' He spoke slowly deliberately.

'The descent also becomes easier Michael.'

'Too negative Georgette!'

Their quiet talk was soothing. It chased away any remnants of sexual tension and gave her food for thought. The feelings still centered on the man seated to her left. Her body wasn't relaxed but her mind, stimulated by the day's undemanding pace, reasserted some of its former sharpness. Michael wanted to debate.

'Sometimes negatives can work for you providing a stimulus.'

'Yes but too much may be overwhelming'

'Not if you analyze the individual factors and deal with them.'

As the words left her mouth she knew that was exactly what she had been unable to do. Michael was right and she acknowledged his point.

'Have you been trying to make me see the error of my ways?'

'Error?'

'I mean my attitude of late. It's the result of being unable to cope with too many negative factors.'

'We were discussing only,' Michael said flustered by her perceptiveness. It wasn't his intention to make any personal references except where it concerned himself. Right now he didn't want Georgette to see him as a doctor or even an old family friend. The honest concession surprised him. He longed to untie the braid which hung down her back. Two years ago, away from the office, her hair was a glorious mass of red which bathed her shoulders. Its fiery colour seemed at odds with the sophisticated personality but the styles she chose added elegance and grace to a unique and intriguing personality.

'We were just talking but it happens that our conversation could be applied figuratively as well as literally to me or to you.'

'Georgette I don't want to pass the judgment on your situation.'

'I know but I think any negative situation could be applied to me if one searched deeply enough.'

'I don't want the search or analysis; I just want to be your friend, to listen. I feel very much distressed by your unhappiness. I would prefer to offer comfort than...'

He halted embarrassed. He liked Georgette, knew their relationship had changed little over the years but found himself wondering why. Georgette never seemed vulnerable before. She was efficient and hard working, as dedicated to her work as he was committed to his own practice. Michael had been hurt before by a vulnerable looking woman whose heart had been made of stone. Much as he liked and admired this beautiful Eurasian woman he would never credit her with any depth except for those few people who she genuinely loved. Her attitude was always aloof, discouraging any intimacy.

Michael even admitted to himself that he was often intimidated by her glossy efficiency. The pause and the unfinished sentence stretched to embarrassing proportions before Michael became aware that he failed to complete a revealing statement leaving the puzzled recipient to wonder exactly what he wouldn't prefer.

She was not to know. Gregory and Stephanie returned bearing a tray with a variety of cheeses, fruits, and small cakes. There was fresh coffee. Any further intimate conversation was impossible. The four sat comfortably in the room discussing Georgette's upcoming trip. Jamaica, they agreed would be an ideal spot to idle away the days, soaking up the sun and enjoying the colourful scenery. The island people were known to be friendly and hospitable to tourists. The honeymoon album was brought out yet again to add some weight to their words.

Throwing up her hands later Georgette declared, 'I've already agreed to go. You don't need to sell me on the idea anymore.'

'I know Georgy. We only want to put you in a good frame of mind for the trip.'

'I appreciate it. I really do,' she replied glancing at the faces of her friends. She said no more feeling very tearful suddenly and not wanting to spoil for them, what had been a beautiful day. Taking a breath to ease the tightness in her throat, she looked at Michael imploringly. 'I think we should be going Michael,' she got out at last.

'Yes, of course.' Rising, they made their way to the front door. 'I'll be in tomorrow Stephanie, just to clear up my desk. Tuesday, I'll come here to see Helen and Christian before I go.'

'Good I can pick you up after work. Why not sleep here Tuesday then I'll take you to the airport.'

'I haven't thought that far ahead, but I'll let you know.'

They bid each other goodnight. Gregory and Stephanie stood arms around each other watching the car disappear down the street waving happily.

'She will enjoy herself won't she?'

'You've done everything you can to ensure that things run smoothly. The rest is up to her.'

****

Michael drove steadily. The usual Sunday night traffic on the highway was faster than normal but the volume seemed worse than most rush hour week days. '*Weekending*' out of town was a popular Toronto practice that often led to long delays getting back into the city from cottages throughout southern Ontario. Michael was about to comment on the heavy but swiftly moving traffic when he had to apply his brakes sharply. Peering out his side window he could see a long line of red lights ahead of him. Shaking his head, he uttered a stream of Hungarian.

'Should I ask you to translate that?'

'No! You should not.'

Georgette smiled, not in the least perturbed. She avoided driving if it was at all possible and this was her main reason. Traffic jams made her blood boil. The stop and start would turn her into a raving lunatic.

'Better you than me Michael.'

'Georgette, I have not the patience for this.' He thumped his hand on the wheel and looked around searching for some way to vent his frustration. Georgette watched him out of the corner of her eye, curious about this new Michael who would display anger over a delay in the traffic and yet remain so calm, in the face of the numerous emergencies, he attended as a doctor.

'I've always admired your ability to withstand the rigors of family practice and yet maintain a very soothing persona,' she said choosing to give voice to her thoughts.

'My practice! I can give all to my patients. I can be in control. If I cannot cope, then there are the services for referral, but this?' He spread his arms out trying to describe his frustration. 'For this I am at the mercy. I have no control. I cannot even see what keeps me confined in my car not moving.'

'Like an unseen force that binds you to its will.' Georgette uttered whimsically. He looked at her and laughed.

'I am silly am I not?...to be so worked up by the things over which I cannot control.'

'It is silly, but very human. I am more often than not the same.'

Michael continued to look at her and smile. She responded shyly. It was the first time in a very long time that she had been understanding and sympathetic to another human without a clinical attitude. In the shadowed car the lights from the oncoming traffic defining and redefining the planes of her face, she seemed the essence of loveliness. The hardened sophisticated look was gone to be replaced by a gentle innocent allure.

Michael wasn't sure if the lights were playing tricks. He did know that he wanted to kiss her.

'Georgette I....'

He leaned across uncaring of whether an invitation was there or not. The seat belt tightened around his neck and he halted sliding his hand to the lock to release it. The blaring of a horn behind him penetrated his mind.

'I think traffic is moving again Michael,' she whispered.

Startled, the hand stopped and he turned surprised to find a big gap between him and the traffic ahead. He drove on saying nothing.

Georgette remained silent too. Something unusual had nearly happened. She could not be sure but Michael looked as if he had wanted to kiss her. She acknowledged to herself that she wanted him to kiss her. She wanted to be in his arms again. Hating the need that arose in her she suppressed it. She had never been attracted to Michael before and refused to allow loneliness to overcome her common sense.

The traffic was still moving slowly. Whether Michael stopped talking because he needed to concentrate on the bumper to bumper mass or just regretted the unguarded moment, he said nothing. She kept her eyes averted, hating the tension that mounted within her. The reminder of the drive took almost an hour. As the familiar lights of the city signs came into view, Georgette was so unsettled it took supreme effort to remain still.

Her thoughts ran ahead picturing the sterile comfort of her condo. Its loneliness offered little solace. The days relaxing pace dimmed and the feelings long since pushed to the back of her mind, resurfaced. '*He must not know how close I came to responding*' she thought fiercely '*nor do I want his pity*'. Michael's car came to a halt in front of the white modern building.

They remained silent. Georgette begged an unseen and unknown God for the strength to bid a pleasant good night and get out before she made a fool of herself.

'I will see you inside.'

'It's not necessary Michael.'

'I think so. We have unfinished business.'

Georgette and Michael avoided each other's eyes staring instead at the numbers lighting up at the side of the elevator. She wondered what he meant by 'unfinished business' but dared not even voice interest. She had no desire to assume anything personal in the comment. '*Suppose I'm wrong,*' she thought distractedly.

'*After so many years why should we change towards each other?*' She took a cleansing breath that seemed to tear through tightened lungs and yet felt no better. Her body began to tremble once again.

'*I don't need this stress!*' she almost shouted but was stilled by a blank unreadable look in Michael's averted profile. The elevator came to a sudden halt and Georgette fiddled with keys as she made her way to the condo door with Michael following wordlessly.

'It's late Michael,' she said pointedly entering the living room, 'but I can make tea if you would like a cup. '

'If it is late, we don't need tea. I shouldn't stay. '

'I just thought you had to discuss....it might be better to......'

'Don't be afraid of me Georgette. I'm not here to hurt you.'

'I'm not afraid.'

His eyes narrowed at the lie. He suddenly wanted her. His stance in the centre of the living room could only be described as cool and relaxed. His jacket, long since discarded, had been left in the car. The white shirt was limp. It had one or two scuff marks and stains from Christian shoes. His hands dug deep in the pocket of his pants and he stood legs apart in his stocking feet, aggressively masculine in the stark white living room.

'*Between this morning and tonight we have passed through a gate and come out two different people,*' she thought. Georgette searched her reserves to try and conjure up some of the pluck that kept her going. The protective armour around her feelings had fallen away in huge chunks and she seemed to be vulnerable to anything.

'Do you want to talk about Christian?'

'No Georgette, I do not want to talk about Christian. I want to talk about you and me.'

'Michael please,' she begged holding up a hand. 'I don't know if I can discuss any relationships right now. I'm just too.....tired. Please?'

'Georgette, I do not want the talk.' Michael's voice was harsh and tortured. Underlying its deep resonance was a plea which penetrated her own fears. She placed a hand at her throat, her eyes widened, the pupils dilated. 'What do you mean?' Her voice was barely above a whisper.

He paused rubbing a hand over his eyes looking tired. Georgette knew that response. She'd seen it often and knew that he was going to adjust himself and avoid the intimate in favour of something else safer. Tension robbed her of the words to diffuse the situation completely. A few months ago a sarcastic or cutting comment would have sent Michael out the door. Right now though, her feelings were overwhelming her, suffocating her and she wanted him to stay, to express himself. She closed her eyes and felt her body sway towards him ever so slightly.

'Georgy?' The diminutive of her name from his lips startled her. It was uttered with such need and longing. Its sound was like music, much different when Stephanie used it. Her eyes tightened at the sweet pain induced at the core of her being, when it washed over her.

'Are you afraid of me?'

'Yes'

'Do not hide what you feel. Open your beautiful eyes.'

She did as he commanded, surprised at the compliment.

'Did you not think that you had beautiful eyes?' he said softly, deliberately not touching her just yet.

'I never thought so. I hate the way I look.'

He shook his head negatively frowning trying to understand why after so much time of friendship and sharing he should develop a physical attraction to this woman.

Without realizing it they had moved closer to each other, continuing to gaze into each other's eyes, not touching just looking. Their deepened breaths mingled. Michael's hand reached up to touch her elbow then slide upwards to the tensely held shoulder. His fingers found the long braid at her back.

'Take it out Georgy. I want to feel the strands in my fingers.'

Her hands moved to hold the braid which he pulled over her shoulder. Without taking her eyes from his face she undid the twisted strands with sure but nervous fingers.

At its straight thickness fell in a long curtain framing her features he ran his fingers along the side of her face and through the soft strands. He exhaled a long breath at the sensuous feel of it unable to hold back a grunt of naked desire. The fingers returned to the face stopping lightly while a thumb caressed the high cheekbones marveling at the velvety feel of the porcelain perfect skin.

He started the journey through the auburn mass again but her parted lips caught his eye. With a groan he covered her mouth with his. Georgette remained immobile. Never had she yearned for a kiss as she did now. Its sweetness and reverence made her want more.

'Miklos' she breathed against the lips just barely touching her own. The hand behind her head increased its pressure slightly. The tip of his tongue probed easily at the parted entrance to her mouth.

Nervous and trembling, she opened her lips in silent response and welcomed his questing tongue. *'Where has this Michael been? Why haven't I felt this before?'*

Unable to think with a rational mind and find an answer, her logic closed down allowing her emotions to rule all actions. She was afraid, desperately afraid, but trust was a big part of her relationship with Michael Czerny and she felt safely aroused by his kisses.

When the kiss ended, she buried her head in his shoulder as she had done earlier but a gentle finger under her chin brought her lips back to his. She saw his desire for a fleeting second before her eyes closed and felt a trembling need rise up within her as she gave in to the desire firing itself from the core of her body.

'Why Michael?' she asked as he released her again.

'I don't know Georgy,' he breathed, but today I find myself seeing you as a woman, wanting you with a desire I do not

understand. I want so very much to make love to you. It's almost
…..it's…' he found he could not continue and held her face with
both hands for a heartbeat before he kissed her on the eyes, nose,
cheeks tasting her before he returned to the full lips, tracing the
edges with his tongue.

Georgette was drowning in a sea of sensuality. She knew
she was lost to all thought. She clutched his shoulders nervously.
Michael picked her up easily carrying her shaking body to the
softness of the stark white couch. Laying her down he sat at
the edge. The top of her blouse was pulled up slightly by their
exertions.

'Please take it off. I want so much to see you….. all of you.'

She did as he requested, without false modestly but
hesitantly.

'You are beautiful dearest. Don't hide from me.'

He spoke tenderly. Michael had given no thought to the amount
of sexual experience in her life. He attributed any hesitation to
the depth of her depression and the unexpected change in their
relationship, nothing more. He wanted her desperately, wanted to
see her animated. It wasn't therapy for him or for her but merely
an uncontrolled sexual attraction between friends; one that he did
not care to analyze to deeply.

'Michael help me,' she murmured when the top was off. He
obliged by undoing the clasp of her bra releasing the small firm
breasts.

'Georgy, my God you are so beautiful' he crooned burying
his face in her neck, kissing the shoulders and making his way
hurriedly to the small peaks begging for his touch.

She gasped at the pleasure of his mouth doing wondrous
things to the hardened peaks.

He stopped only long enough to remove his shirt before he
covered her body with his own. She was aware of his need as he
lay atop her driving himself to her as his desire overcame him.

'Take of your clothes…please,' he gasped.

'Michael….I….Michael?' She made no move to stop him. He was sure she was asking for more.

'Do you want me to stop Georgy? I don't know if I am able.' He breathed the words into her ear while his hands roamed the softness of her skin, seeming to draw the desire out of her as he explored the planes and lines with eager hands.

'No…I just want to go upstairs,' she got out at last. It was a lie. She didn't want him to stop, but fear held her again. She needed a moment. It was her first time. When she took off her blouse, she had committed herself to the act. If she held back Michael would be angry but she knew he would understand. There was however a need born of desire, frustration and aching loneliness. She didn't know why Michael should be the one to awaken the need but he had to be the one to satisfy it.

Nodding her assent he picked her up heading in the direction of her pointed finger.

They disrobed completely. Georgette had experienced her last, second thought, downstairs. She craved what Michael had to offer. She would not tell him this was her first time. The technicality of her virginity was lost to minor surgery years ago and she was taking the pill to control the bleeding that had caused her monthly problems. His eyes questioned the safety of their act and she nodded wordlessly to reassure him before adding a silent invitation for him to join her on the bed.

He went to her outstretched arms the length of his aroused body meeting hers heatedly. He paused to caress the smooth skin before wrapping his arms around her and rolling her body on top of his. She smiled into his face, surprised to find herself looking down at him.

I love your hair,' he acknowledged huskily fingering the strands which fell around her face. Gripping a handful, he let the softness fall through his fingers. 'For years I have watched you curl and style, admired it up, admired it down, but never so much as I do now Georgy.' He ended on a hungry moan finding her parted lips. They kissed deeply as their hands roamed freely over unfamiliar grooves and curves.

Georgette felt stimulated and wondered how she could have gone for years abstaining, denying herself the joy she was sharing with a friend turned lover.

Michael felt the release of her tension, sensed a change in her. Rolling her onto her back, he parted her legs easily. He met with some resistance and felt her stiffen.

'It's been awhile Michael,' she said burying her face in his shoulder to hide the lie.

'Do I hurt you?'

'No…please don't stop.'

'Now I cannot Georgy.'

He entered her with some force and she arched her back, while holding a startled involuntary gasp deep within her. A myriad of sensations flowed from the core of her womanhood upwards to envelop her whole body and send a shock of chills through each nerve ending.

'What is it my dearest?' he managed to ground out. His voice was unsteady, every fiber of being centered on the woman whose moist warmness sheathed him so tightly.

'Don't worry, I am fine. Don't talk, just make love to me please. Don't stop.'

He complied, biting and teasing the long neck, the soft ears and the full lips as he drove himself. Unable to savour and analyze each sensation on a mental level, Georgette gave up trying, relaxed and found herself overwhelmed. She slipped on the merry-go-round of sensuality, flying effortlessly, wanting to stop, yet clinging desperately and fearing the end of the ride.

Frightened by the out of control sensation in a body already tortured and depressed, she held herself rigidly at the end to avoid the unfamiliar feelings of the climax. She feared its power would shatter her fragile emotions.

Michael sensed the rejection and drove harder and faster overriding her silent withdrawal, determined to take her to the heights. She gripped his shoulders mindlessly nails digging into the bulky shoulder muscles. Her head shook back and forth silky strands swirling in a red mist.

'I can't' she gasped

'Come with me Dearest love.'

'I'm so afraid. Help me.'

'I will.'

Georgette cried out deeply as her body took over. Her subconscious mind wondered who could be making that noise. Her return to sanity left her bewildered. The sound of Michael's voice was reassuring.

'Hush my darling. I have hurt you. I am sorry.'

Michael had never heard such heart rending sobs. In his experience no woman had cried with as much abandon as Georgette. She had denied being hurt but he couldn't be sure. It seemed such a radical departure from her usual controlled behaviour. Michael was puzzled and rolled over pulling her with him so that they lay side by side facing each other.

Georgette refused to look into his face hiding her bowed head into a shoulder that had a fine line of puckered scar tissue. She traced the full length of it absently frowning through her tears as she sensed a deep trauma associated with it.

'It is many years old. The memories have faded.' He used a thumb to wipe away the tracks of her tears.

She continued to torture the scar as if trying to wrest its secrets. He captured her hand bringing it to his lips. She tugged lightly but he refused to let go, tightening his hold. He curled his hand around hers and brought it to rest below his chin.

'You have been pulling away from me for years Georgette. Why do you not stop now?'

'I thought we were already friends.'

'We are friends but not to each other. We are friends to Stefania, Gregory and Christian but not to each other.'

Georgette closed her eyes. She felt safe cocooned in his arms. She pondered his words, processed them lazily through her uncluttered mind before accepting the truth of his analysis.

'I understand the difference.' She glanced into his eyes then, still afraid of revealing too much.

'Do you want me to leave?'

'No. Please stay for awhile if you can. Do you mind if we don't talk?'

Whatever Michael felt, he said nothing. His hand rose to brush the hair from her face before planting a light kiss on the soft unlined forehead.

A pastel light which softened the beauty of the room was turned off with a minimum of movement leaving the pair hidden from the world, safe, under cover of darkness.

Chapter 5:

Much later, Georgette felt Michael stir. She had no idea what to do or say. She remained silent. In her mind she pictured him as he dressed, remembering with pleasure the lean lines of his body as she had seen it briefly. He joined her on the bed too quickly for her to admire much of him beyond his face, filled with desire.

Michael always seemed bulky and slightly overweight. His broad shoulders were deceptive. The extra large shirts needed to cover his upper torso, bundled untidily around his slim waist. The preoccupied doctor rarely gave much thought to his attire and consequently appeared sloppy and unkempt.

Georgette, a lover of almost any art form had been pleasantly aroused by the feel of the firm body under her hands. Her eyes flickered in remembrance of the act. Her body stiffened but she held back needing some time to digest and absorb what she and Michael had shared and its possible repercussions.

Forcing herself to breathe deeply was difficult, for no sound emanated from the other side of the bed. She could barely control the natural startle response when she felt his lips just inches from her ear. He knew she wasn't sleeping it seemed. He whispered softly, 'I must go. I have the early call. Please phone me later?'

Georgette mumbled an affirmative response of some sort but she was embarrassed by her inability to carry off the encounter with the aplomb expected of a sophisticated woman of the world.

She heard a few words uttered in Hungarian and held on to them, committing them to memory even as she heard him close the door to the bedroom on his way out.

****

'Have you bought the entire store Georgy?' Stephanie commented, laughingly as she met her business partner at the door of their office building. It was only mid morning and already she had bundles of bags and boxes.

'Don't tease me. At least you could help. My arms are killing me!'

Stephanie ran forward and grabbed a box and bag clearly threatening to fall to the floor.

'In your office?'

'Of course in my office.'

'No need to snap, although I am glad to hear it.'

'Was I always a snapping turtle Stephanie?' Georgette stopped and turned to question her friend, eyebrows drawn together in a perplexed frown.

'Not in a nasty way. I know you just want to keep people on their toes.'

'People?'

'Well mostly me.... Georgy you are so vulnerable right now. Don't analyze everything I say. Just be yourself. I don't want to tiptoe around you every time I make a comment.'

'That would be tough for you, no?'

'Yes....No!' The pair giggled girlishly.

'Stephanie, I don't know what this world would be like without you. Those accents you bring up from nowhere. I wish....'

'Don't wish. Show me what you purchased instead.'

Boxes were unloaded and the bright colourful clothes admired.

'These don't look like you at all Georgy.'

'They are NOT me! I went to a department store instead of my usual boutique. The salesgirl had an effervescent personality which rubbed off on everyone. She had me buying these things before I knew what happened.'

'*Give that girl a promotion,*' thought Stephanie admiring the practical yet festive, tropical clothes. She knew Georgette would never have bought anything like that before but restrained herself from saying so.

'You need not look like that. It's only because I'll be on vacation. I will never wear them ....' Any further comment was halted by phone ringing.

'It must be for me, Georgy. You weren't expected today.' She reached over to answer the phone. Georgette listened to the one sided conversation with increasing anxiety.

'Hello….yes…. Michael, how are you? .... I didn't expect….. no….everything is fine. Yes…just got back…Speak to her? Of course!'

Puzzled, Stephanie handed the phone to Georgette. She did not miss the haunted, fearful look on her friend's face.

'Is anything wrong Georgette?' she said covering the mouthpiece.

'No…no, just a minor problem. I'll get it sorted out.' She spoke into the phone hurriedly. 'Yes Michael, what is it?'

There was a long pause at the other end of the line. Georgette was ashamed of her tone but she was embarrassed and uncomfortable with Stephanie close by.

'I know you are not alone. I hope the way you speak is not the way you feel about me?'

'I'm busy as you know. It's just difficult right now.'

'Stephanie would expect you to speak with me. We have been talking for years.' Clearly his tone was showing signs of irritation.

'But not now! It's different. I didn't expect this.'

'Expect what? We made love last night and I left your bed this morning. I want to see you. You did not call.' Now the words were clipped. Georgette fought for composure.

'You thought I would do something foolish? It won't happen. I promise. I must go. See you when I get back.' She rang off with a hasty goodbye hardly waiting for a further response.

Michael heard the click on the other end of the phone. He was furious. *'That cold hearted bitch. She used me to warm her bed and chase the loneliness for one night. Now I am dismissed.'* A silent rage filled him. For years he suppressed the hurt and anger that often threatened to overwhelm him. The Hungarian revolution, the loss of his parents, that two timing wife, Angela, all served to destroy his faith in everyone and everything. *'What a fool I am to think I deserve any happiness. The joke is on me!'* Behind the anger, disappointment spread outward from his gut. The pain was almost unbearable. *'I know it was difficult for her to speak but the tone held not one iota of warmth. It was almost as if last night was nothing more than an expendable memory to her.'*

Michael could not control his random and self abasing thoughts. No matter what he was feeling, patients waited. Setting aside his own pain, he lifted the intercom on his desk, asking his nurse, Patty, to send in the next patient.

****

Later on the way home, Stephanie observed the stony profile in the car beside her. She knew that something had occurred between Georgette and Michael. She wondered if Michael had gone overboard trying to help her deal with her depression. Georgette's version of the conversation gave the impression of some unwanted conflict or pressure. Never one to side step issues, she took the bull by the horns.

'Did you and Michael fight last night?'

'Fight? What a childish word to use for two adults. No we did not fight.' Georgette was relieved that she didn't have to lie.

'You seemed very tense on the phone earlier.'

'Well I was. I didn't expect him to call. If he needed to speak with me he could have called me at home.' Thankfully the car was pulling into the driveway of her apartment complex.

'But Georgy....'

'Look Stephanie, don't come up. Just drop me at the door. You don't get away early too often. Christian will be glad to see you.'

The mention of the little boy effectively put a stop to any further confidences or arguments. The car pulled to a halt and Georgette quickly jumped out. Ignoring the headache threatening to burst through, she cheerfully grabbed her bags and boxes from the back of the car.

'I'll see you sometime tomorrow. Don't call me. I'll call you and let you know if I decide to stay over.'

'Are you sure?'

'I'm sure.'

The fixed smile was beginning to crumble as Georgette waved the car and driver away. She hadn't really wanted a drive home but Stephanie had been insistent. 'Taking you home will get me out of here early too.' Georgette demurred but didn't press the issue. Now she was free; free to scream, free to cry, free to hide, at least for awhile.

'I am going to take that damn phone off the hook and disconnect it or throw it so far away it will never force me to speak with anyone again. After turning off the ringer, Georgette changed her clothes and went straight to bed. She ignored her body's need for food. The duvet effectively cut off the rest of the world as she sobbed and cried her way through the long night refusing to leave her bed even for a moment.

Hours later, other needs could no longer be ignored and getting up with a disgusted snort and blinding headache, Georgette staggered to the bathroom . She was surprised to find sunlight was straining to get in the small bathroom window. The antique brass bathroom clock showed that it was after 7:30.

'My God! Have I slept over 14 hours?' Georgette peered at her face in the mirror disgusted by the puffiness and ravages of restless night. Hunger made her dizzy and she collapsed on the floor fighting for consciousness. She had not eaten since her meal with Stephanie. The bathroom floor welcomed her coldly but she

had little strength to protest the hard unfeeling tiles. More tears followed the outpouring of words.

'*Why am I torturing myself like this? Maybe I should end it all now. I don't want to die. I really don't want to die but I can't live like this? Where can I find the strength to continue?*'

Out of the mists of pain and self pity, Georgette heard the O'Malley voice, strong, firm and decisive.

'*No O'Malley was ever a quitter.*'

'I'm not quitting Daddy. I just can't go on.'

'*Nonsense. You are quitting!*'

'Is that why you hate me? Because I am not strong enough?'

There was no answer. Georgette forced herself up, fighting to overcome the weakness. Thirst consumed her. She reached for the bathroom tap. The water felt cool revitalizing against her skin. The emotional crisis passed taking only a small measure of Georgette's rapidly dwindling reserves. Like a demanding lover, it would come back, seeking more than it gave, opening wounds, making the hurt and bitterness pour out, leaving her limp and exhausted.

Much later, in the warmth of her kitchen, a fragrant cup of coffee helped to restore a small measure of her equilibrium. She had been shocked by the state of the living room. All the clothes which she had purchased were scattered from end to end. The old Georgette would have been appalled at the disarray. The unsightly mess hardly drew a careless shrug. The answering machine clicked abruptly startling her. She had gotten used to the silence. She glanced at the flickering light knowing that she would hear the message, even if she didn't want to speak with the caller. A now familiar voice cut through her with knife edge precision.

'I know you are there. You don't want to speak, but you will listen. You are a selfish, hard-hearted woman of no feeling. You walk on me. You dismiss me. You care nothing. Let your conscience guide you to Hell.'

****

Georgette felt the weight of her obligations. In another moment of self pity, she wondered how she could just avoid people altogether. It seemed an effort even to call Stephanie and cancel the trip to Oakville, but she knew that to do so would worry her friend even further. The turmoil it caused within her was nauseating. Instead, she set out a plan to avoid a confrontation and called the office with a false smile in her voice.

'Stephanie, I am just a little overwhelmed with packing. Really, I will just drive out and visit with Helen for the afternoon. I'll stay long enough for her not to be mad at me and then come back and finish up.'

'Are you sure Georgy? You hate to drive.'

'Sure I do.' She paused choosing her words carefully. 'Look, you know that I appreciate what you've arranged. It sounds perfect but you didn't leave me much time to pack properly and say my few goodbyes.'

'I was sure you would have changed your mind if I left it too long.'

'No….really I'm happy to get away on vacation. I just don't want to rush what I'm doing now.'

Stephanie had sounded skeptical initially but accepted the reprieve with barely disguised relief. Leaving the office early would have been difficult. Georgette was well aware of the last minute challenges of arranging requests for urgent services which often came into the office during the last hour of the day.

Georgette hung up the receiver and breathed a sigh of relief. She didn't really want to stay over in Oakville for the night. Given the choice of driving or facing more unavoidable questions from her friend, she chose to drive. Helen would be less probing and she could leave early. It all seemed deceitful but necessary.

Despite her bravado, she couldn't get behind the wheel of her car either. Her vision felt distorted and she noted a slight tremor in her hands. There was a hollow feeling at the pit of her stomach which could not be filled. She tried to eat a little before heading out. Unknown to Stephanie, Georgette caught the commuter train to a local station and took a taxi to the house from there.

Helen was none too pleased by the look of her daughter's friend. Once she voiced her opinion, the old lady let the matter drop. Georgette considered Helen to be as much of a close friend as she was a surrogate mother. The two women shared many things beyond a love for Stephanie. Georgette had spent much of her life in England once her father retired from the Navy. Her family home had been within a few miles of the village where Helen had been born. Similar cultural attitudes drew them together. There were many days when Georgette wished her own mother had been a little more like Helen. The afternoon turned out to be quite pleasurable and stress free.

Keeping a close eye on the clock, Georgette did not linger. She arranged for the taxi to return in time to catch a convenient train back to town. She said her goodbyes to Helen and Christian, all the while fighting a sense of foreboding.

****

A very early flight avoided the necessity of any last minute calls. She slipped out of her condo and into another taxi just as the sun was rising. Another pounding headache ruined the beginning of her adventure. Georgette was barely able to settle on the plane and catch a few minutes of sleep. It wasn't restful but the tears held off. Michael's words continued to echo in her ears, long after the call. She felt the pull of his sexuality tugging at her constantly. It did not abate even when mingled with the truth of his words. She shifted in her seat and requested a glass of water.

The pain pills she hastily purchased preflight were needed to still the pounding. As soon as the water hit the empty pit of her stomach she felt the tears fall. Being nurtured by a cold glass of water seemed to symbolize the bland emptiness of her world. Everything to sustain life was contained in a colourless, tasteless liquid. People, like Michael, would readily declare that she was like water; necessary but passionless. She would love to have heard from him whether he also found her passionless. She was too afraid too ask. His telephone message gave every indication that he thought her heartless. Her response to his call at the office had been unforgiveable but she could not face him for reasons which were incomprehensible. He had done her no injustice.

Visions of Michael, aroused and tempting, forced her to turn away and look out the window. Snippets of land were visible below. Georgette pulled down the blind, adjusted her pillow and closed her eyes. She didn't want to think, feel or see. Her disciplined mind closed all emotional doors. When her will failed to keep the thoughts at bay, the drugs soon did their work.

****

No breeze disturbed the moist heat on the beautiful tropical island. Its weight descended on her senses making her sluggish. The long wait through customs and immigration did little to improve her mood. She silently cursed her loving but misguided friend. Georgette had just about given up the idea of enjoying even one moment of her holiday when her bags were whisked away by a slim, dark skinned, grey haired, man of indeterminate age, whose toothy, lopsided grin welcomed her to the island.

'My name is Baxter, Miss O'Malley. I am going to drive you to your destination. Come with me.'

'How did he know it was me?' The Georgette of old would have questioned him thoroughly but the car looked luxurious and air conditioned. She said little, following meekly behind his long strides. She allowed Baxter to assist her into the car. The change, from hot to cold, sent shock waves through her already achy body. She knew without the medication she would have felt much worse.

'We are going to St. Ann's Bay Miss. It will take about sixty minutes. If you prefer, I will say nothing. If you have any questions, please ask.'

'Thank you Baxter. Silence is preferable for me right now.'

Georgette saw little of her journey. She closed her eyes to the sea front drive. Visiting tropical islands was not new to her. The lush palms, inviting green-blue sea and vibrant colours could not hold her gaze.

Nearly an hour later, for the first time in days Georgette managed to give thanks for her friend's ability to match the animate to the inanimate. She was welcomed by Sonia, Baxter's wife, a beautiful coffee coloured woman with soft hair and a face which was truly unique. Her voice, like Baxter's was melodious. She seemed to sing her welcome. The accommodation was not a resort-type setting at all, but the upstairs floor of a large house, close enough to the beach to almost touch the frothy waves curling in from the depths of the Caribbean sea.

Sonia and Baxter lived on the ground floor. From their quarters, they took care of guests, the grounds, and all domestic chores. On the outside of the house was a winding staircase leading to the upstairs. There were two large air-conditioned bedrooms with ensuite bathrooms, living and dining rooms and a small kitchen. A wrap around verandah gave an almost 360 view of mountains and sea. The most beautiful feature was the cathedral ceiling in the living room. At its centre, hung a large fan, actively drawing the heat upwards. The apartment was scrupulously clean and smelled of fresh wax.

Georgette didn't know what to do first.

'Please have a seat Miss O'Malley. I am going to fix a light drink for you. There are some snacks on the table. I will unpack your clothes and then you will rest. When you are ready for supper you just call me.'

Not at all perturbed by the gentle control, Georgette allowed herself to be led into bed just over an hour later where she slept soundly until the following morning.

Rising from the mists of her dreamless state, Georgette was halted by the unfamiliarity of the sunbathed bedroom. It took some minutes for her to orient herself to the change. A glance at her watch startled her out of bed. Once again she had slept for hours. The sudden movement brought a return of the pounding and she sank back to the cushiony mattress waiting a few minutes before making her way to the bathroom. She thought it too early to disturb Sonia. The satiny pillows beckoned and she was soon asleep again.

There was a point where the needs of her body overtook the delight of the bed. She could hear Sonia moving quietly about. After a quick shower she was out into the dining room where the delicious smells of a typical Jamaican breakfast awaited her. Replete from food and undemanding conversation, there was a return of some interest in her surroundings. She changed into a colourful two-piece bathing suit and made her way to the beach. Baxter followed at a discreet distance. He was instructed to ensure that she did not stray too far. Her every need was available in a small cabana on the beach including a jug of delicious ice cold fresh squeezed lime juice, large towels, lotions, and finger snacks.

Later in the day, Baxter took her for a short drive in the surrounding area. The evening was spent quietly. Soft music played on the stereo while Georgette read books about the local culture.

She soon found that evening comes early because the sun sets quickly in the tropics. Before 8 o'clock, Georgette was back in bed, sound asleep. She followed this routine for the first six days grateful for the privacy and discreet response from her 'caretakers'. In fact, she was hardly able to do more. Her anger with Stephanie had long disappeared. Indeed she was pampered and nurtured quietly and efficiently by two people who well understood her need for unobtrusive care.

Few words had been exchanged beyond daily pleasantries but Georgette, who was by nature curious and observant, felt a kinship with Sonia. She had read enough about the Island to know a little of its history and peoples. That evening she stuck up a casual conversation while Sonia prepared dinner.

'Sonia, I know that many people are of mixed races on the island. I haven't seen many others but you look familiar, if you don't mind me saying so.'

'No Ma'am, not at all. I think we both have a Chinese grandmother.'

'What? Well I do yes, but do you?'

'Yes Ma'am.'

'Sonia I wish you wouldn't call me Ma'am. My name is Georgette.'

'I couldn't call you by your first name but I can call you Miss Georgette.'

They both understood the great divide in cultural class systems in other countries and Georgette did not engage in any further pleading.

'Tell me about your grandmother. I am curious to hear how she came to be in Jamaica.'

Sonia was happy to talk about a woman who clearly reigned supreme in her family. The story was amusing and had been told many times. Sonia struggled to avoid lapsing into the patois of the locals. Stories had to be told in a certain way. Georgette knew languages. The dialect was not familiar to her but she listened carefully.

'Mas Ping was my great-uncle who came from China many years ago. He never did tell us how he and Nei-Nei got to Jamaica but I think him sneak 'pon a ship and didn't know where it was going. He set up shop in Moneague and Nei-Nei help him. Uncle Ping never marry. He like business too much. Nei-Nei was called Missy Song.

Busha Bickles did manage a plantation in the hills. Him did come often to shop. Him like Missy Song but Uncle Ping say no! She marry only Chinese. Trouble was Nei-Nei like Busha Bickles too!'

'Sorry to interrupt Sonia. What do you mean Busha?'

'Bickford Ecclestone, my grandfather was named but he was called Mas or Busha Bickles. He was the head man on the plantation up in Brown's Town. He was a tall, fair skinned man. Uncle Ping say him have 'whole heap 'a pickney dey 'bout but no wife. The overseer or head man is called Busha,' she added remembering the question and trying not to get sidetracked.

'I sense a Romeo and Juliet story here.'

'Almost but not quite. One night when Nei-Nei couldn't stand it no more, she sneak out through the window and run across the field to meet Busha Bickles. No one knew how long she did it but when she started to show her pregnancy Uncle Ping vex 'til him couldn't vex no more. Him take out his gun fi go looking for Busha Bickles.' Sonia stopped to take a deep breath. Shaking her head she continued. 'He went to kill him. Only Nei-Nei was able to save her baby father by promising Uncle Ping she would never see him again. She won't say if she did or didn't but five months later my Dada was born.'

'That's an amazing story Sonia. How many brothers and sisters do you have?'

'Nine Miss Georgette! Seven are in America with my parents and three of we are out here to manage the business and look after Nei-Nei.'

'I see. Thank you for telling me the story.'

'You're welcome. I'll go now Miss. If you need anything, please call.'

'Yes thanks, I will.'

The story stayed with Georgette through the night. *'Everyone has a love story except me.'* She shut out a vision of Michael and returned to her troubled sleep.

Chapter 6:

The warm sunny days passed quickly. Georgette had to admit that she felt much better even if the pounding pain was only reduced to a dull roar. She kept any medication to a minimum, moved slowly in the mornings and established a routine. She loved her conversations with Sonia who seemed to know a lot about the Island's history, culture, and people. Her hostess was informative, amusing and a direct contrast to her respectful, steady and mostly silent husband, who seemed quite a few years older. They had no children as a couple, although Baxter had a few from previous relationships.

She travelled extensively throughout the island in the comfortable car. Sometimes Sonia would join them and sometimes not. They went into small and large towns, crossed hills and valleys and looked out from mountain tops over the beautiful expanse of beaches around the island. Georgette mostly enjoyed driving through the mountains where her headaches disappeared. A couple of days with intermittent heavy rain showers did not dampen her spirits. She used that time to sit quietly and think about her life and what meaning it had for her. Michael's touch sometimes invaded her reverie. She tried to think about how she could make amends with him. Possibly he would not even want to resume any kind of relationship. She knew how much he had been hurt before but her own inability to feel comfortable with intimacy held her back.

A lot of time was also spent thinking about her parents and their calm unruffled marriage. It was hard to believe that they were indeed gone. She found it better to shed her few tears and know that some healing was taking place. Deep inside, she could not change the one issue which held her aloof from life. She did not know how to be one with another person. She could not emulate her parent's relationship and she did not know how to create one of her own.

Towards the end of her third week, she was pleased to receive what she understood to be a virtual royal summons from Missy Song.

'Nei-Nei says you are to come Miss Georgette.'

'I would be honoured. Please convey my thanks.'

Early on the following Sunday afternoon the trio headed out to the village of Moneague. It was quite a small place. From Sonia, she had heard that it used to be the crossroads between the north and south coast of the island. All travelers stopped there to refresh themselves before or after tackling the climb over the Blue Mountains. The winding road, bound for the south coast, was aptly named Mount Diablo. In contrast, on the way to Moneague from St. Ann's Bay, they also passed through a nature made tunnel-like road, called Fern Gully. In her travels with Baxter, she had already made the trip, but Sonia added some interesting facts as they headed south to see the elderly Matriarch.

The village wasn't busy. There were a few people in the shop which seemed to be at the front part of the house. They walked through the aisles to reach a door marked private behind the cash counter. A chorus of greetings met them at every step of the way with some voices quietly curious, some just polite and some nosey.

G'afternoon Miss Sonia. Is who dat?' One wizened old man asked outright.

'Mi cousin come from Canada, Mas Joe'.

'Welcome Miss. G'Afternoon.'

Georgette smiled. No one batted an eyelid at her colour or race.

'Sorry Miss Georgette. Dem ask too many questions.'

'That's fine. I don't mind.'

There was a short corridor which led to another door. Sonia knocked and entered. 'Nei-Nei, we come.'

She stepped aside to reveal a pale looking Chinese woman, seated graciously in an arm chair, whose hair was as white as her skin. Her dark eyes were slightly clouded with cataracts, the skin wrinkled with age, and fingers bent with arthritis. None the less she looked up and smiled. There were a few teeth missing from the broad smile but it was one of welcome.

'Come child, come child. Mek I see you.' The accent was quite unexpected. It sounded wholly Jamaican.

'Good afternoon Madam. Pleased to meet you.' Georgette leaned over and shook the outstretched hand.

'Sit girlie. You are too tall fi true.'

'My Father was a very big man.'

'White man…hmm…you resemble mi son.'

Georgette sat patiently while the fingers roamed her face and arms, ending with a light pat of affection. The old lady smiled before tears filled her eyes. Without thinking Georgette spoke in Cantonese. When the old lady frowned, she switched to Mandarin. A big smile lit up her face and she responded in kind.

'Not since Mas Ping died, I have not spoken my language. You very smart Missy George. You speak well.'

Georgette smiled in response and continued to address the old lady. Missy Song waved away her granddaughter and another woman who was clearly Sonia's sister.

'Fix something for the lady. I want to talk to her first.' And talk she did. Georgette heard stories from China to Jamaica; things which could not have been explained to her family. Georgette listened patiently, loving the way in which Missy Song described her adventures. Her eyes and body were declining but the mind was sharp and memory excellent. Georgette laughed and cried throughout the afternoon.

They were served cold drinks and light snacks. Beyond the walls of the small sitting room which appeared to be an anteroom to the old lady's bedroom, she could hear the others laughing and talking. Georgette was quite happy to sit and bask in the warmth of the elderly Matriarch. She had never known grandparents of her own. In her mind she imagined that somewhere in China, there had been a woman just like this, years ago, who would have told her the stories of the family. The anecdotes helped to actualize her limited personal knowledge of a Chinese ancestral history.

In the early evening, the sisters who had been busy in the other part of the house came in to pry Georgette away.

'Nuff said, Nei-Nei. Miss Georgette needs to eat and we want to meet her too.' Extending her hand she introduced herself. 'I am Mary, Sonia's older sister. My husband Winston and I run this shop and look after my Grandmother.'

'Come see me before you leave,' the old lady begged before the door was closed.

Mary extended her hand. She looked vaguely similar to Sonia but there were differences in the shade of the skin and some features. The relationship was, however, unmistakable. Georgette was taken to the very back of the house where a large dining room, kitchen and living room was filled with people. They were all family. On the massive dining table, laden with food, not an inch of space could be found. Someone said grace, finishing to a chorus of amens. People moved around the enormous buffet taking bits and pieces of a wide range of available foods until Georgette lost track. She was encouraged to try everything. Fortunately she had a rapid metabolism and a healthy appetite, which earned her nodding approval from the food loving Jamaicans.

The dinner was delicious. Georgette had never in her entire life experienced family as she did then. As soon as the food was cleared away, people drifted into different groups, some commanding her attention, wanting to know about the snow in Canada. Most of the men went out into the back yard where the teams were set up. The sound of dominoes slapping the tables and the shouts of 'six love' rang out. Albums appeared with pictures of everyone from the Matriarch right down to the smallest member of the family. Once the drinks started to flow, music blared from a stereo in the corner and dancing was soon underway.

Missy Song made another appearance. In response to the music she was assisted from her room and with stick in hand did a small twirl on the dance floor receiving loud clapping from everyone. It was now open for all to participate. Georgette observed the swirling hips and sensuous dancing with some amusement. What she had done with Gregory, Michael and Stephanie, paled in comparison to the rocking hips, grinding in tune to the driving beat which characterized the music, a mix of calypso and reggae tunes.

Rather than feeling shy about participating, she joined in whole heartedly receiving cheers and enthusiastic encouragement from everyone. She realized, in a moment of unrestrained happiness that connecting physically and emotionally with people and not just watching from the sidelines, made life real. She felt a part of the family in a way that was foreign to her usual interactions. In time she would analyze the impact but for the moment Georgette was content to be a partaker rather than an observer.

Hours of energetic dancing and talking passed before Georgette knew she could not sustain the pace of the others. She wasn't as fit as she thought and just before midnight she was tired and wanted to get to bed. She made her apologies. Everyone smiled. They obviously planned to continue with the festivities but wished her well. She stopped as requested at Missy Song's room door. She did not expect her to be awake, but the octogenarian was propped up in her bed, eyes wide. She waved Sonia away.

'Let me speak alone child.'

'Oh Nei-Nei, I won't understand you anyway.'

'Go wey girl.'

Missy Song patted the bed. 'Come Missy George.' Georgette sat at the side of the bed and took the old lady's hand in her own. Missy Song spent quite a while just staring at her guest.

'nǐ zǒu zài yīn yǐng de hēi niǎo' she eventually intoned.

'wèi shé me, nǐ shì shén me yì si', Georgette asked curiously

'wèi le zhǎo dào lù jìng, nín bì xū shì hēi niǎo'.

Even to Georgette the words were cryptic. She asked the old lady to explain. Despite her best intentions the full message was not comprehensible and the headache which had threatened earlier was now a pounding drum in her head. She memorized the words and knew they would come back to her when her mind was clear. She raised the fragile deeply veined hand to her lips in thanks for the day and kissed a soft cheek before leaving.

On their return to the house, Georgette declined any further food or drink. She thanked Sonia and Baxter profusely for sharing their family with her. The evening had been a revelation which Georgette couldn't even begin to process. She took her pain medication and tried to settle to sleep.

Any rest she hoped to enjoy evaded her. She got up and took a drink from the fridge before returning to bed trying again to settle. The sheets were crumpled beneath her and she could not get comfortable. The light came on again. She grabbed a piece of paper and began writing a note to Michael, asking for his forgiveness. The ink was hardly dry on her signature before she tore it up. A few minutes later, the medication began to do its work. The pain subsided a little. She tried to sleep but it would not come. Getting up yet again, and taking a second sheet of paper, she began writing, hoping, she thought with a clearer head. Satisfied with the contents, she folded it neatly, put it in an envelope and addressed it.

The letter was placed under her pillow. She kept her hand on it hoping to infuse some warmth into the words and tried once again to sleep. It came fitfully. She tossed and turned in the bed until the sheets were mangled around her body. She could have screamed in frustration. The Blackbirds which Missy Song had spoken about seemed to fly around overhead calling her. It was then she recalled the message.

'*You walk in the shadow of the Blackbird. You will not be strong until you become the blackbird. It is a smart creature. Knows how to survive, but remember it sings its sweetest song, only when it mates.*' What nonsense, she thought but could not dismiss the message entirely.

A hour later, Georgette gave up, unable to let go of any number of issues fighting for attention in her mind. Pushing the sheets aside, she got out of bed. The blinds were not closed. The light of a full moon beckoned through the slates of the window. She walked out to the verandah, hoping some night air would settle her nerves. The moon shone brightly in the inky sky, spreading its meager light generously. The soft sounds of the surf rolling in and lapping the shoreline, created a magical backdrop. The air was clean, fragrant and moist. Against the advice of Sonia, she walked down the stairs seduced by the sounds and unsure if she was asleep or awake. She felt safe. The road leading to the house was gated and set well back from the road. She was unlikely to be attacked in the early morning hours.

The gravel beneath her feet was sharp through the light slippers she wore. A piece of glass caught the side of her foot and she bent over to see if it was cut. There was no blood, only the shape of a scorpion lifeless on the stones. Its poison spread quickly through her body. Georgette had time to look up once before she fell to the ground. Her last thought was deep concern that a cloud covered the shining light of the moon.

****

Stephanie and Gregory slept peacefully in the large king sized bed. They were back to back but still touching each other. They seemed to turn as one when a change was needed. Soon they would be facing each other, arms and legs wrapped together. Stephanie always looked forward to that moment in the morning when she was face to face with the man of her heart, caressing his features as if she was seeing him for the first time. The sound of the phone shattered that possibility.

'It's for you Gregory. There are never any translating emergencies.'

He reached over for the phone and answered, his voice polite and ready, as if he had been up all night waiting for the call. He listened carefully before handing her the phone. 'It seems there are translating emergencies after all. For you Sunny.'

Unlike Gregory, her sleep laden voice mumbled into the phone. It took a minute before she sat bolt upright. She placed a hand on Gregory's chest to stay his questions until she understood the words and finished the call.

'Call me immediately with any news. I appreciate you informing me right away. Don't spare any expenses and reverse the charges if necessary. Use this number, and if you don't get me then call the office number on file.'

'What is it Sunny?' he asked when she handed him the receiver.

'It's Georgette. She collapsed outside the house early this morning. It seems she was bitten by a scorpion and she's in the hospital.'

Stephanie glanced over and looked at the clock. She couldn't imagine what Georgette was doing walking around at that hour of the morning. 'Gregory, will you look after Christian this morning. I am going to shower. I want to be ready for whatever may come.'

'Of course. If you need me to do anything let me know.'

Gregory didn't worry about his wife. He found out very quickly in their marriage that she was capable of handling almost any emergency with a calm, organized mind. It was quite different from the way she handled almost everything else in her life.

By 2 pm Stephanie had not heard back from Jamaica and she was worried. Her own call went unanswered. She sat at her desk; head bent forward, her hands resting on her cheeks. Soon the call came through from the receptionist and she answered it immediately.

'Mrs. Richmond, Miss Georgette is in the hospital in St. Ann's Bay. The doctor is not sure what is happening with her. He says maybe it is the Scorpion bite but he doesn't know. She won't wake up Miss.' In her anxiety Sonia struggled to make herself clear but she was frightened. Once that message was delivered she lapsed into the local patois.

'Sonia, please listen to me. Don't do anything until I get there. I have a ticket for the 5 p.m. flight. If anything happens that requires emergency care they can go ahead but I will decide what needs to be done when I get there. Just ask your husband to meet me at the airport.'

Sonia subsided in the face of Stephanie's firm tone and agreed to stay calm. They rang off. Stephanie was fully prepared to catch the next flight out. The ticket sat on top of her desk and a small case was packed and waiting in a corner of her office. She was unsure of what would be needed to handle the emergency but she made sure to carry all her identification. She included the power of attorney papers giving her the right to make decisions for Georgette. When they had gotten the legal documents signed at the lawyer earlier in the year after the death of her parents, she never thought it would have to be used. She tried to set aside any guilt about sending her friend to the Island for what she hoped was a holiday but it gnawed away at her insides.

She had a few calls to make. It was important to have a word with her son before leaving although she knew he wouldn't understand what was going on. Christian's voice was cheerful. They had not been parted since her honeymoon with Gregory. It was a wrenching decision to leave him. His sweet voice brought tears to her eyes but she knew that between Gregory, his two grandmothers, and Marguerite, he would be well cared for.

It had been unexpected but the most difficult call had been to Michael. She knew that if Georgette was coming home ill, she would need a physician to accept her. Georgette had always used

Traditional Chinese Medicine to maintain her health but doubted that Dr. Hang Ma, her acupuncturist, would be able to interact with the physician in Jamaica. She hoped that Michael could fill in and called him hurriedly.

'Michael, Georgette has collapsed in Jamaica. I don't know how serious it is. I want to be able to bring her home if she is stable. If the Doctor asks for a physician here would you accept his call?' The pause at the other end seemed interminable. 'Michael?'

'No Stefania.'

'No? What do you mean no?'

'No I won't accept her.' A frustrated silence followed his words.

'I am asking you to help a friend. I can't believe you would refuse.'

'Ask Raj. He will be more help to you.'

'Put me back to Patty. I'll talk to Raj.' Stephanie's tone was clipped. She said nothing further. Fatigue was setting in and she had no desire to get into a struggle with Michael. He had his reasons. Rajinder Dilip Singh was a young man who was among the early graduates of the new four-year Family Practice residency program at the University. He was more than capable and willing to accept Georgette. Raj assumed Michael felt too close to Georgette and did not question why he was being asked. He was a delightful young man. Stephanie breathed her thanks before ending the conversation.

No sooner had she ended the call than the secretary informed her that Gregory was waiting below to take her to the airport. She didn't have a minute to wonder not only about Michael's refusal but also his tone. The tears she held at bay all day could not be suppressed at the moment of her goodbye to Gregory. He held her tenderly, wishing her a safe flight. 'I'll miss you Sunny but I know you need to do this for Georgette. Call me when you get there and let me know if I can do anything.'

'I will. I love you,' she whispered before hurrying to the ramp for her departure gate.

Chapter 7:

Stephanie arrived in Montego Bay well into the night. She was tired and irritable, an unusual circumstance for her. Anxiety over the well being of her friend and the possibility of an extreme outcome left her quite shaky. Unable to sleep on the plane, she dragged herself through customs and immigration.

Baxter waited for her outside and was unable to prevent himself doing a double take. The women looked like sisters. He welcomed Stephanie with every courtesy just as he had done with Georgette. Unlike Georgette, she had many questions and probed for answers until complete understanding of one topic allowed her to move on to the next.

Sonia had prepared the second bedroom. As inviting as the bed appeared to be, Stephanie also spent some time gathering information from Sonia, hoping to piece together a clear picture of what happened. She needed to see it all in her mind's eye, just as if she had been there.

Stephanie declined any food other than a sweet drink to bolster her flagging energy. She made a quick call to Gregory before sinking into the welcoming depths of the bed. The low level air-conditioned room was just comfortable enough for her to sleep.

She rose early, ready to tackle the events of the day. Sonia informed her that she could not go to the hospital until the morning visiting hours. Stephanie put her frustration on hold. A quick dip in the inviting sea, helped to work off some of the anxiety which delays always generated in her. She seemed less sure, in the warm sunlight, what the day ahead would bring. The swim was invigorating and she returned to the house to prepare herself.

Stephanie dressed in a casual skirt and scooped neck top, covered with a short bolero jacket and slip on sandals. Sonia prepared a light meal of fresh fruits, island coffee and some fishcakes. It would be enough to sustain her for quite a while. Like Georgette, Stephanie ate well. They set out for the local hospital by midmorning. The government run facility seemed barely adequate for the burgeoning population who waited outside for some type of care. There were many stares in her direction. She smiled affably when some small children approached her cautiously. She bent over to touch their chubby faces. Their smiles reminded her of Christian. She wondered if he woke up asking where his mother was. Sharp calls drew the children scampering back to their mothers.

Sonia took her straight to the rectangular shaped ward room where beds were lined up against the windows down the length of the vast room. Nurses milled about tables in the centre area. They did their writing and charting in between patient care. Everyone looked up at her when she entered the room. Stephanie had no self consciousness about her height or looks. She had been a standout since the year she grew four inches and stood a flaming red head taller than everyone else in her class. Her eyes scanned the two rows for the trademark matching hair of her friend. Georgette lay, towards the end of the row on the left, unconscious on the bed, side rails up, her red hair fanned out around her in contrast to the white sheets and the pallor in her face.

Stephanie went to the side of the bed touching her friend's cold hand, hoping to infuse some animation into the sleeping body. There was not one sign of recognition. No amount of pleading or crying elicited even the slightest response. Sonia was able to procure a rickety wicker chair and encouraged her to sit. With a minimum of space between the beds for visitors she had to pull up her long legs. An IV ran into one arm and a bag was seen at the other side of the bed. *'In and out...what a sad condition to meet the needs of a flailing humanity?'* she thought. Looking up and down at other patients, she could see they were mostly elderly. Many suffered the same sad state of fluid going in one tube and out another. When she was able, Stephanie looked at the foot affected by the scorpion's sting but apart from a slight redness and swelling, there wasn't anything to see.

It seemed like hours before a young doctor came around to see her.

'I'm sorry about your friend Miss. My name is Doctor Hastings. We are not able to do much here. This is a small hospital with very little equipment. My plan is to transfer her to either Montego Bay or Kingston.'

'Which is the better hospital?'

'They are both good,' he bristled.

'I meant better equipped to deal with her needs.'

'Kingston.'

Stephanie knew that she had to tread carefully. She had no wish to offend anyone. People were sensitive, she was a foreigner and her own nerves were already on edge. Since her arrival, Georgette had not moved a muscle. The nurses, all dressed in white, checked her reflexes, turned her every couple of hours and rubbed her back. There had been no answering response to any of their ministrations. She turned her attention back to the doctor hopeful of an explanation for her condition. Clearly he did not want to talk.

'I will arrange transportation for her as soon as an ambulance is available. We will send her with a nurse. If you organize a ride, you can leave with her.'

Stephanie felt dismissed.

****

263

It was hours before the transportation was settled. Stephanie asked Sonia to return to the house and pack Georgette's clothes and bring both suitcases. She did not want to leave the hospital. She called Gregory's agent in Kingston and asked him to book her into a hotel as close to the University Hospital as possible. When the ambulance finally pulled into the entrance to pick up Georgette, Stephanie was ready.

On her honeymoon with Gregory, the happy couple did not spend time sightseeing. Their passionate love affair was an unquenchable fire. He was the only thing she wanted to see then. Now, as she settled back in the comfort of the car, the passing features of the island held her enthralled. She asked questions and occupied her time absorbing the beautiful vibrant colours so abundant everywhere. Sonia who was full of lore and history to match the passing towns entertained her as much during the drive as time would allow. She shared her plans with Stephanie. Baxter planned to stay in Kingston and assist her with transportation while Sonia would return with the help of another friend to St. Ann's Bay. She only needed to ensure that both Georgette and Stephanie were safely settled.

'We can't leave the house too long Miss Stephanie. The criminals watch the house all the time.'

'Will you be safe alone?'

'Yes Ma'am. Mi cousin will come fi stay. Him bad, yu see!'

Stephanie laughed, despite her grave concerns for Georgette. She truly enjoyed the local dialect. She was checked into the hotel while Baxter and Sonia made their own arrangements. Her suite was luxurious. Once settled, she put in a call to the shipping agent, Mr. Morris and thanked him profusely.

'Anything I can do to help,' he replied graciously.

She changed and waited for Baxter to return. He wasn't long in coming and took her immediately to the hospital. It wasn't far but the traffic was slow moving. Baxter seemed to know the University Hospital grounds pretty well and soon found a good parking spot. He escorted her to the ward where Georgette had been transferred.

It was much the same set up. Only the room was bigger and there were a few cubicles where four beds were walled off from the others. Georgette had been placed in one of these. Stephanie went to speak with the head nurse and found she was to be addressed as Sister Tappin. The introductions were very formal. It seemed as if everything followed a system similar to Britain. She mentally abandoned her Canadian cultural biases and remembered what life was like in England when she travelled there with her mother. She asked if it were possible to speak with the Doctor. Sister promised to try and get a hold of him but, as she cautioned, 'he is a busy man. It may not be until tomorrow.' Stephanie held her smile through the ache in her heart.

Perhaps things were not to be so bad after all. A short while later, a tall man with graying temples strode down the hall. The young nurse, caring for Georgette, came to call Stephanie from the bedside. She was taken to another room, likely someone's vacated office, just off the ward.

'I am Dr. Parsons, he said introducing himself. Are you a relative of Miss O'Malley?'

'We are not related by blood but she is my best friend and business partner.'

'I can't speak with you. I must talk with her relatives.'

'She has none. Both her parents died in the past year and she was an only child. I have a power of attorney allowing me to be responsible for her care in the absence of her own ability to do so.'

'Then you must go to the administration office and provide them with the information. I can't talk to you until that is settled.'

He turned on his heel and left. Stephanie seethed. Protocol!

She was directed to the offices but it was after hours. Someone else sent her to the registration desk but the clerk would only take the information needed for Georgette's admission. 'Sorry Ma'am

I can't help you. You must return in the morning and speak to the Registrar. The office opens at 8:30 a. m.' It was almost the last straw for Stephanie. She decided against spending any more time at the hospital. At the bedside, she hissed into Georgette's ear.

'I know you are doing this just to make me learn to be patient. You can stop now. I get it.'

She kissed the smooth forehead, squeezed the hand lying loosely on the top of the bed spread. For one moment it felt as if there was a return squeeze. Stephanie waited, hoping but nothing happened.

Back at the hotel, she made a few phone calls. Christian was delighted to hear his mother's voice but ended with a tearful sounding goodbye. Gregory quickly came on the line to cheer her up and get the latest news. The normalcy of their conversation allowed her to settle down for the night. Tomorrow was another day.

******

Stephanie took an early morning swim in the hotel pool. After a light breakfast she met Baxter in the lobby. They headed back to the hospital. She presented herself at the Registrar's office two minutes before opening and quickly took care of the documentation. She hoped to be at the bedside during morning rounds so that she could capture the elusive Dr. Parsons. When he eventually appeared, he looked as if she were the last person he wanted to see.

'Miss ….er?' Dr. Parsons queried.

'Mrs. Richmond.'

'Mrs. Richmond. Your…friend is not in a coma but she is certainly unconscious. She responds to painful stimuli but not normal interactions. She did not seem to have a concussion with the fall and the scorpion sting is not responsible for this prolonged loss of consciousness.'

'How do you know that Doctor?' In response to her question, the Doctor elevated his body slightly and drew in a deep breath.

Stephanie knew she had offended him again and tried to make amends with a clarification. 'I am not questioning your information; I just need to understand the difference.'

'Had it been a poisonous sting she would be dead. The paralysis from the venom does not distinguish between groups of muscles in her body. Her respiratory system would have shut down along with everything else and she would have stopped breathing.'

'I see. Thank you.' Stephanie felt the anxious tattoo of her own heart beat.

'My plan now is to do a brain scan and see if there is anything untoward inside her head. I will try to book it for today as well as some additional blood work. I will speak with you tomorrow again.'

'Thank you.'

An hour later, when her own rising blood pressure was under control she said goodbye to Georgette, this time whispering 'You better wake up soon. I am losing what little patience I acquired overnight.' She watched as her friend was wheeled down by stretcher to another part of the hospital. Georgette was accompanied by a nurse and Stephanie was instructed to wait.

Unable to sit still, she stepped outside to get some air. Baxter could sense the frustration flowing out of the young woman in waves. He took her to the Botanical Gardens located quite close to the hospital grounds. Stephanie passed the time walking around admiring the flowers. Many were named along with information about their use in health and healing. It was a calming time. She thanked Baxter for his thoughtfulness and accepted his suggestion of a quick lunch at a restaurant nearby.

She returned to the hospital, ready to sit, read and be silent until it was time for her to return to the hotel. To her surprise, Dr. Parsons returned to the unit to speak with her in the early evening. His face was not comforting. He spoke with her, standing slightly away from the bed.

'Mrs. Richmond, your friend has a brain tumour. It is a pituitary tumour and seems to be growing. Has she been having headaches?'

'Well yes. That was the reason for the vacation. She complained all the time about the pounding head. I thought she was just....'

'Did she have any other symptoms?'

'What are the symptoms of a brain tumour? What would I be looking for? Is it cancer?'

'I don't know at this point but usually they are not. Did she have any other symptoms?'

'No...I don't know...She seemed as healthy as a horse. I don't know what was abnormal for her, other than her menstrual cycles.' Stephanie was getting agitated. Her hands moved in all directions.

'That's what I mean. There are several kinds of reactions with this type of tumour. We need to identify which one of her hormones was affected.'

'Can this be done in Canada?'

'Canada? Are you serious? The woman is unconscious. You will not get any airline to accept her and I will not release her in this condition.'

'Doctor, I have a 2 ½ year old child at home, a business to run because my partner is lying in a hospital bed, and a very patient husband. If she can return to Canada I will see that she gets treatment.'

'And I will not release an unconscious patient. Nor will any airlines take her.'

'That would be the least of my problems. I can't stay here indefinitely and I am not leaving her.'

At that moment both heard a distinct moan from the bed. They stopped arguing and went to bed side. Georgette was moving her head back and forth. 'St...nie....ste..nie.'

'I'm here Georgy. Come back, honey. Come back please. I miss you.'

The Doctor called for a nurse. They unceremoniously pushed Stephanie aside. He ran through a series of tests, looking into her eyes and testing reflexes before smiling for the first time.

'Seems she is coming round, at last. Well.'

Stephanie said nothing. Georgette looked around frantically before settling bloodshot eyes on her best friend. She smiled through pale, dry lips and nodded. Tears fell from Stephanie eyes.

'Am I ever glad to see you,' she wailed, taking the limp hand and pressing it to her face.

'Whe...am...I?'

'I'll explain in a minute Georgy. Just take it easy. I am going to stay with you, and talk if that's ok with the Doctor.'

'We'll let her rest for now. I am going to have the nurses put an hourly watch on her tonight. Don't stay long but use your time to reassure her.'

Stephanie did just that, holding the hand, crying off and on. She kept her information to a minimum, not relating anything the doctor had said earlier. If there was indeed a large tumour which needed attention, it was up to him to share the news with her. Stephanie just wanted to get her home.

****

Two days later, the pair was just about set to depart from Jamaica. Many things had to fall into place. Gregory called in a couple of IOU's and arranged a private jet to fly them both home, with a nurse onboard. Dr. Parson's relented a little when he saw how efficiently Stephanie handled herself. She organized long distance calls allowing him to speak first to Raj and then to an Endocrinologist at Toronto's largest hospital. They arranged for Georgette to be transported directly from the airport to the hospital by ambulance. Georgette wasn't happy about having to remain confined at the hospital until the time of departure. The Doctors were taking no chances on a relapse. She subsided into a brooding pout. If asked, she would have to admit that she was feeling weak. All of the adventures in Jamaica, since her arrival to the unorthodox departure, did nothing to alleviate the headache. 'It would have been worth all the trouble if the annoyance of constant pain was gone,' she had confided to her friend while they waited for the discharge.

The plane cleared the northern shore of Cuba before either Stephanie or Georgette was finally able to relax.

'This has certainly been a challenge. Are you comfortable Georgy?'

'Not in the least. I am deeply grateful for your intervention. I don't know if I would ever have awakened without hearing your fighting voice penetrate the mists in my mind. Talk about the valley of the shadows. I am pretty sure I know what that means now. I'm happy to be out of it. I am, however, worried about the future.'

'I can't reassure you Georgette. I know nothing about what's going on in your head. Raj has taken care of everything back home. He will see you shortly after you get in.'

Georgette longed to ask about Michael. She didn't. Instead, she allowed the gentle rocking of the jet to lull her into a restful sleep. What lay ahead hung heavily on her mind but she pushed it away, trusting in the wisdom of specialists to guide her care.

Chapter 8:

A bright sun flooded her window, casting a stream of light across her yellow bedspread, but Georgette sensed the halcyon days of summer passing quickly. It was already into mid-September and the slight chill of autumn hung in the air during the darkening evenings. Georgette had blossomed in the tropical breezes of the Island. Warmed by the climate, her normally cool skin felt comforted by the dry heat. The air-conditioned room in the large downtown Toronto hospital was a far cry from the ward unit in Jamaica. Its comforts were unmistakable but she felt chilled to the bone and isolated. There were times when the silence was healing. She was able to engage her thoughts and work through the mess her life had become. At other times she longed for quiet undemanding company. She was dismayed to realize there were so few people in her life who could be good company for her.

During the five days since she was transferred from the Island in a sleek private jet, she had been prodded and poked, x-rayed and scanned until she felt as if there was not one part of her body which had not been on display. The neurosurgeon handling her case was due any moment to discuss the overall results of the tests. Georgette hoped to be able to go home. Nothing was certain until she heard from the doctor but every footstep in the hall left her wary. The idea of a tumour was still new. It was already clear that there would never be any guarantees about its status. She did not relish the idea of surgery but mentally agreed to wait for all the results before committing herself to anything.

When the knock came, she was almost certain that deep inside, she could handle any news bad or good.

'Come in!' she called out in response.

'Good morning, Miss O'Malley. I am Dr. Erin Dawson, an endocrinologist. We have a few things to talk about. I spoke with the neurosurgeon this morning and he will be in to see you later. Are you feeling any better?

'I am thank you. The headaches have subsided quite a lot. I am grateful for that.'

'Excellent! Now, as we have hinted you have a Pituitary tumour. It has affected your Prolactin levels. I am quite surprised that you have not sought help before this. Usually fertility issues bring women into care.'

Georgette shrugged. She had heard all this before. 'I used to have irregular periods but I had a D&C years ago in England and the doctor put me on the pill. I just get a new prescription at the walk-in clinic every year. I haven't had any fertility issues.'

'Have you not had your regular Pap tests and breast exams.'

'I understood that I didn't need to, if I am not sexually active.'

'Well, that's true but only if you have never been sexually active. Are you saying you...?'

'Yes. I have never..... until... very recently.' Georgette hated the frown which marred the eyebrows of the doctor. '*Was it a sin not to have sex?*' she thought.

'OK so you are saying you never tried to get pregnant or had any relations with men?'

'That's what I am saying.'

'So you would not have noticed anything unusual about your body or breasts?'

'No. Only the headaches.' Now the look was comical.

'I see. Well this type of tumour usually produces a whole set of symptoms, including non pregnant lactation, decreased libido and infertility. Perhaps you have not felt attracted to anyone?'

'Not really...well.... Until recently.'

'Must have been a powerful attraction?' The eyebrows rose significantly.

'Pardon me?'

'I'm sorry to be so personal but in this day and age these symptoms would not have gone unnoticed for quite so long. I believe you are almost 36 years old?'

Georgette nodded. She began to feel more and more like an oddity. She tried to pay attention while the doctor spoke to her but thoughts drifted towards Michael. *'Powerful attraction indeed!'* One she could not even cope with. She struggled to focus on the final words.

'We are going to use medication to try and reduce the tumour. I will start you out on a dosage which I think will help. You will do follow up blood work with Dr. Singh every week and I will see you in about six to eight weeks. Obviously if things do not improve, we will look at other options.'

Dr. Dawson smiled, patted the hand on the bed and left. Georgette felt like a teenager. Later, the Surgeon came in and repeated much the same story. He hoped not to have to operate but would seriously consider going ahead if the tumour growth did not stop or if there were any further episodes of unexplained unconsciousness. Georgette only wanted to get home. If she was sick at all, the cause now seemed to be her confinement and the repetitive information.

By late afternoon, Stephanie picked her up. She had been away from her condo for almost a month. It had been the planned length of her vacation but she still shook her head at the way life can change in such a short time. Her friend seemed inclined to linger, watchful of any uncertainty.

'I'm fine Stephanie. Really. I don't want anyone to stay with me' she said, hoping for time alone to readjust to all the changes.

273

'Ok, I won't push. Your housekeeper has left some precooked food. You just need to warm it up when you are ready. Call me if you need to talk at anytime but just give me a quick heads up in the morning if all is well. Call Raj, if you feel sick.'

Georgette nodded, knowing that concern prompted the instructions. The friends and partners shared a long hug before Stephanie made her own way to Oakville.

****

Georgette was convinced to stay home for a few more days. She tried doing a little work at the condo and found she quite liked the peace and quiet. The staff needed protocols for a new contract and the home ambience of safety and comfort allowed her to work undisturbed, setting her own pace. She was not able to drive and took to walking along the lake front in the evenings. At the end of a week her self-imposed isolation was beginning to bore her. She returned to the office quietly and without fanfare. She certainly felt better physically. Emotionally there was still a bit of a roller coaster internally but she set it aside focusing on her own health and wellbeing and the work needing to be done.

She realized it was also time for her to get blood work done as the Specialist requested. Her secretary Yolanda was asked to pick up the requisition from the doctor's office but Georgette knew she could not avoid going there for results. It was getting to be quite a challenge, pretending not to care that a momentous event occurred in her life. Everything about the tumour and its effects on her emotions and body seemed to centre on sex and reproductive organs. She couldn't escape the shaft of emotional light piercing, with laser precision, into her deepest self, turned on by a man who surely did not want to see her ever again.

Yolanda was also instructed to call Patty, the receptionist at Michael's office, to find out the days when Dr. Singh would be alone in the office. Clearly there were other days when both men would be seeing patients. Avoiding them was critical to her. Facing Michael anywhere would be a problem. She wasn't sure if she could pull off a face to face meeting. Judging by her behaviour after their interlude, she had no certainty about her reactions if confronted by someone who occupied so much of her thoughts. Fear held her tightly and she couldn't understand why.

Wednesday was deemed to be the safest day to visit. Georgette kept her appointment, feeling confident that she would not have to deal with Michael. In his consulting rooms, Raj seemed surprised that she did not ask about his partner even as a social courtesy. He kept silent and remained professionally focused on her concerns and results. He had not discussed Georgette with Michael at all after Stephanie's first phone call thinking that their rift was professional and not personal, a circumstance he respected.

'Georgette, I am so happy to see you. It was quite a frightening time for you.'

'It was. I am happy to report that I am feeling better. My headaches are down to manageable discomfort and I have energy again.'

She had not seen Raj in his office before and he took an extensive history. Once again she felt like she had to defend her right not to be sexually active.

'Not everyone feels the need to jump into bed at every turn. I never have.'

'Don't get me wrong. I am all for abstinence as a choice but a lack of normal desire or low libido could have been caused by the tumour.'

'I'll keep that in mind as I discover the new me.'

She tried to keep things light. Raj was pleased with her progress and told her so. She just needed to follow up each week to ensure her blood hormone levels remained normal.

Georgette opened his door cautiously, expecting Michael to be waiting in the outer room, ready to pounce on her. He wasn't. As she made her way down the hall, a little disappointment surfaced unbidden. She pressed the button for the elevator trying to avoid processing its meaning. She stood head bent waiting for its arrival. The door would open and swallow her up….keep her safe from

Michael. The prospect was suddenly more scary than meeting him face to face.

****

At the other end of the corridor, Michael opened the door to the stairs exit. He had been on another floor in the large office building discussing a new case with a colleague. One of his patients had been admitted to hospital in serious condition and he needed to check her file. The shock he felt seeing Georgette standing at the other end of the hall, caused him to draw back.

The vision of her created a reactionary pain in his chest, and their last words burned in him. It was like the days of his youth when he ran from gunfire in the streets of Hungary hiding behind walls, fearful of a bullet, just like those which killed his parents. He could not understand how someone he desired so much got tied into the traumatic stress of his childhood. He focused his energy on stilling the pain and breathing evenly.

Michael was relieved that she had not seen his foolish behaviour. He opened the door more cautiously and peered down to where she stood, erect, long hair in a 'swept up' pony tail, the very essence of elegant beauty. His heart beat faster at the sight of her, despite the childish anger which kept him away. He was disappointed when she did not turn around. She was safely in the elevator before he felt able to enter his office wondering how he had gotten himself into this mess.

'Michael, you just missed Georgette. She was here for her first appointment.' Raj spoke naturally despite some misgivings at the wisdom of exploring the unspoken rift between these two old friends.

'That's good. I hope she's feeling better.' His tone did not indicate if he cared one way or another.

Raj frowned but asked to speak with Michael in his office.

'You haven't asked about her. Is there anything you want to know?' He paused giving Michael an opportunity to say something. 'Surgery seems to be off the table for now. It would be a shame to cut that beautiful hair,' he concluded weakly seeing no interest in his partner.

Michael frowned. 'She's your patient Raj. Do what you have to do independent of me. I have no need to be kept aware of her condition or progress.'

'I respect patient confidentiality but I thought you were friends.'

'We were friends.' The tone did not invite any clarification. His face was stonier than the sharp retort.

Raj chose not to intrude further on what was clearly a personal matter. He was not to know that Michael wished with all his heart to speak with someone. Pride held him silent. 'I have to go Raj. Doctor Basine is waiting for me.'

The young doctor was puzzled by the response but did not make any further comment. He had heard Michael talk often of her before. The little boy who was their Godson seemed to be the apple of both pairs of eyes. He shrugged and returned to his next patient.

Michael went into his office hating himself but unable to control his churlish behaviour. *'What had she done? Not called him? It wasn't a crime. She was busy getting ready to go away.'* He rationalized trying to find forgiveness in his heart. When he heard that she had been desperately ill, he behaved like a callous schoolboy. Michael knew that he was upsetting Stefania and now Raj but old habits die hard and his heart had learned searing lessons early and painfully. He collected the chart from his files and returned upstairs.

****

Michael wasn't the only one wrestling with the unspoken but apparent rift between him and Georgette. Stephanie had just about enough. She complained long and bitterly to her husband but was advised to keep out of the relationship.

'How can I Gregory when I love them both so much? Georgette acts as if nothing has happened and Michael just backs off if I attempt to bring up anything.'

It was late in the evening. Stephanie was seated at her dresser brushing the long red gold hair. Gregory sat propped up on the king sized bed, surveying his wife performing her nightly ritual. The effort, in tandem with her overactive emotion was producing only flyaway strands, catching the electricity from the air with each of the long strokes.

'They are adults and need to work it out together.' Gregory sighed wishing some of the energy could be directed towards him.

'How can they if they won't speak to each other?' Stephanie turned to face her husband, not intending to argue but needing to get his point of view.

'Maybe you're seeing something that isn't there.'

'I would love to agree with you, my darling, but my intuition tells me that they have lost something important between them. My only hope is that Georgette will come around now that she feels better.'

'My only hope right now is that you will come to bed and cuddle with me. You use up far too much energy worrying. Time is a great healer. You keep your lines of communication open with them but promise me you won't do anything to push them either way.'

'Alright but….' Stephanie laughed as she turned back to the mirror and surveyed the odd halo around her head.

'Come on my angel,' he said extending his hand. 'You are the only red head I want to think about at the moment.'

'Titian Gregory, titian.'

'Gesundheit,' he laughed before capturing her in his arms. Gregory effectively cut off any further 'buts'.

****

Georgette paced the floor of her apartment. She did feel better in many ways. The days had passed into weeks and with each time frame she was more and more aware of subtle improvements in her sense of well-being. Her energy levels continued to rise giving her a clearer perspective on the life she led. Georgette had to admit to herself that she had only been half alive. Now that her body was returning to a normal hormonal phase, she wondered how she could have tolerated her self-imposed celibacy and retreat from intimacy.

Her only lover had been a one shot experience which she now regretted, but only because in a moment of sheer sensuality, she had allowed herself a glimpse of the real thing. It was too beautiful not to want more. Powerful feelings for Michael lay beneath the surface of their apparent indifferent relationship. She had dated extensively in the past, sidestepping intimacy with a wide array of excuses designed to keep amorous suitors at bay. *'What am I to do now?'* she asked herself in the mirror each morning and each night.

It was but a few days later when Georgette received a call from a friend. She had been a popular, well informed, dinner companion. It wasn't an unusual circumstance to receive an invitation, but timely to her current state of mind.

'Georgette, Pascal here. I tried to reach you at the office but they told me you weren't in today.'

'Nice to hear from you Pascal. I am working from home this afternoon. When did you get in?'

She made small talk in her usual polite manner. Georgette knew he would want to meet with her. Pascal had not seen the new and improved version, recently emerged from behind the shadow of the tumour. *'Would it make a difference?'* she asked herself.

'I wonder if you would have dinner with me tonight. No show or gallery opening, just a delightful meal at the restaurant of your choice.'

Georgette never prevaricated. She loved good food and quickly named a seafood establishment downtown. Pascal was agreeable. He would book the table and send her flowers as always.

Choosing the right outfit for the evening was challenging. Since the death of her parents she had disdained all outfits in black. She did not want to look as if she were in mourning. Suddenly, the colour looked very inviting. Choosing a sheath type dress with a high pseudo mandarin collar, it satisfied her picky evening dress code. There were some light gathers at the shoulder. An oval shaped opening from her collar to mid-spine revealed soft tantalizing skin and a back slit showed a length of leg when she walked.

Nervous fingers quickly twisted the long hair into a double opposing knot, stylishly decorated with two hair sticks her mother had purchased in Hong Kong years before. She looked elegant, sophisticated and untouchable. She would not admit to wanting to end the evening at the restaurant door. Georgette was fearful of changing her ways just yet.

Pascal Meloche was a former client of the Agency who used her services during negotiations with a Chinese manufacturer. The wealthy Montreal businessman had asked her out years ago and she declined pointedly.

'Our office rules prevent me from establishing any other relationship with clients.'

'You are the boss. You can make or break the rules,' he rejoined.

'Georgette grew cold. 'I'm the boss. I set the example. When our business concludes, talk to me then.'

Only a man with supreme confidence could have withstood her icy tone. Pascal feared no one. He called her again and she agreed to a social evening only. It had been the first of many. Pascal was married. It was understood that she was to be a social friend and only if he was visiting in Toronto. After a couple of years of infrequent visits, he changed the rules and pressed her to enter into a long term affair. They parted company. Her very firm 'no' was unassailable. She had missed his cultured presence at the very kind of events which she enjoyed but she was uncompromising. If he wanted their friendship to continue it would have to remain purely platonic.

As Pascal watched her walk towards him, he wondered how he could have let her go. There was an elusive quality about her. He could not define it. The air of quiet confidence which she exuded was powerfully seductive. His heart beat faster. Clearly much had changed for both of them. Pascal's warm greeting was open and inviting.

'You look as elegant and beautiful as ever.' he murmured in a cultured Parisian French, kissing both her flushed cheeks.

'Thank you, Pascal and thank you for the flowers. They cheered me up immensely.'

'Were you sad? Come and eat. A little food goes a long way. I am looking forward to our evening.'

Georgette smiled and allowed the hand at her back to guide her to the secluded table.

How she managed to deftly avoid personal topics throughout dinner was a miracle. Pascal was inclined to talk about his family and she encouraged him to share information about his children. The meal was as delicious as expected and passed without any awkward moments. She began to feel some discomfort knowing that she would have to make a decision by the end of the evening.

Georgette had taken a taxi to the restaurant. Pascal did not drive. Leaving together would have been an open consent to extend the evening at her place or his hotel.

'I'd like to talk a little more Georgette. Can we go somewhere else?'

'They have a lounge upstairs. We could get a coffee for me and a drink for you.' She welcomed the reprieve.

Pascal clearly had something else in mind but acquiesced to her wishes. He escorted her upstairs. Once seated, he smiled at her across the low set coffee table.

'There have been some major changes in my life, since we last met Georgette. My oldest son has taken over the day to day operations of the company. I have more free time and ..... I wanted to travel more than I have in the past.'

Pascal had hinted as much during their dinner talk. Georgette's heart sank. He was truly a kind generous man but she had no desire to be any man's plaything. A strained smile began to crack at the edges.

'My wife has also indicated a need to have a new lifestyle. We are divorcing Georgette. Will that..... make a difference to you?'

She was stunned by the news. Men in his position didn't divorce their wives. She stared at his immaculate white shirt. Clearly, it was hand-made. His suit fit him perfectly. He had abundant hair for a man in his early fifties. Her gaze returned to the perfection of the white shirt. It was replaced by the vision of a rumpled casual sport shirt, well past its prime. She hated to make comparisons and wondered if the tumour was altering her visual field. The shirt changed colour, started to wrinkle and bundle up around his waist. It turned into a scuff marked mess, which she longed to remove from its owner's heated body. She blinked once to stop the mind movie.

'Georgette?'

'I heard your question Pascal. What I know is that I can't live in 'what ifs'. The here and now is what sustains me. You are still not free. So....to answer your question, it would make a difference, but can't at this time because it is not real. You are not yet free.

'I see.' Experience taught him that her answer was final. 'Are you ready to go?'

'I am. If you ask the concierge to call a cab for me, I'll be fine.'

Georgette didn't need to wonder if her evening with Pascal would leave her in tears. It didn't. She was wholly satisfied with her decision.

Chapter 9:

Over the next few days, Georgette gave a lot of consideration to her resolution. From her experience with Pascal, Georgette understood that she did not want to date a married man nor wait for a divorce. She watched Stephanie negotiate that bumpy road. Her friend had loved Gregory and managed her tumultuous year with dignity. Gregory's first wife relocated to Italy and played no part in the courtship. Pascal's wife may have wanted to leave him but who knew the truth of it. She slept with a clear conscience and planned to move ahead with her life. She did not love Pascal enough to make the sacrifice.

It was wonderful to be free and able to make decisions based on her choices rather than being driven by hormones which altered her perception of everything. She had a notable ease in all relationships but one. She also understood that her best friend was worried and concerned by her continued efforts to avoid personal issues in their daily conversations. Georgette admitted as much to herself deftly sidestepping opportunities to get the problem out in the open. It was mid-October when she was faced with a challenge to her friendship with Stephanie. Caught behind the desk in her office late on the Thursday before the holiday, she was dismayed to look up and see her business partner framed in the doorway. The look in Stephanie's eyes was insistent. Georgette knew as well as anyone that whatever she wanted, it would not be denied.

'Are you going to let me spend Thanksgiving alone?'
Alone?

There was a moment of silence. A battle of wills was underway.

Stephanie, you know that I am still trying to work my way through these changes I'm feeling. I am not really up to being around anyone.

'Anyone? like….me?'

'Well not you but…everyone…you know.'

'I said I would be alone.'

Georgette knew that was a blatant lie and frowned to say what her lips could not.

'Uncle Ken is having hip surgery and Helen is going to England to look after him until his daughter can take some time off work.'

A raised eyebrow acknowledged the words and questioned the unmentioned and obvious other member of the family.

'There is a Japanese ship coming in with some serious concerns about the cargo and crew. It will be in Halifax over the weekend and Gregory has to fly down to meet with the ship's Captain and the local agent.'

Georgette felt her heart sink. Surely Stephanie could not be telling the truth. She lifted her head to silently ask about the one person who really mattered.

'Michael is on call and has to stay in Toronto.'

Georgette visibly relaxed although few would have been able to decipher the body language. 'I suppose even you couldn't make up all that. Ok. I will drive down with you on Friday.'

'No! I will come in and pick you up on Saturday. I have to take Helen and Gregory to the airport on Friday.'

'I am sorry Stephanie. Do you think I am being silly?'

'I don't know what's going on with you and I won't press you to share if you don't want to. It will just be a quiet weekend, maybe a drive in the country, a light meals and conversation ….about anything.'

It was indeed just that. Stephanie did not interrogate her friend in any way. Christian was happy to have his Tante visiting. They played games like old friends. She sang with him and told him funny stories. Watching them together, Stephanie knew that Georgette was merging the woman, who loved her godson, with the woman who ran a business. She liked what she saw. The rift with Michael was a troubling aspect of Georgette's healing but she did not allow the fallout to intrude on the weekend.

Marguerite, who had been sent home to spend the holidays with her family, returned on the holiday Monday. She found lots of things to keep Christian busy while the two business women spent a long time discussing strategy and action for the coming year. Stephanie had plans to add to her family but intended to put it on hold until Georgette was fully recovered. They both agreed that the business was currently at capacity. Adding resources or contracts would not be wise unless they took in another partner. Georgette was willing to wait, feeling that the present compliment of staff could handle anything without undue stress. The discussion brought back some painful memories.

'I will never understand how I could have left you alone. I allowed myself to get so caught up in Peter's control that I lost sight of the important things in life.'

'No...I think you did what any woman would have done to make her marriage work. It is impossible to know how we will behave when emotions drive us. I am just finding out what that really means Stephanie.'

'Don't hurt yourself in the process Georgy. I had to make some tough choices. I would have liked a better emotional balance to deal with that year of my life and yet I survived. You will too. There comes a time when it all makes sense. Only you will know when the time arrives.'

Georgette was to ponder those words long after she returned to her condo. It had been a weekend in which she seemed to gain some equilibrium. For awhile, she was able to return to a relationship with Stephanie similar to the one they shared before her first marriage. The freedom to talk openly and honestly had always marked their time together. Stephanie remained true to her word. She neither probed nor searched for hidden meanings. They achieved a consensus about work related issues but most importantly Georgette sensed that whatever decisions she made about her relationship with Michael, she would be supported.

****

Seven weeks after her discharge from hospital she repeated some of the more extensive tests and returned to the specialist for a follow up appointment. There was no doubt about the improvement. Georgette and the Doctor both agreed that the changes were hopeful. Surgery was put on hold as long as progress continued. Dr. Dawson only adjusted the dose of her medication and wished Georgette a happy holiday.

Despite the weather changes Georgette failed to realize how quickly the weeks leading up to the Christmas season loomed. She had spent so much time out of the office working from home, designing new protocols that she let go of her need to be aware of every moment of every day. How nice it was to just sit and allow the days to meld one into the other, she thought.

As she began to immerse herself in shopping, Georgette also realized that she had an enormous decision to make. Her only family, Stephanie and Gregory, were also Michael's only family. The Thanksgiving weekend, alone with Stephanie, was a rare opportunity that would not be repeated at Christmas. Michael would not be on call. She had no idea how to gracefully bow out of a tradition established from years of friendship. Christian would also be celebrating his 3rd birthday. His two godparents were insolvent. It was going to make a very challenging holiday season.

****

In his office, Michael also sat and contemplated the upcoming holiday season. He spent the fall months brooding a lot about his life. Work had always been a panacea to his inner turmoil. No amount of effort could still the churning inside of him. Christmas with Georgette was impossible. He had said too much, revealed secrets to her. He had no wish to expose himself even further to her whims. He conceded that she had been ill, but not too ill to accept his desire. He also conceded that he could love her. He did, in fact, know his heart was already fully engaged. In those moments of deep intimacy he had seen her vulnerability. His mind closed to its seductive pull. His thoughts returned to the feel of her sharp tongue and biting wit. It had often driven him to anger over the years though he would not admit it openly.

He wondered what it was that drew him to women who exposed their vulnerability. His compassion for them was part of the drive which made his practice so successful. On the other hand, he was cowed by women of power even as he admired them. He tried to conjure up a picture of Angela, his cheating wife. She had used tears on him over and over to hide her feigned weakness and infidelity. By the time of the divorce he could see that she was a scheming, dispassionate immoral woman. Georgette was none of those things and yet he could not let go and allow himself the freedom to love her openly. Fear held him tightly. He couldn't identify its source but the façade was crumbling leaving him exposed.

Michael could not excuse himself from attending the celebration of his Godson's birthday. No excuse would ever be sufficient to wipe the hurt from Stefania's face and Helen's heart. Try as he might, he could not conjure up the courage to face either Stefania or Georgette.

****

Back in St. Ann's Bay, Sonia was happy to learn from their US agent that the house had been rented again. She had been very distressed by the events surrounding her last client. She had liked

Georgette, welcomed her into the family. The way in which her visit ended haunted Sonia constantly. It had been delightful. Georgette's fall left her feeling uncertain about the responsibility of caring for strangers. She had almost convinced herself to return to work in the shop in Moneague and let Mary manage the house. A card, sent by Georgette, thanking them for their help and support and sending her best wishes to Missy Song did much to restore Sonia's confidence. The weeks of respite allowed her to get a better perspective on the mishap and put it behind her.

With a happy heart she went to prepare the bedroom for the next couple who would be coming. She removed the protective counterpane which covered the mattress and spread out the fitted bottom sheet. As she tucked in the corner near the headboard, a piece of paper which had been stuck between the headboard and mattress fell to the floor. Sonia bent down and stuck her hand under the bed to grab, what turned out to be an envelope. It was fully addressed but not sealed properly. She felt no temptation to open it. The man's name included the title Doctor. She felt the information was confidential.

If she had any qualms at all, it was to decide if she should mail the letter to the addressee. She thought not. Sonia was pretty certain that the letter originated with Georgette. Unfortunately all the arrangements for Georgette's vacation had been made by Stephanie Richmond. At the time of the fall, Sonia had been grateful to have Mrs. Richmond's number. The tall woman with the striking red hair was an amazing organizer. *'Perhaps,'* Sonia thought, *'she will also be the best person to ensure that the letter reaches its appropriate destination'*. She was unable to make the decision herself. With letter in hand, Sonia dialed the Richmond home in Oakville.

****

Some days later, Stephanie sat in her office. Three years ago she had been in exactly the same position when a call from her late husband startled her out of a reverie. Almost 24 hours later he would be dead and their son would be born prematurely. On the anniversary date, Gregory, who had been a part of her life then, would take the little boy and his grandmother, Helen to some event. She was left to pass the day however she wished.

For the third year she found herself at the office wondering yet again if there was anything she could have done to save her troubled husband. She had been told often enough that he was beyond help. Even as she understood it intellectually, emotionally it was impossible to let go of a need to analyze the impact on her life. She still dedicated this time to him each year.

A retrospective of the good and bad times of their marriage eased her initial feelings of guilt. At the end of the evening she would light a candle for him at the local church. In a few days time the family would travel north to visit Christian's great grandfather. Despite his ill health, he lingered on buoyed by the birth of his last living relative.

Stephanie tried without success to focus on the energy of her dead husband and could not. She knew her body's natural healing was part of it. Gregory's love had done much to restore her faith and strength but she was clearly puzzled and deeply troubled by the rift between her son's godparents. Her mind refused to let go of its insistent intrusion. The celebration of his birthday was officially held on Christmas Eve, the day after his arrival home from the hospital but she was no further ahead in getting a firm commitment from either Michael or Georgette.

The envelope lying in a desk drawer, newly arrived by courier from Jamaica, continued to be a distraction. Georgette had written to Michael at some time before she collapsed. Did the letter contain words of peace or conflict, love or hate? She picked up the phone on her desk and engaged in a short conversation ending with a few final terse words.

'Nothing that you are doing or plan to do is as important as what I have to say. I'm in my office. I'll see you here within the hour.' Stephanie took a gamble. She hoped it would pay off.

Within the hour she heard footsteps and a soft knock. Stephanie waited for a face to appear.

'Come in Michael.'

She got up from her seat and went around the desk to welcome her friend and physician with the traditional greeting. She returned to her chair behind the desk. She had no fear of her childhood 'brother' but he was older and always had an age advantage over her. This office however, was her turf and she intended to use it to bolster her sagging confidence. The summer holiday which had left Michael looking so much younger and vital had waned and the perpetual stooping shoulders were back in place as if carrying the weight of the world. Refusing to get sidetracked by pity, she stretched out her arm and invited him to sit in the comfortable chair on the opposite side of her desk.

'I am very impressed Stefania. It seems impossible to imagine that I have not been here before.'

'Are you on call tonight?' This was a business meeting. She wanted to avoid the personal. She responded in English to his Hungarian.

'No Stefania.'

She stared at him, a half smile tilting the corners of her mouth and plunged on. 'It would take a blind man less time to see what is happening here, than you and my best friend. I grow weary of dodging the ball in your cat and mouse games.'

'I don't know what you mean.'

'Indeed you do Michael. Listen to me.' Stephanie got up from her seat and moved to the front of the desk to plead her case. 'I love you more dearly than if you had been my own biological brother. I don't mind if you and Georgette weren't meant to be lovers but you need to be friends.'

'She has made it clear, she wants nothing from me.'

'And you have made it clear that you don't want to challenge that assumption.'

'That is not fair!'

'You are a man and a physician. Let the physician in you guide your fear, past the effects of her illness, to the man who clearly loves her.'

'Who told you that?'

'You did!'

'No!'

'Oh yes Michael. Georgette asked me to translate something for her. The words came from your mouth even though she never said so. It was a colloquialism which she could not translate. *Ami amire szuksege van ram.*'

'I didn't think she heard me.'

'That's very naive of you. Look at the business we do. Georgette can inhale a language at the drop of a hat. She has heard me speaking Hungarian for years. She could have looked up a standard phrase in any language dictionary.'

Michael looked away. Now it was his turn to look sheepish. Stephanie continued to plead her case slipping into their language when she sensed a softening.

'Miklos Basci, when Papa died, you held me in your arms and gave me comfort and strength beyond your own pain. I know that Angela hurt you badly but she wanted a doctor not a husband. You were too blinded by her beauty to see the obvious. Georgette is as deserving of your patience as I was. What she doesn't deserve is your contempt. You should have saved that for Angela.'

'My God Stefania! You don't know how much I want to believe they are not the same.'

'You fool. They are only the same in the stubborn part of your brain.'

Michael chuckled. This little 'sister' of his knew how to fight. 'When did you get so tough?'

'You forget that I was not only Piotr Droga's daughter. Helen Brownrigg is also my mother.'

Stephanie got up from the chair facing Michael and returned to the seat behind the desk. She felt satisfied with the way she handled things so far. Michael was not angry. She pulled open a drawer, extracting the white envelope.

'This letter was sent from Jamaica. Georgette must have written it, but in the mess after her collapse, it got lost or forgotten. I have not read it. Only Georgette knows the contents but it is addressed to you. Read it or return it! The choice is yours.'

Michael took the envelope and noted his name and office address carefully written in Georgette's beautiful hand. He longed to hold the paper to his face and caress the beautiful handwriting, seeking the scent from her body.

'Where was it found? Or do you know?'

'Behind the bed, if it matters. Now my dear friend, I must go to church. I will light a candle for Peter, but I will also light one for you and Georgette. I will see you December 24th! You have ten days to make things right.'

Michael felt like a small child who had been scolded and dismissed. He wasn't angry but humbled by the certainty that he had been as culpable as Georgette in their estranged relationship. If he had no ties to her it wouldn't have mattered but he did share an enduring relationship with Christian as well as deep feelings. He needed to stop hiding behind the shield of fear which permeated his personal life.

****

Georgette walked purposefully along the avenue leading to her apartment. It was late but she felt confident. Christmas lights twinkled all around her as people were preparing for the holidays. Decorated apartment balconies, vied with store front Christmas scenery, all visual temptations to participate in the festivities. There was so much to see.

She had been to the mall department store where she had purchased her fun tropical wardrobe back in the summer, before the fateful trip. Georgette needed nothing new but longed to interact with the salesgirl who lifted her spirits months ago. Her recovery was progressing and she was no longer depressed but living without the constant pressure in her head and see-saw of emotions required adjustments. In some ways she was testing her new persona in similar circumstances to assess changes in her behaviour, much as she had done with Pascal.

The young lady hadn't been there. Disappointed, Georgette decided to walk through the store, marveling at the shoppers bargain hunting for the holidays. She realized the futility of wasting time walking aimlessly, looking at nothing, simply because in reality she didn't want to be alone. Frustrated by the crowds whose very presence increased her loneliness she turned to retrace her steps when her eye caught sight of a winter coat and hat, hanging in one of those large wall sconces. She went closer to touch the edges and feel the soft material.

'That coat was made for you Miss.'

Georgette turned to respond to the comment. She felt as if she had stepped back in time. A young woman whose unmistakable Jamaican lilt urged her to try on the outfit was a younger replica of Sonia.

'Are you Jamaican?'

'I am. Are you too?'

Georgette smiled. Before her trip, she would have thought the question absurd. 'No I was there recently. You remind me of my hostess.'

The young lady smiled. 'Do you like the coat Miss?'

'I do.' Georgette knew the sales staff was paid on commission. She didn't need a coat, but the situation was surreal. In the back of her mind the words of Missy Song echoed. Her admonishment to step out of the shadow of the Blackbird came through loud and clear.

'I will purchase this coat and hat. Please ring them in and then I am going to wear them home.'

Georgette quickened her pace. Snow began to fall. She had worn comfortable boots, with a moderate heel and gloves to keep her hands warm but she worried about spoiling the fabric of the new coat. The soft flakes soon fell off, swirling around and behind her. She moved with the cutting precision of the wind. Her breaths, leaving her body in short puffs, felt like a release of all the negative thoughts and feelings which she harboured for years. With each step she felt her power and strength return. *'Am I really strong?'* she questioned, *'or is this mantle of mine just a prop?'* She learned the reality of it as soon as she arrived at the front door of her condominium building. Michael waited for her, cold and shivering. His shoulders were hunched against the chill. Hands dug deep into the pockets of his leather jacket. He was out of the falling snow but not protected from the elements. She showed neither surprise nor anger, just polite, friendly courtesy as if she expected him to be there.

'Michael. Have you been waiting long?' she asked, making it sound as if she were late for a prearranged date.

He started to speak, stopped and began again. 'An eternity it seems Georgette.'

'Come inside. I'll make some tea.'

She found it easy to make everyday small talk in the elevator. Her heart was pounding furiously and yet she knew calm had settled on her. The vulnerability, hidden for years behind biting sarcasm, was gone.

She removed her hat and coat in the vestibule, hanging them up carefully before taking Michael's jacket.

'Have a seat. I'll put the kettle on and change these clothes. Back in a minute.'

Michael didn't quite know this new Georgette. She smiled, spoke and reacted with a softened shade of herself. He had been surprised and stirred by the sight of her approaching the condo. She wore a form fitting knee length coat. The neck and hem were feathered as was the hat. She reminded him of a Raven, flying through the flakes of snow. She was elegant and exquisitely beautiful. The hem of the coat fluttered back and forth like wings with each step she took. Her welcome warmed him. He sat on the couch surveying the beauty of her home. Michael longed to explore its personal treasures but remained seated, rooted by his fear of making a misstep.

Georgette returned to the living room, wearing a red and black trimmed quju, the wrap around dress of the Han Chinese. She set a low table to one side before returning to the kitchen to brew the tea. Michael did not see the rituals associated with the preparation but the large tray holding the cups, teapot and some delicate cookies added a touch of formality to the moment.

'Let me help you Georgette.'

'No don't get up.' She kneeled deftly, tray in hand and placed it on the table. She remained on the floor on her knees before sitting back on her heels to pour the tea. Georgette leaned forward to offer him a cup before taking her own.

She spoke a little about her trip, mentioned Christian and her gift choices for him as they sipped the tea. Michael contributed little but his eyes never left her face. He wanted her to talk forever.

'This tea is very fragrant. What is it?'

Georgette launched into a quick tutorial of tea as she refilled his cup. Michael didn't know if it was the warm brew or the undemanding atmosphere but his body felt comforted and relaxed. He declined a third cup before leaning back contentedly and closing his eyes.

'Keep your eyes closed Michael,' she commanded gently.

He did as he was told but struggled to obey her admonishment when his foot was captured. His socks were off before he could draw another breath. Firm fingers massaged tender spots. He bit his lip often, perplexed by her ability to find every sore point.

'I watched my mother do this for my father every time he returned, after an extended period away from home.'

'Did she teach you this skill?'

'No! I hated to watch her do it. I wondered why she would make herself subservient to my father just like a good Chinese wife.'

Michael opened his eyes then, a frown marring his face. 'Then why are you doing this for me Georgette?'

'It took me a long time to realize that wasn't the reason.'

'What then?'

'She did it because she loved him and this was one of the many ways in which she demonstrated her love.'

Michael longed to ask and couldn't. He sought a way around it.

'How did your father show his love to her?'

'By trusting her to manage and care for everything in our lives and treating her as an equal partner in their marriage.'

'Sounds like an exceptional man.'

'My father commanded a ship. When he walked through the door of our home, the Commander stayed outside.' Georgette smiled taking his other foot, grinning openly when he winced at the first pressure.

'You should take better care of your feet.'

'It is obvious I need someone to help me. Do you love me enough to do this for me?'

'Yes Michael I do.'

Up to that point, Michael had allowed his senses to be halted by the pain from her ministrations. The declaration of her love was his undoing. A hand went to his groin to hide the ache which threatened to turn into a raging fire. Still he had to make some rejoinder.

'Georgette, Georgy, I love you enough to leave the tortured boy and the unhappy divorcee behind. I am also happy to leave the physician at the door, if I may come inside.'

'Indeed you may.'

They faced each other for long moments. Neither wanted to precipitate a sudden change though each understood the plane on which their fragile bond existed. Georgette leaned back on her heels, releasing his foot from her lap. The absence of her warmth allowed a chill to return to his feet. Emotions were held in a delicate balance.

'Georgy, when you allowed me to love you before, I should not have. You were ill and vulnerable, perhaps driven by something I did not fully understand. I am not sorry for loving you but I am sorry I put my…needs…before a complete understanding of yours.'

Michael uttered the words in that slow measured way of his, ensuring that his English did not get hijacked by anxiety.

'No matter Miklos. I was ill, too inexperienced to understand what I really needed and used our lovemaking as the wrong way to communicate what I felt inside.'

'Georgy, Georgy, you speak my language like an angel!'

'And you say my name in a way that bends my heart towards yours.' She smiled then and rose to her feet. She halted his movement with a look. Bending over she unbuttoned his shirt one by one and slid it over his shoulders. She unbuckled his belt and pulled off his shirt before the pants and briefs were teased over his knees. Each time he attempted a word, she stalled him with a short kiss. His overall restraint was admirable.

As she moved his pants to the floor, he knew his rising heat could not be contained much longer and yet he remained at her mercy, hoping.

Finally she stood before him and released her hair, shaking it gently to release its fullness. The wrap, which covered her naked body, tumbled to the floor and she stood still, perfection drawn in every nuance and shading of her beautiful skin. She did not encourage him to get up. Instead she moved forward and straddled his thighs placing herself perfectly on his burgeoning manhood. She rested her cheek against his face, her breaths long and shaky, adjusting to the feel of him.

His arms wrapped around her waist, steadying her body, then seeking the angled curves. His lips sought hers, tenderly fiercely, aching, aching for release. He was breathless, delightfully fearful of her power and yet rising to meet it.

She rose slightly to meet his thrust and he captured a breast lightly then with increasing ardour, drawing the most primitive call of love from the depths of her being.

It pushed him to the edge. He made no demands. Pressure drove them both. Her fingers dug into his shoulders, steadying her movement as a cry tore from her body, leaving a shuddering echo in his.

When at last either could speak, words failed. Only long and short kisses, murmurs and sighs punctuated the stillness. There was no shifting to another spot or position for some time. When at last she could release herself from his throbbing warmth, they made their way to a sensuous caressing shower before crawling into her large bed.

'Do you want to talk?' he asked stroking her body lovingly.

'I have something I need to say but we don't have to talk.'

Michael stopped what he was doing and slipped out from under the covers. 'Just give me a minute Georgy. There's something I forgot.'

Puzzled, she watched him walk naked to the door leading downstairs. There was undisguised pleasure in seeing his lean lines, narrow waist and powerful thighs. She considered him a magnificent male. His intellect was matched by an utterly masculine toned body. Georgette realized she had a lot to learn about the private man but knew that she could take the time to do so. He returned quickly with a white paper in hand. Once settled down with her head in the crook of his arm he showed her the envelope.

'Georgy, what is this?'

'That's my writing. It's addressed to you. Where did you get this? There's no postmark on it.'

'Do you not remember writing it?'

She thought for a long time. The letter was unopened. Her mind traveled back over the weeks until it settled on that night. She remembered writing something but as far as she could recall, the letter had been torn up.

'This must have been written shortly before my blackout. My memory is a little fuzzy.'

She received a tight reassuring hug and kiss for the memory of the event which changed her life.

'I only received it tonight. I have not opened it. I was afraid to know if you truly hated me. I was also afraid to know if you truly loved me.'

'And now?'

'I am just truly happy.'

Georgette smiled. She too was afraid to know the contents but her slim finger was soon under the edge, extracting the paper.

'Read it to me. What you said then can only be repudiated by what you feel now, or validated by our declaration of love.'

With those words, Georgette knew this brilliant man would hold her heart for ever.

My Dearest Michael,

I have been lost for such a long time; lost in the mists of my own unhappiness, lost in my failure to find an identity of my own, from which I can offer the best of me, to anyone. You opened me to another possibility, one I have never explored before but I was not ready. My time here has shown me much of who I am. I hope when I return, we can revisit our relationship and start anew.

Georgette.

'Oh my darling, I was too blind to see beyond the moment. If the possibility of being with me gives you hope and renewal, your love does the same for me. I will erase all sadness from my past relationships in support of our love. I hope you can too.'

'I have nothing to erase Michael. I can only build from this moment forward. You are my first and only lover.'

'What???'

'You are my first and only man.'

'Georgy,' Michael let out a stream of Hungarian, part apology, part shame, pure love and before long pure desire. This time

Georgette lay back and allowed him to access her loveliness. He raked her body with kisses from head to foot, sparing nothing in his need to give thanks for a second chance at love. As sighs and sounds flowed from her, Georgette knew the Blackbird was finally singing its most glorious song.

****